Blue Sunrise

Gregg R. Overman

FUTUREWORD PUBLISHING

Blue Sunrise ISBN 9780984589043
Book cover painting Farmhouse Marketing

To have this author as a guest speaker for your event please fax our office at 901-672-6303 or visit our website: **www.futureword.net**

Printed in the United States of America

Trade paperback first edition **01.31.11**

Second edition **06.01.11**

First, I would like to thank my wife, Sheri, for her unending support.

Thanks to Cheryl Haynes and FutureWord Publishing. I can truthfully say this book would never have seen the light of day without Cheryl's pushing me to go for it.

Special thanks for a lesson in airplane design to Charles Burks who saved me from flying the Mars I nose-down into the sands of Mars.

To Barry Lincoln who caught a serious issue that I missed completely.

To Elona Charbonnet for a very thoughtful and helpful critique.

And last but not least, to my beloved godmother, Carolyn Duty Banks, whose kind words of encouragement and sage advice I will never be able to repay.

Much appreciation as well for the many other people who read, reread, praised, critiqued, and challenged various ideas, phrases, chapters and verses. As any author can tell you, it takes a village to write a novel.

To all of my teachers—but especially my father. To him and everyone else who filled my head with the bits and pieces necessary to build a book and who filled my heart with joy and a hunger for more.

And on the slopes of Cheyenne Mountain above NORAD, in parks and in backyards across half the Earth, in the streets and from windows with the curtains barely parted, people raised their eyes and trembled at the sight of Mars burning with a pale, blue flame in the sky above them.

~Gregg R. Overman, Blue Sunrise~

Chapter One
Shuttle Outbound Station
March 25, 2061

Ben Allspot stood in line with some forty-five other people—almost all of them men. Virtually everything he owned was contained in bags at his feet. With a well-muscled physique and standing six feet four inches tall, he stood out in the crowd, but it wasn't his size that made people glance in his direction and then quickly away. There were small scars on his face, especially above the eyes, and his knuckles were large and crisscrossed with white lines. His nose had obviously been broken at some time, perhaps more than once, and hidden under his long, curly black hair, was the reminder of a knife fight he had nearly lost back in his younger days when he had been more violent—and more at peace with himself. But it was mostly the look on his face that caused the men in line to keep a discrete distance. No one considered engaging to him in conversation, and that was just the way he wanted it.

The fact was—he felt horrible. He had managed to pass a drug test earlier in the day, but that was the beauty of carbohydrate-based drugs. As carbohydrates, they were metabolized rapidly, and he had heard of people passing routine drug screens within hours of taking Carbodine. He didn't really know if that was possible, and someone had told him they would be tested again before boarding, so he had not taken a dose since the night before. The rumor of another drug test didn't seem to be true, since they were already filing onto the transport, but goddamn, he felt bad. Ben Allspot was going cold turkey while standing in line for a flight through space.

There was a continual, high-pitched ringing in his ears. His skin felt warm and dry with a peculiar prickly sensation that wasn't altogether unpleasant, but he was slightly nauseous and seriously constipated. He had slept only two hours the night before, and his mind seemed to have shut down. It was as if some vital connections had been severed in his brain, and he had struggled during the last twelve hours to recall commonly used phrases and familiar ideas. Fear had welled up from nowhere on several occasions, nearly overpowering him with its grip, and for the first time in his life, he could appreciate the debilitating paralysis of an anxiety attack.

Over and above everything else, he was massively depressed, and he knew it. He was not without a good education as were most of the men shuffling forward in line. He had almost graduated from college before discovering Carbodine. He knew that Carbodine worked by changing the level of Serotonin and other chemicals in the brain. He knew that the brain was a marvelously adaptive organ and adjusted to new conditions over a period of time. He knew that his depression was a matter of his brain attempting to reestablish the old balance, and that with time he would feel better. But right now, it was knowledge without comfort or understanding—just another piece of empty and meaningless information swirling in a maelstrom of grief and pain. He stood in a world composed of differing shades of gray, preparing to leave his two daughters behind, perhaps forever, and he was far beyond any consolation or potential relief.

The memory of his daughters caused his eyes to fill with tears, and he blinked rapidly as the line moved slightly. He kicked his bags forward. Maybe it was best that they stay with their mother. At least she would keep them well fed and clothed. Of course, he could have done that, and he loved them dearly, but his wife had taken exception to his drug use during the last two years and had finally taken the children and moved up to her mother's house in Shreveport. It hadn't helped that he had gone to jail a couple of times for shoving her around.

He had always been a violent man, although he didn't really think of himself that way. His father had been a hard-drinking, hard-drugging, New Orleans riverboat captain who worked three weeks on and two weeks off. Ben had come to hate the two-week period when his father was in the house. He had come to hate the uncertainty of what his father would do when he came home. Would it be kisses and presents, or rage and angry, painful fists? He had come to hate his mother for not taking them away from it.

Ben had grown up big, strong, and tough with a natural inclination for drugs, alcohol, and bar fights. His marriage and the birth of his daughters had done wonders to calm him down, and his intelligence and strength of will had gotten him almost all the way through college. Those were the good times. He had worked construction during the day and become a supervisor over the crew even while taking night courses. His children had been at home for him to love and care for, and his wife would cook the most wonderful crawfish and shrimp dinners whenever there was a little extra money. It was the time just before a good friend had turned him on to Carbodine.

At first he had done it just for fun. It *was* a lot of fun. Within minutes of taking the small, white pill, a feeling of calm energy would come over him. Things seemed to be clearer, and he found himself engaging in long philosophical discussions of intense interest. Nothing seemed out of reach, and the world would explode in fresh, new opportunities. Even the worst part of his job or schoolwork became a joy to perform, and for a while—a short while—his grades actually improved.

Then one day he decided he needed the Carbodine to keep up with all the work he had to do. School, his job, his family. He decided he couldn't be expected to expend all that effort without a little boost every now and then.

Slowly and subtly the experience changed. His wonderfully adaptive brain desperately tried to find a new balance, and having been induced to produce unnatural amounts of some chemicals, it compensated by producing less and less of others. The calm energy gradually became a frantic need to get certain things done and done exactly as he saw them being done. The fresh, new opportunities became slim lines of possibility that must, at all costs, be exploited before they closed forever.

The frantic needs gave way to bursts of black, murderous rage, and he was fired for nearly killing a worker who had unfortunately misaligned a concrete form. He took a lower paying job and dropped out of school for lack of funds. For reasons that now seemed unclear to him, he had taken a short course in piloting the small fusion tugs that were used on the moon.

And he had gone to jail. Not for the first time, but for the first time in a long time, and with some regularity.

He didn't feel like his life was exploding. It was imploding—closing in around him with alarming speed. When his wife left with his daughters, all that he had ever loved went with them. He lost his new job due to missing work from a stint in jail, and in the midst of all this, with the world spinning around and crushing down upon him, there was only one thing that relieved the pain even for a moment—Carbodine.

It became the focus of his life. How much did he have left? How long would that last? Where could he get more? Where could he get the money to buy more? How long had it been since his last pill? Could he safely take more right now, or should he wait?

Frantic questions. A frantic need.

From within this desperation, it slowly dawned on him that he had become a drug addict, and that he could either break free of his situation or die.

He had been thinking about dying quite a bit for the last few weeks. Fantasies of his death would float up unbidden in idle moments as if they had a life of their own. A large caliber gun in the mouth would be the best way to go. It was quick, like turning off a light, and as sure a way as he could think of.

And it wasn't so much that he wanted to die—he just wanted to be dead. The fear of what it would do to his daughters was all that kept him from it.

He knew he hadn't been the perfect father, but he had never laid a hand on either of them. He had done the best he could for them, and he loved them with all his heart. But they had watched as he beat their mother. They had seen the police come to pick him up. The memory of those eyes, big as saucers, haunted him still. The vision of those faces would come to him of its own accord, just as thoughts of suicide often did. He could not forget it, and he could not fix it.

No, they would probably be better off if he never saw them again, but how much pain would it cause them to know he had killed himself? He couldn't bear to think about it. He had done them enough harm.

"I am well and truly boxed in," he admitted to himself at one point. "I can't stand it, and I can't leave it behind."

The solution had come to him in a flash. The airwaves and newspapers were filled with advertisements for work on the Moon, and looking back on it, he couldn't understand why it hadn't crossed his mind before. Companies were screaming for experienced construction hands. The pay was good, and with the course he had taken in piloting lunar tugs, he would be a shoe-in.

He had walked out of his apartment and taken a bus to the nearest application office. After filling out several pages of forms, he was admitted to a tiny office where a small man wearing a crisp, white shirt and a red tie sat waiting behind a desk littered with paper. There was a filing cabinet behind the man and a single chair in front of the desk. The walls were completely bare.

The man took the forms and began reading through them without so much as a glance in Ben's direction. Ben sat down in the chair.

"Well, Mr. Allspot, you have some excellent credentials. I don't think we'll have any problems placing you immediately. Is there anything else I need to know?"

Ben looked down at his feet. "I've had a little trouble with the police."

"I see that listed here. Any felonies?"

"No."

"Are you currently on probation or parole?"

"No."

"Then we've got no problems. If you'll sign right here."

He reached across the desk with a piece of paper, and for the first time, looked straight at Ben.

Ben was suddenly and acutely aware that he hadn't shaved for several days and that his shirt was filthy.

The man was speaking. "This piece of paper authorizes us to check your personal file. We'll have that information in a few hours. The minimum tour is three months. You can get an added bonus if you stay for six." The man hesitated for a moment, and his voice took on a slightly more serious tone. "You'll be required to report for a drug test the morning of the day you leave."

Ben scribbled his name and passed the paper back across the desk. "I want to leave tomorrow."

The man raised an eyebrow but pulled another piece of paper from one of the piles in front of him, signed it, and gave it to Ben. "Report to this clinic at 10:00 tomorrow morning. The directions are on the back. There is a shuttle leaving for Lunar Base Three at 5:00 tomorrow afternoon. You'll need to be at the entrance of the tube transit by 3:30. Pick up a packet from the secretary, and read it. There are some very strict limits on what you can bring with you. Be sure to have a current ID card.

Ben stared dully at the piece of paper for a moment and stood to leave. "Thanks."

"You'll be working for Lexam."

"Okay."

The man leaned back in his chair. "Do you want to know what it pays?"

"No," Ben said, and walked out.

~

The line had moved forward considerably, and Ben was soon facing a clerk with dark black skin and tired eyes.

"Place your bags on the scales. Are you carrying any drugs or weapons?"

"No."

Ben picked up his bags with one hand and put them on the scales.

Another clerk recorded the number on the scale and opened the bags to look through them before quickly slipping a plastic tag into the handles.

"Name," the black clerk said.

"Huh."

"Name," the clerk repeated and looked up at Ben.

Ben felt his throat tighten, and his heart began to thud in his ears. Black spots swirled in his vision and the ringing in his ears increased in both pitch and volume. This man wanted something from him, but what was it?

"Dude, your name?"

"Uh, Ben Allspot."

The clerk scrolled through a list of names on the screen in front of him and hit a button on the keyboard. "I need to see your ID card."

Ben fumbled in his pocket, handed the card over, and watched as the clerk slipped it into the reader.

The clerk scanned the screen, hit a few keys, and returned Ben's ID card along with a small tag. "You'll need this tag to claim your things when you arrive on the moon. You're cleared to board. Take any available seat."

Ben turned toward the loading ramp.

"You might want to put that tag in your pocket," the clerk said.

As Ben shuffled away, he heard the clerk speaking in a soft voice to his companion. "Man, they'll take anybody these days."

Ben slipped the tag in his pocket and walked on.

Chapter Two
Mars Orbit
March 26, 2061

"Braking maneuver will commence in fifteen minutes, Commander Thon."

Ki Thon looked over at Mike Cochran, the pilot, and wished they didn't insist on calling him Commander. He was more used to being called Doctor Thon, although Ki would have been just fine. "Steady as she goes Mr. Cochran. Bring up the surface on visual when you get a chance."

A small screen blazed to life in front of him almost before he finished speaking, and Ki allowed himself just a few moments to savor the view. The surface of Mars was unremarkable from this distance except for the fact that he would soon be the first man to set foot on it.

Ki considered that to be a shame. The first manned expedition to Mars could have taken place at any time during the last fifty years, but money ruled all decisions, and the mining of He_3 from the Moon was so profitable that it had edged out all other concerns.

"Magnification sir?" the copilot, Adrian Melancon asked.

"No, just leave it as it is."

The panorama moved slowly as their ship, the Mars I, went through its last orbit. Some of the deeper valleys stood out in deep contrast to the larger mountains and the rare, wispy clouds, but mostly it was indistinct shades of red. *Dust and rocks and water in reasonable quantity if we're lucky*, Ki theorized.

The pilot, copilot, and Ki were the only three people in the cramped cockpit. Ki was totally out of his element here and completely useless except for some rudimentary navigational duties that had already been performed, but mission protocol had him in this seat, and that is where he would stay until the ship touched down. It grated on his nerves to be sitting with nothing to do, and he used the slowly gliding view of the surface of Mars to help him relax.

Five other people, the rest of the crew, were in the middle of the ship, and Ki thumbed his throat microphone to talk to his second in command. "Braking maneuver in less than fifteen minutes, Mr. Fielder. I trust you have everything secured."

"All ready for braking maneuver, sir," came the raspy reply of Tom Fielder's voice over the headset.

Ki spoke again. "As per the drills, we will have an audible countdown beginning at T minus one minute."

"Aye, Commander," came the reply.

It was unlike Tom to speak so formally, and Ki realized his second must be more nervous than he would let anyone know. But that was Tom's way—all wisecracks and brash in-your-face attitude, cloaking one of the most brilliant engineering minds Ki had ever known. They had met as students at MIT and slowly became friends simply because that was the only way to become friends with Tom. Ki remembered the days spent talking in the student union about everything from religion to psychology—Tom had a disdain for both—and wondering what the future would hold for them.

Although Tom was the older of the two of them, Ki had risen faster in the ranks of the NASA hierarchy, and Tom eventually found himself working for his old friend. It had actually worked out well for all concerned. Ki got the best engineer at NASA on his staff, and Tom got a supervisor who could sometimes protect him from himself. Tom had simply never learned the blunt truth that bureaucrats don't care to hear the blunt truth. Ki had even tried to talk to Tom about it once, and Tom had replied, "Okay, so you're telling me I'm supposed to kiss some pencil-neck, bean counter's ass? Look, if they don't want to know the answer, they better not ask me the damn question."

The memory brought a smile to Ki's lips. It was strange in a way. The very traits that made Tom so popular in college had become a hindrance to his career.

"Braking maneuver in five minutes, Commander. Bringing up the fusion engine now."

A low steady whine filled the cockpit as He_3 was crushed together and ignited by a laser at the rear of the ship. The pilot and copilot became more animated as they went through a rigorous checklist of gauges and sensors.

"Status, Mr. Melancon?" Ki asked.

"We are all green, Commander," the copilot replied with his slight Cajun twang.

Speaking of nerves, Ki said silently to himself. He didn't normally interrupt someone at his or her job without an extremely good reason, but he had to restrain himself from calling Tom once more to make sure that everyone and everything was secure.

He concentrated on deep breathing and relaxing his muscles—forcing his mind to stay clear but alert. The engine increased in pitch slightly as the pilot brought up the flow into the fusion bottle.

"We'll be in the insertion window in . . . " the copilot paused to look at a display, ". . . 65 seconds."

The pilot spoke, "Initiating burn countdown at your discretion, Commander."

"Begin, Mr. Cochran."

The whine increased to a scream, and soon a computer voice announced, "Engine burn to commence in T minus 60, 59, 58 . . . " The two pilots were feverishly checking gauges and flipping switches. Ki sat with his hands on his legs. His palms were sweaty, and his feet were cold.

The ship was flying upside down and backward above the surface. The engine burn would almost, but not quite, stop their motion relative to the Martian surface.

"Three, two, one." There was a boom, and the scream of the engine became a roar as it acquired lower harmonics. Ki was pushed deep into the acceleration couch as the ship slowed. He tried to watch the screen in front of him, but the vibration was so intense it was a blur. *I wonder how the pilots can see what they are doing.*

Suddenly the engine went back to a low whine and Ki rebounded slightly in his chair as weightlessness returned. Now came one of the tricky parts. Just like the old shuttles used in the Twentieth Century, the pilot, together with the flight computer, would have to flip the ship end for end as they fell toward the atmosphere so that the wings could catch the thin air. The ship would then land almost like a traditional airplane. But this was all educated speculation. No one had actually tried to fly an airplane on Mars before, and the flight of the Mars I was going to be more guided-fall than flight. The nervous hollow in the pit of his stomach grew deeper as he remembered the prototypes that had been lost during testing in Earth's upper atmosphere. Of course, changes had been made since then, but the debate continued over procedures for flying in the Martian atmosphere. The only thing everyone agreed on was the low margin for error. The air was just too thin for major course adjustments.

Cochran and Melancon continued to scan gauges and flip switches. "We are solid in the window. Initiating pitch adjustment now," said Cochran.

A low whistle joined the whine of the engine as the nose of the ship began to lift away from the planet's surface. A wave of dizziness flowed over Ki as his inner ear gave signals in conflict with what he could see. The view on the screen was shifting quickly, and the horizon of Mars slid upward into star-filled darkness as he watched. He closed his eyes and took a few deep breaths.

Another low whistle blended with the first and then both stopped.

"We have proper horizon and should feel atmosphere in about five minutes," Cochran announced. They were dropping like a rock toward the surface.

Ki thumbed his throat mike. "Turn-over is complete, and we will enter atmosphere in about five minutes."

"Aye, Commander," came Fielder's reply. "Make sure he brings us in close. I don't feel like walking."

That is more like Tom, Ki thought. "I'll see that he gets the message."

The pilots continued to manipulate the instruments for a few moments. "All computers are on line, and autopilot is fully engaged." Melancon leaned back in his seat. "I hope it went to Martian flying school," he said.

That was the plan. The computers were to guide the ship down as it dropped like a stone onto the Martian plane near the 53 boxes of supplies that awaited them. They would then taxi in close, gather up the supplies, and set up camp for the next three years.

A low hiss, like sand on glass, slowly filled the cabin. "Entering atmosphere, Commander," said Cochran. He was silent for a moment while the hissing grew louder. "We are drifting to starboard in the window."

Ki could not see Cochran's face, but he could almost hear the frown. There was a slight lurch as the ship tilted to left.

"Autopilot is correcting." Cochran was silent for another moment. "We are now drifting to port."

There was a stronger lurch to the right. "Drifting strongly to starboard and," Cochran hesitated, "we are out of window."

The craft lurched sickeningly to the left, but this time it was accompanied by a low boom and a creaking sound as the structure of the ship complained of the stress.

Ki could barely hear the pilot as he shouted over the noise of atmosphere and the popping of the ship's skin. "Going to manual landing on my mark," Cochran shouted to Melancon. ". . . Three, two, one, mark."

They seemed to fall out of the sky and Ki's shoulder straps tightened as he floated out of his seat. Melancon shouted, "We are fifteen hundred feet below and six hundred feet to port of window."

The engine noise rose above the hissing and booming. There was a sharp lurch to the right, and Ki settled back down into his seat. He could see the pilot Cochran's right hand increase the throttle as he pulled back slowly on the yoke with his left. The engine noise grew louder, but the ship suddenly veered wildly to the right. The craft was tipping over, and a warning buzzer added itself to the din and the general confusion.

Cochran fought the controls. "Damn," he said in a barely audible voice.

Melancon began to reel off numbers. "Skin temperature is at red line. Altitude is 9,000; 8,900; 8,800; 8,600," and all the while the ship slammed them in every possible direction.

Cochran screamed through the noise, "She's not responding. I have negative effect to rudder control." He glanced at a gauge. "Ground speed is near zero

Melancon yelled back, "Nose it down. Nose it down. We've lost almost all forward vector!"

"I'm supposed to nosedive this thing into the sand?"

"Belly-flop or nosedive, we've got to get some forward speed."

Cochran swore and pushed forward on the yoke and the throttle. The engine noise modulated upward, and the shaking began to increase in tempo. There were popping noises from all over the craft.

Melancon yelled across at Cochran, "She's not going to take much more of this without breaking up."

Just as he spoke, the shaking went up again in frequency and then faded out. The buzzer stopped, and even with all of the wind and engine noise, the plane seemed eerily quiet.

Melancon continued to call out numbers. "4,400; 4,300," he hesitated for a moment while Cochran gently pulled back on the yoke and increased the throttle. Ki could almost feel the slight adjustments to the flaps as Cochran nursed the plane back into near level flight. "4,200," Melancon continued, calmer now, and leaned back into his seat slightly. "4,100 and dropping steadily. Skin temperature is coming out of red line." He pulled up another display. "We are still four hundred miles from the landing site. At this rate of drop we will hit ground approximately 75 miles shy of target. That puts us down right in the middle of the western Kasei Valles canyon. Altitude is 3,900."

Cochran leaned over to scan the copilot's display and grimaced at the numbers. He looked back at Ki and then glared out of the small windshield for a few seconds. "Prepare to fire belly jets," he said.

Ki raised an eyebrow but said nothing. The belly jets were intended for use only during the last stages of the flight just before they touched down. Even with the best aircraft that could be made for Martian flying, the thin air required too much speed for a safe landing. The flight plan called for a long, powered fall through the entry window with a last minute drop in air speed and firing of the jets located on the underside of the plane to maintain lift. But they were a long way from the flight plan now.

"Belly jets?" asked Melancon in an even voice.

"Give me another option and I'll try it," said Cochran. "There is no way she'll fly level. She wasn't designed for it. The only other thing I can think of is standing this baby on its tail to gain altitude, and with the way she's handled so far, I'm not real eager to try it."

Melancon replied simply, "Altitude is 3,700 and dropping."

"Okay Melancon, you take over belly jet throttle control and just bring them on slowly until we are holding altitude. I'll see if I can hold this thing in a straight line. Hopefully the flight-surface computer can keep up with what's going on. Begin throttle-up on my mark."

Ki watched Melancon's gloved hand reach out to cover a small set of throttles located just to the right of the main throttle controls.

Cochran began his countdown, "Three, two, one, mark."

The copilot pushed forward slowly on the throttles, and yet another whine began to grow in the cockpit, but the plane remained stable. Ki watched the altimeter slow and finally stop at 3,590. Melancon kept his hand on the throttles for a moment and then drew it back. There was silence in the cockpit.

"3,590 and holding, sir. We are at fifteen percent throttle on the belly jets."

Ki spoke, "Analysis of what caused all this, Mr. Cochran."

"Momentarily, Commander," he replied. "Mr. Melancon, I am going to hold this altitude and vector. Run a status check, and pull up the data starting from just after atmospheric entry. See if you can figure out what happened. It felt like we lost rudder control."

Ki thumbed the mike at his throat, "Mr. Fielder, we . . . "

Tom cut in, "What the hell . . ."

Ki stopped him. "Mr. Fielder, let me remind you that whatever you say will be recorded for posterity." He paused for a moment and then continued, "We have experienced some control problems, which the pilots are now investigating. We will hold this altitude until Mr. Cochran feels that it is safe to continue." He turned off his mike without waiting for a reply, knowing full well that Tom would hear the click as the signal terminated.

Ki returned his attention to the cockpit as Melancon was saying, "Skin temperature is dropping to normal. All control surfaces are functional. Sensor check shows no malfunction, and there is negative damage to the craft."

Cochran kept his hands on the controls. "She feels good right now, but we need that data. I can't fly straight out forever."

Melancon was watching a screen full of numbers in front of him, occasionally hitting a keypad to scroll downward. No one spoke for several minutes.

Finally, Melancon said, "We didn't lose rudder control, but it looks like we lost rudder effect. Sensors show rudder movement with no corresponding shift of craft position. The autopilot tried to use the flaps to bring us into the window, and we rolled badly. Those lurches were the wings dipping left and right."

"But we have rudder now, "Cochran said.

"No doubt about that," said Melancon while he pushed numbers on the keypad and read the displays as they popped up in front of him, "or we'd be splashed all over the sand right now."

"We need an answer and fast," said Cochran. He was looking at the guidance radar. "We are well below the entry window but still more or less in line port to starboard. This thing won't exactly turn on a dime, and we will reenter the window in about three minutes."

Melancon continued to work with the computer for a while. "It's hard to say for sure, but it looks like rudder blanking."

Ki was far from being an Aeronautical Engineer, but he had thoroughly studied the design of this aircraft and now understood more about aircraft design than he had ever wanted to know. He recalled that there were times when the structures of an aircraft could shield a control surface from the airflow that allowed those surfaces to change the aircraft's path. It was a serious problem for some planes, and many a pontoon plane had crashed when the pilot had pitched it back in such a way that the pontoons shielded the wings from airflow.

Ki spoke up, "But this craft is designed for a great deal of rudder blanking. The rudder is over thirty feet tall."

Of course, everything on the plane was larger than normal. It had been designed for a guided drop through Martian atmosphere and had been built in orbit around Earth. The wings were twelve hundred feet from tip to tip and would have snapped off in Earth's dense air or dragged the ground in an attempted Earth landing.

Melancon continued to scroll numbers across his screen. "Best I can tell it was an upper atmosphere effect. On closer look, we had some response to rudder movement, but it wasn't enough to make any difference. Remember the big fight about handling during entry? Some of the engineers wanted to come in under attitude-jet control until we dropped below 6,000, but they got overruled by the big cheeses who were just sure this thing would fly in the upper atmosphere. I reckon we just proved who was right."

Cochran swore, "Goddamned engineers. I'd like to get one of those bastards up in a good fighter jet for a joy ride." He glanced at the console. "So we should be fine since we're below 6,000."

Melancon actually chuckled, "Only one way to find out."

Ki watched Cochran's helmet bob in agreement. "Right you are, Mr. Melancon. Position?"

Melancon flipped several switches and looked at the display. "We will enter the horizontal aspect of the window in precisely 57 seconds, but we are slightly to starboard."

Cochran paused for a moment. "Alright, we'll keep to this heading for another 60 seconds. That will put us slightly above the window. At my mark, cut the belly jets and I'll bring her to port and into the window. We should lose enough altitude on that maneuver to put us right where we need to be."

Ki tapped his throat mike and spoke. "Mr. Fielder, we are going to make a slight course adjustment in just under one minute. This should put us back into the entry window." He clicked off without waiting for a reply. Tom would have plenty to say when and if they landed, and Ki was not in the mood to listen to it.

Ki rolled his head back and forth as much as his suit would allow, loosening the muscles in his neck while Cochran and Melancon went over more checklists. Time seemed to stretch out forever.

Finally, Melancon reached up to put his hand on the belly jet throttles. "We got five seconds to target . . . three, two, one. Above window and cutting jets." He pulled back slowly with his left hand, and the whine of the belly jets faded to a whisper and disappeared. Ki could feel the aircraft begin to drop slowly. Cochran turned the yoke to the left, and the plane lurched slightly but began to bank.

"Touchy, touchy," Cochran said.

A small light went from red to green on the console in front of Melancon. "We are solid in the window," he said.

Cochran ever so slowly turned the yoke back to the right and then straightened it up.

"Vector is correct and we are still in the window," said Melancon.

Cochran reached up to touch a switch. "Engaging auto-pilot."

He flipped the switch and pulled his hands away from the controls. The plane flew on without so much as a bump.

No one spoke or moved in the cockpit for several minutes until Melancon called out, "She's looking good, my friend."

"Don't get cocky," Cochran answered, "we still have to land this thing."

"Ah, she's flying now. Dollars to donuts the autopilot takes her right on down."

Ki felt himself relax slightly and tapped his throat mike again. "We've got green lights up here. The autopilot is engaged, and we can expect landing in…"

"Fifteen minutes," Melancon filled in.

"Fifteen minutes. Thon out,"

Cochran and Melancon kept themselves busy with systems checks, but the next fourteen minutes were the longest Ki could remember. Finally, Melancon spoke again, "Altitude is 1,200. Belly jets should engage in five seconds."

Ki counted it off to himself and felt the belly jets fire up right on cue. There was another sensation of being pushed down and forward in the seat. Loud thumping noises could be heard as the landing gear deployed.

Even though the forward camera gave a better view of things, Cochran strained forward in his harness to look out the front window. "I have the landing field in sight, and it is reasonably clear of debris. We should have nose up in ten seconds and touch-down in twenty."

One of the main difficulties in choosing a landing site was finding a place that was flat and without too many large rocks. The wheels on the Mars I were nearly twenty feet tall and resilient, but a large boulder could still cause problems.

Ki was pressed down into his seat and felt the nose of the plane tip up as the belly jets roared through the final seconds of flight.

Melancon watched the numbers streaming by in front of him. "Ground speed is dropping right on line. We should hit sand right about…" There was a lurch as the back wheels hit, and the plane tipped forward onto the nose gear. "Now," he finished. "Welcome to Mars, Commander."

"Excellent job." Ki hit his mike, "Welcome to Mars, Mr. Fielder." There was cheering in the background. "All we have to do now is taxi in to the base site."

"One hell of a ride," Tom replied. "Tell Cochran I'm voting to have it included as the thrill of the century at the next World's Fair."

"I'll relay the message," said Ki and blanked the connection. "Mr. Cochran, I believe you have the wheel. Let's go pick up our luggage and unpack."

The plane had not stopped rolling, and Cochran increased the throttle slightly as the plane lurched and dipped over the uneven surface. It would take them nearly an hour to reach the site of their base camp, but that was okay with Ki. He began to cycle through the various outside cameras, pulling up one view after another. There were mountains to the north, and the Mars I bounced roughly toward the foothills. Red sand and irregular rocks covered the ground under a light yellow sky.

Ki was not superstitious, and it didn't bother him that their expedition was off to a rough start, but of course, he couldn't possibly know what the next few months might bring.

Chapter Three
Time Unknown
Place Unknown

Space is mostly emptiness. Concentrations of matter are more exceptional than normal. Even within the galaxies, where matter is pulled together by the warm embrace of celestial attraction and great dark black holes, most of the space-time continuum is far from the curving influence of gravity and is therefore essentially flat, remaining in its naturally smooth and undisturbed state but for the ever so brief winking of virtual particles and a fifteen-billion-year-old, resonant hum as the universe rings still from the primordial explosion.

The stars fill the background in their slow, revolving dance and lend but a faint, cold light to this region far out on a spiral arm, but it is the flatness of this place that is important to what is about to happen.

Distant stars will not reveal their motion except on a time scale that few if any beings can appreciate, but here, in this instant, they might be seen to tremble; ever so slightly at first, but with more and more agitation—in the manner of objects wavering in the distance through heated air. It is not air in this place but gravity itself that sends photons scattering away from their arrow-straight paths.

Titanic but highly localized forces ripple and spread, and space-time demonstrates its annoyance by projecting great streamers of hard radiation that bloom and grow quickly stronger until, with a brilliant burst, the stars form themselves into a perfect circle of light around an opening filled with more stars—stars of a different and distant locale. From this breach, what appears to be a polished silver ball floats lazily forward. It is followed closely by a long cylinder so black and non-reflective it can only be seen when it eclipses the ring of light and the remaining, undisturbed stars.

The cylinder clears the opening, the ring snaps shut, and the bright pinpoints of the stars can be seen to quiver for a moment as if shivering from the cold as they return to their accustomed places. A slight burst of gamma radiation spews from the rear of the cylinder, and it begins to gain upon the ball. When a collision seems imminent, the front of the cylinder opens like the jaws of a shark, and the shining ball vanishes from view. The shark closes its jaws and floats forward for an instant before small jets of radiation erupt from its sides. It begins to spin along its long axis.

Several antennae rise up out of the sides of the cylinder, and it scans a vast array of frequencies in a search for a very specific type of modulated, electromagnetic wave. It has done this countless times before, for many thousands of years, with very little success; but here, in this place, it finds the object of its endless quest. In a broad range surrounding 100 kHz, there is a huge amount of information being transmitted, but the cylinder has not been programmed to care what is contained in the modulated waves. It does not even bother to record them.

It takes careful measurements concerning the waves' direction and an even more precise survey of nearby stars so that its own position might be known. A large burst of sustained radiation erupts from its tail, and it accelerates away at nearly ten gravities on a tangent to the source of the waves—all the while tracking the direction from which the modulated waves emanate.

For days it travels, triangulating the position of the modulated waves until a set criterion for positional precision has been satisfied. The cylinder then flips end-for-end and decelerates till it comes to what it references as a dead stop. The cylinder takes more measurements of its position from nearby stars, and short bursts of radiation from its sides align it perfectly with a new target almost directly away from the source of the modulated waves.

Another burst from its tail and the cylinder drifts slowly forward opening its jaws wide to release what can now be seen as a series of interlocking hoops. The hoops begin to spin rapidly and soon blur to the point of invisibility as the shining ball is reborn. The stars begin to waver and tremble while radiation leaks from the rip in space forming around the ball, and once again, a ring of light forms a window into the distance—a window into which the cylinder, mouth now shut, sedately drifts.

The ring collapses around the tail of the cylinder, and the stars quiver for just a moment before resuming their slowly revolving dance.

Space is flat here and undisturbed but for the ever so brief winking of virtual particles and the low, solemn ringing of the universe as fifteen-billion-year-old hydrogen sings its tuneless chorus.

Chapter Four
Surface of Mars
March 27, 2061

Tom Fielder called over the broadband com of his suit radio, "Is everybody suited up and checked out and ready for day two of the great Mars adventure?" A jumble of assents came in answer.

"Hold it," he said, "Let's go down the list."

Mike Cochran and Carlos Espanoza rolled their eyes as Tom reeled off the names.

"Commander Thon?"

"Check," came the reply.

"Mike Cochran?"

"Check."

"Adrian Melancon?"

"Check."

"Evelyn Weiss?"

"Check."

"Kaitlin Geller?"

"Check."

"Pamela Krazinsky?"

"Check."

"Carlos Espanoza?"

"Check."

"Alright," Tom said, "Starting decompression now."

He reached over, flipped the red top from a button near the door, and pressed the button firmly. There was the soft thump of a valve opening somewhere below the floor, followed by the whine of a pump and a slight whistle as the air pressure began to drop. Under these small noises was the unrelenting hum of the idling fusion engine.

Tom looked around at the crew huddled in the belly of the Mars I. It was a cramped space even in weightless conditions, but in the three-eighths gravity of Mars, there was hardly room to move without bumping into someone.

He scanned the duty roster in his hand. "One more time for the record. Cochran, Weiss, and Krazinsky are wearing the video recorders for today. I've got Cochran and Geller locating supply boxes. I show all boxes retrieved except number thirty-six and forty-two. Weiss, you'll be working on the temporary quarters with Melancon. That leaves me, Commander Thon, Krazinsky, and Espanoza to continue the dismantling of the Death Trap."

It was the only name he had used for the Mars I since they landed. He had taken the time to look at the flight tapes and was truly amazed that Cochran and Melancon managed to get the craft under control, but that didn't keep him from needling them about it, and it damn sure didn't make him fond of his current home. They had lived on the Mars I for two months already. He couldn't wait to move into the temporary quarters and begin the process of building their permanent home from pieces of the long, flat wings and tail section.

"I'm sure everyone is raring to go after that rousing breakfast of squeeze-tube oatmeal."

There were mumbles from the crew, and a light above the single hatch on the starboard wall went from red to green as he spoke. Kaitlin Geller was standing closest to it, and Tom called to her. "Ms Geller, if you will do the honors, we'll get this show on the road."

She spun the wheel on the door, popped it outward, crawled through the hatch, and began climbing down the ladder to the ground. The crew followed her one by one out of the Mars I. Tom was the last to leave. He pulled the hatch shut and pushed a button to re-pressure the cabin to keep it warm. As he dropped the last few feet onto the sand, he saw Cochran already sitting in the driver's seat of the rover. Kaitlin Geller was standing at the rear of the vehicle detaching a thick cable trailing from the underside of the Mars I.

Tom hit his com button. "How does she look, Cochran?"

"All charged and ready, sir. I have a good signal from forty two, but thirty six is still not showing up."

"Bring in forty-two, and then start a spiral search pattern for thirty six. It's probably behind a hill somewhere."

"Aye, sir."

Tom turned to the work at hand. The skin of the Mars I was made of an extremely light but stiff Carbon composite. Recessed bolts held large plates of the composite in place. They would need to unbolt these plates and slide them down to the ground for use as the exterior walls and roof of the permanent housing. When they were finished, the Mars I would be a skeleton of high-strength alloy struts sitting on three large tires with the fusion engine exposed right down to its shielding. The air scrubbing equipment, heaters, escape hatch and several other items on the Mars I were also destined to become part of the new building. Evelyn Weiss and Adrian Melancon were working on the temporary housing they would use during the few days when neither the Mars I nor the permanent housing was habitable.

All of the plates on the underside of the left wing had been removed, along with most of the plates on top, and Tom could see the thin storage bin that filled the wing between the structural supports. It had been emptied yesterday, and the tools and spare parts it had carried to Mars were piled neatly a few yards away. He walked over to check the stability of the scaffolding along the wing's backside. The broad feet of the scaffold were still solid and had not sunk into the sand, and he signaled for Krazinsky and Espanoza to go up and begin removing plates from the top of the wing.

He keyed his radio, "Start on the bolts next to the body of the plane. Commander Thon will be down here to guide the panel down."

The landing gear of the Mars I were close in toward the body of the plane, and the right-hand wing had been braced with another scaffold to insure that the plane did not tip over from the loss of weight on the other side as the plates were removed. Tom walked under the plane to make sure it hadn't shifted during the night. It too seemed to be firm and solid in the sand, and he saw Evelyn Weiss finishing up one of the temporary structures just a few yards to his left as he started to walk back under the plane. She was a shapely woman, but he was a bit surprised to see how well it showed through her space suit, and he decided on the spur of the moment to check her progress.

The Martian gear wasn't at all like traditional space suits. It was fairly tight fitting, allowing only a small layer of air between the skin and the inner fabric, and the inner fabric served mainly to reflect infrared radiation back to the skin. The outer fabric was thin by comparison with what was needed in space, partly because Mars had an atmosphere—it was only 7 millibars compared to Earth's 1,000—but it was still more hospitable than full vacuum.

Tom bounced unsteadily toward the nearest structure where Evelyn Weiss had just finished shaving the outer edges of the doorframe.

Building the temporary quarters was simplicity itself. A plastic guide resembling the ones used to line flowerbeds was pushed down in the sand to act as a form. A quick curing, two-component urethane was then sprayed inside the form to make the foundation. After the urethane hardened, a large plastic balloon in the shape of an igloo was inflated and placed on top of the foundation. Urethane was then sprayed on the balloon all the way down to the plastic guides. After cutting away the plastic from where the door would be, a quick spray of urethane was applied to the inside walls and floor, and the door was shaped to accept the hatch. A few fittings were glued on for heated air, the hatch was glued into place, and that was it.

Tom looked around. The mountains were to his back, and the partial skeleton of the Mars I rose up to the yellow sky just to his right. To his left, just past the temporary shelters, were neat stacks of plastic boxes waiting to be opened. The boxes were stacked directly in front of him pointing to the smooth location where the dwelling would be erected. Evelyn Weiss was working on the door of the second temporary shelter. The brick-red sand was littered with tools and thin slices of urethane that were light enough to blow away in Mars' thin winds. The air-supply hose lay in a heap, and the partially disassembled urethane application equipment was scattered amongst the tools.

Tom keyed his radio by pushing a button on his left wrist. "Let's get this urethane picked up before the wind carries it off."

Evelyn turned her head toward him. He could see her blue eyes and slightly upturned nose through her faceplate. "What are we going to do with it?" she asked.

Tom's reply was clipped, "It'll make great confetti for the parade when we get home. Now let's get it picked up." Evelyn was a decent engineer, but she was a truly superb technician.—even if she did tend to be a little messy, and they had worked together for over a year in preparation for the mission. He knew the measurements on the door would be perfect.

He picked up a small black box lying at his feet and pressed it firmly against the doorframe while holding down a button on the front. Within a second, a laser beam shot out in four directions—precisely up and down and precisely left and right. He adjusted the beam with a dial on the front of the box until the red light just touched the frame. He then repeated the process from several points on the door.

As he expected, it was perfectly square and level.

Evelyn was watching him as she placed the last of the plastic strips into a bag. "Is everything alright?"

"It's close enough," Tom replied without turning around. "Go ahead and fit up the hatch, and I'll get Cochran and Geller to start building the bunks. I want to get it pressured up and warm by tomorrow morning."

He pushed another button on his wrist. "Cochran, come in."

"Cochran here,"

"What have you got?"

"We've got forty-two loaded up, and we are headed back. I found a weak signal from thirty-six. It looks to be somewhere northwest of here."

"Good. Drop off forty-two and come over to the number one temporary. Bring crate number five. You and Geller can start putting in the furniture while Weiss finishes the airlock. We'll get box thirty-six later today."

He didn't listen for the reply but turned and began walking toward the Mars I. From where he stood, he was looking almost straight into the back of the engine. The exhaust had been baffled and pointed upward, and a slight wavering of heat could be seen above the body of the plane as the reactor idled. The two wings of the plane, the left one a mere skeleton now, drooped slightly at the ends even in the weak Martian gravity, and he could see Krazinsky and Espanoza near the body of the plane as they struggled to remove the last plate on the top of the wing above the landing gear. Thon stood on the ground below them waiting to catch the plate and gently lay it down once it was removed. It seemed to be taking longer than it should.

Tom spoke into his radio. "Espanoza, how's it going?"

"Okay I guess." His voice was labored, and Tom could hear him panting slightly from exertion. "The last bolts on this side just don't want to let go."

Tom saw a cloud of dust out of the corner of his eye and turned to see Cochran returning to camp. Cochran pulled the rover up next to the neatly arranged boxes on the far side of the temporaries and jumped out to offload box number forty-two from the wagon.

Evelyn Weiss was at the igloo door, rechecking it for level, and Tom chuckled to himself. *Damn, she's as good as any I've ever seen.*

Just as Tom turned back to the Mars I, there was a popping noise, and he saw the structure of the plane tremble. Espanoza straightened from his crouched position on top of the wing and Krazinsky stood up next to him. Tom realized with horror that the left wing was now drooping lower than the right wing. Ki stood frozen in place directly underneath.

Tom frantically pushed his radio button and screamed, "Ki, run! She's coming down!"

It was too late. Even as he ran toward the plane, the screeching sound of ripping metal filled his helmet, and the wing bent down from where it attached to the side of the plane until the far end touched the ground. It flexed slightly, and Tom believed that it might hold, but with a snap, it broke off from the body of the plane and fell to the ground.

Dust and sand billowed out, and Espanoza and Krazinsky fell fifteen feet in slow motion from the low gravity to land on top of the plate they had worked so hard to free. Espanoza bounced to his feet, but Krazinsky grabbed her ankle and doubled up where she had landed.

There was a babble of voices as everyone keyed their radios, and Tom roared as he bounded through the swirling dust. "Everyone off the com! Off the com now!"

The dust quickly cleared in the brisk wind. Commander Thon was nowhere to be seen.

Tom called out, "Espanoza, Krazinsky, suit integrity. Check your gauges."

Espanoza replied first. "My gauges are fine. I'm okay."

Tom bent over Krazinsky who still lay curled on the wing plate. "Krazinsky, are you with me?"

Krazinsky answered in a strained voice, "I twisted my ankle, but I don't think it's broken." She lifted her right arm and looked at the gauges near the wrist of the suit. "My gauges look good. Where is Commander Thon?"

Tom stood up. "Ki, can you read me?"

A weak reply came. "I appear to be largely unhurt."

"Where are you?"

"I am in a small space. I cannot move my legs, but I think it is because they are pinned by one of the support struts. My suit gauges look good, but it is already uncomfortably cold."

It's the sand, Tom realized with horror. *The suits were made to keep us warm in Martian air. Being in the sand is like hugging a steel pole on a cold day. He must be under the storage bin.*

Tom hesitated for a moment. "You must be under the storage bin." He called out to the crew, "Espanoza, get Krazinsky off the wing and into the cabin. Leave it depressured, but close the hatch and get back down here. Everybody else, break open crate number eighteen. It's got some shovels in it. Bring them over here, and let's start digging now. He'll go hypothermic in that sand in . . . Krazinsky, you're the doctor. How much time does he have?"

Espanoza had picked up Krazinsky and was carrying her toward the ladder. Krazinsky's voice came over the radio. "It's hard to say. It depends on how much of him is buried in the sand. Anything past thirty minutes will be pushing it."

Tom looked at his watch. It glowed back military time: 0815.

Tom called out again to Ki. "Commander, can you bang on the storage bin? I need to find your location."

"I . . . I can try, but I cannot easily move."

Tom picked his way through the struts until he was standing over the storage bin, but he could hear nothing. "Are you hitting the storage bin?"

"I am trying, but I cannot move my hand very far. I am not able to apply much force from this position."

Tom placed his gloved hand on top of the storage bin and could feel a faint vibration. "That's good. I can feel it. Keep it up."

Tom moved slowly through the struts while keeping his left hand on the storage bin, but he could feel no difference from one place to the next. He looked up and down the bin from where he stood. It was nearly one hundred feet long. He realized he would be better off just guessing where Ki was trapped from his last observation of where his friend was standing when the wing broke off.

"Ki, this is not going to work. I can't tell where you are. Can you dig some of the sand away from you? The more deeply you're buried the faster you're going to . . . He stopped.

"Freeze to death," Ki finished for him. "I heard Krazinsky's estimate. I am lying on my stomach. One of the support struts is across the back of my thighs. I do not think my legs are injured, but the strut has pushed me down into the sand. I am attempting to move some of the sand away, but the angle is bad, and I will not be able to move very much."

Tom screamed into his radio, "Where are those goddamn shovels?"

"We're on our way," came Cochran's reply.

Tom worked his way out of the wing supports and bounced several feet away to turn and look. He tried desperately to remember where Ki had been standing when the wing fell. Espanoza was coming back out of the Mars I, and the rest of the crew came bouncing up with the shovels.

"We've only got four shovels," Cochran said.

"I know," Tom replied. He decided on a point about fifteen feet down from where the wing had broken off. The storage bin was six feet wide, and there were two support struts that ran the entire length underneath it on both the front and backsides. Every ten feet there was a cross brace under the bin. The struts and braces formed small boxes under the bin. Ki was trapped in one of these. Tom called out. "Ki, can you reach out and touch any of the struts to your left or right?"

"I—I can only touch the strut behind me."

No help. Tom could hear Ki's teeth chattering. He looked at his watch: 0822. He cursed under his breath and pointed at a section of the wing. "Everybody with shovels, start digging there."

Krazinsky spoke up from her place in the cabin of the Mars I. "Commander Thon, you need to move your arms or anything else you can to generate some body heat. Try moving your legs in a walking motion. Even if they won't move, the muscle contractions will help the blood to circulate."

"I will d--do that," came the reply.

Cochran, Melancon, Weiss, and Geller worked their way through the struts and began flinging sand away from the point where the backside of the long strut had pushed its way into the sand. Tom paced back and forth watching. It was going to be slow work. The extra support beams were in the way of every move—preventing the crew from easily throwing the sand out of the way. Cochran and Geller were on the outside, and they had it a little easier because they could dump the sand to the side, but Tom realized they might be covering up the spot where Ki was trapped.

"No," he said. "Throw the sand back out of the way. Not to the side."

All four of the crew stopped and turned to look at him. "Cochran, Geller, back toward me, not to the side."

They went back to shoveling and Espanoza broke in. "What do you want me to do?" he said.

"Stand there and shut the fuck up!" Tom screamed.

Ki's voice came over the radio. "Th--they are doing all they c--can, Tom."

All of the coms were open and Tom could hear the labored breathing of the crewmembers with shovels. Melancon slipped and almost fell backward over one of the struts, and Tom went closer to look at the progress. He could see that it was not going to work. They couldn't back far enough away from the holes they were digging because of the struts, and as they shoveled, their feet were beginning to push sand into the area they had already cleared. He looked at his watch again: 0826. They were not going to make it.

Tom climbed out of the wing and kicked a nearby box in frustration. There had to be something else he could do. He took a few deep breaths to clear his mind and then began walking in a tight circle, looking everywhere around the camp for something, anything that would help remove Ki from under the wing. Finally, he stopped and stared at the temporary shelters for a few precious moments. His eyes shifted to the pile of material that had been removed from the storage bin and then to the rover. He took a step toward the stack of plates already removed from the wing, then stopped and held his hands up to his helmet.

He whirled around. "Cochran, bring the rover around to the back of the Mars I and park it under the air-hose outlet. Weiss, use the wagon on the rover so you can open the access plate and remove the pressure regulator."

"Sir?"

"I said take the regulator out of the air line. Now move it!"

He turned to Espanoza, "Go get the air line for the temporary and bring it to Weiss. Weiss, as soon as you get the regulator out of the line, hook up the air hose and bring the other end over here."

Cochran and Weiss were already climbing through the wing, and Espanoza bounded toward the temporary shelters.

Tom turned back toward the wing. "Melancon, look through what we pulled from the storage bin yesterday. There are three spare, temporary-shelter balloons. Bring one of them over here. Geller, take all of the shovels and plant them as deeply as you can along the front of the wing right up against it." He pointed to four positions starting from the tip of the wing and leading back to about half way down the wing. "Here, here, here, and here. There's a large hammer in the pile of stuff with the spare shelter balloons. Bring it over, and pound the shovels in as deeply as you can."

Melancon was dragging one of the extra balloons through the sand. Tom pointed to an area about ten feet down from the broken end of the wing. "Okay Melancon, put it right about there. Unfold it and flatten it out just like we were going to make another temporary shelter, but turn it upside down. I want the flat bottom pointed up."

"Aye, sir."

Tom made it to where Weiss stood on the back of the rover in three long leaps. She was spinning the regulator off of the line, and she turned with it in her hand. Tom held out his hands, and she dropped it to him. "You're going to need a coupler," he said.

She pulled a coupler out of a pouch at her waist and began to spin it on to the pipe. "I picked one up from the temporaries," she said.

Tom laid the regulator on the wagon. Espanoza arrived with the airline in tow and dropped it at the rear of the rover. Tom reached down and inspected one end of the airline to make sure the valve was closed and the quick-connect was attached. He handed that end to Espanoza. "Take this end and stretch the hose out to where Melancon put the temporary shelter balloon. Then get Melancon to help you bring one of the wing plates and put it right behind the balloon. Cochran, hand the other end of the air line to Weiss when she's ready."

"I'm ready," said Weiss.

"Okay Weiss, turn the air valve on full when you get the hose tightened up. Cochran, unhook the wagon and bring the rover around to the front of the wing directly across from where Melancon put the balloon. I want the tires of the rover snugged up tight against the wing. We've got to keep the wing from sliding forward."

Evelyn was twisting the hose onto the air outlet pipe. "Mr. Fielder, there's over a thousand pounds of pressure on the other side of this valve. If that hose breaks, it will exhaust our air supply and may cause some damage."

"It's double wire-braid hose. It should hold, but don't open the valve until I have the other end in my hand, and stay where you are. If the hose breaks, close the valve."

Cochran was already climbing into the driver's seat. "Mr. Fielder, what the hell are we doing."

"We're getting our commander out of a very dark and cold place."

Tom bounded back to where Espanoza had placed the end of the air hose and looked at his watch: 0837 "Commander, how are you doing?"

Ki's voice sounded weak. "F--fine," he said.

Tom reached down and got a firm grip on the hose. "When you're ready, Weiss."

"Opening valve now," Evelyn replied.

The hose twisted in the sand like a living thing as the pressure built up, and he could almost feel Weiss cringing with the expectation that it would burst. Tom stood with the hose writhing in his hands. If it broke anywhere near him, the blast would shred his suit and possibly him as well. He was facing away from the body of the plane. The back of the wing was directly to his right, and the flattened out balloon was several feet to his left. The rover was coming in to view on his right as Cochran pulled it up against the front of the wing. "Everybody back off," Tom cried. "We're about to do a little sandblasting, and a direct hit will cut through your suit."

He didn't wait for a reply but slowly opened the valve at the end of the hose with his right hand. Air hissed out and the sound quickly rose to a shriek as Tom continued to open the valve. He leaned forward more and more to keep the force from pushing him over backward, but the hose began to slip through his hands.

Tom closed the valve with a curse. "Damn it! Melancon, come over here and get right up behind me. I can't hold the hose by myself, and it's trying to push me over."

Melancon was behind him in one jump, and Tom felt him nestle into his back like two spoons laid together. The hose moved as Melancon picked it up.

Tom gripped the valve and tensed his muscles. "Okay. Hold on tight."

Tom opened the valve slowly until the air screamed from the hose. He gripped the valve with all the force he could muster, and the hose pushed them back a step, but they held, and Tom began to direct the air toward the underside of the wing. Sand blew out in huge clouds. He leaned down and played the air back and forth under the support struts, blowing sand toward the tip of the wing. He found that with the angle just right, the air would blow the sand out of his vision, and he could see what he was doing.

Within a few minutes, they had excavated a broad, shallow pit under the struts. He closed the valve and laid the hose in the sand. "Melancon and Espanoza, drag the balloon under the struts and into this hole, and make sure I can get to the air inlet. Cochran and Weiss, pull the wing plate in behind them, and put it on top of the balloon. Move it people. We are running out of time."

Tom looked at his watch yet again: 0840. "Commander, we will have you out in just a few minutes."

There was no response.

"Commander, can you hear me?"

Still no response.

Tom shouted, "Ki Thon, can you hear me?"

"I hear something," came the reply. It was Ki's voice, but it had a soft, dreamy quality, and Tom could no longer hear Ki's teeth chattering. "Ah yes, it is my old, dear friend Tom."

"Ah shit," Tom said. Ki had used that term for him only once several years ago when Tom had managed, with great difficulty, to get Ki slightly drunk. "This is not a good sign. Hold on, Commander. It won't be long now."

Cochran and Weiss were sliding the wing plate in between the balloon and the underside of the wing struts, and Tom leaned forward to find the air inlet on the balloon. He picked up the air hose and pushed the end of it into the quick-connect fitting. Ever so slowly, he began to open the valve. There was a hiss of air and the balloon started to inflate.

"I want everybody standing on the back side of the wing," he yelled. "The first one to see Commander Thon call out."

The balloon began to inflate and the wing plate lifted with it until it touched the struts. It stopped there as the pressure continued to build.

He heard Espanoza. "Won't it burst?"

Weiss answered. "No, the round part of the balloon is twelve feet across. That gives you about one hundred ten square feet of surface area. Even at just one pound per square inch that comes out to," she paused to do the figures in her head, "something like 16,000 pounds of lift."

"Cut the chatter," Tom said. But the backside of the wing began to lift out of the sand.

Several of the crew cried out, but Tom shut them up. "Keep your mouths shut and your eyes open."

The backside of the wing continued to lift, and the entire wing slid forward a few inches but stopped, held firm by the rover and the shovels.

Geller cried out, "I've got him! I can see him."

Tom continued to let air into the balloon. "Geller and Melancon, crawl under the struts, and let me know when you can drag him out."

The two crewmembers dropped to their bellies and began crawling under the wing. Within moments, Melancon's voice rang through Tom's helmet. "I've got his arm. He's coming out."

Tom turned off the air valve and stood up. Geller and Melancon were backing out from under the wing, dragging their Commander by his arms behind them.

"Melancon," Tom said, "get the Commander into the cabin. Dr. Krazinsky, you've got incoming."

"I'm ready to get an I.V. started as soon as you can get him up here," came her reply.

Melancon outweighed Ki by almost one hundred pounds on Earth, and he easily picked up the Commander and slung him over his shoulder. Ki flopped around like a rag doll, but he was still semi-conscious and babbled incoherently while Melancon carried him up the ladder.

"Okay," Tom said, "everybody gets in the cabin but Weiss and me. Cochran, button it up and get the heat on. I need status on hydraulic fluid and air as soon as you can get it."

"Aye, sir."

Krazinsky broke in. "Mr. Fielder, I have to get Commander Thon out of his suit to start the I.V. We will not be able to let you back in until we get the commander suited back up."

"I am aware of that, Dr. Krazinsky. Weiss and I have a little clean up to do. Give me a report of the Commander's condition when you finish your examination."

The crew was climbing the ladder into the cabin, and Weiss stood there looking at Tom. "What do we need to do?" she said.

Tom raised a hand and pointed to where the wing had broken off. Wires dangled, along with several hydraulic lines. One of these dripped hydraulic fluid slowly. The fluid was warm from passing close to the reactor, and most of it boiled away in Mars' near vacuum, leaving a thick, brown residue in the sand below the body of the plane.

"One of the emergency cutoff valves is leaking through," Tom said. "We'll need to plug it from this side. Box twelve has a bunch of extra fittings and a tubing cutter. Bring a half-inch pipe plug, the tubing cutter, and a half-inch tap. We'll just cut it off flush, tap some threads, and use the plug to seal it. We need to let the air out of the balloon and put the regulator back in the line. I'll take care of that."

Weiss turned and walked toward the boxes. Tom turned to the balloon and then called out, "And get the field microscope out of box thirty-nine. It should be right on top."

"Yes, sir."

Tom bent over the balloon and made sure the valve on the air hose was securely closed before pulling a small utility knife from the pouch at his waist. There was no release valve on the balloon, and it would need to be cut to let the air out. It could be patched later if it was needed.

He selected a spot so the air would not blow back on him and made the smallest possible hole in the thick plastic. Air whistled out in a soft whisper, and the wing began to settle back down even slower than it had lifted. Tom pulled a marker from his pouch and made a small "X" near the hole.

"Mr. Fielder?" It was Cochran.

"Yes."

"The hydraulics look good. We haven't lost much fluid at all, but the air is a different story. We're down to about fifty percent of what we should have. That looks like about two months supply before we have to start using water to make oxygen."

"Does that include filling the permanent dwelling?"

"Yes, sir."

"Alright, send a message to NASA and tell them to get some water and some LOX headed this way."

"Will do. They're not going to like it."

"They'll like it just fine if Ki lives."

"Yes, sir."

"Mr. Fielder." It was Krazinsky.

"Yes."

"Commander Thon is going to be fine. His temperature is coming up nicely. He has some very bad bruises on his legs but no serious muscle or bone damage. He'll need strict bed rest for the next twenty four hours and limited duty for a few days after that, but he's going to be fine."

Tom blinked rapidly and took a deep breath. A smile came over his face even as tears formed in the corners of his eyes. "Now that is good news. How is your ankle?"

"It's not too bad. The suit kept it compressed, and I elevated it and put a cold compress around it as soon as I got up here. I'll need to patch my suit to fit the swollen ankle, but Commander

Thon and I will both be limping around the camp by tomorrow or the day after."

"Excellent," Tom said. "Just excellent."

Most of the air had leaked out of the balloon. Tom walked around the wing, got in the rover, and drove it around to where the airline hung from under the Mars I. He got out and stood on the platform to close the air valve and then jumped off and bled the excess pressure by opening the valve at the other end.

Evelyn came up just as he finished putting the regulator back in its place. Tom climbed over the back of the driver's seat and sat down behind the steering wheel. "Hop on the back," he said, "and we'll get that hydraulic leak fixed."

Tom pulled the rover under the wing and reached around to pick up the field microscope. "Take care of the leak while I get a look at something."

Weiss stood up to work on the hydraulic line, and Tom set up the field microscope to look at the broken end of the wing.

Evelyn Weiss had a messy job in front of her. There was no way to block the dripping fluid as she cut the line and tapped threads on the inside surface, and the fluid covered her gloves and ran down the front of her suit while she worked. Before long, she was covered with a brown, sticky residue.

Tom was still looking at the struts when she finished and hopped down from the platform. "What's it look like?" she asked.

Tom straightened up and moved out of the way. "See what you think."

Evelyn looked through the microscope and adjusted the focus. For several minutes, she moved the microscope to look at different areas on the broken end of the strut. "It would be nice to have an X-ray diffraction or an electron microscope," she said, "but it looks like stress fatigue cracking. There's a wavy appearance to the top side that looks like compressive forces and micro-cracks radiating outward from that. Then you can see where it tore loose when the wing fell."

"Yep," Tom said. "I'd say our little flutter through the sky on the way down did more damage than we knew. The wing plates were the only things holding the wing on. They kept the struts from breaking until we unbolted them." He shook his head and looked up at the Mars I. "I may have to rename the Death Trap.

She managed to bring us down safe with a broken wing. That's not too shabby."

Evelyn turned, and Tom got a look at the front of her suit. "Goddamn," he said with a chuckle, "You're a mess."

"Yeah, I guess so."

Tom stretched his hands above his head and rolled his shoulders. "Let's see," he said, looking at his watch, "it's 10:00. Why don't we take a break?"

"I could use one."

"Krazinsky," Tom called, "How long before we can come back in?"

"I'd like to leave Commander Thon hooked up to the I.V. for another couple of hours at least," replied Krazinsky.

"Fine," said Tom, "We're going to take a break in the temporary shelter. At least we can sit down without getting too cold.

~

Evelyn followed Tom as they trudged over to the temporary building she had been working on, and Tom walked straight in the door and immediately laid spread eagle, face down on the fresh urethane surface. He was obviously exhausted. The only light came from the doorway, and Evelyn almost stumbled over him when she walked in. She sat down next to the wall, pulling her knees up to her chest, and wrapped her arms around her legs, resting the chin of her faceplate on her knees.

She was in awe of what he had done. She felt that no one else could have reacted as quickly in that length of time or organized everyone to do it with such precision. Tom Fielder had saved Commander Thon's life with nothing more than the keenness of his intellect and the strength of his will.

She looked at him lying on the floor. In the dim light, she could barely make out the back of his head and the steady rise and fall of the air tanks on his back as he breathed.

For the first time since she had become involved with the project, she understood why Commander Thon had insisted that Tom be second in command even to the point of risking his own position as commander of the first Mars expedition.

Tom spoke without moving. "Quit looking at me."

Evelyn scowled at the back of his head. *Damn him.*

Chapter Five
The Planet Harmony
Exact Time Unknown

From his position on top of the hill, the Tree saw the Koombar vehicle approaching from some distance away, and, at any rate, his young had alerted him to its imminent arrival. The car pulled up on the side of the road, 800 feet away at the base of the hill, and six large and well-armed Koombar piled out quickly and came to attention in two neat rows on either side of the back door. Their eyes probed the area, and their rifles were held at ready. One of them opened the vehicle door with a flourish, and a single Koombar emerged and began walking to where the Tree waited. A soft, modulated hum came from the Tree, and his young scattered into the surrounding brush. The Tree's forward eyes carefully inspected the approaching Koombar, and he noted its relative youth and the orange sash of royalty about its shoulders

Ah, so that's what this is about, the Tree reflected. *I am to teach this one.*

Just as it had been from the early days of the Great Migration, the young of the Koombar rulers were sent to learn at the hands of the oldest Tree in the region. The ruler of this area had recently become the Supreme Watcher, so this would be his oldest son. The Koombar believed that the Trees considered it an honor to teach the son of a Supreme Watcher, but of course, the Koombar didn't really understand. They understood so little.

The Tree sent out another modulated hum, and one of its young emerged from a small, nearby building (the only building in sight) with a device resembling a lawn dart and drove it into the ground near the base of the Tree. The Tree reached down and stroked the head of his son.

The young one looked up to his father and spoke in a series of high-pitched hums, squeaks, and clicks; and the Tree responded with its usual modulated hums. They were speaking two different languages. The adult Trees spoke by vibrating their roots in a complex harmonic song and would open their mouths when speaking to the young so that the vibrations could resonate in the air and be heard by children. Otherwise, adult Tree speech would have been nearly inaudible to those without roots. The young could not duplicate the adult speech and spoke a syntactically related but tonally different language. While the adults could speak the language of their children, they generally did not do so except with the very young—those who might still suckle and sleep in the hollow at the base of the trunk on the opposite side of the mouth and the forward eyes.

The old Tree looked down at his son and noted that its gray fur had none of the coarse appearance that signaled the end of childhood. The child's two eyes were large and deep black—situated in the front of the face for binocular vision and just above a nose that consisted of three holes. The mouth was a simple lipless slash below the nose. When the child spoke, the Tree could see the strong teeth common to omnivores and a tongue that lashed back and forth to make the clicking sounds. There were two arms jointed at the elbow and ending in hands with just three digits—two fingers opposing a strong and well-developed thumb. The young one stood erect on two legs and had a long prehensile tail that twitched absentmindedly behind him. The race of Trees could not know it, but their children closely resembled Earth-born, New World monkeys except for the hands and the upright posture.

"Father, why does this Koombar come to your glade?"

The Koombar rarely frequented the areas inhabited by adult Trees—much preferring to deal with the less intimidating young, and a Koombar in this place could mean trouble.

Adult Trees shared little in common with conventional vegetation, having no leaves and with thick bodies abruptly capped by a flat top, but they sometimes reached fifteen feet in height, and the three arms, spaced equally around the trunk, superficially resembled bare branches. Each arm split at the elbow into two forearms that ended in large, scabrous hands with the same three digits as their young. There were three sets of eyes—each pair situated above and between each of the arms—and one large mouth capable, it was said, of swallowing an adult Koombar in one bite. It was a false rumor, but one the Trees tried not to confirm or deny.

"This one comes so that I might teach it," said the Tree as he stroked the back of the young one. One of his other hands adjusted the communicator that had just been driven into the ground at his base.

The young one opened his mouth in surprise. "What could a Koombar need to hear from you?"

The old Tree sent out a very short vibration that roughly translated to: "It is not for you to understand." The phrase carried the connotation that it was something only adult Trees need worry about, and the young ones grew used to hearing it soon after they began to roam from their parent's side and ask questions about the world. The phrase could also have been translated, "It is too complex for you to grasp," and this would have been true for a lot of things. The juvenile Trees were not exceptionally intelligent. They had prodigious memories and could carry out the most complex tasks imaginable with just one telling of the instructions, but their problem-solving skills were limited—not much better, in the Trees' opinion, than those of the adult Koombar.

The young one pondered his father's response for a moment, then laid his head against the old Tree's thick body. "He will have a good teacher."

The Tree held his son close. "A teacher is only as good as his student," he replied.

The child looked up into the large black eyes of his father and wrinkled his nose in a grin. "Well then, this one will have a terrible teacher."

The Tree boomed a low rumble of laughter. "Away from me, insolent one. I have business to attend."

The young one ran off into the brush to await its parent's calling, and the old Tree watched as the Koombar continued climbing the low hill. The glade was lush with late summer growth on three sides, but a broad path opened down the hill to the road. The luxuriant grass of the path was trampled from the traffic of children, but flowers grew at the edges of the opening. Insects hummed and flew through the air while puffy, white clouds moved slowly eastward in a mild breeze. It was a beautiful place—the home of the old Tree for over 400 years, and only twice before had a Koombar left the road to speak with him.

The adult Koombar—just slightly larger than the Tree children—were covered with ragged, brown fur and could walk upright when necessary but preferred to walk on all fours. Two bulbous eyes were set almost directly on top of the head and allowed 360 degrees of vision whether the Koombar was upright or bent down on its hands. Two large, slow-moving lids blinked at regular intervals up and over the eyes from the sides of their heads, and the eyes would sink slightly into the skull with each blink. The front of the face was completely taken up by a muzzle resembling that of a terrestrial dog except that the mouth, which had slightly protruding teeth, was open only at the front. They had no tongue, and teeth covered the entire top and bottom of the mouth. The cheeks on each side of the muzzle were thick and well muscled to aid in swallowing and in speech, and there was a small hole hidden in the fur below the throat that served as a nose. The hands had three digits and an opposable thumb, but the digits of the back feet were fused into a fleshy pad for walking. They wore clothes only for the designation of rank, and this one was wrapped in a swath of royal, bright orange fabric.

The Koombar walked to within twenty feet of the tree, stopped, and stood up as straight as it could.

The Tree waited for a moment. Protocol dictated that the one of lesser rank should speak first, but the Tree couldn't help making the little Koombar fidget just a bit.

Finally he spoke, "This one is greatly honored to be in the presence of such a fine specimen of the Koombar heritage."

The communicator picked up the vibrations of his speech from the ground and translated it into the high-pitched squeaks and whistles of the Koombar language. The young Koombar jumped slightly from the sound.

Well, the Tree realized, *he's scared to death.*

The Koombar clacked his teeth together. "I am Skrin—son of the Supreme Watcher. I have come to you for instruction. I will call you Tree"

The communicator did not translate this. Young and adult Trees alike understood the Koombar language perfectly—the reverse was generally not true.

The Tree swept his arms forward and then down to the ground. "You will pardon that I do not prostrate myself before you."

Skrin visibly relaxed. "The limitations of Trees are well known," he said.

"And how might this limited one instruct the exalted son of the Supreme Watcher?" the Tree said, knowing that the irony would be lost on the young Koombar.

"My father has told me that the Trees have much knowledge of things which are of no concern to most Koombar but may be of help in the many and varied duties incumbent upon the Supreme Watcher."

"What might these things be?"

"My father has told me I should know of such things as Biology, History, and Philosophy."

Skrin stumbled over the words, and it was obvious they were new to him. "Interesting," said the Tree, "And how will these things help you to destroy your enemies?"

"My father would not tell me that. He has told me to come to you for instruction." Skrin squatted on his feet and leaned forward till his elbows rested in the grass. It was a posture of repose for the Koombar. "Instruct me," he commanded.

"Very well, where should we start?"

"What is history?"

"History is the study of the past—the things that were done in the past and how they turned out."

Skrin shook his head in derision. "And what good is that? The past is gone and cannot return."

"Oh, but it does. The Trees have a saying: 'Trees not rooted in the past will be washed away by the present.'"

"What foolishness is this—roots and washing away. The Koombar can run from floods. We are not tied to one piece of ground as you are."

Tree folded his two forward arms together and contemplated for a moment. "I believe you have been taught military strategy?"

"Of course," replied the Koombar, "I received the highest marks in my class."

"Most commendable, but where do you think this knowledge of how best to fight war came from?"

"It is the way to fight war. It is how war is fought and won. The Masters of War are taught these things from the older Masters. It is the way things have always been."

"No," said the Tree. "In truth, it has not always been this way. The Koombar have fought many wars in many different ways. The winners learned from these battles. They studied what the losers had done and learned how war could be lost. They learned what not to do. Those who lost and were allowed to live learned from their oppressors as they came to understand how they were beaten. The military strategy you have learned is a result of thousands of wars and the knowledge that was gained from each of them."

The young Koombar was growing restless, but he seemed to be thinking about it. "I suppose that could be true, but what then is history?"

"History is the study of the people and places in which these events occurred. The Koombar have learned the lessons but have forgotten what made the lessons important. You have eaten the rind from the fruit of the Skaal bush and thrown the rest away."

Skrin shrugged his shoulders in irritation. "The Koombar do not eat such things."

The Tree sighed. Teaching its own young was a pleasant but at times trying experience. This one was going to test his patience. "Very well, it is like eating the skin from the Jikry and leaving the flesh to waste."

"But if the skin is good and filling, what does it matter?"

The old Tree mentally scolded himself. The use of allegory was a complete waste of time when dealing with the Koombar. "Let me put it this way. Learning of the circumstances surrounding a war and the motivations of the people involved might give the Masters of War a deeper understanding of the strategy. This deeper understanding could give them greater flexibility during the battle and allow them to respond more appropriately to unforeseen circumstances."

Skrin considered this for a moment. "I suppose I can see something of what you are saying, but it seems like a great deal of trouble for a marginal advantage."

"Wars are won and lost by virtue of marginal advantages," said the Tree.

Skrin inflated his cheeks in a gesture of agreement. "This is true. Teach me then, of some history."

The old Tree wrinkled its nose with pleasure. The adult Trees spent most of their sessile lives caring for and instructing their children, and it gave them great satisfaction. In fact, the Tree intelligence had developed from a need to instruct their children. In the prehistory of the Tree home world, their young had wandered free soon after birth and had died in great numbers at the hands of predators or from an inability to coordinate their efforts in the search for food. The adults had few natural predators but were unable to move from the place of their rooting and could starve to death with food in clear view.

The young mobile Trees developed a rudimentary intelligence and an incredible memory for details under the evolutionary pressure for survival, but they were idiot savants. It was not until three children fused together to form an adult that any real intelligence was born.

The adult Trees began to teach their young how to hunt in groups and later how to plant crops and raise animals. The children would gather around the adult in large groups and listen for hours as the adult instructed or simply told stories. The young, in turn, cared for and brought food to the adults, and the Tree civilization had grown and spread to every corner of their long-lost home world.

So it was with pleasure that the old Tree began the instruction of the young Koombar. The urge to teach was built deep in its genetic code, and the pleasure that teaching brought was only slightly muted by differences in the student. This very pleasure had contributed much to their current status.

The old Tree spread its arms and spoke, "Very well, young Koombar, I will tell you the story of how the Trees and the Koombar came together, and how it is that the Trees do the bidding of the Koombar."

Chapter Six
Exact Time Unknown
Place Unknown

There is a flash in space, and the cylinder follows its shining ball out of the ring of light and into a region that seems as empty as where it came from. It swallows the ball as before and then unfolds a single, dish-shaped antenna. The antenna swivels back and forth for a short time, looking for an extremely weak homing signal that it eventually locates and locks. A simple program checks fuel levels and finds them to be adequate. Another program runs a series of tests to determine the integrity of the specialized shielding surrounding its engine and finds it to be adequate.

It then transmits a set of coordinates over and over again in a tight beam. The coordinates are transmitted 4,096 times before the antenna is retracted. It does not wait for an acknowledgement, nor would it receive one, but simply disgorges the ball and disappears in a flash of hard radiation.

Space is mostly flat here, being far from any strong gravitational forces, but a delicate instrument might find an extremely small but powerful gravitational source about one light-week distant. The source swallows everything that ventures too closely—even light, but telescopes of various kinds would reveal a great deal of activity.

Radiation spews forth on a number of wavelengths from the spinning edge of the source. Even in visible light, the view is interesting. Occasional bright flashes can be seen at the point where the radiation originates, and in a wide halo around the source, there is a twinkling of radiation and visible light as subatomic particles give up one or two photons each before disappearing forever into the maw of the source. Surprisingly, a preponderance of this radiation consists of gamma rays in the range of 500 million electron volts.

Higher magnification would reveal slowly moving vessels drifting through the halo and a great black ball in orbit around the gravitational source but some 300 million miles from it. The vessels and the great ball are made of the same non-reflective material as the cylinder and are nearly impossible to see except when they occlude the stars in the background or the twinkling of the point sources.

As time goes by, vessels can be seen emerging from the black ball, accelerating to the halo, and drifting there for a time before they return. Occasionally the black ball releases a small and unnaturally dense object that accelerates at nearly fifty gravities toward the gravitational source. These small objects continue to accelerate until they strike the edge of the gravitational source at a precise tangent, producing huge gouts of radiation and particles. The radiation screams upward out of the gravity well and is gone, but some of the particles, under the influence of unseen forces, stream out to the halo and curl lazily into orbit. These particles are different from the universe in which they find themselves, and the black vessels move carefully among them, gingerly harvesting mirrored matter for later use.

Space is flat here and undisturbed but for the ever so brief winking of virtual particles and the low, solemn ringing of the universe. In the distance, a most peculiar dance of light, radiation, and jet-black vessels can be seen.

Chapter Seven
March 29, 2061
Surface of Mars

The crew had just left the Mars I and the cabin was still depressured. Tom climbed back through the hatch and sat down on the bunk across from where Ki lay in his suit. He pushed a button on his wrist to activate their private channel then reached up and pushed a button on a small box fastened to his chest. The blinking red light of his video recorder went out.

"You're not supposed to do that," Ki said.

"These things drive me nuts. I feel like Big Brother is watching."

"Big Brother NASA *is* watching."

"Well," Tom said, "Not right now."

Tom looked over at his friend. "So how do you really feel?"

"Not too bad. I am very weak, and my legs hurt, but Dr. Krazinsky has given me something for the pain. I'm afraid I slept through the duty assignments. What is scheduled for today?"

"Don't change the subject. I want to know how you feel."

"Tom, I will be fine in a few days. Dr. Krazinsky's earlier estimate of my quick return to duty was a bit optimistic, but do you really think she would lie to you concerning my condition?"

Tom frowned and looked at the floor. "No, I guess not."

Ki looked at Tom and noted the hunch of his shoulders and the way he had begun to absentmindedly rub his knee through the thick fabric of his suit. "Perhaps we should talk about how you feel."

Tom pulled away a bit and groaned. "Couldn't you let me work up to it just a little bit?"

Ki laughed weakly. "We could do that, but I imagine there are other things you need to be doing."

Tom picked up the duty roster. "Espanoza and Melancon are wearing the other two recorders. I've got Cochran and Krazinsky on the never-ending search for box thirty-six. Weiss is finishing up the work on temporary number two. She should be finished by tomorrow."

Ki broke in. "You are ahead of schedule."

"Yeah, well. I helped write the schedule. I've pulled Melancon off the temporary buildings to help Espanoza and Geller with the Mars I. We should be finished taking it apart by tomorrow. If Cochran can retrieve thirty-six, I'll put him on laying the foundation for our permanent home, and Krazinsky will be opening boxes until I can think of something else that will keep her off her feet. I'll be in charge of walking around waiting for something else to go wrong."

Ki frowned slightly. "What is that supposed to mean?"

Tom hesitated. "I've got a bad feeling."

Ki waited for his friend to continue.

"I think we're snake bit," Tom said.

"Snake bit?"

Tom stood up and tried to pace in the small cabin, but he kept bouncing in the light gravity. He turned to Ki and put his hands in the air. "Haven't you ever been involved in a project that went bad and never got better? We almost smash up trying to land, you almost died yesterday, half our air supply is gone and . . . "

"Snake bit?"

"It's just an expression. It means that everything you touch is bound to turn to shit. It makes sense in Texas. I guess Yankees would say something like 'snowbound.' Hell, I don't know. I just know we've had way too much trouble already, and I can't shake the feeling that it's just beginning."

"You surprise me, Tom. I've never thought of you as the superstitious type."

Tom tried to rub his face but succeeded only in bumping his hand against the faceplate of his helmet. "It's not superstition. I've just got a bad feeling."

"There have been a few problems," Ki said, "but this has been a successful mission. The Mars I landed safely. I am alive. You were listening to the transmission from NASA last night. Rick Jelton himself, the head of NASA Central, said the video footage of the rescue has played almost nonstop on every network. The net result has been greater interest in the mission. NASA didn't even complain about the water and the liquid oxygen shipment. Rick said they could ask congress and the Europeans for the moon and we would get it. You have become a hero."

Tom snorted.

Ki continued. "We weren't planning on flying the Mars I back to Earth. This is a permanent settlement. About the worst that could happen is that we would need to set up the electrolytic unit to convert some of our water to oxygen, and if we're lucky enough to find water, we'll be doing that anyway.

"We all have bad days, Tom. You are the best engineer I have ever seen, and yesterday proved that you deserve to be here. I'll be up and around in a few days, and the permanent quarters will be finished in two or three weeks."

"Two," Tom said.

"There you are. I think we'll all feel better when we can walk around without bumping into each other."

"That's . . ." Tom started but was interrupted by a pop of static on his radio.

"Mr. Fielder, can you read me?"

Tom switched his radio frequency. "What is it, Cochran?"

"Sir, I think we found thirty-six."

"I'm not in the mood for games, Mr. Cochran. Did you find thirty-six, or are you just thinking about finding thirty-six?"

"Uh, well sir, you might want to come out and take a look at this. I'm heading back to camp and should arrive in about five minutes."

"I'll meet you outside in three. Fielder out." Tom switched back to their private frequency. "I gotta roll, Commander. Get some rest."

Tom was through the air lock and down the ladder before it occurred to him that he wasn't sure if Ki had responded.

Chapter Eight
Surface of Mars
March 29, 2061

"This better be good, Cochran. I've got better things to do than chase after a box full of Espanoza's farm tools."

"Yes, sir. I've got a signal, but I think it's down in a crevice."

"What?"

"It'll be easier to show you."

The rover rolled easily across the sand with a rocking motion from the many small dips and hills. Cochran swerved expertly around the larger rocks, and Tom took a moment to look around. The camp was already out of sight behind them, hidden except when they topped the taller hills, and the small talk of the crew had faded from their com sets. From the tops of the hills, the reddish sand and boulder-strewn plain seemed to stretch on forever to their right as they headed northwest and away from the sun. It was, he decided, pretty unremarkable in a way. The sand was a strange color, and of course, there was no vegetation of any kind. Otherwise it could have been almost any desert on Earth. They were in the foothills of a large mountain range that rose up quickly to meet the sky in front of them, but it was the sky itself that gave it all away. Pale yellow and cloudless but for the rare wisp of carbon dioxide; it was not the sky of Tom's childhood, and in his current mood, it hurt his eyes to look at it.

"I don't think we're in Kansas anymore," he mumbled.

"Sir?" Cochran asked.

"Nothing. So you're telling me this box fell in a crack?"

"Yes, sir. That's why we had such a tough time tracking it. I think the homing signal is bouncing off the sides of this crack and spreading out as it goes up. We're getting a diffuse signal from a broad area, and the tracking software can't settle on an exact direction." He pointed to a large rock in the shape of an obelisk that had weathered unevenly, giving it the appearance of a totem pole. "This is about where we were yesterday when you called us back to help Ms. Weiss. Take a look at the map."

Tom leaned over to look at the map on the console. A red X indicated the base camp, and the location of the rover was a small, barely moving circle. Inside the circle was an arrow that should have been pointing straight at the location of box number thirty-six. As he watched, the arrow moved lazily through several degrees of arc. The rover seemed to be moving in the right general direction, but that was all the map could tell him.

The terrain was quickly becoming more rocky and less sandy. Tom looked over his shoulder at the camp as they topped another rise and realized they had been moving up for some time. Cochran was following the tracks of his earlier trip to find the box, and it took them on a winding course around boulders the size of houses and large, rocky shelves thrusting up from the sand.

Tom looked at the map again. "What are we, ten miles from camp?"

"Pretty close."

"So this box comes down ten miles from where it's supposed to be and lands in a crack."

"That's about it, sir."

Cochran had to cut the wheel sharply to maneuver through a tight passage, and the rover heeled over as the tires rode up on the edge of a steeply projecting slab of rock.

"Snake bit," Tom said.

"Sir?"

"Never mind." Tom tightened his seat belt and held on to the roll bar with one hand as the rover rocked violently back and forth over the uneven ground.

Cochran drove them through a narrow channel between two rocks towering thirty feet above them. "It's right through here."

They came out at the bottom of a monstrous, rocky plate perhaps six hundred yards long from its base to its top and jutting upward in front of them at an angle of twenty-five degrees. Cochran stopped the rover and pointed upward. "I think it's in there."

Fifty feet from where they sat, the slab of rock had split nearly level with the horizon. It looked as if the bottom part had then shifted downward, opening up a gap about twenty feet across at its widest point. Tom looked to the left and right. They were near the middle of the slab, and the cleft stretched for two hundred yards in either direction.

"Now that's pretty damned amazing," he said. "This box travels all the way from Earth and manages to fall in this crack. What are the odds of that?"

"I've had a little time to think about it," said Cochran. "The prevailing winds are into the mountains. Once the box got this far over, all it had to do was land somewhere on the upper part of the slab. It just slid down until it fell into the crack."

Tom looked up at the rock. "Okay, make it one in fifty billion."

Tom turned to Cochran. "Have you gone up and looked?"

"Yes, sir, but you can't really see anything. I made sure we had some flares in the tool box before we left camp."

"Good. Get a few of the flares, and let's see what we can see."

Tom began climbing up the steep incline. He had to bend forward till his hands almost touched the ground, but the surface was free of sand, and the rubber soles of his boots offered good traction on the rock. Cochran followed behind with the flares in his hand.

Tom dropped to his stomach at the lip of the crack and leaned his head and arms over the edge. The angle of the sunlight was such that he could see only about ten feet into the depths of the fissure as the crack slanted away from him. The rest of it was covered in darkness. Cochran came up on his left and lay down next to him.

"Do you want me to throw a flare?" Cochran asked.

Tom looked around. "No. Give me one of the flares. I'm going to walk about a hundred yards that way." He pointed to his right. "You go down about the same distance in the other direction. We'll drop flares at the same time and see what we can see."

Tom took two of the flares and began walking to his right. He held his arms out for balance, and his left hand almost brushed the surface as he moved across the face of the rock. When he was in position, he dropped down to the rock and looked to his left. Cochran was already lying down with his head over the crack and a flare in his hand.

"You ready?" Tom called.

"Say the word," Cochran replied.

"Alright. Let's go." Tom twisted the top off the flare then turned the top over and scratched the end of the flare with the abrasive till it sparked and began to burn. He dropped it into the crack. "Try not to look directly at the flare."

The flare skidded away from him down the slope of the crack and fell about fifty feet before it began tumbling to the left. He could see Cochran's flare tumbling down and to the right at nearly the same depth. Tom's flare hit an outcropping and stopped some one hundred feet deep and sixty feet to his left. Cochran's flare continued to tumble downward and to the right till it reached the middle of the crack and seemed to disappear. *That's odd,* Tom thought, but he was distracted by the sight of box number thirty-six wedged over one hundred feet down near the middle of the crack where it narrowed toward the bottom. The parachute was wrapped around it, and the bright blue plastic of the box could barely be seen through the fabric and tangled lines.

Both of the men continued to hang over the edge of the crack, and neither of them spoke for a few moments. "Do you think we can get the winch-hook around one of those lines?" Cochran asked.

"Only one way to find out," Tom said. "Go down and move the rover. Park it right below where I'm standing." He looked at the jagged edge of the split. "We need something to keep the cable from rubbing."

"Got it covered," said Cochran. "I didn't know what we might be heading into this morning, so I packed a little rock climbing equipment. There's a few pitons in the tool box."

"Perfect. Bring up a couple of those and a hammer."

Cochran backed his way down the rock on his hands and feet, and Tom walked toward the middle of the crack until he was directly above the box. Cochran moved the rover to a point just below Tom, pointed it toward the rock, and scrambled up, towing the winch-cable behind him. Tom took the end of the cable and cocked the safety latch out of the way before throwing it into the crack. Cochran sat next to him pulling more cable from the winch, and Tom lay down, watching the hook slide down the steep slope to where the box waited.

"Hold it!" he called as the hook brushed the side of the box. Just then, the flare burned out, and all went dark.

"Damn it," Tom swore and pulled the other flare from his pouch. He twisted it apart and scratched the top before throwing it off at an angle to his right. The flare skidded down and away on the inside face of the rock and then began tumbling toward the middle of the crack as the other flares had. It disappeared beneath the box and went out.

"What the hell?" Tom said. "With all the money this mission cost, you'd think NASA could have bought decent flares." He turned to Cochran. "You got another one?" he asked.

"On the rover."

They looked down the rock to where the rover sat. "Maybe I can snag it in the dark," Tom said. "There's parachute line sticking out all over it. Give me the pitons, and go back down to the rover. If I can get it hooked before you get there, we won't need another flare."

Cochran handed the pitons and hammer to Tom who found a small crack and drove one of the pitons deep. He then leaned over the edge and began to move the cable up and down, fishing for the box. Before long, he felt resistance.

"Aha. I've got it."

He snapped the cable through the piton while holding tension on the cable. Cochran was just arriving at the rover. "Start taking up slack real slow. I don't want to tear through the parachute."

Cochran leaned down and pushed a switch on the front of the rover. The cable began to wind up on the winch-spool. "I hope it's not wedged too tight," he said.

Tom let go of the cable when it began to tighten slightly. "We're gonna know pretty quick," he said. The winch pulled the cable tight until it went in a perfect straight line down the rock. There was an anxious moment when nothing seemed to happen, and then the cable jumped and began to wind into the spool. They could see from the tension that the box was still hooked. "Alright, box thirty-six is ours." He leaned over the crack and watched the cable reeling in from the darkness. "Stop the winch when I raise my hand," he said, but something was bothering him. He just wasn't convinced that two of the flares could have been defective. And why had all the flares tumbled to the center of the crack? An idea began to form in his mind. Just then, the parachute came into view at the edge of the light. He raised his hand. "Whoa."

Cochran stopped the winch.

"Okay," Tom called, "raise it up real slow just a little at a time till I say stop."

Cochran began to bump the winch on and then off. Tom watched the parachute and then the box ease up out of the dark crevasse. "Come on," he repeated every few seconds. "Just a little more."

Finally the parachute was all the way up to the piton and Tom called for Cochran to stop the winch. "Come up and help me pull it over the edge. And bring some more flares and some rope."

Cochran opened the toolbox, pulled out three flares and a large coil of lightweight rope, and scrambled up to where Tom sat at the edge of the split in the rock. Together they pulled the parachute up and then dragged the box over the edge until it sat between them.

"I'm going to leave the cable through the piton," Tom said. "Go down and start letting the winch unwind. The box should just slide right down to the rover. And give me the flares and the rope."

"What did you need the rope for?" asked Cochran.

"This is where it gets a little weird, Mr. Cochran. I'm going into the crack."

Cochran hesitated. "Say again, sir."

"I said, I'm going down into the crack. Now give me the flares and the rope."

"Why do you need to go into the crack? We've got the box."

Tom felt irritation sweep over him with a sensation that made him feel as if his skin was shrinking. "There is something I want to see," he said. "Now hand over the stuff, and get back down to the rover."

The tone of Tom's voice didn't invite further conversation, and Cochran handed over the flares and rope. Tom held the box until Cochran reached the rover to release the brake on the winch. He gave the box a slight shove, and it began skidding down the slope straight to the front of the rover. Tom watched the box slide down for a moment, then moved over several feet and busied himself with driving the other piton into the rock. He tied one end of the rope to the piton and the other to a ring on the side of his suit. He then threw the coil of rope over the edge of the crack and watched it unwind into the darkness.

When the box reached the bottom, Cochran pulled the winch-hook from where it had snagged one of the parachute lines and looked up at Tom. "Let's unhook the cable from the piton and go home," he said.

Tom ignored the comment. "Pull in the winch-cable until I can grab the end. I can use it as a lifeline while you lower me down."

Cochran stood at the front of the rover without speaking or moving. "Mr. Fielder, I'm not sure this is such a great idea."

"It's a wonderful idea, Mr. Cochran. Now pull in the cable till I can hook the end to my suit. You will then slowly release the cable from the winch just like you did to bring the box down the slope, but this time you will be lowering me into the crack. When I'm finished looking around, you will pull me back out."

"Mr. Fielder, this seems a little reckless."

Tom gritted his teeth in irritation. He choked back what he wanted to say and took a few deep breaths. When he spoke, it was slowly and with great precision. "I understand your feelings, Mr. Cochran, but I have done a good deal of rock climbing in my day, and this is not a difficult task. The inside of the crack is sloping away, and I can easily walk myself down with the winch-cable. I am also wearing one of the recorders. Your objections will be noted."

Cochran hesitated for a moment still. "Yes, sir," he said.

Tom relaxed just a fraction. "We'll take it slow."

Tom held on to the cable as it snaked back through the piton. He waved at Cochran to stop the winch with about three feet of cable extending past it and set the hook's safety latch back into position before snapping it into another ring at belt level on the front of his suit. He then stood up and began to lower himself over the edge, taking care not to rub his suit against the sharp lip of the crack. The outer skin of the suits was tough, but there was no point in pushing his luck. When he was over the edge, he grabbed the cable and lowered himself down until he hung from the hook in his belt. He pulled his feet up and stood against the severe slope of the rock, holding the cable in both hands. Tom was nearly horizontal to the ground, but the cable held him upright and against the rock. "Okay, Mr. Cochran. Real slow."

"Releasing brake now," came the reply, and Tom began to walk backward down the inside face of the crack as the winch-cable unwound.

"That's just about right," Tom said. "Don't let it go any faster than that." As he dropped further into the crack, darkness enclosed him till all he could see was a band of light at the top spreading out to his left and right. He turned on his suit lights, but they were not bright enough to show the ends of the crack.

"Okay," Tom said, "hold it there for a minute while I get one of these flares lit."

The cable stopped, and Tom pulled out a flare and scratched the top. Sparks flew and the flare erupted in brilliant white light. Tom held it away from his suit and looked left and right.

"It's just as I suspected," he said. "The crack is filled with sand almost to the top at both ends, but it slopes down into the middle."

"I don't get it," Cochran said. "Shouldn't the sand be level across the bottom?"

"Yes it should," answered Tom.

"Then why is it sloped?"

"Well, Mr. Cochran, I think we've found ourselves an hourglass."

"I still don't get it," said Cochran.

"Start lowering the cable again," Tom called. "I'll explain once I get a look at the bottom."

The cable began to reel out and Tom backed further down the crack while holding the flare away from his suit with one hand and the cable with the other. Cochran spoke. "Are you alright, sir?"

Tom grimaced. "Yes, mother, I'm just fine."

Cochran groaned. "I'm sorry, sir, but this is making me a little nervous."

"Look, Cochran, if the cable breaks and the rope breaks and I fall to my death, you'll see the cable and the rope pop straight up out of the crack. If you don't see that, then don't worry."

"I wish you wouldn't talk like that, sir."

Tom almost laughed. "What is bothering you? When I was younger, we used to climb straight up the sides of rocks three times this tall with a lot less than a Titanium-alloy, braided cable. And in one full gravity I might add."

"I never cared much for rock climbing, sir," Cochran said.

"What were you planning on doing with the rock climbing equipment you brought?" Tom asked.

"I guess I'd have used it if I'd had to, but I wasn't looking forward to it."

Ideas were turning in Tom's mind as he continued down into the crack. "You like Ferris Wheels, Cochran?"

"Can't stand them, sir."

"Cochran, are you telling me that NASA's best pilot is scared of heights?"

"Flying is different, sir," Cochran said indignantly.

Tom laughed out loud. "What about roller coasters?"

"Roller coasters are pretty cool."

"You're weird, Cochran."

"If you say so, sir, but it seems to me that going down into that crack is a little weird too. If you don't mind my saying so."

Tom chuckled. "Yeah, I might have to give you that one."

Tom kept moving backward. "Keep it coming, Cochran. I'm near the bottom." The sloping sand to his left and right was getting closer as he dropped further down into the crack, and the opposite wall at his head was closing as the crack narrowed. Before long, his helmet brushed the other side of the crack, and he told Cochran to stop the winch. The flare in his hand was nearly spent. He twisted around to look over his shoulder and dropped it. The flare fell straight down through a small slit in the bottom of the crack and disappeared from sight.

"Well I'll be damned," Tom said.

"What is it?" Cochran said anxiously.

"There's an opening in the bottom of this crack. I'm going to try and see what's on the other side. Hold up while I get myself repositioned. I'll tell you when to lower the winch some more."

Tom pulled himself up on the cable and let his feet slide down the rock, catching himself with both hands as his chest swung forward. He was now hanging against the slope in front of him. The opening was only ten feet below him, but he would have to use his hands to keep his suit from rubbing against the rock.

"Okay, Mr. Cochran, We've got about ten more feet to go."

The cable spun out once more, and Tom walked his hands down the rock. The crack narrowed to a slit less than three feet wide at the bottom, and Tom found he could reach across to the other wall and hold himself in the middle while he descended. He reached over and began walking himself downward with his hands on opposite sides of the crack.

As he approached the bottom of the crack, he had Cochran slow the descent to a crawl. First his feet and then the rest of his body dropped through the slit until his hands reached the bottom edge of the crack. He called Cochran to stop the winch.

His suit lights shown out across a roof of rock. The crack was a thin line disappearing into darkness some eighty feet in front of him. He was dangling by a small, braided wire cable and a piece of rope above he knew not what.

"Mr. Fielder," Cochran called.

"I'm with you, Cochran. I'm hanging out of the bottom of the crack, but I can't get my suit lights pointed down to see what's below me. Hold on while I light a flare."

Tom wrapped one arm around the cable to keep his body from falling backward and pulled a flare from his pouch. He scratched the top and threw it sidearm along the crack as hard as he could. The flare fell down and down and then bounced and began tumbling away from Tom before coming to rest some three hundred feet below him.

"Good God!" Tom cried. His voice shook with excitement.

"What is it?" exclaimed Cochran.

"This place is huge." The force of throwing the flare caused Tom to spin lazily on the cable. Over half the room lay in the shadow of an incredible pile of dull red sand some forty feet below him, and as he spun back around, he could see the floor of the cavern and the far wall some five hundred feet away down the crack. The roof of the cavern slanted with the overlying rock, and the wall to his left was lost in darkness. The sand spread out to his right and left as far as he could see, but he noticed the floor of the cavern had the same slope as the roof.

"Hold on, "Tom said, "I'm going to throw my last flare."

Tom timed the throw so the flare went out at right angles to the first one and down slope to fall somewhere under the point where the rover sat on the surface. The flare tumbled as before, down the sloping sand, but this time, it seemed to tumble forever. Finally, it came to rest over twelve hundred feet away and more than five hundred feet below him.

"Holy shit," Tom said.

"What's going on?" Cochran asked. The tension was obvious in his voice.

"Everything's fine, Mr. Cochran, but you won't believe the size of this place. The sheet of rock that cracked and trapped our box is the roof of a cavern, but we're only seeing the very end of it from the surface. Both the floor and the ceiling slant downward for as far as I can see. I'd estimate," he paused for a moment, "hell, maybe a half mile range of vision, and I bet it just goes on down and out from there. Mr. Cochran, you are standing on the roof of the biggest cavern I have ever seen or heard of."

"I hope that's not supposed to make me feel good, Mr. Fielder."

Tom reached up and grabbed the lip of rock at his head to stop his spin. He was looking in the direction toward where the rover sat above him. The rock of the cavern ceiling was streaked gray and brown and had flaked off in large patches. Both the ceiling and the floor sloped down from where he hung suspended above a two hundred and fifty foot, cone-shaped pile of sand. As he looked past the flare, he could just make out some of the features of the far wall. He realized the ceiling closed on the floor in the distance. Looking closer to the flare, he saw a lighter colored channel winding its way on the floor of the cavern toward the wall. His eyes followed the channel till it disappeared at the wall in an uneven patch of darkness. He tried to estimate its width, but there was nothing for comparison, and he finally decided the dark area was somewhere between fifty and two hundred feet across. With one hand he reached up to activate the magnification on his faceplate and zoomed in on the area of darkness.

There appeared to be an opening in the cavern wall where the light-colored channel met the converging floor and ceiling, and he could see a few slender, pale spikes hanging down at the entrance like teeth in a huge mouth, but he couldn't quite make out what they were. He brought the magnification up to maximum, but vibration caused the image to jump around in his vision. Tom placed both hands against the rock at his head, took a deep breath, and let it out slowly. The image stilled for a moment.

Tom couldn't believe what he was seeing. He let out the breath, and the image began to bounce around again. "Mr. Cochran," his voice was trembling. "I'm not sure, but we may have just hit the jackpot."

"What is it? Are you okay?"

"I'm fine, Mr. Cochran. Give me just a minute."

Tom tried to still his breath to get a better view of the opening, but it was too far way, and his arms were already getting tired from holding them above his head.

"It's too far," he said. "I don't know what it is." He pushed with his hands to reverse his spin and untangle the rope from the cable, and let his arms drop to his sides.

"What does it look like?" Cochran asked.

Tom started to answer, but stopped himself. "There's an opening at the back of the cavern behind where the rover sits. It's got some interesting outcroppings, but I'm not sure what they are."

"What do you think they are?"

"Cochran, I don't want to get a bunch of crap started over nothing. I'm going to stay down here and get plenty of video. We can look at it later on tonight. Commander Thon is the geologist. He should be the one to decide what they are."

"What's it going to hurt to tell me what they look like?"

"It would just fuel a lot of useless speculation. You'll get a chance to see the video along with everyone else. Now, cool it."

Cochran lapsed into silence, and Tom continued to occasionally reverse his spin at the end of the winch-cable until the flares burned themselves out. He braced his hands against the edges of the slit and called to Cochran. "Okay, Mr. Cochran, I've got all the pictures I can take. Bring me up."

"Starting winch, Mr. Fielder," came the reply.

Tom worked his way through the small opening and then planted his feet against the rock to walk himself the rest of the way up. At the top, he unhooked the winch-cable but left the rope hanging down in the crack. He backed his way down the slope to the rover and sat in the passenger seat while Cochran secured the winch. There was a small door resembling a glove compartment in the dashboard, and he popped it open to reveal a computer keyboard. He typed a few commands and turned to look at the map on the console. A black "X" had appeared with the words "Cave Opening" next to it. He closed the box, secured his seat belt, and took a long pull of nutrient broth from the straw in his helmet. He was more thirsty than hungry, but this would take care of both, and he greedily sucked down the cherry flavored liquid.

Cochran swung himself into the driver's seat and backed the rover away from the tilted rock shelf in front of them before turning it back toward their base. "I really wish you'd tell me what you think you found," he said.

"Don't beg, Cochran. It just pisses me off, and I'm not sure what I saw. So until we can get the video off of my recorder and have Melancon work his computer magic on it, you'll just have to wait."

Chapter Nine
Surface of Mars
March 29, 2061

They drove the rest of the way back to the camp in silence. When they pulled up next to the temporary shelters, Espanoza called from where he was pulling one of the last plates from the topside of the wing. "Hey, I see you found my stuff."

"We also found a cave," said Cochran, "and something in it, but Mr. Fielder won't tell me what it was."

There was an immediate babble of voices over the common radio. "Cave?" "What did you find?"

"Everybody cool it," Tom said. The com fell silent. "Cochran and I found the entrance to a large cavern at the bottom of a split in a rock shelf. I'm sure it's all real interesting, but I couldn't see well enough to make out the details." He paused to look at his watch. "We've still got several hours work ahead of us. Let's take care of that first. We'll knock off a little early, and Melancon can run some enhancements on my video."

Tom gave Cochran a dirty look that Cochran probably couldn't see, and the crew slowly returned to work.

"A cave, Mr. Fielder?" It was Ki on their private com.

Tom switched frequencies. "Yes, sir, and a big one at that."

"Fascinating," said Ki. "And what did you find that you don't want to talk about?"

"I'm not sure. It was almost a half mile away, and I couldn't make it out very well, but I may have found evidence of water."

"One half mile?" Ki said incredulously.

"It's a big cave. That was the limit of what I could see, but it continues down from there."

"What incredible luck," said Ki. "Did you actually see water?"

"No I didn't. I'm not even sure I found a good case for water being there. That's why I don't want to speculate too much until we can look over the video."

There was a moment of silence before Ki spoke again, "That is probably for the best. I will look forward to seeing this video."

There was a click as Ki turned off the private com, and Tom tried to focus on helping Weiss with finishing the work on the second temporary building, but he noticed there was less chatter on the radio, and he knew all the crew was looking forward to seeing his video. He hoped it was worth seeing.

~

The sun was low over the horizon, and Tom was walking around the two igloo-shaped temporary quarters, staring intently at the foundation and the doors. Evelyn Weiss had just pressured them up while injecting a harmless, green smoke. Tom was looking for leaks.

"It looks good, Ms. Weiss. Tomorrow night we sleep in here."

"That will be nice," she said.

Tom looked at the sun and checked the time. Though they might have worked for another twenty minutes, he called a halt. "Alright, gang. Let's wrap it up. Commander, if you could depressure the cabin."

Commander Thon responded, "Depressurizing now."

"Good," Tom said. "Melancon, if you could carry Dr. Krazinsky to the vessel and help her up the ladder."

"I can make it on my own," said Krazinsky.

"Melancon, carry Dr. Krazinsky to the vessel and help her up the ladder," Tom repeated.

"Aye, sir," from Melancon. He bounced the fifty feet or so over to Krazinsky and effortlessly scooped her up from where she had been sitting on one of the empty boxes while sorting parts from another.

The light at the top of the hatch turned green as Espanoza was climbing the ladder, and he popped the hatch and climbed through. The rest of the crew filed in—Melancon with Krazinsky hanging from his back.

As soon as the cabin was pressured up, everyone began to pull off their helmets and strip out of their gear. Tom unclipped the twin cameras from the sides of his helmet and carefully pulled the data-box from the chest of his suit. He laid the cameras and data-box on his bunk, pulled off his helmet, and slipped the air tanks off of his back before popping the seals and peeling his suit off. The cabin was soon filled with the rank smell of sweat.

"Whew," Tom said, wrinkling his nose, "we are one fragrant bunch of Martians. Somebody turn up the re-circulation rate."

Cochran twisted a dial on a console toward the front of the cabin, and the whir of fans went up in pitch. Adrian Melancon and Pamela Krazinsky were helping the commander out of his suit, and there was a gurgling noise coming from the back of the cabin as Carlos Espanoza emptied a full bladder pack from his suit.

Evelyn Weiss was stowing gear in an overhead compartment, and she flipped her straight, sandy brown hair out of her face with one hand. Tom could see her fine features in profile, and he noted the clear complexion and the strong set of her jaw. She turned and saw him looking at her and slowly blinked her pale blue eyes.

"How about a good hearty dinner of freeze-dried beef stew," Tom said.

"I'm really not hungry," she said.

A "Me neither" came just a little too quickly from Espanoza, and it was followed by a chorus of assent from the rest of the crew.

Tom looked around the cabin. He knew they were lying. NASA said they could live for months on the nutrient broth in their suits, but it was hard to believe it after having eaten no solid food all day. Tom's stomach was growling even at the idea of reconstituted stew, and he knew the rest of the crew was just as hungry.

Everyone was looking at Tom expectantly, and he realized they had talked about this beforehand. The suit radios were not designed for privacy, but the signal strength could be manually adjusted, and with a little fine-tuning, they could be made to broadcast only a few feet.

Tom stood for a moment looking back at them, and a lopsided grin came across his face. He looked at Ki. "Commander Thon?" he said.

Ki grinned back at him. "I am not especially hungry either," he said.

Tom nodded his head slightly. "Well gee whiz," he said, "what you say we watch some home movies instead?"

Melancon bounced in one stride to the front of the cabin and sat down in front of a computer screen. "Sounds like a winner to me." He called over his shoulder, "Let me get my video tools up. Can somebody hand me Mr. Fielder's recorder?"

There were two computer screens in the front of the cabin to the left and right of the entrance to the cockpit. Adrian Melancon was easily the largest member of the crew, and his broad shoulders almost hid the left screen from view. A rugged giant of a man and a fitness nut to boot, Melancon was easygoing and all but unflappable, and Tom actually liked him in a distant sort of way. He could see the muscles ripple as Melancon moved the pointer and spoke to the computer in soft mumbles. With his straight black hair, dark complexion, brown eyes, and high cheekbones, Tom reckoned that women probably found Melancon irresistible.

Mike Cochran was pretty much the opposite. He was a small man with a pinched face and a whiny voice that could set Tom's nerves on edge almost instantly. Cochran had unplugged the data box from Tom's cameras and was handing it over Melancon's shoulder.

Tom moved to the front of the cabin as Melancon spoke to the computer. "Download video, Lt. Commander Tom Fielder." He turned in his chair to address the crew in his soft Cajun accent. "I'm going to send this to both screens. The right-side screen doesn't have 3D capability, but the resolution is higher."

"Download complete," announced the computer.

"Okay," Melancon said over his shoulder, "Y'all pull up a chair and gather round. Does anybody know about what time the interesting part started?"

"I'd say about 9:30," said Cochran.

"That sounds about right," Tom said, "but hold up a minute." He was helping Ki off of his bunk, and Weiss came over to lend a hand. Together they all but carried the commander to the front of the cabin and sat him down in front of the right hand screen. Ki grimaced when his legs flexed from settling into the chair.

Melancon tapped a few keys. "9:30 coming up." The scene was down the rock face. Cochran was talking. "Mr. Fielder, I'm not sure this is such a great idea."

Cochran looked at the screen. "Fast forward through this," he said. "This is before Mr. Fielder goes into the crack."

Tom said nothing, and Melancon bumped the video forward. The scene was a close-up view of the interior rock face of the split. Tom had just lit the flare, and the view swiveled left and right as Tom looked at the sloping sand on either side.

"This still isn't the important part," said Cochran.

"Let it run," Tom said. "This is what started me thinking something strange was going on. I noticed the flares we threw down from the top of the crack all fell to the middle, and two of them seemed to go out when they hit the bottom. The sloping sand on either side was a clue that there was an opening in the bottom of the crack. That's why I decided to go down." Tom had been listening to the audio portion of the recording with half an ear and timed his little speech just right. All eyes had remained glued to the computer screens, but when Tom stopped talking, the audio filled the cabin. Cochran looked at Tom from where he stood behind Melancon and said, "Ah man." The crew listened to the next exchange between them.

Cochran: "I wish you wouldn't talk like that, sir."

Fielder, laughing: "What is bothering you? We used to climb straight up the sides of rocks three times this tall when I was younger with a lot less to hold us up than a Titanium alloy braided cable."

Cochran: "I never cared much for rock climbing, sir,"

Fielder: "What were you planning on doing with the rock climbing equipment you brought?"

Cochran: "I guess I'd have used it if I'd had to, but I wasn't looking forward to it."

Fielder: "You like Ferris Wheels, Cochran?"

Cochran: "Can't stand them, sir."

Fielder: "Cochran, are you telling me that NASA's best pilot is scared of heights?"

Cochran: "Flying is different, sir."

There were snickers from some of the crew, but Ki turned and frowned at Tom. "Let's get down to where you actually see the cavern," he said.

Melancon moved the recording forward in a blur until the scene changed to a lengthwise view of the crack from when Tom had turned and begun walking himself down with his arms outstretched.

"Right about here," Tom said.

They all watched as Tom descended through the roof of the cavern and threw the first flare. There were exclamations from the crew at the first sight of the huge cavern, but Tom hushed them. "It gets better," he said.

They watched the second flare arc away and tumble down the pile of sand and continue to tumble across the sloping cavern floor. The image spun slowly from Tom's rotation at the end of the cable, and there were more exclamations as everyone drank in the sight before them.

"Fascinating," Ki said. "Mr. Melancon, can you get a distance on that far wall?"

"Hold up a bit," said Tom. "I stopped my rotation to get a better look at the far wall. That's what really got me excited."

Melancon allowed the recording to run until the image stopped with a good view of the channel in the cavern floor and the dark area against the cavern wall.

"Okay," Tom said. "Stop it right there."

The picture froze, and several lines jumped across the screen as Melancon used the images from the binocular cameras to triangulate the distance to the wall. "Just shy of eight hundred yards," he said.

"Absolutely fascinating," Ki said. "This cave could not exist on Earth. It would have long ago collapsed from its own weight."

Tom leaned forward to point at the dark area. "Zoom in on this."

The image jumped forward, and they could easily see a smaller cave extending down and away from the cavern. "Pan up just a bit," Tom said.

The image slipped on the screen and one of the slender pale spikes came into view. "Right there," Tom said. "Zoom in on that."

The picture jumped forward again till the spike filled the screen. "Jackpot," Tom said. "Commander, I believe we are looking at a stalactite."

Ki was beaming. "Indeed we are, Mr. Fielder. Indeed we are."

Cochran looked at Tom and spoke with thinly veiled sarcasm. "Don't most caves have stalactites?"

"That's not the point, Cochran," Tom said. "Didn't you take Geology in college?"

Ki broke in quickly. "Stalactites are formed by water dripping from the roof of a cave over many hundreds or thousands of years. The water partially evaporates near the tip of the stalactite and deposits minerals, and so the stalactite grows longer. These particular stalactites may have been formed many thousands or perhaps millions of years ago, but it is our first direct evidence of liquid water on Mars." Ki studied the screen for a moment and then turned to Melancon.

"Mr. Melancon, can you give me panning control of this image?"

Melancon hit a few keys. "You have independent control of that screen. Right click to zoom in, left click to zoom out, and just drag the pointer to the edge of the screen to pan."

"Thank you," Ki replied and began to flick the image in and out and scroll it around with dizzying speed. He settled on the edge of the light colored channel and zoomed in. "Look at this," he said. "It appears the upheaval of rock that formed this cavern interrupted an existing flow of water. The water then formed a new channel on the floor of the cavern." He paused and leaned forward as if it might give him a better view. "Hmmm." The image danced about once more as Ki moved to the edge of the dark area and zoomed in. "Can you enhance the image past this opening?"

Melancon began to mumble arcane commands to the computer, and the image on Ki's screen slowly lightened and seemed to reassemble itself several times as it was transformed into a somewhat grainy picture of smooth, bulbous outcroppings and small, slick grooves pointing away from the camera angle.

"This is incredible!" Ki exclaimed. The excitement was obvious in his voice. "Look here." He pointed at the screen. "And here." His finger moved over slightly. "The area past the opening is much older than the channel on the cavern floor. What we have is a fracture cave giving way to a water cave. This opening is the beginning of what was once an underground river. The stalactites were formed after the water receded."

Ki rubbed his hands together and leaned back in his chair, half-turning to face the crew. "Ladies and gentlemen, if we are going to find water on Mars," he pointed to the screen, "we will find it in this cave."

"Ms. Weiss," he continued, "I believe you have considerable experience in caving, do you not?"

Weiss answered, "Yes, sir."

"There is much work to be done, and we should eat now," Ki said, "The building of the permanent quarters must take priority, but we will explore this cave at the earliest opportunity. Mr. Fielder, your climbing experience will be useful. I want you to work with Ms. Weiss on a plan for the exploration of this cave. Mr. Melancon, please rewind so that I can get a good look at the outside of the rock, and let it run from there. You can blank the audio. I will need to prepare a report for NASA."

"Yes, sir" replied Melancon, and the computer screens jumped to the outside view and began to run forward. Ki remained hunched in front of the computer, but the rest of the crew went about preparing their meal.

Tom found himself sitting on a bunk across from Weiss. He spooned up a bite of beef stew. "I remember something about your spelunking experience from your personnel file. Where did you do most of your caving?" he asked.

"It is my hobby," she replied. " I spent many summers exploring the caves in France: La Grotte de Mons and Grottes de la Foux near St. Cézaire, the Grottes du Chat, and many others. Caves have always fascinated me."

Tom pursed his lips and nodded his head. "Well," he said, "I guess the French habit of taking two months of vacation every year can be good for something."

Weiss' eyes flashed. "And what is that supposed to mean?"

Tom smiled his most innocent smile and actually batted his eyes. "Why nothing, Ms. Weiss. I'm just glad to know you've spent your spare time doing something that was educational and of use to all of us and to this mission."

Tom leaned back against the bulkhead and finished his meal. He was tired but exhilarated. There was hardly anything he enjoyed more than baiting Evelyn Weiss, and his earlier anxiety over the mission was far from his mind.

Gregg R. Overman

Chapter Ten
Exact Time Unknown
Place Unknown

The great black ball receives a message that has been transmitted 4,096 times. It reads the message eight times and compares each reading for accuracy. Thereafter the message is ignored. No effort is made to determine its origin.

The message contains a simple set of coordinates, and in response to it, four black cylinders are readied for launch. They are different from the first cylinder. They contain almost no instrumentation except for a rudimentary guidance system, a simple radio receiver, and a device for detecting gravitational sources. They are slightly longer than the first cylinder, and each of them carries four small cylinders strapped in a ring just above the tail. The smaller cylinders are little more than engines with infra red detectors, but they carry a web of extremely strong wire folded tightly in a compartment at the nose where the shining ball might be held. . The small cylinders will not require a shining ball of their own.

A large door opens in the side of the black sphere, and the cylinders are flung out one by one through the action of a magnetic sling. They wait a respectable time before radiation erupts from their tails, and they begin to accelerate at nearly ten gravities away from the black ball.

Inside the black ball, another, much smaller, probe is prepared. It also lacks sophisticated instrumentation, but its guidance system is slightly better, and its destination is more precisely known than that of the four, larger cylinders. The magnetic sling pushes it out in a slightly different direction. Radiation spews from its tail, and it moves off at an angle to the other four with an acceleration of nearly ten gravities.

The four cylinders and the small probe travel outward for weeks—climbing slowly away from the space-curving effect of the massive gravitational source around which the black ball orbits. The large cylinders, each with their four smaller cylindrical passengers, move together at first, but no two engines are exactly the same, and they have no instruments or programming that might allow them to check their position relative to one another. As days go by, one of them begins to pull slightly ahead, another to lag behind.

Finally, one by one, they arrive at a region where space is flat, and they each disgorge a shining ball that rips a small and very temporary hole in the fabric of the universe down which they, one by one, disappear.

The smaller probe reaches its own region of flat space and performs an identical atrocity on the flesh of time and space. Its only cargo a small bit of information.

Space is very flat here and mostly empty, but in the distance, a terribly beautiful sparkling of light can be seen.

Chapter Eleven
The Planet Harmony
Exact Time Unknown

The old Tree cleared its mind and called up memories of the first contact between the Koombar and the Trees. The Trees retained an excellent capacity for memorization even in their adult form, and since the adults were born from the fusion of three of the young, they carried three separate sets of memories from their childhood. Aside from that, there were excellent computer records dating back over a million years, but they would hardly be necessary for this work. The story of the Trees' enslavement by the Koombar was a popular one and had been told endlessly in the large gatherings of young Trees. There was much to be learned from it.

The roots of the Tree began to hum, and the translator clicked and whistled the Koombar language as he spoke. "This is a tale of many ages gone by," the Tree said. "It is of a time before the Trees came to know and understand the Koombar."

The young Koombar lay twenty feet in front of the old Tree's forward eyes with his arms out in front of him. He was absentmindedly licking at the fur on his forearm. "Was this when you were young?" he asked.

There was a booming hum from the ground as the Tree laughed. "No. This was long before I was born."

"You are said to be the oldest Tree."

The Tree considered that for a moment. There were several Trees who were slightly older than his four hundred years of adult life, but some of them had gone to sleep and might never awaken. At any rate, they were half a planet away. He didn't want to divert the discussion into Tree Biology, and it was unlikely this young Koombar would see an older Tree during his short lifetime. He was therefore the oldest Tree this Koombar would ever meet. "That is correct," he said.

"But Trees live almost forever."

"No. Adult Trees may live long enough to see fifteen generations of Koombar—about seven times longer than a Koombar might live, but we do not live forever. The story I am about to tell began over one million years ago."

Skrin narrowed his eyes in a frown. "One million years?" he said.

"There have been more than one hundred thousand Supreme Watchers since this story began."

The Koombar turned his head in suspicion. "Truly?" he asked.

"Truly," replied the Tree.

Skrin plucked some grass from the ground in front of him and sniffed at it. "It is also said that the Trees do not lie."

The old Tree considered that for a moment also. It was generally true that Trees did not lie. They could misdirect conversations with the greatest of skill, but the blatant telling of false information with the intent to deceive was unnatural to them. "The Trees do not care to deceive those they talk to," he said.

Skrin plucked another piece of grass, laid it in his palm, and blew on it so that it lifted and swirled away from him. He was trying hard to appear nonchalant. "Would you do me any harm?"

"The Trees harm nothing except to eat or in the case of immediate need for self defense. Often we choose to die rather than to do harm."

"That is insane," said the Koombar.

"There are times when the ways of the Koombar appear as insanity to the Trees."

Skrin shook his head in consternation. "Very well. Tell me of this story so old that it can be nothing but useless."

"Excellent," said the Tree. "Let us begin.

"Over one million years ago, the Trees and the Koombar did not live on the same planet. The Trees lived on their own world and the Koombar lived on theirs. The Koombar knew nothing of the Trees, but the Trees listened to the radio waves from the Koombar planet and eventually translated the Koombar language and began to understand something of what was happening on the Koombar home world.

"It was not a good time for the Koombar. Your race is not known for its understanding of the interdependence of living things or for the need to develop and use renewable sources of energy. Almost all intelligent life forms begin using coal and oil from the ground for their energy needs, and the Koombar were no exception to this. Some races quickly understand that their need for energy will eventually outstrip their supplies of oil, and they develop other methods of generating energy. The progression is usually from oil and coal to nuclear fission followed by nuclear fusion. Some races have turned completely to solar energy or to the energy that can be gained from the wind and waves or from heat in the ground. To our knowledge, the Trees are the only race that has tamed anti-matter.

"Less than five hundred years after the Koombar discovered and began to use the oil of their world, the oil was almost completely gone, and the Koombar had not developed the science that might have led them to other, cleaner ways of producing energy. And energy, by that time, was not the worst of their problems. The Koombar had no will or desire to temper their growth by spending any time or effort in developing controls for the gaseous pollution produced by the burning of oil and coal. They had also paid little attention to the many strange chemicals they had been pouring into the rivers and streams for all those years. Those rivers and streams emptied into the oceans of Koombar.

"When the Trees discovered the Koombar, your planet was dying. The temperature had risen nearly ten degrees, and the equatorial regions were uninhabitable and had reverted to desert. The oceans were polluted to the point that few fish could live, and many thousands of species of plant and animal had died. Some of these species had been purposely exterminated. Still, the Koombar burned oil without precaution, fought wars with what little oil remained, and dumped chemicals into streams without regard.

"I know that the ways of Trees seem strange and unusual to the Koombar, but we could not begin to understand what your race was doing. We only understood that soon you would all die, and an intelligent race would be lost to the universe.

"The Trees are a curious race, and we had sent probes to many regions of the galaxy to gather information and return to us. This is how we found the Koombar. Understand that we had no desire to visit these places. We are, after all, rooted in the ground for all of our adult life. Physical exploration of distant objects does not interest us, but still, we wanted to know more about the universe.

"The discovery of the plight of the Koombar set up a terrific debate among the Trees. We had found few systems where carbon-based life, or life of any sort, could flourish and grow. Most of space is simply empty, and where matter concentrates, there are frequently nearby sources of hard radiation or wild variations in the amount of incident radiation. The proper combination of stability, heat, and light is rare. The Trees view all life as sacred, and our deepening understanding of the scarcity of life simply reinforced this view.

"How then were we to consider the sanctity of intelligent life? In over fifteen thousand years of exploration, the Trees found less than ten thousand planets that harbored life. Of these, only twenty-five held life that we could understand as being intelligent. We had surveyed only a small fraction of the galaxy, but it seemed obvious that intelligent life was a most rare and wonderful thing.

"Understand also that we had contacted none of these races. It is not in our nature to interfere. We take pleasure in watching the Great Cycle of Life, but we do not generally presume sufficient understanding of that cycle to alter it in any way. It is our belief that such things should be left to the will of the one who created all things. It is part of our [*untranslatable*]." The translator squawked.

Skrin raised his head. "What is this word that cannot be translated?"

The old Tree looked down at the translator. "There is no Koombar word for this thing." He hummed briefly to the translator. "I will give it a name you can pronounce. We will call it religion."

"And what is this re-li-gion?" asked Skrin.

The Tree chuckled to himself. The idea of attempting an explanation of religion to a Koombar was a novel concept, and he would enjoy the challenge, but it would take them far away from their current story. "Briefly, religion is a set of beliefs which help the Trees to define their place in the universe."

"The Koombar make their own place in the universe," answered Skrin.

"Religion, in itself, does not conflict with that concept," said the Tree, "but it would take many hours to explain religion, and even then, some parts would remain unclear. Let us return to our story. We can talk of religion at some other time if that is your desire."

Skrin inflated his cheeks. "Very well. Continue with this story."

The Tree continued, "We found ourselves in the middle of an extremely difficult question. Life was sacred to us—intelligent life even more so. It is part of our belief that the universe is evolving toward greater harmony with . . ." The Tree paused for a moment. He was about to use the word "God" but decided better of it. "With itself," he said. "We believe that intelligent life is a part of that evolution.

"What were we to do? The Koombar were involved in their own cycle. It seemed wrong to interfere with that cycle. On the other hand, it seemed wrong to simply watch the Koombar exterminate themselves and remove an intelligent life form from the universe.

"The debate raged across our planet. Some said interference was wrong, and the Koombar should be allowed to complete their cycle and die. Others said we were a part of the Koombar cycle by virtue of our having gained knowledge of the Koombar predicament. If we were now a part of the Koombar cycle, then we had a duty to save them.

"And so the debate went on. For over one hundred years we talked and struggled with these ideas. Meanwhile, some four generations of Koombar came and went. The number of Koombar had decreased drastically, and your planet was deteriorating ever more rapidly. It became obvious that if we did not act soon, the Koombar would be beyond any effort we might make on their behalf.

"What finally tipped the debate was the understanding that your planet was now beyond repair. The degeneration your pollution had set in motion could not be reversed. Life would continue on Koombar, but only in the form of microbes and some very simple plants. It would be tens of thousands of years, if not millions, before the planet could recover. It seemed that, if we were to save the Koombar, we would have to move them to another planet.

"This played into the hands of a segment of the Tree population that had long advocated a migration to another planet. These Trees had no desire to spread the Tree civilization about the galaxy, but they believed we should colonize at least one other planet to insure the preservation of our race. They pointed out that some strange disease could destroy us, or that our sun could suddenly become unstable. None of this seemed terribly likely, but there was another segment of the Tree population that was enamored of the adventure it posed and yet another group excited over the engineering challenges. All of these groups argued that, if we were going to move the Koombar to another planet, we should go there first to prepare the way for them. The Trees and Koombar would then live together on this new planet.

"It is probably not possible for me to explain the massive realignment of Tree philosophy that was necessary before we could consider saving the Koombar. Our own children die from misadventure quite frequently, and we do little if anything to control them or to guide their natural curiosity. A basic tenet of the Tree religion is that the Cycle of Life—the universe itself—is under the guidance of a force far greater and more intelligent than we can imagine. It was considered by some that the saving of the Koombar constituted blasphemy or heresy."

The Tree looked wistfully into the distance, and his arms dropped to the ground. "Subsequent events proved that we had made a grave mistake, and the Tree principle of noninterference is now sacrosanct."

The old Tree stood without moving for a time. "At any rate, Trees are known to debate the finest of points for decades and longer, but we also tend to work in concert once a reasonable majority is reached. And so the work began. It was a task on a scale of nothing we had ever before attempted. Even the construction of our anti-matter generator did not compare to the scope of this work. Land was cleared, and factories were built. New sources of metal were located, and mines were dug. Our planet wide consumption of energy went up by a factor of thirty.

"We had never before made spacecraft for transporting adult Trees. Almost all of the work we had done in space was previously handled by computers and automated machinery. There had been a short time when some of our children had been sent to aid in the building of the anti-matter generator near the black hole, but even that ran now without personnel.

"We had experience in transplanting adult Trees from those times when landslides or other things made their rooting place unlivable, but it was a difficult task made more difficult depending on the age of the Tree. Our roots continue to grow throughout adult life and may reach forty or fifty feet in length. For this reason, only younger adult Trees would be moved to our new planet.

"Before we were finished, some six hundred ships were built for transporting young and adult Trees. Nearly the same number were built for transporting the Koombar to their new home. It was decided the new planet would be called Harmony. It was hoped that the presence of the Trees would temper the warlike nature of the Koombar and that our races might learn from one another. It was a time of great excitement and endless optimism."

The old Tree paused here for a moment and reached down to pick up a feather near its base. In unconscious mimicry of Skrin, he blew the feather out of his large hand and watched as the wind caught it and carried it away. "Our culture was young then—less than twenty thousand years of recorded history. We had much to learn about ourselves and even more to learn about the Koombar.

"So the great fleet was built. We began sending young and adult Trees to Harmony. The ships would leave, drop off the occupants, and return for another load of passengers. We sent the ships designed for transporting the Koombar into orbit around your home planet.

"By this time, the situation on Koombar was extremely serious. Your planet was habitable only in the polar regions, and there were roughly one hundred thousand Koombar in the north. These Koombar were separated into two camps and were continually at war. There were about one hundred and twenty thousand in the south, and they were divided into three factions. What little technology the Koombar possessed had deteriorated markedly. No radios functioned on the planet, and the main source of heat was from the burning of wood. It is possible that, with such a small population, the Koombar might have stopped their wars, but the livable area of the planet was shrinking year by year—forcing you to compete fiercely for available resources. The Trees had arrived to save you from all of this.

"A single ship was dropped from orbit to land in the middle of a vast plane before the walls of the largest city in the north. External speakers began to broadcast a message of peace and hope, telling the Koombar that we could bring them to a new home with food and water aplenty.

"The people of the city attacked the ship. Of course, there was little danger they would do it harm. The best weapon at their disposal was a single shot projectile device of limited range and projectile velocity. The pellets simply bounced off the ship. Watching the scene from orbit was a single adult Tree. Not knowing what to do, he did nothing, even though he could see the Koombar building a catapult that might be capable of toppling the ship.

"Fortunately, the catapult was not completed by nightfall, and the Koombar tired of watching their ammunition careen off the skin of the ship to land randomly on the plane.

"Darkness spread across the plane until only the light of torches could be seen without the enhancement of light amplification or Infra-Red. The Tree watched with interest from his ship as a group of twenty Koombar left the city from the far side and circled around, giving wide berth to the walls as they approached the ship. The Tree opened the hatch and the Koombar ran in to safety."

Skrin raised his head. "The Disaffected," he said.

"Yes," said Tree, "The Disaffected, those without hope, those who feared their lives might end soon. These came to us in small groups under cover of night. It seemed the evacuation of Koombar would not be the timely and orderly process we had envisioned. We parked our ships at various points next to all gatherings of Koombar, but we took care to place them where routes to the ships would not be in full view of the general populace. Slowly, we began to move Koombar to Harmony. We tried to convince some of the Koombar to return to their planet and explain that we had truly come in peace and that Harmony was a wonderful planet with food and water for them all, but they refused."

Skrin blinked slowly. "Wisely I would say. The Koombar do not look favorably upon loss of personnel during war."

Tree stretched his arms in front of him. "This process took nearly three hundred years. At one point we dropped video machines into some of the cities with views of Koombar eating and playing on Harmony. Your people took the machines apart and used the screens as windows in the walls of their cities. It seemed to have no impact on the number of Koombar boarding our spacecraft.

"In the end, your planet died and thousands of Koombar with it. We left many ships standing on the surface in the hope that some would finally understand their only chance for life lay on Harmony. These ships are there still, although they must have run out of fuel by now. The rest of the ships were sent to our generator for use as scrap, and even that proved to be a mistake.

"On Harmony, things grew and evolved. The Koombar tended to keep to themselves, and with seemingly limitless space and resources, there were few real wars. Occasionally one group would find itself in disagreement with another, but it usually resulted in only a minor skirmish, and the weaker force would withdraw. We gave them energy in abundance, and this planet was chosen for its bounty of food and water. Life was good for the Koombar, and the Koombar changed—at least to some extent.

"With the abundance of food and energy, the need to reproduce was lessened, and the Koombar population stabilized, of its own, at near the current level. Where before issues had been settled always by force, negotiation began to play a role. The Trees actively promoted this change, and for some time it seemed that the dream of those long-dead Trees would be realized—the Trees and Koombar would learn from one another and live together in peace.

"Then came the birth of Cheswan Swi Geberak."

Skrin interrupted, "I know of him."

"As well you should," said Tree. "Cheswan was born of the ruling class. His father was the Watcher for one of the largest groups on Harmony, but Cheswan was born with deformities. He was abnormally small, and his limbs were twisted. As is the custom with the Koombar, he was brought out into the wilderness to be killed, but for reasons we will never know, he was simply left to die. One of our children found him and brought him to an old Tree rooted nearby. The old Tree took pity on the small Koombar and fed him."

"So it is true," said Skrin, "that Cheswan Swi Geberak was raised by Trees."

"It is true. The old Tree not only fed the babe but also began to teach him when he grew to an age of understanding. It became apparent that Cheswan was a brilliant student. Our own children are not terribly intelligent but have an excellent capacity to carry out the desires of the adults. Most adult Koombar have no desire to learn the technology of the Trees, and we have found almost no Koombar who were capable of understanding it. Cheswan was different. Not only did he hunger for the knowledge, but he easily grasped most of the ideas. He was particularly interested in the concept of our anti-matter generator, and although he never really understood the underlying principles, he came to know much of the practicalities involved.

"Eventually, Cheswan desired to be with his own kind. We cautioned him of the danger, but he was insistent, and we prepared a vehicle he could operate and sent him on his way.

"According to Koombar legend, Cheswan drove to his father's city and demanded his place as heir to the Watcher. We presume this to be false, but it hardly matters. We had no reason to believe anything was amiss until several years later when one of our probes impacted our home planet. At first it was believed the probe had malfunctioned, although no one could see how this was possible. Then another probe impacted our planet, and then another. Altogether, eight probes smashed into our planet and ignited their anti-matter engines. The resulting radiation and increase in temperature destroyed almost all life and killed every Tree on the planet. Nearly one billion Trees, adult and young, died as a result of what Cheswan had learned.

"We discovered later that Cheswan had reprogrammed the computers on the anti-matter generator from one of our stations here on Harmony. A simple process really, and one that we would never have considered to guard against. It no longer mattered. The damage was done. Not just that our home planet had been destroyed, but the Koombar now knew that the Trees were vulnerable. A Watcher who claimed to be Cheswan's father came to us demanding that we furnish him with weapons. We refused. This Watcher then burned the Tree that refused his request, and when we did not retaliate, he burned another, and another, and yet another.

"Thousands of Trees died in a massacre that went on for years until the Koombar understood we would never give them weapons. They finally grew bored with the whole thing. Occasionally, one of the Koombar Watchers will make the same request or other requests that the Trees cannot honor, and more Trees die. Such it has been since Cheswan Swi Geberak was raised and educated by Trees."

"Why will you not give us weapons?" Skrin asked.

"Weapons would simply allow the Koombar to destroy each other in greater numbers. War would be the outcome. Eventually the Koombar would destroy the Trees, and this planet would become as your home planet."

Skrin hesitated for a moment as if he were afraid to ask the next question. "Could you destroy the Koombar?"

The sun was beginning to set, and Tree watched the sky turning pink in the west. He was growing tired of this for some reason. "It is technically feasible," he said, "but we are not capable of such an act."

"I don't understand," Skrin said.

Tree wrinkled his nose in a grin at the little Koombar. "Sometimes I don't understand it either," he said, "but the day is at an end. Your guards grow restless. Let us take this up another day."

Skrin looked about in surprise at the long shadows. "Yes," he said, "I must be going, but I would understand why the Trees do not destroy my people. This is an important issue."

Tree scratched at one of his six eyes with one of his six hands. "It is important to the Trees also, but it involves our view of the universe, and that view is a result of our evolution. To understand evolution we will need to speak a little of biology."

"Biology." Skrin stood and faced the Tree. "Yes, we will speak of biology next time." He turned to go but stopped for a moment. "And this was history?"

"An example of it, yes," replied the Tree.

"Hmmm," said Skrin, "I still fail to see the use of it, but it was an oddly interesting story. I will return when my duties permit."

Tree bowed as low to the ground as he could. "By your leave, sire." But Skrin was down the hill and did not turn to acknowledge him.

Chapter Twelve
Surface of Mars
April 17, 2061

Tom Fielder woke up to the soft ringing of the morning bell and remembered, finally, not to sit up and bump his head on the curving wall. Each temporary building held four people. It gave them a little more elbowroom than the Mars I, but not by much. After two weeks, the place still smelled slightly of urethane sealant and glue, but under that was the aroma of human sweat. It reminded him that they needed to find water.

Not that there wasn't a lot of water on Mars. Someone had calculated there should be enough water on Mars to cover the surface some 100 meters deep, but the Martian water wasn't on the ground—it was in the ground. Several of the Mars probes found significant amounts of water mixed into the sand and rocks just below the surface, but recovering that water would be difficult and time consuming.

"Rise and shine," he said, "Today we move into the mansion on the hill."

Espanoza and Cochran made grumbling sounds. They were tired. He had pushed everybody pretty hard over the last few days, and Ki had spoken to him somewhat forcefully about pacing the crew. "We will be here for three years," he reminded Tom. "We can't get everything done in the first few weeks." Tom grudgingly agreed to slack up a bit, and the conversation had been nothing like the chewing out he had received for embarrassing Cochran during the replay of the cave video, but he was already forgetting every bit of it as he eagerly looked forward to getting into their permanent home and exploring the cave. The lab was a few days from completion and still open to the Martian atmosphere, but the living quarters should be pressured up and warm by now. They had moved all of the furniture yesterday afternoon, sealed the lock, and turned on the air and heat.

Tom couldn't help it. He felt like a kid on Christmas day. Not only would there be space to move around in, with a real dining area and kitchen, but he would, for the first time in months, have a room to himself. This was not a luxury shared by most of the crew. Only Commander Thon, Tom, and Dr. Pamela Krazinsky had their own rooms—Ki and Tom by virtue of their mission rank, Dr. Krazinsky by virtue of her position as Medical, and the fact that her room doubled as an examination room and sick bay. Evelyn Weiss would share a room with Kaitlin Geller, and Adrian Melancon would bunk with Carlos Espanoza. That left Mike Cochran alone in a room built for two, but nobody seemed to mind.

Tom rolled out of his bunk and stretched his hands up to touch the ceiling. "Let's get some more of that delicious squeeze-tube oatmeal and check out our new digs."

Ki stood up across the room. "Why don't we go to the permanent quarters first," he said, "I have something I want to show all of you."

Espanoza and Cochran stopped and turned to look at Ki. "Uh, Commander," Tom said, "I'm kind of hungry."

"Nonetheless," said Ki, "Let us suit up and visit our new home."

Tom looked at him carefully. Ki had the enigmatic grin on his face that always meant he was up to something. Espanoza and Cochran remained frozen in position.

Tom turned and roared, "You heard the man. Let's get dressed."

There was a burst of activity as everyone began to slip on their suits.

Seals popped and lines began to hiss as they jostled around each other in the small space. Espanoza and Cochran tried desperately not to bump into Tom or Ki while they suited up. Within a few minutes they were checking each other's fittings and connections.

Tom checked Ki's suit thoroughly. "What are you up to?" he said in a near whisper.

"Why, Tom," Ki said, "It just seems to me that we might enjoy eating breakfast in our new home."

Tom knew that, that wasn't it, but by now he could see little more than Ki's eyes through the faceplate. And anyway, Ki could be a deadly poker player when he felt the need.

"Okay, whatever. Just leave me in the dark. I'm only the second in command here. There's no need in my knowing everything."

"Exactly, Mr. Fielder."

Tom frowned but turned and allowed Ki to check his suit. Espanoza and Cochran were standing and ready to leave. "Alright," he said, "hit the button, Cochran."

A pump kicked on to depressure the small room, and a green light soon flashed above the door.

Cochran twisted the heavy handle that popped the hatch outward and then pushed it open. There was a slight whoosh of air as the door opened, and they stepped out onto the cold sand. Tom checked the bottom of the door-seal for sand before he closed it and looked up to see the rest of the crew waiting outside the other temporary building. The sun was barely over the horizon, and an unsubstantial frost covered everything in sight with a thin, white coat that glinted and sparkled from the oblique rays of the weak light. Rolling hills shaped the horizon just under the rising sun, and pockets of icy fog could be seen sliding along low places in the sand as the sun warmed the ground and stirred a breeze in the thin air. The nearby mountains sent jagged teeth into a sky painted with streaks of pink from the rising sun, and Tom stood for a moment simply looking. The black walls and clear, domed roof of the permanent housing just 100 feet in front of him were also covered with sparkling frost.

Tom realized that something was wrong. He looked around carefully and then hit a button on his left wrist to activate the private channel between him and Ki. "Commander, Melancon is not here."

"That is correct. Shall we go?" was all Ki had to say about it.

"So you're not going to tell me what is going on or why I'm missing a crewmember?"

"Patience, Tom. All will be revealed in time. You really should practice some of the meditations I have tried to teach you."

"Yeah, right," Tom said, and kicked at the sand with the toe of his heavy boot. "Live within the moment and all that Zen stuff."

He thumbed the general com button on his suit radio. "Okay," he said, "Let's move it before we turn all white and sparkly."

The crew bounced off to their new home with Tom and Ki bringing up the rear. Tom noticed that Ki was barely limping. "In the lock four by four," Tom said. He and Ki stood outside as the crew cycled through the door.

Ki was perfectly still and staring into the sun. "Truly a splendid morning."

"Yeah. Real nice," Tom said, "and not a hint of rain."

They took their turn through the lock and emerged into the communal room. This was the largest room in the building. The clear, slightly domed roof was nearly twelve feet high at its center and allowed the light of Mars to give an open, airy feeling. The internal wall between the kitchen and the communal room was actually an eight-foot partition, but the living quarters had a more standard ceiling and roof for greater privacy and noise control. The laboratory roof was of standard construction for containment purposes. The wall to his left was a huge computer screen that doubled for watching movies. It was blanked to a dull gray and would remain so until the computer system was connected. Directly across from Tom was the entrance to the kitchen. A table surrounded by eight chairs and offset slightly to the right of center, occupied most of the communal room. There were couches and other chairs to Tom's right, and a door leading into the living quarters with its separate bathrooms for men and women. Access to the lab was through the kitchen and through an internal airlock that would be used when experiments required Martian atmospheric conditions.

"Home sweet home," said Tom just as he realized that the rest of the crew had removed their helmets and was standing around with strange grins on their faces. There was some small talk going on, but Tom was having trouble hearing it through his helmet. He quickly popped the seals on his helmet, twisted it to the left and pulled it off.

He was instantly overpowered by the smells. There was the odor of fresh urethane and sealant just like in the temporary, but on top of that was something he had trouble identifying for a moment.

"I'll be damned," he said, "bacon." He continued sniffing. "And coffee."

Just then, Melancon leaned out of the doorway leading to the kitchen. There was a towel draped across his shoulder, and he held a spatula in one hand. "We got bacon, sausage, cheese omelets, biscuits, and hot coffee for anyone that wants it. No bread for toast yet, but I'll have that taken care of by tonight. And I'm not real proud of the omelets, but you can only do so much with powdered eggs."

A cheer erupted from the crew. They had been living on ship's rations for nearly two months, and the idea of eating real food at a real table with real silverware was something they had tried not to think about. The smells were driving everyone crazy, and the crew surged toward the kitchen.

"Hold it," Tom said.

The crew froze in place. "We ought to at least get out of our suits first, and I believe we have Commander Thon to thank for this surprise. It would be appropriate if he served himself first." The crew began to peel out of their suits. There was a row of lockers next to the airlock, each one with a crewmembers' name at the top. The room was filled with the sound of lines popping, and the tearing sound of Velcro fasteners as the crew removed their air tanks and stripped out of their suits. In record time, the suits had been put up and the crew stood around with an air of expectant urgency.

Ki stood beaming with his hands behind his back. He was a small man of five feet six inches with thinning, straight black hair and oriental features. His round face was accentuated by his tendency to gain weight, and even though he had trimmed down for the mission, he easily carried more body fat than any of the other crewmembers. It was one of the things that had helped him survive his encounter with the fallen wing.

Tom turned and gave a bow to Ki. "Commander Thon, after you."

Ki gave a short bow in return. "Thank you, Mr. Fielder. I believe I will."

He began walking to the kitchen, and the crew parted in front of him.

"Alright," Tom barked, "single file."

The crew formed a snaking line through the kitchen door, and Tom walked past them and into the kitchen. The large stove to the left was covered with pans full of steaming food. Ki had taken a plate from the counter to the left of the stove and was piling bacon and eggs onto it. The counter to the right of the stove held pitchers of reconstituted orange juice and milk. Just to the right of that was a thick door leading to a large un-insulated pantry that jutted out of the side of the dwelling. It was not heated and stayed at whatever the Martian temperature might be.

The crew was going to eat well while on Mars. Some things, like fresh fruits and vegetables, were out of the question unless and until they could get the greenhouse up and running, but the perfect deep freeze was just an airlock away, and most foods, if they were sealed to prevent freezer burn, would last for months or years just sitting on the sand.

Tom scanned past the pantry door and found what he was looking for. Another counter on top of the ultrasonic dishwasher held two large decanters of coffee. Creamer and sugar and cups and spoons lay beside them.

"Sweet mother of God," he mumbled to himself as he walked across the room, "Real coffee in a real cup."

He poured himself a cup and stood there just holding it in his hand, savoring the warmth and smell for a moment. He took a sip and looked at the cup with raised eyebrows for a moment before moving over to the island in the middle of the kitchen to get out of the way as crewmembers stopped to fill their cups. Holding his cup with both hands, he leaned over and put both elbows on the counter and took another sip while he watched the crew demolish the piles of food on the stove. Adrian towered over him to his left with his own cup of coffee.

"This is some righteous coffee, Melancon."

Adrian was grinning from ear to ear. "It ain't exactly the Café du Monde, but it ain't bad. I had to do a little experimenting to get the right mix in the pressure pot."

"Oh yeah," Tom said, "I guess cooking in 0.7 atmospheres is going to take some getting used to."

Adrian took the towel draped across his left shoulder and began wiping up a small spill from the counter. "That's not really a big deal," he said. "You just got to put anything you want to boil or simmer in a pressure pot, but this damned high-oxygen air makes things taste funny. I put a little cinnamon in the coffee, and that kind of brought it around, but cooking bacon in this gravity was just about more fun than I could stand." He pointed to the stove where a large hood came down almost on top of the cooking surface. "The hood helps a lot, but I found out real quick you got to use a splatter screen or you get grease flying everywhere."

Tom sipped his coffee and watched the crew filing across the far side of the kitchen. "How long have you been here, Melancon?"

"I've been here all night. Commander Thon told the girls he needed to talk to me and I'd be sleeping with y'all. I slept in my suit till about three this morning. Then I got to lie down in my own bed for a couple of hours."

Tom didn't comment but continued to sip his coffee. They stood in silence watching the last of the crew fill their plates. Tom chuckled and shook his head. "This gang is sure as shit going to ruin your buffet."

"I reckon so, Mr. Fielder. You might want to get in line before they start coming back for seconds."

Tom walked over and filled a plate high with sausage, eggs, and bacon before joining the others in the communal room where he sat down next to Ki and Evelyn Weiss.

With the first bite of food, all other concerns vanished from his mind. There was no talk at the table for several minutes while everyone shoveled down food in ways that would have thoroughly embarrassed their mothers.

Finally Ki slowed down enough to take a long drink of his orange juice. He looked around the table. "I wonder how many of us are going to end up on sick call before the day is out?"

Tom looked up and spoke in a loud voice. "Hey, slow it down. This isn't your last meal. I don't want to hear about any stomachaches later on today. We've got plenty of work to get done." He yelled toward the kitchen, "Adrian, what's for dinner?"

A voice came from the kitchen. "Fried chicken, mashed potatoes with gravy, corn and fresh bread if I can get it to rise right."

Tom put down his fork and spread his hands before him. "See there. Now that's not the kind of food that anyone with an upset stomach should be eating. Do I make myself clear?"

There was a muffled chorus of "Yes, Sir" as people spoke around mouthfuls of food.

Evelyn spoke between bites. "Well put, Mr. Fielder."

Tom looked at her and turned his head slightly to the side. "Thank you, Ms. Weiss," he said. "You have grease on your chin."

Evelyn colored slightly, and Ki covered the grin on his face by taking another drink from his orange juice.

"Well," Ki said, "today we get a look at the cave. How long will it take to get the gear checked out and ready?"

Tom forked some eggs. "I had Weiss and Melancon check out the gear before they turned in last night. We can be ready to roll in about one hour."

"Excellent, Mr. Fielder, and don't forget to pick up a recorder before you go."

"I hate those damned things," Tom said.

"Regulations, Mr. Fielder."

Tom and Ki locked eyes for a moment. "And if you think there is any chance yours might break, I would suggest that you wear two of them," said Ki in an even voice.

Tom continued to glare at Ki for a moment and finally raised the bite of egg to his lips. "Well put, Commander."

"Thank you, Mr. Fielder. And by the way, you have grease on your chin also."

Evelyn couldn't help herself and burst into a peal of laughter. Tom's eyes narrowed for just a moment, but then his expression softened. Finally, he said with a grin, "Okay, okay. I get the message. I'll take good care of the damned recorder."

"Good," Ki said and took a last bite of sausage. "This is truly wonderful." He stood and tapped his glass with a fork. "Everyone, listen up," he said. Stillness fell over the table as the crew put down their eating utensils and turned to look at Commander Thon. Adrian appeared at the kitchen door with a towel in one hand and a skillet in the other.

"Today we celebrate our first good meal on Mars. I believe Mr. Melancon deserves a round of applause." The crew clapped their hands and hooted. Adrian flashed his teeth in a grin and bowed expansively, fluttering his towel to the side for emphasis. "We have accomplished much in our first three weeks here. We enjoy our food in the first permanent dwelling on Mars. The laboratory nears completion, and with luck, Mr. Fielder and Ms. Weiss may find ice in the cave to the northwest. I want all of you to know that it is an honor and a privilege to serve with you on this historic mission.

"In appreciation of your efforts thus far, I think we all deserve a few hours off to accustom ourselves to the luxury of our new home. I hereby declare the first Mars half-holiday. We will resume normal duties at 12:00.

The crew erupted with a cheer, and Commander Thon sat down, but Tom had a stricken look on his face. "Commander," he asked in a voice only Ki and Weiss could hear, "what about my schedule?"

"We'll get caught up, and the crew needs some rest."

"But Commander, the cave."

"The cave has been there for thousands of years and will surely be there tomorrow. I suggest you concentrate on getting the platform set on top of the pile of sand. That will give you all day tomorrow for exploration."

Tom shook his head. "I don't see how we can get everything done if we lose four hours this morning."

"Mr. Fielder, knowing your predilection for padding schedules, I have no doubt we will be back on track in a few days."

"But Commander, the schedule calls for…"

Ki cut him off and looked straight into Tom's eyes. "Screw the schedule, Tom, and don't whine."

Weiss spewed most of a mouthful of juice across the table with a loud, uncontrollable outburst of laughter. The entire crew turned to look, and she pushed herself away from the table while grabbing her napkin and wiping her mouth. "I'm sorry," she said, but there were tears in her eyes, and she continued to giggle helplessly.

Tom found himself grinning in spite of himself, and Ki lifted his glass of juice in a salute to Tom as he also smiled. "Enjoy the morning," Ki said.

Weiss stood and began wiping the table, but she couldn't stop giggling and finally grabbed her plate and glass and retreated to the kitchen where they heard her erupt once again with uncontrollable mirth. Krazinsky and Cochran looked down the table at Tom and Ki with quizzical expressions.

Tom looked at Ki who was leaned back in his chair and still smiling. "You enjoyed that, didn't you?" Tom said.

"Apparently not as much as Ms. Weiss," Ki replied, "but yes."

Tom shook his head but chuckled. "She did get a kick out of it." He took one last bite of bacon and finished his cup of coffee. "How about I get Espanoza and Cochran to clean up the kitchen while Melancon and I finish the computer connections? We could get the news piped into the big screen," he waved to his left, "and everyone would have a chance to send some e-mail in the privacy of their rooms."

Ki appeared to consider it for a moment. "That's probably a good idea. How long will it take?"

"Forty five minutes tops."

Ki simply nodded, and Tom picked up his plate and began walking to the kitchen but stopped and turned halfway there. "We should still have enough time this afternoon to go to the floor of the cavern after we get the platform set up. Do you want me to bring Weiss?"

"Yes. And bring back some rocks."

"No problem."

Chapter Thirteen
Surface of the Moon
April 17, 2061

On Earth, his head would have been hanging forward on his chest. In the low gravity of the Moon, it simply tilted slightly and wobbled slowly with each breath. His hands were crossed in his lap, and his eyes were closed. His mind was far away.

Ben Allspot sat in a small room with five other men, waiting for his turn in the Lunar Tug Simulator. The room, like everything else on the Moon, was painted a dull cream color. The walls, floor, and low ceiling were made of a Steel/Titanium alloy. There were no computer screens, no pictures, and of course, no windows. Scratchy pop music played softly through an intercom near the door.

Three of the men were engaged in an animated discussion concerning what they would do with their money when they returned to Earth. One of the men sat nervously tapping his foot and glancing at the door every few seconds. The last man sat with a book titled "Lunar Communication Systems" propped on his crossed legs. The chairs were of tubular and sheet-steel fabrication without padding of any kind. The man with the book turned a page and cleared his throat without looking up. Ben, although he appeared to be asleep, was in a state of effortless concentration. He was completely oblivious to the conversation, or the men around him, the music, the room itself, and his presence on the Moon. Lacking an immediate distraction, his ideas had slid easily into a tight focus. He usually wasn't aware it was happening. He only knew his thoughts seemed lately to spiral down to a single point, as if that point had some kind of psychic gravity.

His days were spent in the Lunar Tug Simulator, or desperately trying to pay attention during orientation classes, or lying in his bunk staring upward. His emotions were inexorably pulled down into contemplation of his own misery.

The effects of Carbodine withdrawal had not significantly abated during his three weeks on the Moon. He still felt as if he couldn't think, he was monstrously constipated, his ears were ringing constantly, and he ate mechanically at mealtimes, neither tasting nor caring about the food, only knowing that he should eat. Perhaps worst of all, he could sleep for only two or three hours at a time and would awaken with his mind full of disturbing images and his focus clouded by stray bits of strange dreams. He would then lie in his bunk for hours, his head awhirl with the mean, dark circumstances of his life.

The dreams were usually about Carbodine—either using Carbodine and the wonderful excitement he could barely remember, or using Carbodine and experiencing nothing more than a crushing guilt, or being offered Carbodine and refusing it.

But last night he had dreamed about his children. He had been back in New Orleans in the small apartment they had rented while he was going to college. He was in the living room in the first part of the dream, talking to his wife and sharing the day. The conversation was lively and interesting, and he remembered feeling nothing but affection for his wife and small family. He stood up to check on his two girls, and, as he walked down the hallway, a feeling of dread came over him. With each step, the fear rose in him, and he became certain that something terrible was about to happen. He lumbered on down the hall, his heart in his throat, coming ever closer to the door to their room. His hand closed on the doorknob, and the door swung open.

The two girls stood looking at him, but they were emaciated and hollow-eyed. Each held a vial of Carbodine, and small white pills littered the floor. "We got this from you," his oldest girl said with a deadpan expression.

The feeling of dread evaporated—replaced by a cold determination as the true horror of the dream unfolded. He walked calmly into the room, ignoring the screams of his children, and grasped his oldest by the neck. Her eyes bulged and there was the crisp sound of bones cracking as he dispassionately and almost gently squeezed down till she hung limp and lifeless. He dropped her to the floor and turned to his youngest, repeating the procedure with the simple thought of, *This is what must be done.* He could still feel the warmth of their throats in his large hands and hear the screams. "Daddy, Daddy! We'll be good! We promise!"

Ben became dimly aware of the room he was sitting in and the men around him and realized every muscle in his body was taut with the memory of the dream. It occurred to him that he was on the brink of insanity, but it was a useless bit of information. There was nothing to be done about it. He couldn't very well go to a counselor or his supervisor without losing his job and returning to Earth. No, he would have to do this on his own or die trying. The notion caused a cynical smile to form on his lips. *Death, where is thy sting?*

It was the video he received yesterday that had done it. He hadn't remembered to check for messages from Earth, but the barracks monitor had walked in and told him he had e-mail waiting. Ben had jammed himself into the tiny computer cubicle and was soon watching his two daughters wave and smile at him from the screen. His wife stood in the background and prompted them from time to time. Charlene, the oldest at eight, did almost all of the talking while her sister Connie stood looking around and occasionally picking her nose. They were beautiful children, with their father's black, curly hair and their mother's fine cheekbones and large eyes. Charlene rattled on, interspersing short stories about school with questions about living on the Moon. Finally, she looked into the screen and pursed her lips. With a short stomp of her foot, she frowned and said in a determined voice, "We want you to come home, Daddy."

Their mother had quickly terminated the session over Charlene's strenuous objections, and as the screen flicked a message asking if he wanted to replay or save his e-mail, Ben felt something on his forearm and realized there were tears streaming down his face.

There was a loud scrape of a chair on the steel floor, and Ben looked up to see the other five men in the room coming to their feet and heading to the door. He stood up with them. "What's up?" he asked.

One of the men with big plans for his money turned. "Man, you were out of it. The intercom said the simulator is broke down and we can have the rest of the afternoon off. Be here 7:00 sharp tomorrow morning."

Ben nodded and looked at his watch. Two extra hours to do what? He bounced lightly to the door, entered the busy hallway, and automatically turned toward his barracks. A voice stopped him.

"Ben? Ben Allspot? Is that you?"

Ben looked down on a small man with a sharp nose, short brown hair sticking out at odd angles, and slightly buck teeth. There was a courier pack hanging from the man's shoulder and he wore the uniform of a parcel distribution service. "Weasel?" Ben said. "I damn sure didn't expect to see you here."

Weasel looked up and grinned, showing his large, uneven teeth. "Ben Allspot, as I live and breathe. How long you been here?"

Ben actually smiled. He had known Weasel McCormick since high school, and they had run together for years until . . . well, until Ben had gotten married. "Less than a month."

Weasel laughed. "Still a Sorehead, huh?"

Ben rubbed the top of his head and admitted that it was a little sore. The ceilings on the Moon were usually less than eight feet tall to jam more people into smaller volumes. It took a while for the newcomers to learn the long gliding strides useful for traveling in the Moon's low gravity, and Ben, like most first timers, had spent the first few days banging his head on the ceiling. Sorehead was the universal term applied to all newcomers.

Ben pointed to Weasel's uniform. "I can see what you're doing. How long have you been here?"

Weasel waved at his uniform. "Shit man, I got the best damned job on the Moon. Get to run around all over the place, don't have to suit up very often, and I know every swinging dick that's worth knowing. This is my tenth tour. I been up here a long time. It's great. I do three months, go home with a bag full of money, spend every penny of it on whores and good times, and come back for more. But there's good times to be had even here if you know who to ask."

Ben heard the words tumble out of his mouth as if someone else was talking. "Can you get me some stuff?"

Weasel smiled and bowed low. "Weasel McCormick at your service." He looked at his watch. "I got to deliver these papers. Buy me a beer at the Cock and Ale, and we'll talk over old times and invent some new ones. Three hours sound good?"

"Sure," Ben said. "Where is it?"

Weasel was already gliding down the narrow hall. "Consolidated Helium Complex, dome three, level four. Just ask around."

Ben stood with his hand half-raised in parting while Weasel disappeared around the next corner. His mind spun with hidden thoughts and emotions, and he was rooted to the spot till someone bumped into him. Ben mumbled an apology and dropped his hand. His first step cracked his head against the ceiling, and people snickered as they loped past him. He rubbed the top of his head and moved down the hall with a little more care. *Stuff on the Moon.* It had never crossed his mind that he might find drugs here.

Chapter Fourteen
Surface of Mars
April 17, 2061

"Okay," Tom said, "just bring it down real slow." He stood in sand nearly up to his knees on top of the giant pile in the middle of the cavern. One of the supply boxes had been folded up and was just coming through the crack in the ceiling above him. His suit lights had been improved considerably over standard issue, but he still could not see the far wall where the water cave had chewed through the rock. Melancon and Weiss were at the top of the large crack where a winch had been installed. Melancon reeled out cable, and the box dropped till it sat on the sand in front of Tom.

"That's it," Tom cried. "I've got it."

Tom unhooked the cable and called for Melancon to pull it up. He had flattened out the top of the sand pile as best he could, and he went about unfolding the box so that the bottom of the box sat on top of the pile and the four sides of the box drooped down the slope. He then stood on the box and jumped up and down to seat it into the sand. He locked the four sides into position with special clips they had fabricated for just this purpose. The result was a four-sided cap on the pile of sand. The bottom of the box would give them a platform to work from, and the sides of the box stabilized the platform to keep it from sliding. There was a piton bolted into the middle of the platform for running cable down to the floor of the cavern, and handles had been attached to the sides of the box to help them climb back up.

Just as he finished, Weiss came dropping through the crack above him. Melancon lowered the winch till her feet touched the platform. She called for him to stop, and unclipped the cable from her belt.

"Welcome to the underworld," Tom said.

Weiss stood for a moment and then began to turn in a slow circle. "This is incredible," she said. "I cannot see the walls in any direction. It's as if the cavern goes on forever."

Tom pointed away in a line perpendicular to the crack in the ceiling. "Our cave is over there. Last one down's a rotten egg," he said and jumped off the platform.

Weiss watched him fall perhaps twenty feet and land softly on the sloping sand. Before she could move, he had pulled his boots from the sand and jumped again. She launched herself off the platform, and they bounded down the sand to the cavern floor, their suit lights dancing wildly about as they fell, stopped, and fell again.

Tom saw the edge of the sand pile below him and began to pick his way down the slope just as Weiss sailed past him and landed, knees bent, on the cavern floor. "I believe that makes you a rotten egg," she said.

"You shouldn't pick on an old man like that."

"And you shouldn't pick on young ladies, but you do."

Tom laughed and turned around, bending over backward to shine his lights up the sloping sand. "It's not going to be near as much fun going back up," he said.

"You are just 42."

Tom grunted his agreement.

"Forty two is not so old," said Weiss. "I'm almost thirty."

"Ooh, pushing the big three zero," Tom said. "Well, like my Daddy used to say, pushing thirty don't seem so bad once you start dragging it around behind you." He pointed in the direction of the cave. "Shall we?"

The floor sloped down steeply in the direction they were walking, and the surface was littered with small, irregular, flat plates of brown and gray rock that had fallen from the roof of the cavern and shattered on the granite floor. Tom labeled a small plastic bag and picked up a few of them to bring back to Ki. As they came to the edge of the channel, they could see that the long-lost flow of water had cut the floor some two feet deep before disappearing. Tom jumped down and looked at the bed of the old stream. It was lighter in color than the rest of the floor and there were fewer of the flat rocks. Tom labeled another bag and stuffed more rock chips into it.

There was a burst of noise from his radio, and he could barely hear the voice of Melancon through the static. He sounded frantic. "Mr. Fielder, can you read me? Come in. Someone come in."

"We read you, Melancon. What's the matter?"

Melancon continued to plead, "Ms. Weiss, can you read me?"

Tom looked back to the pile of sand. He could barely see the small crack in the ceiling from where he stood. He reached down and twisted a small dial on his wrist all the way to the right, increasing the signal strength on his radio to maximum. "We read you, Mr. Melancon. Everything is fine," he said.

"Thank God," said Melancon, "I can barely hear you. What's going on?"

"Nothing really. We are having reception difficulties because we moved away from the crack. I had to turn up the gain on my radio before you could hear me."

"Scared me half to death," Melancon said. "I've been screaming into the radio for the last five minutes. I had to turn mine all the way up before you answered."

Tom turned and began walking down the channel. "We'll have to set up a relay antennae tomorrow. You might want to let everyone at camp know we're okay. Your signal is probably going half way around Mars."

"Yes, sir."

Tom and Evelyn continued to walk in the bed of the old stream as they listened to Melancon reassure the crew that all was well. They could not hear any response from the camp, and the reception of Melancon's signal continued to drop slowly as they walked farther from the sand.

They were soon standing at the entrance of the water cave and Tom was surprised to see that it was somewhat smaller than he had estimated. The top of the cave was just twenty feet above their heads, and the stalactites hung down no more than four or five feet. They turned so that both of their suit lights shown into the cave.

There was a drop of about six feet where the rocky shelf ended and the water cave began. It was like looking into another world. The large, fault cavern they had entered from the crack in the ceiling was painted in shades of brown and gray and was all sharp angles and more or less straight lines. The water cave was smooth and undulating, with rounded edges and streaks of deep tan fading slowly into grooves of nearly white rock, all pointing down and away from them. There were small patches of quartz that sparkled and shimmered in their lights, and white stalactites hung above their partnered stalagmites at irregular intervals for as far as they could see—like strange teeth in the throat of some great, stone beast.

"Mon Dieu," Weiss exclaimed breathlessly, "it is beautiful."

Tom stood silently for a moment then jumped down to the floor of the cave. "Stay where you are," he said. "I want to see something."

The floor of the water cave sloped down but not nearly at the angle of the cavern floor, and Tom began walking slowly through the wonder that surrounded him. A cross section of the cave would have been roughly in the shape of an egg lying on its side. The left side of the cave was taller and slightly more rounded. Tom soon came to a bend on his right, and he could see where the rushing water of millions of years gone by had hollowed out a large shallow depression in the left-hand wall. He kept to his right where the footing was more even, and disappeared from Weiss' lights as he rounded the corner some fifty yards in front of her.

"What are you doing?" she cried.

"Let's see if this works," he said. "Melancon, can you read me?"

There was silence, and Tom repeated the call. Still there was silence.

Weiss spoke into her radio. "Mr. Melancon, can you hear Tom?"

Tom listened but could hear nothing of Melancon's reply

Evelyn spoke again. "Tom is about fifty yards down the cave and around a bend. I can hear him, but he is out of range of your radio."

Tom had continued down the cave for some distance as Weiss and Melancon talked. He was looking for something in particular, but time was running out. The sun was close to setting outside, and he didn't want to navigate the rough terrain and narrow passages of the path back to the camp in the dark.

Just as he was about to give up, he saw it. There was a large, flat plate of rock that had fallen from the roof of the cavern and washed down the cave to fit neatly into a depression on the floor. He bent down and got part of his gloved fingers under it and heaved upward till it tilted and fell to the side. Underneath was a shallow dip filled with sand. *Even better!*

He leaned forward and dug through eight inches of sand till he felt the rough bottom of the cavity. Using both hands, he scooped out the sand and threw it to the side. When he had cleared a small spot, he bent down further and looked closely at the bottom of the hole. It had the appearance of sandstone, but there was a curious glint to it from his suit lights, and the surface seemed almost translucent.

"Mr. Fielder, what are you doing?"

"Collecting samples, Ms. Weiss. I'm almost finished."

He pulled a hammer from his belt, held it high over his head for a moment, and slammed it down as hard as he could into the exact center of the pit. Splinters flew in all directions. Tom looked down and then hit the bottom of the hole several more blows until he had dislodged a sharp-edged piece about five inches long. He held it up to his face.

It was mostly sand, but the lights of his suit seemed to penetrate into the surface, scattering thin beams of light as he turned it in his hand. The sand was glued together with the very thing they had come here to find. Tom was holding a small piece of ice.

"I've got ice, Ms. Weiss," he said.

"You found ice?"

"It's not exactly enough to take a bath in, but by God, I've got ice." He took out another bag and labeled it.

"Where did you find it?" Weiss asked.

"Right where you'd expect to find it—under a rock."

He placed the ice in the bag and stood up. There was another bend in the cave just fifty yards from where he stood, and he was sorely tempted to see what lay on the other side, but it was getting late. He turned and began to retrace his steps out of the cave but stopped for a moment to look back at the curve where the cave disappeared into darkness. It was all he could do to resist the impulse to peak around that corner, but duty finally won out over curiosity. It would have to wait until tomorrow.

Chapter Fifteen
Surface of the Moon
April 17, 2061

Ben returned to the barracks and flopped down on his bed to stare at the springs of the bunk above him. His mind was like a hidden machine, furiously at work behind the scenes. There was a tumult somewhere within him—he could feel it, but his conscious mind was blank and strangely calm. He had read that Carbodine withdrawal would dissipate after a few weeks. He could expect a return of appetite and improved sleeping patterns within a few days. A good night's sleep could do wonders for his disposition under normal circumstances, but these were not normal circumstances. Sleep would not return his family or his children. A good meal would not improve his performance in the simulator.

He was in real danger of being rejected as a pilot, and it was ridiculous. He had passed the course on Earth at the top of his class. There was nothing difficult about the flight tests. He remembered the ease with which he had performed more complicated maneuvers just over a year ago. He had the skills for this. He had proven it. But he needed to prove it here and now. If they would give him time to get his mind clear, the simulator would be no problem, but he kept freezing at the controls. The correct move seemed obvious in the moment just after he botched a docking or landed too hard, but he couldn't push through the fog in his head fast enough to matter. He had always delighted in the ability of his mind to quickly assess options and take proper action. Not now.

The Tug Shuttle course on Earth had been fun and gratifying—the tug controls like an extension of his mind and body. He now fumbled his way through the exercises, thinking frantically but to no avail about every move. He recalled the clerk at outbound station asking his name and the difficulty he had in understanding the question. How long would it take before his powers of concentration returned? Would they ever return? How much time did he have before the instructors tired of watching him bend simulated landing struts and damage virtual docking rings? Just yesterday, two other men had washed out of the shuttle pilot class and had been sent to work construction. Would he have been next if the simulator hadn't malfunctioned?

It was probably a good thing the simulator had broken. Likely he would be getting fitted for a construction suit and a tool belt otherwise. Of course, he wouldn't have run into Weasel if he hadn't walked out of the waiting room at that precise moment. There was a certain symmetry to it.

But was it all worth it? If he waited long enough, his brain would readjust, his ears would stop ringing, and his mind would clear. At least that was the theory, but after the agony of these last few weeks, it was hard to believe he would ever feel normal again. What was normal anyway? He couldn't remember.

Had Carbodine ruined his life? At times, he felt it had, but things had not been perfect before Carbodine. There were fights and disagreements before Carbodine. Carbodine hadn't taken his daughters away, his wife had.

Carbodine wasn't some brand new drug. It had been around for at least forty years. Lots of people took Carbodine all their lives without adverse effects. He had simply let the pressures of work and school push him into using too much too often. This wasn't the time to stop using. As a pilot, he could send more money home to his children. Construction hands made less than half as much. He just needed a little help getting through the class. He would taper off after that.

Somewhere deep in Ben's mind, a voice was shouting with alarm, but it was largely hidden from him, and he ignored it—becoming a pilot was the important thing for now. He would take care of the rest of it later. He folded his hands on his chest and went to sleep.

~

The sound of men returning at shift-change woke Ben, and fragments of a dream whispered to him softly for a moment, then disappeared. He rolled out of his bunk and laced his fingers above his head, stretching till his knuckles popped loudly.

The communal bathroom was at the far end of the barracks, and Ben launched himself in that direction, nearly hitting the ceiling with his first step. He splashed water on his face and rinsed his mouth. The nap had left him feeling unsteady and disoriented, but not much more than usual. He ran his hands through his hair and looked at his watch. It was time to go. Consolidated Helium complex, dome three, level four. Or was it dome four, level three?

Crap, my mind is shot.

Despite all attempts to control and organize the growth of towns and industrial complexes on the Moon, the rapid expansion of profitable business had resulted in a patchwork of factories and living areas. Most companies built their own company towns adjacent to construction sites or factories. Such was the case with Lexam, the company Ben worked for. The Lexam complex consisted of 14 domes of various sizes. The smaller of these domes were barracks for housing employees. One served as a cafeteria, and the rest were storage facilities, refineries, and laboratories. Lexam had no extra space for lease, but that was not true of all companies.

The rapid growth of the fusion industry and its appetite for He_3 had sent many visions for profitable business on the Moon into the dustbin. What started as a government research effort quickly became an industrial race as company after company realized trillions of dollars were at stake. Early law enforcement efforts were tied up for years by jurisdictional disputes. A Lunar Police Department was eventually formed, but funding for law enforcement on the Moon was not a high priority with politicians whose constituency was on Earth. The individual companies were forced to employ security personnel whose only real responsibility was keeping theft to a reasonable level. The few laws that had been enacted were generally enforced only when safety issues were involved.

The net result was the blooming of a vigorous underground network. While hardly anyone was foolish enough to discharge a projectile weapon on the Moon, other black-market commerce flourished and with a population of over one million, drugs were more readily available on the Moon than in many of Earth's inner cities.

Of course, Ben didn't know this yet. Companies with interests on the Moon didn't care to advertise such things, and there was enough strife on Earth to keep the media busy and the populace occupied. Ben had spent his time on the moon either in class or staring upward from his bunk, and the men in his barracks had given up on making conversation with him. So far, it had suited him just fine, but there were a lot of things about life on the Moon that Ben had yet to learn.

He left the barracks and walked nearly a quarter mile down a featureless, cream colored hall to the transit tube station. There was a network of maglev trains connecting all the various complexes, and every complex had at least one station. The small room was crowded with shift-change traffic, and he looked around for someplace to sit.

The few steel benches were taken, and Ben leaned against the wall, watching the people as they talked and told jokes. Two women sat dressed in work clothes on a bench by themselves. Neither of them was particularly attractive, but several men kept glancing in their direction. One man in a group of three pointed to the women and said something that caused them all to burst into laughter. One of the other men punched the first one lightly on the arm and said with a grin, "You ain't right, man."

They might as well be Aliens. Ben brooded.

With the low rumbling of the approaching train, people began to shuffle toward the turnstile. Ben held back and was the last one to walk through the small gate. He pressed his palm on a plate to the left of the turnstile and said, "Consolidated Helium." A mechanized voice informed him that Consolidated Helium was the third stop and that no transfers would be required.

He sat down next to a slightly overweight man with greasy hair. "Where you going?" asked the man with a smile.

Ben turned his head and looked the man straight in the eyes, then turned back without a word and looked forward as the train accelerated out of the station. He replayed his recent strategy in an endless loop, but there seemed to be nothing he could add or take away. The man next to him got up at the first stop, but Ben hardly noticed, and he almost missed Consolidated Helium even though it was announced twice.

The station at Consolidated Helium was bigger and busier than the one at Lexam, and Ben found himself jostled by the crowd. He stopped a man at random and asked where the Cock and Ale could be found.

The man looked up at Ben. "Dome three, level four. Take a left out of the lift and go about two blocks down. It's on the left." He squinted and surveyed Ben more closely before speaking again. "It's a rough crowd, but you look like you can handle yourself," and he was gone.

Ben followed the signs to dome three and took the lift up to level four. The door opened on a world he had not known existed on the Moon.

Consolidated Helium had suffered financial losses and was forced to cut back its lunar operation. This entire level had once been occupied by small labs and administrative offices, but the elevator doors opened on a scene reminiscent of a wild afternoon on Bourbon Street during Mardi Gras.

The usually blank walls of the hallway had been cut open and windows inserted. Signs stuck out above almost every door, reading "Jim's T-shirt Shop," or "The Fry and Burger." There were shoe stores, clothing stores, novelty shops, bars, strip joints, and a tattoo parlor almost directly across from the lift.

And there were people, real people. People having a good time. The hall was narrow, with room for only five or six men to stand shoulder to shoulder, and it was packed solid. Some stood in small groups, drinking and talking, while others moved about, elbowing their way through the tightly packed crowd. A man leaned with his back to the wall between two of the shops. His eyes were closed, and his head lolled to the side. The press of the crowd around him seemed to be the only thing holding him up. Music blared from several of the old offices, and Ben felt himself caught in the crossfire of differing beats and rhythms.

The doors to the lift started to close, and Ben muscled his way forward and into the swirling mass. He stood for a moment letting it sink in, and something stirred within him. Tears welled without warning in his eyes. He blinked them back and took a deep breath. The unrefined odor of humanity came to him along with the sweet, bread-like aroma of spilled beer. There were sharp, pungent odors he didn't want to think about, flower-like fragrances of perfume and cologne, and the pervasive smell of food cooking. From the "Fry and Burger" came the odor of hot grease and frying meat. Someone was cooking sausage and sweet peppers nearby, and even the smell of barbecue was in the air, though Ben could not imagine how it was possible without setting off the smoke alarms.

A young woman wearing a skimpy halter-top stumbled into him and looked up, blinking her eyes with the effort of focusing. "Whassup, big guy?" she asked.

Ben had to yell over the noise. "I'm looking for the Cock and Ale."

She jerked a thumb over her shoulder, and her breasts bounced nicely against the thin fabric of her shirt. "Down there on the left," she said and danced away with her drink held carefully in front of her.

Mental note to self. There are no sagging breasts on the moon.

He started working his way through the crowd. There was another hall at right angles to the first one about one hundred yards from the lift, and he could see that it was jammed with people also. The crowd began to thin slightly as he moved forward, and the outside wall of the dome at the end of the hallway was in sight when he spotted a metal rooster jutting out above a door on his left. There was no window, and he opened the door to step into a room seemingly near pitch darkness. Before his eyes could adjust, there was a call from across the room. "Ben-ja-min!"

Weasel sailed across the floor in one bound and landed at Ben's feet. "Dude! I still can't believe you're on the Moon." He then turned and shouted, "Hey, everybody. This is my old runnin' buddy Ben from Earthside." Ben was beginning to make out a few details, and he could see some of the people raise their hands in a desultory wave.

"Let's get you fixed up with something to drink," Weasel said and steered Ben to the bar where a truly huge man stood with a towel stuck in his belt. "Spiral, this is my man Ben. Whatever he wants is on me. At least for tonight."

Ben experienced the strange sensation of looking up at someone and could see instantly how the bartender had come to be known as Spiral. His head was shaved, and he wore large, hoop earrings in each ear. But it was his facial tattoo that impressed Ben.

In stark black and white, beginning at the bridge of Spiral's nose, was a spiraled tattoo covering his eyelids, head, ears, and as far down his neck as Ben could see. There were two rings tightly pierced on both sides of his lower lip, giving the impression of silver fangs, and shiny, black teeth glinted in the dim light when he opened his mouth to ask what Ben wanted.

"I'll take a beer," Ben said.

Weasel craned his neck. "Be right back," he said and bounded to a corner of the bar.

Spiral looked at Ben carefully while he drew beer from a tap as if wondering whether he could take Ben in a fight, or if he would need to. Ben returned the gaze without blinking but without malice.

"You known Weasel long?" Spiral asked as he put the beer on the bar.

"Since high school," Ben replied.

"Weasel's nuts."

"So am I," said Ben

"Ain't we all?" asked Spiral with an easy laugh. "Ain't we all?"

Ben picked up his glass without smiling. "Thanks."

Spiral eyed Ben carefully. "No problem."

Weasel had moved to a booth against the wall and was waving at Ben to join him. Ben carefully glided over to avoid banging his head or spilling his beer. "Spiral is a big guy," he said as he sat down.

"Oh yeah. Just don't piss him off."

"I wasn't planning on it."

Weasel leaned across the table. "What are you looking for?"

"Carbodine."

"That's an easy one," Weasel said. "Here's how it works on the moon. Synthetics are easy to find and cheap. Heroin and cocaine are expensive and tough to get because they have to be imported from Earth. You can't find anything that needs to be smoked. If you decide to smoke something and set off an alarm, shame on you. You'll be back on Earth before you know it."

"Carbodine's fine."

"Okay. Just hold what you got." Weasel bounced across the room and began a conversation Ben couldn't hear.

Ben took a sip of the beer and set it down on the table, watching the bubbles rise in slow motion through the amber liquid. It was surprisingly good. He was just beginning to ponder the step he was about to take when Weasel slid into the seat across from him.

"That'll be one hundred dollars," Weasel said and slipped his cupped hand, palm down, onto the table.

Ben automatically covered Weasel's hand with his own, and as Weasel pulled his hand away, Ben found himself holding a small plastic vial. He pulled it to his side next to the wall and popped the lid. There looked to be nearly a week's supply of Carbodine in the vial. He shook out one small, white pill and popped it in his mouth.

"Damn, Weasel. Just like that? You can walk across the room and pick up this much shit just like that?"

Weasel grinned from ear to ear and pointed both thumbs at his own chest. "I am the man. I told you I got the best-damned job on the Moon. I make more money movin' shit around than I do carrying packages. Hell, I can find half of anything you can name in this bar, and I can find the other half before I get to the lift. This is the Moon, man. Anything goes as long as you don't break any safety laws."

"But it's cheap," Ben said. "This looks like three hundred dollars worth in New Orleans."

"You got fifty tabs. I told you synthetics are cheap. We got more chemists up here than in all of Louisiana and Texas combined. Something like five percent of the population are chemists, and some of them are making tons of money turnin' sugar into somethin' sweeter."

"Damn," Ben said, "this is weird."

"Oh come on, Ben. You're not thinkin' right. You been to jail before, haven't you?"

Ben nodded. "You know I have. It seems to me you went downtown with me once."

Weasel frowned for a moment, then smiled. "Oh yeah. We never should have rearranged that sign."

"Not in broad daylight anyway," said Ben with a grin. "But I couldn't help myself. It was too obvious. When you look up and see a sign that reads 'Seersucker Suits by Joe Cocks,' what are you going to do?"

Weasel was giggling uncontrollably. "The judge called it defacing private property."

Ben laughed for the first time in weeks, and it was like a dam broke within him. He could hardly draw a breath, and tears rolled down his face. "Defacing, my ass. We just made it read true."

"Those were damned sure some shitty lookin' suits," Weasel said between gasps.

Ben wiped at his eyes as the laughter ebbed. He realized that the entire bar was looking at them, and he raised his glass to Weasel. "Here's to truth in advertising."

Weasel held up his own glass. "To truth in advertising. But gettin' back to what I was sayin' about jail, you remember seein' drugs in the lockup?"

Ben raised his eyebrows. "Yeah."

"Well, if they can't keep drugs out of prisons, then what's so weird about havin' drugs on the Moon."

Ben stood quietly, contemplating his nest words. "I don't know. It's just strange."

"Just enjoy it Ben-ja-min. The Moon is one wild-ass place. We're gonna have ourselves a party. Just like old times."

Ben shook his head and laughed as he took another swallow of beer. "Just like old times." He downed the beer and put it on the table between them. "The beer is pretty good too, but it's a little flat."

"Low air pressure. It'd fizz out of the glass if they made it like on Earth. The beer is good, but the whiskey ain't worth drinkin', and stay away from anything they call Tequila unless you want to be sittin' on the pot all day. You want another beer?"

"Sure," Ben said, and Weasel slid out of the booth to politely ask Spiral for two more beers.

Ben leaned back and looked around. It was almost too bizarre for him to absorb. Drugs on the Moon. He supposed there was prostitution and gambling too, but neither one had ever interested him.

A jukebox was playing some new hit song he'd never heard, and he suddenly had the urge to see a live band. Weasel would know where to go.

Right on cue, Weasel slid into the seat across from Ben, placed one of the beers on the table, and lifted the other in a toast. "Here's to us," he said.

Ben lifted his own beer. "Here's to us. To the old times and the new." They each took a swallow, and Ben looked over at Weasel. He had known Weasel for almost twelve years. They had been through just about everything he could imagine, and now he was sitting with him in a bar on the Moon toasting their friendship.

"When do you need the hundred dollars?" Ben asked.

"Don't worry about it. You get paid in a couple of days. You can pay me then."

A feeling of affection came over Ben. *Yeah, Weasel is a true friend.* Something else was coming over him, and Ben realized he was hungry. "Let's go get something to eat," he said. "I'm about to die from cafeteria food."

"It's your night, dude," Weasel said and went to settle up with Spiral.

They walked together into a crowd that had grown even larger since Ben arrived.

~

The approach to the docking ring was a little fast, but Ben checked a gauge and saw that he was massing only 200 tons. He allowed the tug to coast for a few more minutes, and then his hands slid over the controls, coaxing the tug into a smooth deceleration. There was a slow drift to port, and he realized one of the retrorockets was out of alignment. His hands moved again as he manually tweaked the thrust on the starboard retro. The tug moved back to dead center on the docking ring. The relative speed gauge dropped slowly and was nearly at zero when the proximity indicator beeped. Ben cut all thrust, and the tug drifted sedately into the docking ring just two feet away. With a soft thud and a dull rumble, the tug mated up with the orbital lab. Magnetic grapples held it firmly.

The screen went blank, and the door of the simulator swung open. Light poured into the cramped cockpit. A technician in a white coat stood outside with a small computer in his hand, looking at the numbers.

"Damn, Allspot, did you take your vitamins this morning? That was a perfect ten."

Ben climbed out and jumped down, landing lightly with his knees bent. "I've been having a little trouble sleeping," he said.

"Fine job. We were about to wash you out, but that was a nice adjustment on the misaligned retro. If you keep this up, we'll have you flying real cargo in a couple of weeks."

"Sounds good to me," Ben said with a broad grin. "I'll see you tomorrow."

"You're first up in the morning," said the technician. "Be here at seven sharp, and get a good night's sleep."

"I can promise you I will," Ben said, and he was out the door, bounding easily down the hall. It was amazing what a good night's sleep had done for him—a good night's sleep, a decent breakfast, a cup of coffee, and one small, white pill—simply amazing.

He moved cheerfully down the hall, smiling and nodding at everyone he passed. The world lay at his feet, and life was good.

Chapter Sixteen
Surface of Mars
April 18, 2061

His room was as neat as a pin. There was a notepad perfectly aligned with the edge of the desk and a pen lying diagonally across it. The bed had already been made, and a pair of sandals, exactly centered at the foot of the bed, were the only things on the floor. There was a small bookcase above the desk with a joyous Buddha in the middle, and the books surrounding it had been arranged with the larger ones to the outside and the smaller ones toward the center, making a sort of V. Above the bookcase were pictures of Commander Thon's wife and two children. Commander Thon sat at the desk in front of a computer screen built into the wall. He was typing rapidly.

"Knock, knock," Tom said.

Ki blanked the computer screen and turned in his chair. "Good morning, Tom. I trust you slept well."

"Like a baby," Tom said. "I hope I'm not interrupting anything."

Ki gestured to the computer. "I was just composing some e-mail to my wife. We are already too far away from Earth to make conversation worthwhile."

Tom nodded. "Yeah, waiting almost fifteen minutes to hear the answer to a question tends to get a little tedious."

"Come in. Sit down," said Ki. "What could I do for you this morning?"

Tom moved into the room and sat on the bed. "Nothing really. I was looking at the progress reports on the Lab this morning. It's moving along well. We may be able to pressure it up and warm it tonight. I need Melancon at the cave today to help with the relay antennas and some other stuff, but he can probably break loose to set up the computers and some of the Lab equipment tomorrow. We might be able to get an analysis of that piece of ice the day after that."

"Excellent," said Ki. "It will be interesting to see what might be dissolved in the ice."

"Or what might be living in it," Tom said.

Ki chuckled. "So you have been watching the television also."

Tom grinned back at his friend. "All you have to do is turn on any channel, and there it is: 'Possible Life on Mars, film at eleven.' Anyway, I was talking to Melancon, and since we're setting up relay antennas, it wouldn't be too much more trouble to broadcast live video feed from our suit cameras back to here. You're the Geologist, and we really need to get you down in the cave to look around. Since you're still on light duty, the next best thing is to let you look over our shoulders. That way you can direct us to look at whatever seems interesting."

"Wonderful idea," said Ki. He paused, in contemplation. "Our broadcast satellite will be in line with Earth till about 3:00 today. I'll tell NASA what we're up to. They will probably want us to pipe the feed to them for a real-time, live broadcast. I wonder what the ratings on that will be?"

Tom shook his head. "I'm not sure I would have agreed to this mission if I'd known it was going to be a media circus. Somebody leaked my e-mail address, and I got over fifty thousand messages in just two hours. Marriage was in the subject header on over two hundred of them. I was afraid to look at the attachments."

Ki threw back his head and laughed. "Those would have been some interesting pictures I'm sure."

"Somehow I wasn't interested. Let's go get some breakfast."

"Good idea," Ki said and stood up, looking at his computer screen and slipping on his sandals. "I can finish this later. What are we having?"

"We're having that wonderful southern tradition: grits and eggs."

"Grits and eggs?" Ki said. "I guess I've never eaten grits before. What are grits?"

They walked down the hall as Tom explained grits. He was still talking when they walked into the communal area. ". . . They're a great source of fiber and naturally low in fat with zero cholesterol, but none of that really matters because they're not edible unless you put tons of butter on them."

Ki frowned for a moment. "So these grits are really more of a carrier for butter and salt than anything else."

Tom beamed. "Ah, Grasshopper, the light of understanding glimmers within you."

The large computer screen on the far wall was acting as a television, and the news was playing footage of Ki's rescue from under the wing of the Mars I. "Ah crap," Tom said, "won't they ever get tired of that."

Most of the crew was already seated at the large table with steaming plates in front of them, and Tom and Ki exchanged good mornings as they walked into the kitchen. Tom spooned grits high on his plate and put several large pats of butter in the middle of the pile.

Melancon was almost hidden by a cloud of flour near the dishwasher. "We've got to get another vacuum hood over here," he said. "This low gravity is driving me nuts. Everything goes everywhere. If I try to make bread, I get flour all the way into the living quarters."

Tom looked at the layout of the room. "It shouldn't be a problem. We'll take a look at that as soon as we get the Lab up and running." He stood there for a moment surveying the existing hood and formulating what it would take to extend it to the nearest counter. Without thinking, he took a bite of the grits on his plate.

"Damn, Melancon. This is the best grits I ever ate. What's the secret?"

Melancon turned with a grin. "Just the slightest touch of garlic, Mr. Fielder."

Ki looked up. "Shouldn't that be, 'These *are* the best grits?'"

Tom shook his head. "Only a Cajun would think of feeding you garlic first thing in the morning." He walked toward the dining area. "Grits: Collective Noun or Not. The debate rages on."

The television was showing Ki being pulled from the wing and hustled off to the Mars I. "Not my most flattering pose," said Ki.

They sat down across from Evelyn Weiss. She was cleaning her plate by wiping a piece of toast across it. "That's okay, Commander Thon," she said with a wry grin. "I understand you will be first in line to receive your complimentary Tom Fielder Action Adventure Toy,"

"Oh puhlease," Tom said.

The scene on the wall changed to a view from the new Sagan telescope. The permanent quarters and the skeleton of the Mars I were barely visible in the grainy picture.

Cochran pointed. "If you look real close, you can see Mr. Fielder saving the world."

There were laughs from around the table, but Tom's face reddened. "That's enough," he said.

Commander Thon had just taken a bite of his grits, and he looked over at Tom with a beatific smile on his round face. "These grits is good," he said.

Tom burst out laughing. "That's just not going to work. Let's try, 'These grits are good.'" He shook his head and laughed again. "Yankees eating grits. What can you expect?"

Ki laughed with him. "Well, they are quite good."

Cochran was getting up from the table, and Tom called to him. "Mr. Cochran, I need you and Ms. Geller to modify my suit and Ms. Weiss' suit so we can broadcast the video straight into the camp in real time."

Cochran nodded. "Live from the caves of Mars, eh?" he said. "No problem. We should have them done in about thirty minutes."

"We're leaving in twenty," Tom replied.

"Yes, sir." Cochran disappeared into the kitchen, and Kaitlin Geller stood up to follow him.

Evelyn stood up. "I should be getting ready. I'll let Mr. Melancon know we're about to leave."

Ki took another bite of grits. "These are really splendid. I must tell my wife about them." He paused for a moment to take a sip of his juice. "This should be a fascinating day."

Tom looked at his watch. "It will take us about an hour to get into the cave and another hour to get the antennas set up. That will give us almost eight hours for exploring."

Ki looked at his watch also. "I need to contact NASA."

Tom gobbled down his food. "And I need to get with Melancon on the video link."

Chapter Seventeen
The Planet Harmony
Exact Time Unknown

A group of thirty young Trees sat in rapt attention as the old Tree instructed them in the techniques they would use for the repair. A large cultivator had broken down a few miles away, and pictures relayed to the old Tree showed a damaged axle. It would take days to repair even with this many young on the project.

Hydraulic jacks would need to be brought to the site. The ground would have to be stabilized to keep the jacks from sinking. Welding equipment was needed, and specialized tools were required for part of the work. A small crane was being driven to the site and should arrive in two days.

Removal of the old axle was an intricate process, and the decision had been made to replace the hub-bearings and all of the bushings. The new axle was being manufactured at a plant nearly one thousand miles to the north. With a bit of luck, it would arrive just as the old one was removed. If not, the young would disperse and go about their usual playful explorations till they were called back to finish the work.

A three-dimensional picture of a hub bearing seemed to hang in the air in front of Tree. He reached out with one of his hands and made a twisting motion. In response, the bearing turned in the air, presenting a side view. Tree hummed to the computer, and the bearing grew larger until a small groove was clearly visible where it attached to a spindle. A tool appeared in the air beside the bearing, and Tree grasped it with one of his other hands. The hologram reacted by moving the tool with his hand as Tree demonstrated the procedure for releasing the bearing from the spindle. The bearing twisted slightly and slid free of the spindle.

The young Trees sat, hardly blinking. Each move was recorded with near perfect clarity in their minds, and they would carry the memory till they died.

Tree recalled an incident from one of his childhoods when a bearing had frozen to a spindle. *It would not hurt to explain what we did in that case,* he decided. Just as he began the presentation of those procedures, the hologram dissolved, and a simple message was displayed—a Koombar transport was approaching.

"That would be Skrin," he said. The children tilted their heads and frowned at the non sequitur.

Tree hummed instructions for the children to disperse and requested one of them to bring his translator. The young Trees instantly erupted in roughhousing as groups of three and four pushed each other about and tumbled together on the ground before jumping up to run into the surrounding woods. Tree grinned at their antics with a wrinkling of his nose.

A lone child walked somewhat stiffly to the nearby storage shed and returned with the translator. As the child drove it into the ground, Tree noted the coarse and whitened appearance of the young one's fur. He bent slightly to more closely examine his son and parted the child's fur, finding secretions already present.

"You are close to maturity," Tree said.

The young Tree bent his neck with difficulty, and looked into his father's eyes. "Yes, father."

"Have you found your mates?" the old Tree asked, but he knew the answer.

"No, father."

Tree reached down and scooped up his son, cradling him in his arms. "How do you feel?"

"I am tired."

Tree reached with one of his other hands and stroked the face of his aging child. The child lay still for a moment with his eyes closed and then looked up. "Father," he said, "I am afraid."

The words pierced the heart of the old Tree, and he held the boy closer. "Do not fear. Soon you will rest. You will sleep and begin to dream. Slowly, you will become a part of those dreams. You will have a different life, a better life than you have known before. You will join with all of the young and the old who have gone before, and, after a time, I will join you."

Tree continued to stroke his son's face, and the child closed his eyes and snuggled closer to his father's chest. Tree was filled with sadness. Though this had happened many times, it was heartbreaking, and he began telling the story of "The Farming Tree and His Son." It was a simple tale, with repetitive verse and an easy, rhyming rhythm, and it was usually told only to the very young. The story had no real instructional value but served only to illustrate the affection that Trees had for their children.

Tree felt the child relax in his arms as the story unfolded. When it ended, his son opened his eyes and looked up. "Thank you, father."

The Koombar transport came into view and stopped at the bottom of the hill, disgorging its armed guards.

Tree held his son close and rocked him gently, humming softly for a time. Finally, he placed his son on the ground and stroked his face one last time. "It is time for you to find your dreams," he said.

"Yes, father." The young tree hugged his father and stepped back. "What shall I do?"

Skrin began climbing the hill, but the old tree remained fixed on his son.

"Go into the forest. Find a place where the sun can greet you in the morning and where you can sit in comfort. Face in the direction of the rising sun, and rest. Your dreams will come before daybreak."

The child turned and walked with a laborious, short stride toward the woods.

"Son," called the old Tree.

"Yes, father."

"Know that, if you hear my call, it is not for you, but for those whose time has not yet come. Simply rest and dream. I am very old and will join you soon."

"Yes, father."

Tree watched his son disappear into the brush while Skrin stood with massive impatience some fifteen feet away. Finally, he turned his eyes to Skrin and spoke. "This one is greatly honored to be in the presence of such a fine specimen of the Koombar heritage."

Skrin remained standing on his back feet. "What could be of such importance that I, Skrin, Heir to the Supreme Watcher, should be kept waiting?"

Tree swept his arms forward and leaned toward Skrin, approximating a prostrate position as nearly as possible. He straightened and stared for a moment without blinking. "My son is dying. I shall see him no more."

"And of what concern is that to me?"

"It is none of your concern but only of mine."

"This is unsuitable," screamed Skrin. "Do you think I have no obligations? Do you think I can stand waiting at the whim of some Tree? Do you think I have time to waste on such things as the death of your son? I should have one of your arms removed for this insolence."

"That would be most unpleasant," replied Tree.

Skrin continued to rant and rave. Tree gazed at him but mostly ignored the threats and the attempts at intimidation. This is what the Koombar did. The Trees had been a long time understanding that the Koombar were prone to overstatement and posturing. He supposed it served to release their tensions and calm them, but right now, he really didn't care. His focus was on the son whose cycle was coming to an end even as this Koombar stood screaming in his glade. It made him think about the end of his own cycle and for perhaps the first time in his nearly four hundred years of life, to long for it.

Skrin continued to scream. It occurred to Tree that they were wasting even more of Skrin's ever-so-valuable time with all this agitation, but it seemed impolitic to mention it. Finally, Skrin's tirade ended and he stood waiting.

Tree bowed low again. "My humble apologies, sire. I deeply regret any loss of time this may have caused and wish to assure you I will make every effort to see that none of my sons dies at a time that would be inconvenient to you."

"See to it then," said Skrin, apparently missing the irony of the statement just as most any Koombar would.

"Shall we begin our lesson in Biology?" asked Tree.

"Very well," Skrin said and settled down with his elbows on the ground and his feet drawn up beneath him.

This one bears watching, observed Tree.

Chapter Eighteen
Below the Surface of Mars
April 18, 2061

Tom and Evelyn stood at the mouth of the cave. "Testing, testing," Tom said into his radio.

"We read you clear," came Ki's reply. He was sitting alone in the comfort of the communal dining room at the base camp. A computer keyboard sat on the table in front of him. The rest of the crew, with the exception of Melancon, was busy carrying equipment into the Lab.

"Initiating video feed now," said Tom, and he pressed a button on the side of his helmet as Evelyn did the same.

The screen on the wall of the communal room went blank for a second then sprung into life with two, three-dimensional views. In the corner of the left-hand screen was the name Evelyn Weiss. The corner of the right-hand screen bore the name Tom Fielder. The pictures bobbed and swung as Tom and Evelyn moved about, and the walls of the cave sparkled from the occasional bit of exposed quartz.

Ki tapped at the keyboard, and a computer screen superimposed itself on the pictures from the cave. He hit a few more keys, looked at the display, and then tapped one more key to remove the computer screen from the video.

"We are getting perfect 3D video in the camp," Ki said, "and our satellite is ready to accept and send the signal on to NASA. I am initiating that sequence now. You might want to watch your language from this point on, Mr. Fielder."

"What about Ms. Weiss?" Tom said. "Shouldn't she watch her language too?"

Ki rolled his eyes. "Yes. Ms. Weiss also. Initiating video stream on my mark." He pressed a single button on the keyboard. "Mark."

Tom bowed and gestured with his palm up to the opening in the back wall of the cavern. "After you, Ms. Weiss."

"Thank you, Mr. Fielder," she replied and jumped down to the floor of the water cave. They walked through the smoothed tube of the old underground river until they came to the first bend.

"The footing is a little better to the right," Tom said. "You can see where the water hollowed out a bowl on the left hand side."

They made their way around the bend but had not traveled more than a few feet before Ki broke in. "The video is starting to fade badly."

Tom walked back a few feet to the bend. "That's much better on yours, Mr. Fielder," Ki said, "but Ms. Weiss video is still breaking up."

Tom pulled a small box from a clip on his belt and laid it on the cave floor. He then extended an antenna from its side and flipped the single switch on its top. A tiny red light gleamed in response. "How's that?" Tom asked.

"Much better," said Ki.

Tom and Evelyn turned and continued their exploration. "We're probably going to need a relay for every bend in the cave to keep the video feed," Tom said. "We only have three more with us, and there is another bend in the cave just fifty yards ahead. Hopefully we'll have a long, straight stretch after that."

Tom looked down to where he had hammered the ice from the floor. "That is where I found the ice. You can see the piece of rock I moved lying next to the depression."

Ki cut in again. "Perhaps you could explain what compelled you to look under a rock, Mr. Fielder."

Tom grimaced but began talking. "One of the things that most people don't realize is that ice can sublime. Sublimation is a term used for the process of solids turning directly into a vapor. Some of you who live in cold climates may have noticed that snow will begin to disappear even when the temperature stays below freezing. Snow can evaporate just like water evaporates from an uncovered jar. Water and ice on Mars will do the same thing. It occurred to me that if I was going to find ice, it would have to be covered up to slow down the process of sublimation. I was lucky that the ice in the bottom of this hollow was also covered with sand. The sand helped to slow the process of sublimation, and the rock kept most of it trapped. It's kind of like putting a cap on a jar. If the sand and the rock had not covered the ice, it would have evaporated thousands of years ago."

Tom and Evelyn continued down to the next bend and were once again forced to deploy one of the relay antennas, but the cave ran straight with an even but fairly steep slope for as far as they could see.

They started walking again. The floor of this part of the cave was almost completely free of debris due to the angle of the floor. There was the occasional stalactite and stalagmite pair, but Tom detected that something was changing as they went deeper into the cave. For the moment, he kept it to himself.

"Commander Thon," Tom said, "is this cave any different from what you might expect to see on Earth?" He figured that would be enough to get Ki going.

"Not really, Mr. Fielder. The fracture cave that lead us to this water cave was formed by a folding of the planet's surface in the same manner that forms mountains and similar structures on Earth. The only thing remarkable about this particular fracture cave is its size. On Earth, it would have collapsed of its own weight, and we would have found a pile of rubble instead of the intact slab of rock.

"The water cave in which you and Ms. Weiss are currently walking appears to have been temporarily interrupted by the Mars quake that formed the fracture cave. The channel that was cut on the floor of the large cavern when the flow of water resumed is clearly visible. The depth of this cut indicates the quake that formed that cavern occurred long after the water cave was formed.

"Water caves such as this one are produced by the downward percolation of water through existing rock. The water tends to carve channels by dissolving certain minerals. If there is a vein of Calcium Carbonate, or Limestone as it is called, it will dissolve faster than the surrounding granite because it is much more soluble. In this way, channels are cut, and caves are formed.

"Of course, one of the reasons for this expedition is the hope of finding some clues that would help explain some of the oddities of Martian geology. We have seen many things in satellite photos that are difficult to understand. For example, there are places on the surface that look as if water has burst from the ground. This is not terribly unusual, but the flow from these sources appear to be very large, and most mysteriously, there is no indication of where the water went. We can see where the outflow pushed huge amounts of rock and sand forward, but it simply fans out and disappears. On Earth, we would find evidence of an old riverbed that once led to an ocean."

Ki actually chuckled softly. "Mars has always held a strange mystical relevance for mankind, and there are many puzzles here. Even the two moons are strange—very small and irregularly shaped." He paused for just a moment as if contemplating this last fact.

"Another puzzling matter is the appearance of many of the craters on Mars. The ejecta of some craters suggests that the surface was in a liquid or semi-liquid state when the meteor struck. It is difficult to formulate a decent hypothesis as to why this might be so. By retrieving rock samples from several areas on Mars and studying outcroppings and various other things we hope to gain an insight…"

Ki kept up his dialogue, but Tom reached out his hand to stop Evelyn. He looked intently down the cave and then turned and looked back in the direction they had come. He repeated this several times before he broke in.

"Commander," Tom said, "does it appear to be getting brighter in here?"

"Brighter?"

"Yes, brighter. Look at the walls of the cave. It seems to me there is more quartz on the walls at this location than where we started.

Tom was analyzing his surroundings. "I have a suggestion, Commander. Roll back the video to the beginning, and set up a view side-by-side with where we are now. Let me know if I'm just dreaming."

Ki hit a few keystrokes and then held down one key and watched as Tom's video whirled backward in a blur to the beginning. He froze the picture and compared it to Evelyn's view. He frowned at the pictures for a moment. There was a sprinkling of quartz in the walls at the beginning of the cave, revealed by glints of light from the crystals, and this was not unusual for a cave, but the section of the cave where Evelyn and Tom were standing was peppered with spots of light.

Ki cocked his head to the side and considered the situation. "There does seem to be a greater amount of quartz at your current location," he said. "It might be just normal variation, but it is a bit strange. May I suggest that you continue down the cave, and we will see if this trend continues?"

Ki toggled the view back to real time, and the video began to bob and weave as Evelyn and Tom resumed their exploration.

"We're rolling," Tom said. "Maybe you could tell us a little bit about how quartz is formed."

"Certainly," Ki replied. "Quartz is actually a crystal of Silicon and Oxygen. It is formed when water evaporates and deposits the dissolved silicates . . ."

Tom turned his radio almost all the way down so that only Evelyn could hear him. "The entire planet of Earth drops off to sleep."

Evelyn turned her radio down also and scolded him. "You are simply being mean. Commander Thon is really quite a good lecturer."

"Yeah, but he tends to get over everyone's head pretty fast."

Tom changed the subject and pointed around him. "What do you think of this?"

"I don't know. I'm not a geologist, but I find it strange that the amount of quartz is changing so quickly." She looked around at the sparkling walls. "It seems also that the rate of change is increasing as we move downward. Have you noticed that the floor is becoming more and more littered with small stones? Quite a few of them are primarily quartz. There is something strange here, but I don't know what it might be."

Ki was still talking as they conversed. ". . . of course, quartz has a hexagonal structure, actually a twinned trigonal structure that gives it many interesting properties and makes it useful for the manufacture of piezoelectric devices."

Tom reached for the dial on his radio. "I've got to rescue these poor people," he said and twisted the dial up.

"Commander Thon."

"Yes Tom," replied Ki.

"Ms. Weiss has observed that we are seeing more rubble on the floor of the cave as we continue. As you can see, most of it is quartz. I noticed when we first entered this part of the cave that the floor was almost completely clean due to the steep slope. The slope has not changed, but there is more debris. I am going to pick up some of these rocks for samples, but I was wondering what your input might be on the subject."

There was a long pause. "It is difficult to speculate at this time," said Ki. "I have noticed that the cave is getting larger as you progress. At the same time, the walls are becoming smoother, and I am a bit surprised at the lack of any major twists or turns." He paused again. "It is almost as if something wore down the cave in a rapid but violent fashion. I would suspect steam or extremely rapid water-flow, but this cave was obviously an underground river. I cannot see how steam could have been generated in such high volume, and the fact that the cave is narrower in the upper parts than it is here rules out rapid water flow. If the cave was becoming more narrow, then the water velocity would be increasing in the direction you and Ms. Weiss are traveling, but the reverse is true."

Evelyn picked up a few rocks and labeled a bag for them as Ki talked. They continued onward and were soon walking on a rough carpet of shining gravel and larger stones. Ki did not speak for some time, and Tom could almost hear the wheels turning in his commander's head as the scene became more peculiar with the appearance of larger and larger rocks.

Finally Ki spoke. "This is most strange. Larger rocks are always dropped at the beginning of a flow of water, while smaller stones and sand are carried further. We saw this at the mouth of this cave. Some of the larger plates from the fracture cave had been carried just a few feet into the water cave, whereas the smaller ones were found several hundred feet further along. This is one of the mechanisms by which rocks become sorted by size. What we are seeing here would indicate that you are walking against the direction of water flow, upstream if you would. But the slope is steeply downward. I cannot imagine what would have made water flow uphill."

Neither Tom nor Evelyn had an answer, and they walked on in silence for a time. Tom began to get the impression that the slope of the cave was leveling off, but then he noticed that the ceiling was closing in.

"Commander Thon, as you can see, the roof is getting closer. We are apparently now walking on a reasonably thick bed of rock that is getting thicker as we move forward. If this continues, we will find ourselves at a point where the cave is plugged by debris."

"That would be most disappointing, Mr. Fielder. Let us hope that there remains sufficient clearance for you and Ms. Weiss to continue."

Tom and Evelyn walked perhaps another half-mile before Evelyn spoke. "Look. Can you see it?"

Tom squinted into the glare of quartz but was unable to make out anything. "What? It looks like more of the same to me."

"No. The floor rises sharply ahead of us. I cannot tell if there is an opening at the top."

They quickened their pace. "Time for me to get a prescription faceplate," Tom said.

They soon came to the base of a pile of large rocks that seemed to block the way. The roof of the cave was still some twenty feet above their head, and the steep angle of the rock pile made it impossible to see if it met the ceiling or allowed room for them to crawl through.

They stood for a moment surveying the situation before Tom spoke. "Let's climb up and see what we've got."

Side by side, Tom and Evelyn scrambled up to where the rocks met the ceiling. At the top was a small opening, just large enough for one of them to crawl through. Tom bent over so that his suit lights would shine into the passage.

He stood up and motioned to Evelyn. "Take a look," he said.

Evelyn squatted in front of the small channel and moved her head back and forth for a moment. "It's difficult to tell what I'm seeing. The passage does not appear to be very long, but I am not sure that I am seeing the end of it. This may just be the top of this pile of rocks. Perhaps it slopes down on the other side, and we can continue."

Tom pulled out another relay antenna and laid it down next to the opening. "That would be nice. Do you have any experience with crawlways?"

"Oh yes," Evelyn replied. "There were several caverns in France that could be accessed in no other way."

Tom waited. Ki had been silent for some time. "Commander, can you read me?"

"Loud and clear Mr. Fielder. I have been watching closely. Ms. Weiss has experienced similar situations in the past and may be more able to recognize a dangerous circumstance. I believe she should go into the opening while you wait outside. If the passage is more than twenty or thirty feet long, we may have to reconsider our current objectives."

"Aye, sir," Tom replied and gestured to the opening. "Be very careful not to tear your suit."

Evelyn dropped to her hands and knees and began to slowly and carefully move into the passage. "Yes, sir. At least this passage is not so small that we will need to drag ourselves through on our bellies. That would be very difficult."

Tom dropped down to watch her progress through the crawlway and flipped the switch on the relay antenna.

"It is not so bad," Evelyn said after she had gone about ten feet. "I can see the end of the passage just a few feet ahead. I will be through in just a moment. Unfortunately, I cannot see what is on the other side because my suit lights are all pointed down. I will let you know as soon as I can stand up and look around."

Tom could still see her moving on all fours through the crawlway. "Just be careful," he said.

"How do you say, 'A piece of cake,' eh? I am coming out now."

There was a brief pause and then "Mon Dieu!" followed by a string of French much too fast for Tom to translate. Ki began to chatter into the radio. "What in the world! I have never seen anything like this!" he said.

"Will someone tell me what the hell is going on?" Tom screamed. "Evelyn, are you alright?"

"I am fine," she said and lapsed into rapid French once more. "Come, come," she said. "Excuse me, but I have no words."

Ki continued to exclaim as Tom started into the passage. "My God! It's a geode!" he gasped. "But this is on a scale I would not have believed possible."

Tom pulled his way through the last of the crawlway and stood up. "Holy shit," he said softly.

He was nearly blinded by the light from their suits. They stood on a ledge some twenty feet from the floor of a roughly spherical cavern the size of a large auditorium, but all other impressions were lost in the appearance of the walls. Every inch of the room—ceiling, walls and floor—was covered in quartz crystals of various sizes and colors. Although red predominated, there were streaks of blue and amber, and their suit lights bounced brilliant rainbows back and forth as they turned left and right. The chamber only suggested the shape of a ball, and there were soft dips and large undulating waves across the walls where the crystals had grown at different rates. At the very top of the room, some fifty feet above their heads, an especially large growth of crystals hung down like an impressionist chandelier. The chandelier held a deep rose color in its heart and shaded to mauve where it merged with the rest of the ceiling.

Tom was struck speechless and stood looking about with his mouth open. The far wall was nearly one hundred feet away, and at first, he could not find even the smallest spot that did not reflect sharp flashes of colored light.

Ki was still chattering away in his helmet about the formation of geodes on Earth and the slow precipitation of Oxides of Silicon. Tom was not paying the least bit of attention.

Evelyn had, had a little more time to absorb the features of the room and she interrupted the commander. "Commander Thon," she said, pointing down and slightly to her right. "What could this be?"

Tom's eyes followed her outstretched arm to the floor of the room, and he felt the hair on the back of his neck rise up as he tried to make sense of what he was seeing. In the middle of the floor was an oblong area nearly lost in the glare from the crystals. It too reflected light, but the color was a translucent grayish green, and the surface was smooth—unlike the jagged quartz of the walls and ceiling. But it was far from featureless. There were small domes and sharp spires with fluted sides, some of them three feet tall and more. One area had a series of small ridges resembling ocean waves, and there were twisted columns in strange shapes projecting upward at odd places—all leaning at slightly different angles.

There was complete silence over the radio for almost a full minute as no one dared to say what was on their minds.

Evelyn finally broke the silence. "It looks like a strange abstract sculpture."

Tom's mind seemed to have shut down momentarily, but Evelyn's words jolted him. He could not accept that this was an Alien artifact. There had to be another explanation, and his mind whirled around the problem for another minute or so. Suddenly he nodded his head vigorously.

"Sublimation," Tom said.

"Pardon?" from Evelyn.

Tom pointed to where the shapes caught the multicolored reflection of their lights. "Sublimation," he repeated. "This is what we came here to find. This is ice."

"Of course!" said Ki. "This room was probably once filled with ice. Over time, the ice has sublimed as Tom described earlier, but it is an uneven process. Small air currents and pockets of dissolved gases and other things would have caused the ice to evaporate faster in some areas than in others. These things sculpted the surface, resulting in what we see now. Congratulations, Mr. Fielder and Ms. Weiss. You have collaborated in what may be one of the most important discoveries of this expedition."

Tom was already pulling a piton from his belt, and he signaled for Evelyn to loosen the coil of rope from her shoulder. "I'm sure you'll want a sample of the ice," he said. "We're going to rappel down this wall and get a closer look."

Tom hammered the piton into a crack near his feet, clipped the rope into the eye, and placed another antenna on the ledge. Tom went first, and they were soon standing on the rough floor of the cavern. "We need to be especially careful with all of this jagged crystal," he said.

The ice lay about thirty feet away, and they walked carefully across the floor till they stood at the edge of the wind-carved ice. Evelyn was gawking like a tourist. "It is like standing in the middle of a diamond," she said.

Tom gestured to the ice. "This stuff is worth more than diamonds right now." He looked up at the roof of the cavern and considered for a moment.

"Commander Thon," he said, "it's a long way through the cave and up the crack. It won't be very efficient to carry blocks of ice that far. We may want to think about drilling in from the top. We'll need to set up a heater to melt the ice and a small pump. If we heat trace the pipe back to the surface, we can just let the pump run continuously. All we'll need at the surface is a hollowed out spot with a piece of plastic in the bottom. The water will freeze as soon as it hits the ground, and we can carry it back to the camp in chunks."

"That seems reasonable, Mr. Fielder," replied Ki, "but it sounds like it might require a good bit of power."

"It will," said Tom, "but we've got those big rolls of solar-cell sheets for emergency use if the fusion reactor fails. I'll need to go through the calculations, but I think just one of those will be sufficient. After all, we don't need to pump the melted ice very quickly."

"We have many things to do before we begin harvesting this water," said Ki, "but it sounds like a good plan. We will of course obtain several core samples from this site before any melting of the surface. One of the questions that needs to be answered is how deep the ice is, but there are no other exits from this room. I suspect you and Ms. Weiss have found a virtually inexhaustible vein of water."

Tom grinned. "Does this mean we can have full showers tonight?"

Ki chuckled. "I believe the two of you have earned that right for all of us."

"Life is good," Tom said and stepped out onto the ice. His feet immediately went out from under him and he landed flat on his backside in the crystals at the edge of the ice. "Damn it!"

Evelyn leaned down to lend him her hand. "Are you alright?"

"I'm fine," Tom said as he stood, but a red light bloomed in his helmet. "Crap, I've got an air leak."

Evelyn was suddenly all business. "Turn around," she said.

The tear was easy to find by the small plume of water vapor condensing and freezing as it left the hole in the butt of Tom's suit. She pulled a small repair kit from a clip on her belt. "Bend over."

Tom bent at the waist and tilted forward with his legs held straight till his gloves touched the ground. "How bad is it?" he asked.

"It is little more than a pinhole," Evelyn replied and selected a round patch from her kit. She struggled for a moment to remove the backing with her gloved hands and then pressed the patch over the small hole. With the thumb of her right hand, she rubbed the patch firmly onto the surface of Tom's suit. "You had best not be enjoying this," she said.

"Let's see. My life is hanging in the balance, and the whole world is looking at a picture of my can sticking up in the air. Not exactly my idea of a good time."

Evelyn inspected the patch for evidence of more air leakage and stepped back. "That should do it."

Tom stood up and watched the red light in his helmet dim and go out. "I've got green lights," Tom said. "Let's get a quick sample of ice and head back before the patch decides to let go."

Evelyn took a hammer from her belt and squatted near the ice. "From here this time." She turned and looked at To "What ever possessed you to step onto this ice?"

Ki had been silent for the last few minutes, but he spoke up too. "I must admit I was wondering the same thing."

Tom's embarrassment at the situation deepened. "No excuse, sir. I simply didn't think about how slick it would be. I guess growing up in Houston Texas doesn't leave you with the right instincts for such things."

Ki did not respond, and Tom stood watching as Evelyn tapped at the ice till several large pieces broke off. She labeled a bag and stowed the ice for later examination. They turned without speaking and walked carefully back to where the rope hung down from the ledge.

Tom looked up at the ledge. "This is going to be easier said than done."

Evelyn was looking at the wall in front of her. "Look how strange," she said, pointing here and there along the wall.

Tom could see a series of holes spaced evenly along the wall from the base up to the ledge. Neither one of them had noticed the holes on the trip down in their excitement at finding the ice. "Looks like good toeholds to me," he said and grabbed the rope. "I'll go up first."

He pulled himself up slowly, hand over hand. Using the holes in the wall for grip helped tremendously, and he was soon at the top. Evelyn followed him up, and he helped her over the lip of the small ledge. "I'll go through the crawlway first," Tom said. "Wait till I get through before you start."

Evelyn didn't reply but turned to look at the cavern. It was easily the most incredible thing she had ever seen. As Tom bent to enter the passage, the light dimmed slightly, but it only added to the beauty as the colors deepened. She turned her body this way and that and watched the play of rainbows against the ridges and rolls of quartz. Adding to the splendor was the green, fabulously sculpted ice in the center of the cavern. She imagined how it might look if lit by hundreds of burning candles—their flickering flames casting moving shadows here and there around the room. Her breath caught in her throat.

"Okay," Tom said, "I'm through."

Evelyn shook herself from her reverie and bent to enter the crawlway. Something was bothering her about the holes in the wall, but it slipped away as her mind returned to the excitement of what she and Tom had found.

Tom was waiting impatiently at the exit of the passage. "Let's roll," he said.

They started back up the cave at a fairly good pace. Tom kept to himself, and they listened to Ki explaining the process of finding the drill site by setting off small explosions on the surface and measuring the returned vibrations as the shock waves bounced off the cave. The commander had not said another word about Tom's fall or the hole in Tom's suit, and Evelyn could almost feel Tom's mood blacken as they walked up the slope toward the fracture cave.

Finally, she turned her radio down and spoke. "Anyone could have made that mistake."

Tom turned his radio down before he answered. "It was stupid."

"It wasn't stupid. You just weren't thinking."

"That's just it," Tom almost wailed. "I wasn't thinking. And have you noticed that Ki," he paused, "Commander Thon has said hardly a word about it? I can hear it now, 'Tom, we must remember that we are in a very hostile environment and should be vigilant at all times. As second in command, you must set the example.' Christ!" Tom swore, "I'd rather take a beating than listen to that crap."

Evelyn chuckled softly. "You do a pretty good impersonation of Commander Thon."

"I should have just laid down on the ice and let my air leak out."

"Nonsense! Don't talk like that. Commander Thon will speak to you just as he would speak to anyone on this mission. I think he does these things not so much because he thinks they are necessary but because he believes, as mission commander, he must do these things. You are having difficulty with this because he has been your friend for so long."

Tom slowed his pace and looked over at Evelyn who smiled at him through her faceplate. As much as he hated to admit it, she had a point. The thrill of actually finding ice had caused him to let down his guard. Ki was going to chew him out because he deserved it, and Tom had never been one to whine about getting what he deserved.

Evelyn sensed that he was softening and spoke again. "The world will remember that we found water on Mars for all of history. Your slip on the ice will be forgotten with time."

Tom nodded. All of history. It was a daunting notion.

"And we get full showers tonight," he said.

"Yes, full showers," said Evelyn. "Now if I had asked you this morning if you would trade a pinhole in your suit for a full shower, what would you have said?"

Tom felt as if a cloud was lifting from him, and he laughed. "Well, when you put it like that."

Evelyn laughed with him. "You may want to brace yourself for some of the pictures though."

"Oh?"

"Mr. Fielder, the sight of you bent over with all of that mist escaping from your derriere…"

Evelyn's voice trailed off into laughter, but it had a pleasant sound to Tom, and he found himself laughing with her. "I guess it did look pretty funny."

They walked for a short while without speaking, and then Tom began to talk. "We'll need to sit down when we get back and look at the power requirements. I wonder if we have a good number on the depth of the cave? I think we can do it with just one roll of solar cells, but we'll have to see."

Evelyn was only half-listening while Tom rambled on about heating factors for the water and the head pressure at the pump. He was such a study in contrasts—brilliantly competent and driven to excel—but strangely vulnerable. She smiled to herself as they walked along. *It would be so easy to become involved with this man.* But she recoiled from the idea. *We are so far from home. He is my direct superior. What would my mother think? Mon Dieu.*

Chapter Nineteen
Near the Orbit of Pluto
May 3, 2061

Space and time are unpretentious out past the orbit of Pluto. Distance from the sun and the larger planets lends virtue in the form of simplicity to this place. Here, on the outskirts of the Solar System, where the large gravity wells of massive bodies are attenuated by their range and the sun itself begins to find the limits of its influence, space approaches its linear resting state, and time can be said to move forward in near straight lines. There is little to disturb the slumber of this almost perfect vacuum except for the occasional passing comet and the endless dance of virtual particles as they wink in and out of existence quickly enough that the universe never knows of their blatant disregard for matter conservation.

But on this date and in this place, something different happens. Where before there was nothing, a great gout of radiation blooms. Photons and other particles scatter in every direction. Strong but highly localized gravitational forces erupt where no mass can be found, and a circle of light forms. A shining ball floats lazily out of the circle, followed by a long black cylinder with four smaller cylinders strapped to its waist. The circle collapses in another burst of radiation just as the cylinder passes through, and the cylinder accelerates slightly to swallow the shining ball in its shark-like mouth.

Two simple detectors are engaged on the cylinder. The first looks for radio waves in a particular band of frequencies and begins a process of determining their origin. The second searches for gravitational sources and begins to carefully map them.

The first detector almost immediately finds and marks the birthplace of a large amount of radio traffic. The second detector maps one gravity well after another. A simple computer program compares the coordinates relayed by the two detectors to find which of the gravity wells matches the radio source. There is an indeterminate passage of time before the second detector gives up coordinates in congruence with the first detector. The cylinder then accelerates away at nearly ten gravities. It will continue to accelerate till it has reached a velocity of almost three million miles per hour.

Just as the first cylinder begins its journey, there is a burst of radiation, and another circle forms. Two more will follow, and this place will not return to its simple slumber till all have passed and gone.

All of this takes place many millions of miles from Earth—out near the orbit of Pluto where space is flat, cold, and quiet, and where the complexities of the space-time continuum are minimal. No one should have noticed these briefly radiant events. Objects such as these have rent the fabric of space many times before in other places and in other ages without discernment or premonition. There seems little reason to believe that anyone might be watching.

But this time, only by chance, someone watches—and knows not what he sees.

Chapter Twenty
Somewhere Outside of Enid, OK
May 3, 2061

It was 11:00 at night, and Gary Marler had been driving north out of Enid Oklahoma for more than an hour. Country music played softly on the radio, and highway 81 was nearly deserted. The electric motor in his old model '50 truck hummed quietly down the road. He had made good time, keeping mostly to the speed limit, and the farm road he was looking for came into view as yet another remake of "Unchained Melody" filled the cabin. He braked hard and turned right, driving another four miles until the gravel road crested a hill. He pulled to the side and opened the door into the crisp air.

A cold front had come through that afternoon, sweeping the last gasp of winter into the Midwest, and it was unseasonably cold. He grabbed his coat from the front seat and fought the stiffness in his joints as he pulled it on. The weather was playing hell with his arthritis, and sharp streaks of pain surged through his shoulders from the effort. He grunted softly and struggled with the zipper.

At the age of 93, Gary Marler had learned not to complain of such things. "God grants long life at a price," he would say. Sometimes he wondered if God wasn't just wearing him down bit by bit till he was ready to go. He tried not to think like that, but it hadn't been easy these last ten years since Jackie went home to Jesus. They had been married for fifty years to the day. Jackie had died unexpectedly on the morning of their anniversary.

She had come to him that morning and complained of not feeling well. A twinge of guilt rose in him as he recalled the irritation he had felt. They were expecting all the children and grandchildren, and he didn't see how he could get all the food ready. Thank God, he hadn't said anything to her. She had kissed him on the cheek and gone to lie down. Two hours later he found her dead. Her eyes were closed peacefully, and her hands were folded across her chest as if in prayer, but a single tear had fallen and left a wet trail down her cooling cheek. There was a moist spot in her gray hair where it fanned out on the pillow, and he lay down beside her, mingling his own, fresh tears with the last of hers.

For six months, he had just been lost. For a year after that, he had cursed his life and questioned why God hadn't taken him first. Jackie could have handled his death so much better than he was handling hers. Finally, he just accepted it, and feelings of gratitude returned—fifty years of living with his best friend at his side was more than most people got.

He turned up the collar of his coat and slipped on a pair of thin gloves. The cold front had done more than lower the temperature. The morning rain had rinsed the air clean of dust and smoke, and the sky was ablaze with stars. The Milky Way spread its glory across the night sky in a haze of light.

A shooting star plowed a brief furrow of disintegration into the air as it melted and died. *A good omen,* thought Gary, and he slipped into effortless prayer.

It was an old prayer. One that he had used countless times over the last eight years. It was worn smooth from use and slid easily through his mind. "Lord, thank you for this day and for the many days before it. That I might be granted the wisdom to find thy path and the strength to follow it. Thank you for the time I had with Jackie, and thank you for taking her quickly. I hold her in my heart as you hold her in your arms till we meet again. In Jesus' name. Amen."

It was a perfect night. He could not remember when it had been this clear, and the moon had already set. He felt a certain thrill as he leaned over the side of the truck to pull back the cover and pick up his telescope. He strained a bit to lift it over the edge. It was an expensive piece of equipment, and his daughter had gently chided him for spending so much on a hobby. He had to admit it was a lot of money, but it was his one extravagance since Jackie had died. A man of small needs, he had lived in the same house for over 30 years. His truck was 11 years old, and it took him wherever he wanted to go. He had looked across the table at his daughter and said with a smile, "Maybe you're right. Maybe I should take up drinking whiskey and chasing wild, wild women." There had been a few nervous snickers, but that had been the end of it.

He picked up the case containing the clock motor and slung it over his shoulder. A small folding chair lay in the bed of the truck, and he picked that up as well. His arms complained of the weight, but he balanced the load and began walking up the short rise near the edge of the road. *This is getting to the point where I'll need to make two trips.*

He gently laid down the chair and the telescope and slipped the clock off of his shoulder. With practiced motions, he unfolded the chair and assembled the telescope. Mars was high in the sky and, at less than 70 million miles away, just past its closest approach to Earth. He could have looked up the settings for viewing Mars from here, but it was too much trouble for something this easy to find. He took off his glasses and leaned over to look through the small sighting-scope till Mars swam into view. He then looked into the main scope and adjusted the focus out, but Mars was nowhere to be seen. Looking back into the sighting scope, he realized it needed to be moved a bit to his right and looked back through the main scope with his hand on a knob. And stopped.

"Now that's weird," he whispered. There was a strange, bright star almost dead center in the field of his scope, and it got brighter as he watched.

"What the hell . . . ?" His hand fumbled along the side of the scope. There was a button for recording video, but he almost never used it. He felt the button through his glove and pressed down. A small red light appeared in the bottom left of the scope. The star changed color as it grew brighter, sliding through the rainbow from red to yellow to deep blue—and then winked out.

Gary pulled a phone from his pocket. He belonged to a small amateur astronomers club, and on a night like this, it was a cinch his friend Paul would be out stargazing somewhere nearby. It seemed to take forever, but there was a click, and Paul came on the line.

"Hello."

"Paul, this is Gary. Are you set up?"

"Yeah, what a night."

"I don't have time to explain. Set your scope to these numbers." Gary checked the settings. "Attitude: 46.29, Azimuth: 35.32.

"What's up, Gary. I never heard you sound so excited."

"I don't know what it is, but I saw something."

Paul laughed. "Flying saucers maybe?"

"No. Maybe a nova or something like that. Just please dial it in."

"Calm down. I'm dialing it in." He paused for a moment. "Got it."

There was silence over the line as both astronomers looked through their scopes.

Paul broke the silence. "I hate to say this old timer, but this doesn't look very…" There was a twinkling that built rapidly to a sharp burst of light in the space of less than a second. It had the effect of a flash bulb, and both of the astronomers were momentarily dazzled. ". . . interesting," said Paul.

"Hah!" cried Gary. "Now what was that?"

Paul hesitated. "I don't have a clue, but it was damn sure bright for just a second. Did you record it?"

"The first part was different, and I missed part of it, but I got the last burst."

"What did the first part look like?"

Gary shifted the phone to his other ear. "It was slower to develop and changed colors from red to blue. Then it winked out. What do you think?"

"I don't know. Was it centered in your scope?" Paul asked.

"Dead center," replied Gary.

"It was pretty much dead center in mine too. Are you on the farm road off of 81?"

"Yeah. My usual spot."

"Well, old timer, we got ourselves something strange then. I'm at least fifty miles southeast of you. If it was real close, it wouldn't have been centered in both the telescopes." Paul mulled it over it over with his eye glued to his scope. "I tell you what. I've got my computer with me. I'm going to put this out on the Internet and see if anybody else saw it or might know what it is. Send the video to my e-mail address."

"Now that might be a problem," said Gary. "I never tried to do that."

"It's no big deal," Paul said. "That scope of yours has more bells and whistles than you even know about. You can send it to your phone and then on to me."

Paul talked his older friend through the process of transmitting data from his telescope and sent a message to astronomy groups on the Internet describing the phenomenon and giving coordinates for those who might want to look with their own telescopes. Paul soon had the video on his computer screen.

"This is some kind of strange," Paul said as he watched the light go from yellow, when Gary had turned on his recorder, to blue and then disappear. "It's not a nova. A nova would last a lot longer than that." He clicked a few keys on his computer. "I'm sending the pictures out on the net. Maybe somebody's seen this before." He watched again as the point brightened, flared to brilliance, and winked out in less than a second. "Curiouser and curiouser," Paul muttered to himself.

"I've got an idea," Paul said. "We can set up a live video feed from your telescope to the net. If this happens again, it will go out in real time."

"Uh, okay," said Gary. "How do I do that?" His arm ached from holding the phone up to his ear, and he switched it back again.

"Basically it's the same thing we did before with one twist at the end," Paul said.

Paul walked Gary through the process of setting up the live feed while his computer beeped with ever-greater frequency to tell him he had received an e-mail message.

"Well," said Paul, "We've generated some interest. I've gotten about twenty messages in the last ten minutes and they're starting to come in at about four per minute." He turned off the audible alert and hit a few more keys. "Okay, old man, that's got it. From your telescope, to your phone, to my computer, and straight to the Internet. I hope we get something else. It's going to take a week to clean up my e-mail files."

Gary had been glued to his scope while Paul completed the Internet hook up. "Gary," he said, "take a look. Do some of the stars at the center seem to be twinkling?"

Paul leaned forward and saw the whole thing from the beginning this time. The background of stars shimmered for a moment in a very small spot. A dull red glow spread from this center and brightened before going to yellow and then to green and finally to blue and purple before disappearing.

Paul was struck speechless, but Gary felt a thrill run through him. "We got it! Did it go out over the net? I wonder how far away it is. I wonder what it is. I wish …" He stopped. He had been about to say, "I wish Jackie was here to see this." It always amazed him that his wife would spring into his memories whenever he got excited about something.

"Damn," Paul said. "I really didn't think it would come back. That color change is interesting. Red light has less energy than yellow, which has less energy than blue. I bet this thing is cycling up through ultra violet. Hell, it wouldn't surprise me if it's sending out gamma radiation right now."

They waited and watched as the source flared like a flashbulb and disappeared.

Paul looked down at his computer. "It was about twenty minutes between the first colored light and the second one. It'll be interesting to see if it keeps to that schedule."

Gary was hardly listening. Thinking of Jackie had calmed him and made him consider the broader implications of what had just happened. Was this the purpose of his long life? Would he soon find himself with Jackie? The prayer slid through his mind again. "Lord, thank you for this night and what I have found. That my act might serve your purpose for the world," he added.

Paul was going on about the number of e-mail messages he was receiving as hundreds of astronomers turned their telescopes to the coordinates he had posted on the net.

Only Gary and Paul saw the first flare of light in their scopes. Perhaps twenty managed to turn their scopes to the proper setting to see the second flare. It was nearly an hour before the third light bloomed and died in the night sky, and hundreds of astronomers over the entire western hemisphere watched with excitement and consternation while it went through the colors of the rainbow, disappeared, then flashed brilliantly for less than a second. It was followed ten minutes later by the last occurrence of what was already being called "The Marler Phenomenon."

It would be some time before its significance was known.

Chapter Twenty-one
The Planet Harmony
Exact Time Unknown

Tree watched the young Koombar rolling in the grass just twenty feet in front of him. *How am I to teach Biology to this Koombar? Just thirty seconds ago he was threatening to remove one of my arms and now he spins on the ground like one of my young.*

"Master Skrin, If you will recall our last conversation, this excursion into Biology is prompted by your question concerning the ability of the Trees to destroy the Koombar and the reason why we are not capable of doing so. You do recall this, do you not?"

Skrin turned on his back with all four feet in the air and wriggled like a snake to scratch his back. "I remember it clearly," he said.

"Good. With that in mind, we will approach the study of Biology from the standpoint of the Tree and Koombar evolution. It will not, strictly speaking, be a study of Biology but a study of the biological forces that have determined how our minds work and social norms.

"You may also remember that you expressed some measure of surprise that the Koombar and Tree history encompassed over two million years. To understand the forces of evolution, we must go back, not millions of years, but hundreds of millions of years."

Skrin interrupted, "What silliness is this? Hundreds of millions. The number means nothing to me."

Tree felt irritation rise in him and quelled the impulse to tell Skrin to shut up and listen. It would serve no purpose, and even adult Trees found it difficult to comprehend time on such a scale. The Tree life span of four hundred years simply did not prepare their minds to think in terms of millions of years. He could hardly expect that a Koombar, with limited abstract capabilities and a life span of seventy years, might easily grasp the concept.

Tree knew that he needed sleep and that it was affecting his temper, but there was much to be done, and at his age, he might not awaken. It would have to wait, and he would have to control his irritation.

"The time is of no particular importance," Tree said, "but you should understand we are talking of a time before the Trees or the Koombar were intelligent—a time when our forebears were like the animals and knew not what they did or who they were."

Skrin frowned with a squint. "You are saying my ancestors were like animals?"

"No, Skrin, I am saying that your ancestors *were* animals."

Skrin shrugged with disgust. "This is plainly ridiculous."

"It is plainly true—just as the ancestors of the Trees were animals."

Skrin plucked at the grass in front of him. "You have evidence of this?"

"The evidence is overwhelming and encompasses such diverse studies as archeology, geology, genetics, and cosmology."

"I know nothing of these things."

"Of course you don't."

Skrin moved as if to stand. "You waste yet more of my time."

"You have asked me to explain why the Trees cannot destroy the Koombar. Do you wish to know the answer?"

"I have asked the question."

"Very well. It is not a simple question. There is no simple answer."

"Begin."

"I have been attempting to do so." Tree paused for a moment to collect his thoughts. "Let us first consider the Koombar." Skrin stirred, but Tree raised a hand to stop him. "It will be easier for you to grasp your own circumstance. An understanding of the Koombar evolution will be instructive in itself, and the differences between it and the Tree evolution will cast the Tree thought processes in the proper context."

Skrin settled back down into a resting position, and Tree continued. "Most of what I am about to tell you has been inferred from the present social structure and morphology of the Koombar. We had no opportunity to study the fossil record of your planet, but it can be assumed that the Koombar were then as they are now—pack animals. It is tempting to believe that the ways of our animal progenitors are lost and that we start anew when intelligence is gained, but this is not the case. In fact, a basic tenet of evolution is that new things are built atop the old, and little, if anything, is discarded.

"So, if we go back to the Koombar world of perhaps two hundred million years ago, we might find packs of animals, closely resembling the present day Koombar, roaming the land. We must consider how these animals fit into their world. Although the Koombar do not now remember, your home planet was populated by many large predators. The Koombar were small in comparison to these predators and easily fell prey to them. As with all worlds, there are predators and there is prey. The Koombar were the prey. The predators were, of course, meat eaters, and the prey were, for the most part, herbivores." Skrin moved as if to speak, but Tree silenced him with a wave of his arm. "Some few, like the Trees on our home planet, developed the ability to eat both meat and vegetation or fruit.

"Now, Skrin, you were about to say something."

"You said the predators were meat eaters. The Koombar eat no fruit or vegetation. Are we not then predators?"

"The Koombar are much too small to have been serious predators on your home planet. The atmosphere there was somewhat more dense than the air of Harmony and the gravity slightly lower. There were several species of birds that routinely made meals of full-grown Koombar, and there were many predators massing six or eight times that of the average adult Koombar. Many predators hunt in packs, and even a band of twenty or thirty Koombar would not venture forth unarmed."

"Yet we are meat eaters," said Skrin.

"Yes," said Tree, "but what sort of meat do you prefer?"

"I prefer the meat of the Jikry."

"That is not what I meant." Tree paused for a moment. "If there is food aplenty, and you are not hungry, and if someone kills a Jikry, what would you do with the meat?"

"I would set it in a warm place for a week or more, so that it might ripen."

"Exactly. The Koombar do not eat fresh meat unless they are extremely hungry—preferring instead the flavor of meat that has decayed slightly. Why do you think this might be so?"

"This is a silly question. Because it tastes better."

"The Trees eat meat also, and we disagree. No, the Koombar prefer the taste of decaying flesh because that is what they have always eaten. The Koombar are, in fact, carrion eaters—scavengers."

Skrin rolled over on his side in a show of boredom.

Tree entertained a brief fantasy of heaving a large rock in Skrin's direction but continued. "These circumstances influenced not only your social structure but also the shape of your body. For instance, the Koombar eyes are placed directly on top of the head and allow 360-degree vision. This is a perfect adaptation for a species in danger of being attacked from any direction. Your snouts are long and allow you to reach inside a carcass through the rib cage or through a tear in tough, outer hide to reach edible flesh that might not be gotten otherwise. Your noses are placed low on the throat to allow breathing while you eat in this fashion.

"But it is the social structure of the Koombar that gives us the best evidence of the early Koombar life. Let us consider what life might be like for the early Koombar. They live in packs—beset by predators—and huddling in burrows or other shelter at night. During the day, they venture forth in search of food, hoping to find the leftover carcass of some other animal or perhaps another Koombar. Their problem, of course, is that the predator may return to the site of his kill, or another predator may arrive while the pack is feeding. It is a reasonable strategy in such a case to post a lookout. We have seen this behavior in animals of extremely limited intelligence. The lookout will be in the greatest danger and will not eat unless food is brought to him."

Skrin rolled upright and his small ears rotated forward.

"This behavioral adaptation is the framework for the Koombar social structure. The position of lookout became prestigious and desirable to insure that individuals, even in the face of great personal danger, would seek it. More precisely, those groups where the lookout became a prestigious position were more likely to survive than those groups in which no Koombar would properly discharge that duty.

"The act of giving food to another is considered an act of obeisance among the Koombar even today. You have no need for lookouts on Harmony because there are almost no predators and your weaponry is reasonably sophisticated; yet the position of lookout persists. They are called . . ." Tree waved his forward arms at Skrin, " . . . what?"

"Watchers," replied Skrin.

"Excellent," said Tree.

Skrin scratched at his chin with one of his back legs. "You are saying this is the reason Watchers are the last to be fed at state functions?"

"Exactly."

"I always felt it was to insure the meat had not been poisoned."

"That is also a consideration. The post of Watcher is still a very dangerous position, but the danger comes now from the Koombar themselves."

"Truly," said Skrin. "Murder is common in the general population, but I cannot remember when a Watcher of any nation died from old age."

"Yet the position is actively sought," said Tree.

"It is a position of almost absolute power."

"And even now you plot the death of your father."

Skrin blinked slowly. "I am a bit young for that."

"But not too young to entertain the idea," said Tree.

"It is the natural order for succession to the Watcher position."

"And your father awaits this plot."

"With great interest. He will be sorely disappointed if my attempt is not resourceful and inventive," replied Skrin.

"Keep in mind," Tree said, "there is a selection process at work here. These murders must be carried out in such a way that the perpetrator is obvious, but the perpetrator must not be killed in the process. It takes a near suicidal courage to attempt such a thing. More importantly, it requires a great deal of intelligence to succeed. The Watchers are fully aware they are liable to be murdered at any time. They would not be in the position if they themselves were not highly intelligent. The new Watcher must also have his retinue in place and ready to take control instantly. All of this insures that only the most intelligent Koombar will become Watchers or keep the position for any length of time."

"It is indeed a most interesting and complex game," said Skrin.

"But it is a game which satisfies a need in the Koombar psyche," said Tree. "The world of the early Koombar was a place of unrelenting danger. Predators were likely to drop from the sky or spring from any nearby bush. As the Koombar technology grew, these dangers lessened to the point of insignificance, but the Koombar still view the world through the same frightened eyes. This expectation of danger demanded a focus.

"Skrin, you have said murder is common among your people. I would say it has been raised up to the status of an art form."

Skrin picked at the ground while he considered what Tree had said. "It is true that artful murder for demonstrable gain is greatly appreciated no matter the level of society in which it occurs, but accidental deaths or murders from rage or intoxication are severely punished."

"I am not denying that there are rules to this deadly game," said Tree, "but I would ask a hypothetical question. What would be the effect on Koombar societal interaction if you suddenly, tomorrow, stopped killing each other?"

Skrin was silent for a long time as he contemplated the possibility. "I cannot even imagine such a world. How would property be acquired? How would Watchers come to power? Most of an adult male's time is consumed with plotting murder or avoidance of murder. What would we *do*?"

Tree waved one of his arms back and forth. "It need not be this way, but the Koombar have made their world into a reflection of what their genetic makeup demands—a place of great danger, requiring constant vigilance to avoid death. If there is no danger, you will create it or imagine it. The Koombar, in the view of the Trees, suffer from a deeply-imbedded genetic paranoia."

"But it can be no other way," complained Skrin.

Tree raised all of his arms to the sky in triumph. "This is exactly the point I have been trying to make! The Koombar are trapped in their perception of the world just as the Trees are trapped in theirs. The Koombar will continue to murder each other because they have no choice, and the Trees," he paused for a moment, "the Trees will never do much of anything."

Skrin had been startled by Tree's outburst, and he settled back down to gaze at the old Tree for a time. "I suppose this has some pertinence to my question," he said.

"All the pertinence in the world," replied Tree. "Let us now consider the prehistory of the Trees. On our home planet, animals reproduce by a process of fusion. This seems to be an exception to the rule as almost all the other planets we studied had males and females who reproduced sexually.

"The Trees begin life as small, mobile creatures superficially similar to the Koombar. The fusion of three of these young Trees produces an adult Tree. If you were to look at the Tree home planet million of years ago, you would find these young Trees roaming about in great numbers and dying in great numbers. Death to predators was a part of this, but most of them died from starvation or misadventure. You would also find adult Trees scattered about here and there. It is important to understand that the adult Trees had no natural predators. Although we lack mobility, we are fairly large, and stronger than you might think. This, coupled with an almost wood-like skin, makes us an unlikely target for hungry carnivores. But even the adult Trees died in great numbers from starvation and drought.

"We have some safeguards against this. The adult Trees will slip into a state of hibernation when food or water becomes scarce. Life functions will slow down considerably, and the Tree will dream till food appears or rain falls. We have this need for extended sleep even when resources are plentiful. I am myself experiencing a need for such a time of rest and dreams.

"Although we are quite happy with our lives as they are, there are some inherent frustrations to immobility. It was possible, in the prehistory of the Trees, for an adult to die from starvation with food just a fingertip away. If fruit did not grow within reach, or if the migratory patterns of animals changed due to drought or other factors, the Tree would simply sleep and dream till it died.

"The two important points for our discussion are that Trees have no fear of predators, and we do not go in search of food. We are conditioned to wait for food to come to us.

"Intelligence grew in the Koombar from a need to communicate and organize their efforts at avoiding predators. Intelligence grew in the Trees for quite different reasons.

"Studies on our home planet indicated that prehistoric, adult Trees lived for about 150 years. We are capable, under suitable conditions, of producing one child per year. It takes three children to form one adult. If you run through the math, you will find our entire planet would have been covered with Trees within a few generations if all the progeny lived and produced adults. It was mainly the death of our children that kept our population in check.

"Our children are of limited intelligence even now. We can presume they were of lesser intelligence in earlier times. Plainly put, they are not capable of caring for themselves. They have no means of defense against predators, and as you may have observed, they are energetic and curious. Many of them die on Harmony from simple accidents. This was much the same on our home planet where they were the favorite food source of several species, but many died from simple starvation.

"The role of the adult Tree increased in importance with time. Those adults who instructed and cared for their children were able to keep more of their children alive to adulthood. Those children eventually learned to bring food and water to the adult in times of need, and the adults lived longer and produced more children as a result. This was the evolutionary pressure that brought the Tree intelligence into being, and it has made the bond between father and son very strong."

Skrin interrupted. "You said that your son was dying."

Tree took a deep breath, and it whistled from him with the sound of a soft wind. "Yes. One of my sons is dying even now."

"Is he injured?"

"No," said Tree quietly, "he is old."

Skrin looked puzzled. "But the Trees live long lives."

"Let me explain. Our young live but twenty years or so. At the end of that time, they must mate. Their hair becomes coarse and whitened. Under the best circumstances, they will find two other children at the same point of readiness, and they will mate. But the timing is precise. The time for fusion lasts little more than a day. They develop a secretion from the skin at the last stage. If they have found mates, the three of them will dig a small hole in which to place their tails. They will then sit with their backs together in a kind of triangle. Their upper arms and their heads must be touching. They must look forward, and their legs must be straight out in front of them. The secretion will then flow freely to cover the three children and will quickly harden to the consistency of tough plastic."

His voice dropped and he looked off in the distance for just a moment before continuing. "The children will remain thus encased for almost six months. It is a difficult but wonderful time. As the secretions harden, the young begin to dream. Slowly they come to understand that two others share their dream. Finally, they dream a common dream and with a similar ideas. It is a deeply spiritual experience but painful in both a mental and physical sense. There is the time of fear when the self begins to slip away. There is the pain of bones fusing with those of your mates. The back of the skull must split open so the brains can merge. The legs wither and become surface roots. The tails intertwine and fuse to become the deep root.

Tree's voice became yet softer till the ground barely hummed. "If all goes well, and frequently it does not, the new adult will begin to move at the proper time and break out of the shell in a state of great weakness and confusion. The case falls to the ground and emits a sweet odor as it decays. This odor is attractive to insects and to the animals that feed on insects. Thus, our young adult is offered his first meal.

"But as I said before, the timing is critical. Those children who do not find mates at the proper stage will sit down alone and form their shells. They will dream their dreams and then they will die."

The translator was programmed to mimic volume and speed of speech, and Tree was speaking so slowly and softly that Skrin could barely hear him.

"And this saddens you," said Skrin.

"Greatly."

"But it sounds as if this happens frequently."

"I have birthed 248 children. 236 of them have died. I have mourned the loss of each one."

"Why?"

Tree looked at the Koombar and let his limbs drag the ground. "They have listened to my instruction and done that which I asked of them. They have fed me, and I have rejoiced in their presence. Do not try to understand the bond between a father and his son, Koombar. It is beyond you."

Skrin stiffened. "This Koombar is glad of it. What use are such feelings?"

"To know the pleasure of love is to know the pain of loss. To rejoice in camaraderie is to mourn its absence."

"Agh," Skrin spit out in disgust. "You continue to waste my time."

Suddenly, all of the Koombar froze in position and became rock still. Tree was puzzled till he saw one of Harmony's small birds flying from the woods to his right. The bird swerved in its flight and came straight at him. One of the old Tree's arms twitched in a move too fast to see. There was a pop, and feathers showered down. With a squawk and a light crunch of bones, the bird was gone. Tree stood casually chewing his meal.

Skrin screamed in fear and backed down the hill on all fours. His guards came running with weapons held high, not knowing quite what to do.

Tree held all of his arms out. His roots hummed and the translator spoke as he chewed "Calm," he said. "No one has been injured. None of you are in danger."

Skrin's voice was high-pitched and loud with his fear. "What have you done!" he screeched.

"I was offered a meal, and I took it."

"That was disgusting."

"The meals of the Koombar are not easily contemplated by Trees. I am not surprised you would find our eating habits unpleasant."

"That bird was alive."

"No longer," commented Tree.

Skrin rubbed his muzzle with both hands and waved his guards back down the hill. His voice still squeaked with emotion. "You ate a live bird," he said in wonder.

"Yes."

"But you ate a living bird."

"Yes."

"It was alive!"

Tree stared at the young Koombar for a moment and then spoke slowly. "It's life has ended."

There was quiet as the Koombar and the old tree simply looked at each other. The guards fidgeted at the bottom of the hill.

Skrin moved a little closer to Tree but kept a slightly greater distance than before, and his ears twitched with Koombar laughter. "In retrospect," he said, "it is somewhat amusing."

"I am glad you find it so."

Skrin wagged his head from side to side. "To see a Tree eat a live bird. Now that will be a good story for my classmates."

"It may also have some instructional properties," said Tree.

Skrin settled to the ground. "How so?"

"Observe our different reactions. The Koombar froze when the bird appeared."

"All Koombar hate birds of every type."

"Yes," said Tree, "but your reflex was to become very still. This is useful behavior on a planet where you are likely to be picked up and eaten by a bird. Your brains had you freeze in place to avoid detection, but on Harmony, where the birds are few and very small, it makes little sense.

"My reflex was to wait quietly till the bird came within reach. Even though I am not particularly hungry, I did not have to think about snatching the bird from the air."

Skrin sat for a time without speaking and considered what Tree had said. "This is actually interesting. You are saying Tree and Koombar alike are bound by these behaviors even when they do not make sense, and that we will rationalize them wherever possible."

Tree was surprised at the Koombar's insight. "Yes," said Tree.

Skrin pondered the idea for a while. "I will have use for this knowledge," he said, "but you still have not answered my question."

"Ah yes," said Tree. "Why the Trees cannot destroy the Koombar."

"I do not know if I can make you understand, Skrin, but consider; the Trees do not go in search of food—we cannot. Except when our children feed us, we wait patiently for food to come to us. Our children die in great numbers, and we mourn their passing, but we do not interfere except to insure that they do not die from starvation. The Trees live long lives, and we have a great appreciation for the cycles of birth, life, and death. I have told you the Trees hold all life to be sacred."

Skrin interrupted. "You just ate a live bird."

There was a low booming noise as Tree chuckled. "The bird's cycle connected with mine when it came within my reach. I did not kill it indiscriminately but for sustenance. It is now a part of me. In the Tree way of thinking, the bird did not die but was transformed. This transformation, as it represents the Cycle of Life, is sacred to us. The Cycle of Life stands at the center of our religion and our philosophy, and interference with it is considered sacrilege. This belief was greatly strengthened by the results of our meddling with the Koombar on your dying world."

Tree looked at Skrin for some kind of reaction, but the young Koombar wiggled his ears and muttered, "A live bird."

Tree sighed and continued. "I have also told you the Trees hold intelligent life to be sacred above all other. The Koombar and Tree cycles have become intertwined and are now one. We could no more destroy the Koombar than you could eat a live bird."

Skrin puffed his cheeks. "That is an image easily understood, but it seems you might compensate for this in some conscious way."

"We would say that the one time we did so resulted in disaster."

"It still seems that knowing these behaviors for what they are would allow you to avoid them."

"I suppose, with practice and conditioning, the Trees might overcome their perception of the situation, but it would be a perversion to us. We are coming back to the vision of a Koombar eating a live bird."

Skrin stood. "The hour is late. I must be going."

Tree bowed low. "By your leave, Sire."

Skrin turned to go, but Tree called after him, "Skrin, I have need of sleep. I may sleep for weeks or even months. Given my age, it is possible I will become lost in my dreams and not awaken. We may not see each other again."

Skrin stood looking at the Tree. "Very well. If we meet again though, understand that I am not so stupid as to believe you could arrange the death of your children to suit my schedule, and your not-so-subtle innuendo regarding my ability to remember our prior conversations serves no useful purpose."

Tree was shocked and embarrassed. "Understood."

"Good. We are in agreement." Skrin turned and ambled down the hill. "Trees eating live birds," he said. "What a day."

Tree watched as Skrin and his guards climbed into the car and drove away. A Koombar had just dressed him down, and he had deserved it.

"I must be getting old," he sighed.

Chapter Twenty-two
NASA Central
May 4, 2061

Rick Jelton was the last to enter the room. His tie was loose around his neck, and the top button of his shirt was open. There were dark circles under his eyes. He normally arrived early, perfectly dressed, and with an air of easy confidence. His associates watched warily as he moved quickly to a chair at the head of the long oval table and sat down. Rick was not only the head of NASA Central, but its spokesperson also. With his dark, full head of hair and even features, he usually had the look of a television anchorman, but he was anything but photogenic this morning. His bloodshot eyes and rumpled suit, the same one he had been wearing the day before, indicated he had spent the night in the building, and Marilyn Lindsay, his second in command, noticed that his hair was still damp from a recent shower.

The table and chairs were the only furniture, and reports and photographs of the Marler Phenomenon were scattered everywhere. Top-ranking NASA Central staffers, fidgeting with nervous energy, occupied most of the chairs. One entire wall was a computer display screen showing a 3D picture of the Earth taken from Moon orbit. The picture was realistic enough that some of the staff purposely sat with their back to it to avoid dizziness.

The Secretary of Defense of the United States of America, flanked by two high-ranking generals, sat across from Rick at the other end of the table. The Secretary—an older man with thin, gray hair and a heavily jowled, florid face—had a haggard look also, as if he and Rick might have spent the night out drinking and carousing. The two generals sat ramrod straight and unmoving with nearly identical close-cropped hair and chiseled features.

Rick eyed the two generals suspiciously, rubbed his face, and took a second to gather his wits before nodding to the Secretary. "It is a pleasure to have you with us today, Mr. Salness."

"Thank you, Mr. Jelton." The Secretary pointed to his right and then to his left. "This is General Laurence and General Walker. They are here at my request." Rick said a silent prayer of thanks that General Laurence was black and General Walker was white. Other than the perpetual grimace on General Walker's face he felt that he might have otherwise found it difficult to tell them apart. The two generals nodded almost in unison without speaking, and the Secretary continued. "Perhaps we should start by having you tell us what you know about the Marler Phenomenon."

Rick thumbed through the papers in front of him but didn't bother to look at them. "I'm afraid we don't have much to report. We have several hundred photographs and videos taken by amateur astronomers from Alaska to Northern Chile. Unfortunately, this event did not come to the attention of the regular scientific community until several hours after it was over. We have since targeted some of the orbital telescopes and radiation detectors on the area, but whatever it was seems to be gone.

"The photographs, however, are extremely interesting. We know there were four separate incidents. The first of these was incompletely recorded by Gary Marler. Each incident consists of two parts: An initial slow build of light from infrared through ultraviolet followed 4.82 minutes later by a very quick reversal of that sequence. The reverse sequence happens so quickly that it appears as a simple flash of light. It was necessary to slow the videos down to confirm this aspect of the second flash. Although the time between the initial build up and the second flash of light is very precise for every incident, there appears to be no pattern to the timing of the individual events.

"We have been able to triangulate the position with some accuracy and have found that the events occurred just outside the orbit of Pluto. We cannot state with certainty whether it was the same source emitting light on four separate occasions, or if it was one source for all events, but there are indications the events were separated slightly in space."

Rick hesitated for a moment. "There is something else. Some of the recordings made with the better telescopes and under good viewing conditions show an apparent movement of stars in a very tight area surrounding the light source just prior to the initiation of the event and just after the flash of light at the end."

Rick folded his hands on the table. "I'm afraid that is all we have, and I'm sure everyone at this table has heard all of this before."

Secretary Salness had hardly moved during Rick's brief speech. "Speculation, Mr. Jelton?" he asked.

Rick grimaced and shook his head. "If you want speculation concerning what caused these lights, all I can tell you is we don't have a clue. There was a tremendous amount of energy expended in an extremely short period of time by some mechanism that follows no known models. There were bursts of radio static recorded from several satellites and from stations on the moon whose timing strongly suggests they may have been related to this phenomenon. The build up of light energy from infrared to ultraviolet and then quickly back suggests radiation coming from the area even while it was not visible. It seems reasonable to assume a continuing rise in energy past that of visible light and into the region of X-rays and perhaps even gamma radiation followed by a quick drop back through the visible light spectrum. Again, it is unfortunate that no sophisticated instruments could be targeted on the area during the events.

"The most troubling aspect of all this is the apparent shift in position of the background stars. Obviously, these stars did not in fact move. One almost has to imagine the appearance and rapid disappearance of an intense gravitational source, not once, but four times, and that seems ridiculous. If there was a black hole in the region, it would still be there, and the stars would still be out of position. Pluto is currently on the other side of the sun. That leaves Neptune and Jupiter as the closest planets. We are performing a careful survey of their orbital paths and a survey of some of the closer asteroids for evidence of orbital perturbation, but it will be a few days before that information is complete."

Secretary Salness took a deep breath and nodded his head, causing his heavy cheeks to quiver. He looked around the table slowly, catching the eye of everyone present except for the two generals at his side. "That seems to be the consensus of the scientific community at large," he said, "but I am privy to some information you do not have."

The Secretary placed his hands flat on the table and leaned forward. "Before I begin, I need to emphasize the delicate nature of what I am about to tell you. Everyone in this room is cleared at the highest level, but the following information is being given to you strictly on a need-to-know basis. There will be no leaks tolerated. Do I make myself clear?"

Everyone nodded in assent, but several people sat up straighter and some of them picked up pens or shuffled papers briefly, as the tension in the room notched upward.

Secretary Salness looked around once again before continuing. "Apparently, light in various wavelengths was not the only thing emitted by the Marler Phenomenon. There are a few institutions around the world doing work on gravity itself. Their aim has been to detect a gravity wave. Up until last night, none of them had been successful." He paused for emphasis. "Last night, two of the three known gravity experiments reported four separate gravity waves passing through the Earth at precisely the time of our four incidents. It is assumed that the third experiment is, in fact, not capable of such detection. It is possible the experiments detected not a gravity wave as such, but a gravity pulse of some kind.

"One of the successful experiments is in the United States. The other is in a country friendly to us. The personnel from these experiments have been detained, and the sites are now manned by military units."

The Secretary paused once again and looked straight at Rick before speaking. "Perhaps you can now begin to appreciate the serious nature of the information you are about to receive."

Rick was shocked. There were almost no restrictions on scientific experimentation in the United States. The few laws that existed were aimed at public health issues, mostly genetic engineering and cloning. He had never heard the slightest rumor of the government shutting down something like a physics experiment. And the scientists had been detained! It could only mean national security issues were at stake. The presence of the two generals began to make sense, but he didn't like it one bit. He looked at Marilyn, but she refused to meet his eyes.

Rick pursed his lips and nodded. "I understand, sir."

"Very well, Mr. Jelton. Let me stress again, leaks of any kind will not be tolerated."

Rick cleared his throat. "I'm sure I speak for my entire staff. We have handled many delicate matters in the past without. . ." He stopped himself. ". . . with very few problems. Given the possible repercussions of a leak in this instance, I am sure we will have no trouble keeping this information to ourselves."

Rick looked around the table. Two of his staff were pale and looked vaguely ill, but no one stood to leave or objected to the obvious penalty for disclosing what they were about to hear.

The Secretary settled back in his chair and began to speak. "Ten years ago, the military spent a great deal of time and money on research aimed at developing a hyperspace drive. There were indications it might be possible to open a wormhole through normal space and deliver personnel or equipment through it to any point on Earth. It would be the perfect weapons delivery system—no warning of any kind, and the weapons could be sent instantly from any point to any other point.

"Almost all of this work was theoretical in nature, and the concept was found to have several serious problems. Calculations showed that it required huge expenditures of energy to open a wormhole of any reasonable size. To put this in perspective, it would take several terawatts of power, expended over no more than a few seconds, to open a hole big enough for an apple. It would take significantly more power to open a hole large enough for a man.

"The other problem involved determination of the exit point of the wormhole. I'm sure all of the scientists in this room understand better than I do the effect that mass has upon space. Even in the Twentieth Century, it was known that gravity is actually the curving of space time—the larger the mass, and the closer one comes to the mass, the larger the measured curvature.

"It seems that wormholes interact with curved space in such a complicated manner that no conceivable amount of computation could solve the equations. In practice it means we could open a wormhole here on Earth and put an apple in it, but we would have no way of knowing where it would come out. Similarly, if we opened a wormhole in a region of flat space, far from any large mass, we could not calculate an exit point anywhere near a massive object.

"To summarize, hyperspace travel might be possible if we could find sufficient power, but then only from one region of flat space to another region of flat space.

"You all know that our sun is an extremely massive object, and that it curves space for billions of miles around. Our scientists found that any meaningful experimentation in wormhole generation would have to be carried out just beyond the orbit of Pluto."

Secretary Salness waited for the importance of his last statement to sink in. "Mr. Jelton, you said the emission of radiation from the Marler Phenomenon followed no known models. That is not precisely true. We never opened a wormhole for several reasons. One of the more important reasons was the calculated rise in radiation from infrared through ultraviolet, X-ray, and gamma radiation. The calculations indicated that the gamma emission would continue while the wormhole was open and then rapidly drop back through visible light when it closed. Some models also predicted a gravity pulse.

"While we might have succeeded in opening a small wormhole, its tactical value would have been nil because of the size limitations inherent in the power requirements and our inability to predict the exit point. Worse than that, everyone within several million miles would have known we were up to something."

No one spoke for some time. Rick's staff exchanged wide-eyed glances at each other. The two generals sat still as gargoyles on either side of the Secretary of State.

Rick straightened some of the now useless paper in front of him. "Somebody opened four wormholes at the fringe of our Solar System?" he asked.

"It fits our data," said the Secretary in a level voice. "Bear in mind, there should be no discernible difference between the entrance and exit of a wormhole. Our researchers tell me that the entrance and exit is actually one and the same for any given wormhole. I don't pretend to understand this, but they seem convinced two objects separated by billions of miles can be one object."

The Secretary dismissed the subject with a wave of his hand. "Putting the theory aside, there is no way to know if two probes were launched into wormholes and then returned through two new wormholes, or if four objects were launched and lost. We can't even know if any probes were actually launched into the holes, but it seems likely."

Rick drummed his fingers on the table. "I would think they'd want their probes back," he said.

"I would think so too."

Rick frowned as something occurred to him. "You said a small wormhole would alert everyone for several million miles around. This happened four billion miles away. Do you have any estimates of the size of these wormholes?"

Secretary Salness laced his fingers together. "That, Mr. Jelton, is one of the more disturbing aspects of this incident. The calculations contain a great deal of guesswork, but we estimate the holes to have been between five and thirty feet in diameter. It seems that someone burned up the equivalent of half our planet's daily power output in just over one hour with this little maneuver."

The Secretary went on before Rick could speak. "And that brings us to our main concern." He turned to his right. "I will ask General Laurence to explain."

The General looked directly at Rick. His complexion was light for a black man, but his eyes were of such a dark brown that, from where Rick sat, the pupils blended seamlessly into them. He spoke without preamble. "Although there was some military research done in this area, I do not want you to have the impression we were close to opening a wormhole. We had several physicists who agreed on the theory. Some parts of that theory were tested and found to be valid. Disregarding the power requirements, we were at least ten years and several trillion dollars away from making an attempt.

"We have intelligence data indicating the Chinese were engaged in similar research. It was our understanding they had abandoned their efforts also. This seems now to be in doubt.

"The ability to open a wormhole is troubling. The implications of the ability to generate that much power are far more disturbing.

"You are all well aware of our strained relations with the Chinese. The tactical uses for wormholes would appear to be almost nonexistent. The tactical uses for energy production on this scale should be readily apparent."

Rick held up one hand. "Is there any chance this energy was produced using fusion generators?"

"None," replied the General. "As a matter of policy, the United States closely monitors the Chinese' consumption of He3.

These events do not represent a trivial amount of He_3. The Chinese' shipments and purchases of He_3 are roughly in balance with their usage. It is also nearly inconceivable that they could have built a generator of this size without our knowledge. This, coupled with the difficulty of transporting the generator four billion miles, puts the idea out of reach."

General Laurence looked around the table. "Gentlemen, ladies, we are looking at an extremely powerful and portable energy source. This is something new—something the United States does not have and has not started working on. There can be no doubt that the security of the United States and the stability of the world's political system are in jeopardy."

"Are we sure it's the Chinese?" Rick asked.

Secretary Salness answered. "They are the only ones with the resources to transport something this far. There is no question, Mr. Jelton—the Chinese are behind this."

Rick pondered that for a moment. There was an unasked question, but it would do no good to bring it up. These were military men. He didn't need to be branded as a UFO freak right from the beginning, and he decided it didn't matter. His job would be the same regardless of who had opened the wormholes. Whatever that job was supposed to be. He looked again at Marilyn, but her eyes slid away from him. No help.

"This is all fascinating information," Rick said, "and I can see why it would be on a need-to-know basis, but I am wondering why NASA Central needs to know. What, exactly, do you expect from us?"

Secretary Salness stirred and turned to his left. "For that information, I will defer to General Walker."

General Walker nodded to the Secretary. "Thank you, Mr. Secretary. Mr. Jelton, perhaps you are aware of the presence of the Alpha 2 surveillance craft?"

Rick was caught flatfooted. He couldn't immediately remember if he was supposed to know about the Alpha 2 or not. "Um, I have heard rumors, like most people."

"Yes," said General Walker. "It's not one of our best kept secrets. For those of you who may not be aware of its capabilities, it is a fusion-powered, automated surveillance vehicle outfitted with state of the art equipment. In addition to the very best cameras and sensors available, it has a highly sophisticated guidance computer and is capable of making real-time decisions. It is potentially able to sustain an acceleration of eight gravities till it runs out of fuel and twelve gravities under emergency thrust.

It was constructed to overcome some of the difficulties involved in obtaining surveillance information on the moon and in near space. Orbiting satellite surveillance cameras are worthless when countries move equipment and materiel off of the planet. The Alpha 2 has been used to gather information in such cases.

"We will need your help with a few items. The Alpha 2 was not designed for long flights and will need to be retrofitted with extra fuel cells. We are also installing a gamma ray detector. We will require the use of the Hawking Detector you planned to orbit next month."

Rick almost jumped out of his chair. "You can't do that. The Hawking Detector is part of an ongoing research project that ties into several other projects. It's not just some souped up Geiger counter. It took ten years of planning and five years of building to get it ready for launch. Besides that, it's in a laboratory in Boston being tested."

Secretary Salness spoke. "Not anymore. Please continue, General Walker."

"The Hawking detector was airlifted to a military launch site," the General looked at his watch, "one hour and 20 minutes ago. It will be launched into orbit soon after this meeting ends. The craft carrying the detector will dock with the NASA space station before the day is out. We will need your personnel to help attach the detector to the Alpha 2."

Rick pleaded, "Secretary Salness, the Hawking Detector contains seven separate instruments. They weren't designed to be deployed until the satellite was in orbit. They will not withstand anything near eight gravities."

"So noted," said the Secretary. "I know that a lot of people have put a great deal of effort into building this satellite. We are not taking this action lightly. My engineers tell me that the gamma detector is quite sturdy. It should easily withstand the acceleration and will allow us to pinpoint gamma sources. We need this capability."

Rick rubbed his forehead. "Damn it!" he said. "I don't suppose there is any route of appeal for this decision."

"These orders come directly from the President himself." The Secretary turned once again to General Walker. "Please continue."

General Walker looked at Rick. "We are pressed for time, Mr. Jelton. You can take this up for review at a later date if you wish, but the Alpha 2 has been instructed to dock with the space station in three hours. Another craft, carrying extra fuel tanks for the Alpha 2, will arrive in five hours. We are deploying equipment and men to aid your personnel in the attachment of the fuel tanks and the Hawking Detector. There will also be some modifications made to the communications module to facilitate transmissions to and from deep space."

General Walker set his jaw, and his eyes drilled into Rick as if he was spoiling for a fight. "The Alpha 2 will begin outbound acceleration, one way or another, by 0800 tomorrow at the latest."

Rick threw his hands in the air. "Great, just great."

"We're not finished," said Secretary Salness.

Rick struggled to regain his composure, but he glared across the table and spoke through clenched teeth. "Yes sir, Mr. Secretary."

Secretary Salness returned Rick's look without blinking. "The surveillance equipment at the disposal of the U.S. military consists mostly of infrared and visible light cameras designed to photograph Earth or objects near Earth. NASA, on the other hand, has direct control of a number of scientific instruments designed to detect events in deep space. Those you don't control can be commandeered by NASA without arousing undue suspicion."

You will immediately begin a detailed survey of the area surrounding the Marler Phenomenon and the area of space between Earth and the Marler Phenomenon."

Rick spoke slowly as if biting each word in two. "You are talking about four billion miles of space, and I have an expedition on Mars to think of."

"The expedition on Mars can take care of itself," said the Secretary, "and Mars is more or less on a straight line between Earth and the region of interest. I would advise you to assign one of your staff members to supervise the immediate concerns of the Expedition."

The Secretary's voice dropped low, but every word was audible. "Don't fight us on this, Mr. Jelton. You'll be gone in a blink if you do, and frankly, we need your expertise."

Rick's eyes slowly rose from staring at the papers in front of him to meet the gaze of the secretary. "I understand."

"Excellent. General Walker will remain in this building until the Alpha 2 departs the space station. General Laurence will be with you for the duration of this crisis. You can refer to him if you have any further questions."

Rick was furious, but he knew the value of graciously accepting inevitable defeat. He smiled and lied. "I look forward to working with them."

Chapter Twenty-three
Surface of Mars
May 16, 2061

Commander Thon, Tom Fielder, and most of the crew sat at the table eating their evening meal. Rick Jelton, the head of NASA Central, was several times larger than life on the wall screen. He was surrounded by microphones and unruly reporters. One of the reporters waved a notepad, and Rick pointed to him.

"Mr. Jelton, it has been a week since the sighting of the Marler Phenomenon. Can you give us any information as to what this was or what effect it may have on us?"

"NASA is still in the process of examining the hundreds of photographs and videos taken by the astronomers who viewed this event. Together with the world's scientific community, we are trying to determine its cause. However, at this time, I can only tell you that it does not appear to match any known phenomena. I would like to stress that there is no cause for alarm. Triangulation of the many photographs has shown conclusively that the light came from somewhere around the orbit of Pluto. This puts it just over four billion miles away. It was not visible with the naked eye, and at that distance, even another star would have little effect on the Earth. I hope this will put to rest any concerns that people may have regarding possible radiation exposure.

"As you all know, there was no time to aim some of the more delicate scientific instruments in the proper direction. We might have learned a great deal more concerning this event. The available video tells us nothing more than what has been talked about on all of the networks: The light goes up in energy from infrared to ultraviolet and probably on through X-ray and perhaps even gamma radiation. There were short bursts of static on some of our satellites whose timing suggests they may be linked to the Marler Phenomenon. This would be consistent with our belief that the energy level went up well above that of visible light. I would like to again stress the distance from Earth and the margin of safety this gives us. Even if this light was still blinking on and off today, we would not be receiving enough radiation to be of any concern."

The reporters erupted in a frenzy of shouts and waving arms when he finished. Rick pointed to a woman in the second row.

"Mr. Jelton, are you aware that the Twenty-first Century Literalist Church has said we have angered God by sending men to Mars and that the lights were the entry of the Angels of Vengeance into our solar system? Are you aware they are calling for the immediate recall of the Mars Expedition?"

To Rick's credit, he didn't smile. "I am aware they have issued this statement. It is the considered opinion of NASA that God would have sent the angels a little closer to Earth if this were the case." There was laughter from the reporters.

Rick was glad of an opening to change the subject, and he eagerly launched into a Mars update. "There can be no possible connection between the Marler Phenomenon and the Mars Expedition. The Mars Expedition has, in fact, been a spectacular success. The discovery of water will greatly reduce the overall cost of the expedition, and with the lab up and functioning, we should soon have explanations for some of the geological peculiarities of Mars that have puzzled the scientific community for over one hundred years.

"The ice in the cave has been found to be 300 feet deep, at which point it is believed the cave makes a turn. Core samples have been taken and are currently in the Mars' lab for analysis. With luck, they will be pumping water to the surface by the end of the day tomorrow.

"Construction of the greenhouse has already begun, and the crew will soon be growing vegetables in a hydroponic garden and attempting to grow certain plants in an enriched Martian soil. We are currently doing studies to determine the feasibility of sending livestock and perhaps another two crewmembers to Mars on its closest approach next year. This expedition will answer many scientific questions, but let us remember, we also hope that Mars can be colonized one day. This expedition will answer that question also."

The reporters again clamored for attention, but Tom Fielder was growing bored with the whole thing and leaned back in his chair with the last of his iced tea. "Man, that is one job I would not take," he said.

"He looks tired," said Evelyn.

Commander Thon took a bite of fish. "A difficult position to be sure," he said, "but I can see where it might have some rewards." He took another bite from his plate. "This fish is delicious."

"Oh, you'd be a natural for it," said Tom. "I, on the other hand, would have told them exactly where to stick their Angels of Vengeance."

Tom looked down the table at Kaitlin Geller. "Geller, you're the physicist. What do you make of this Marler Phenomenon?"

Kaitlin dabbed her mouth with a napkin. "Rick has shared all the data he has, and I've spent some time in the last few days going over the videos. The Marler Phenomenon is just. . ." She shook her head. "I don't know. Rick is right in saying there is no danger of radiation on Earth, but this was an extremely energetic event. High-speed collisions will emit radiation, but it requires speeds approaching that of light itself, and nothing can explain this ramping up of energy followed by the little flash of light at the end.

"The amount of energy released is hard to comprehend. It makes you postulate things like matter falling into a black hole, but this follows none of the models for that kind of event, and a black hole this close to the solar system would have perturbed the orbits of the planets already. You can be sure NASA has checked this very carefully, and it has not happened. If we could only have gotten some decent instruments targeted on the event, we might have an explanation, but frankly I doubt it. This thing is just weird."

Tom looked over at Ki and grinned. "Just weird, huh. Cool."

Ki rolled his eyes and shot back, "And you will be pumping water tomorrow?"

"Yeah, right. Rick knows better than that. He gives me all kinds of hell about using the solar film to power the pump and then wants to brag about how wonderful it is that we'll be able to supply our own water."

"Rick has valid concerns over the safety of our mission."

Tom put his cup on the table. "Don't you start. We can't run wire all the way out there, and if the fusion generator fails, we can just bring the solar film back."

"Rick has a duty to voice these objections."

"He has a duty to cover his ass."

Ki smiled and nodded. "Ah, Grasshopper, you begin to understand."

Espanoza piped up from across the table. "I'm still not too happy about using some of the scaffolding from the greenhouse reflectors."

Tom took a deep breath. "We've been through this before. I can't lay the solar film on the ground or it will be covered with dust in less than a day. It won't generate much power if it's covered with dust."

Espanoza frowned and looked down at his plate. "If I can't get the reflector film positioned properly, we will have barely enough light to grow mushrooms."

Tom shook his head in irritation. "And if I can't get power to the pump, you won't have enough water to grow anything."

Ki stopped them. "Relax, gentlemen. We will pump water for two months. You can then have your scaffolding back. Why don't you work with Ms. Weiss and see about running some auxiliary lighting in the interim?"

Espanoza was still not happy. "It will ruin the experiment."

"We are going to be here for three more years," Ki said. "You will have ample opportunity to determine the feasibility of your reflector system before we go home."

The screen on the wall switched to a recorded interview with Gary Marler. He stood in a frayed jacket with his few strands of gray hair blowing in the Oklahoma wind. A pair of old-fashioned glasses sat perched on his nose, and he smiled easily at the question about the Angels of Vengeance.

"Nah," he said, "I don't reckon the Lord is going is punish us for going to Mars. Seems to me, he gave us brains to think with and curiosity to make us get up and move around. Since we got the brains and the guts, my guess is we just weren't meant to stay on this little planet forever."

Evelyn smiled at the screen. "He seems like such a nice man. He reminds me of my grandfather."

"I'm just glad to see that not all Christians are morons," Tom said. "And on the plus side, it's knocked pictures of my butt off the evening news."

Everyone laughed, and Melancon walked out of the kitchen wiping his hands on the ever-present towel on his left shoulder just as Pamela Krazinsky bustled past him and went over to talk to Espanoza. There was a hurried exchange of whispered conversation, and Espanoza stood to follow her back through the kitchen. Tom watched them disappear into the lab through the door.

Melancon waited out the last part of the interview with Gary Marler before speaking. "Dinner is headed to the compost heap. Better fill up now."

Ki stood up with his plate. "I think I will take some more fish," he said, but he stopped in front the cook. "Oh yes, Mr. Melancon."

Melancon towered over him. "Sir?"

"I received a memo from NASA Central today concerning our consumption of butter."

Melancon grinned. "Oops."

"We are very much enjoying your cooking, but you are the dietician. I must rely on you to bring our diets into balance."

"Well, they're not exactly out of balance."

"Mr. Melancon. . ."

"Yes, sir. I'll see to it."

Tom stood and picked up his plate. "Let's get rolling. I want to go over tomorrow's duty roster before we call it a night."

Kaitlin picked up her plate, but Evelyn sat watching the news and picking at her food as Tom looked around the room. "Where's Cochran?"

"He finished early," Evelyn said. "I think he went back to his room."

"We're going to have a staff meeting in 15 minutes."

"Do you want me to go get him?"

Tom considered. "No, I'll go after him later."

Tom followed Kaitlin into the kitchen and found Commander Thon standing near the laboratory door with Carlos Espanoza and Pamela Krazinsky. "Carlos agrees with me," Pamela said. "These structures do not appear to be crystals."

"What's up?" Tom asked, and the three of them turned as a unit to face him.

"Dr. Krazinsky has found some interesting material in the ice-core samples," Commander Thon said. He gestured to Krazinsky. "Perhaps you should explain."

Krazinsky began to talk animatedly, telling Tom things he already knew. "The ice is exceptionally clear down to a depth of about 250 feet, and it becomes progressively more turbid down to the rock surface at 300 hundred feet. The last few feet are more frozen sludge than ice.

"I took some of the core samples from the region of 275 feet. It is difficult to handle because of concerns with contamination, but I prepared some slides and stained them with several preparations. I couldn't see anything of consequence in most of them, but I just finished looking at one prepared with a simple Acid Fast Stain such as might be used for detecting Tuberculosis. The results are… Well, I'm not sure what I am looking at."

Espanoza spoke up. "I believed at first they might be salt crystals of some sort, but…"

"Hold it," Tom said. "Why don't we all go take a look." He turned to Kaitlin. "Ms. Geller, you are the Geochemist of the group. I suspect you have looked at more crystals than any of us. Would you join us in the lab?"

Kaitlin Geller placed her plate on the counter and followed them through the open airlock door at the back of the kitchen.

It was the largest room in the permanent building except for the dining area. Directly across from the airlock leading into the kitchen was another airlock that opened to the outside. A pair of high-tech vacuum hoods flanked the outside airlock, and there was a door to the left of them into a freezer similar to the one in the kitchen. Stainless steel counters lined the walls, and two large, rectangular islands took up the entire center of the room. The islands were covered with so much equipment that hardly a square foot of work surface remained. The various tools of chemistry, biochemistry, geology, biology, and engineering stood shining with the gleam of new glass and the sparkle of polished steel. Hums in several frequencies permeated the room from the idling equipment, and a soft, rhythmic popping sound came from under one of the counters as a compressor labored steadily. Already there was a slight chemical twang to the air from Krazinsky's work in staining the slides

Tom made a mental note to check the airflow around the kitchen door and looked around with satisfaction. He knew it wouldn't stay like this for long. Labs tended to get messy at about the same rate as sock drawers, but right now, it was a beauty to behold.

Dr. Krazinsky walked over to a computer screen that popped into life as she approached. The small group gathered around behind her, but nobody said a word for several minutes. No one wanted to say what they were all thinking.

The screen showed a standard light microscope view at a magnification of 750X. The picture was cluttered with strange shapes—all colored pink from the Acid Fast stain. Some were simple hexagons or octagons. Others were wild spirals with pink hair around the edges. One resembled nothing so much as a carousel with strange blobs in the place of horses. Almost every structure contained between two and four darker pink areas within it. Close examination showed light pink rods attaching these areas to the outside walls.

Tom spoke first. "Have you looked around on this slide very much?"

"No," said Pamela. "I got Carlos as soon as I put it under the microscope."

"Why don't you drop the magnification and look around a little bit?"

Dr. Krazinsky hit a few keys and the magnification dropped to 50X. Using the arrow keys on the keyboard, she scrolled rapidly around the slide.

"What are we looking for?" asked Espanoza.

"I think we'll know it if we see it," replied Tom.

Something large slid across the screen, and Pamela backed up till it was centered and then zoomed in. Perhaps fifty irregular shapes were fused seamlessly together in a near perfect circle. Each shape held the hint of darker interior areas, but it was difficult to see at this magnification. Along the outside of the circle, rectangular shapes were attached and joined end to end to form long, spidery legs. One of the legs had broken off and was curled half under the circular body.

"That's what we were looking for," said Tom.

Espanoza blew out a deep breath. "Well I'll be damned," he said.

"It's the same basic morphology as a jellyfish," said Geller.

Commander Thon spoke. "Congratulations, Dr. Krazinsky. You have just become the person who discovered that Mars was at one time alive."

Krazinsky stood with her mouth open. She was white as a sheet. "I think I need to sit down," she said.

Tom grabbed a nearby stool, and Espanoza guided her to it. "Put your head down on the counter," Espanoza said.

Dr. Pamela Krazinsky sat down and leaned forward till her head touched the keyboard, but she immediately began talking. "Simple, multi-cellular life. I can't believe it. I never… I guess I never really thought about it. To see it with my own eyes. There were indications . . . indications it should be here, but . . ."

She stopped talking and raised her head. "Good Lord, we have a lot of work to do!" she exclaimed.

Tom burst out laughing. "That's the spirit."

She pointed to Espanoza. "Carlos, you'll need to take care of most of the taxonomy. I've got to figure out how these things lived. I wonder if we can actually get some of them to grow. Of course, we'll need to do a thorough analysis of the water first so we can put them in the right medium, but we can set up some incubators after that's done and see what happens. I wonder what their respiratory cycle is like. We know there wasn't enough oxygen to be useful. My bet has always been some form of sulfur. There's lots of sulfur on Mars, and it has multiple valence states. Thiotrix bacteria on Earth use sulfur in a photosynthesis reaction. Mr. Fielder, you're our inorganic chemist. I desperately need your help in analyzing this water."

Tom held up both hands with a smile. "Hold up, Doc. I've got a pump to get running."

Krazinsky got a pained expression. "Mr. Fielder, please. Some of these things may still be alive."

Tom raised an eyebrow and continued to grin. "After several million years?"

"We won't know till we try."

Commander Thon walked over to the intercom and pushed a button. "All personnel report to the Laboratory." He repeated the call, and they could hear the whispering echo from other parts of the living quarters.

"Commander Thon," Tom said softly, "please tell me you're not going to use this to call another holiday."

Ki laughed. "No. I expect I would have to lock Dr. Krazinsky in her room to keep her away from these Martian bugs."

Adrian Melancon and Evelyn Weiss walked in. "What's up?" asked Adrian.

Tom pointed to the screen. "Check it out. Dr. Krazinsky just made the history books."

Everyone gathered around the screen, but Dr. Krazinsky continued to plead with Tom. "Please, Mr. Fielder. I need to get some of this incubating as soon as possible. It could take days to know if anything still lives in that ice. We can't just dump them in deionized water. We need to know the salt balance to make an appropriate medium."

Tom shook his head. "I'm really sorry, Dr. Krazinsky, but the pump has priority. I may be able to spare Ms. Geller for a few hours tomorrow. She's probably as competent a chemist as I am."

Dr. Krazinsky looked as if she might be about to cry.

"Look, I've got an idea," Tom said. "If you don't mind going down-and-dirty with the experiment."

"I'm listening."

Tom gestured to the freezer built into the left-hand wall of the lab. "You've got more core samples than you need in that freezer. If you need more, we can get them. Why don't you just take some of the water from around 100 feet down and use it for the medium. It's not very elegant, but if these bugs are going to grow, they'll grow in that."

She turned away and began issuing orders before he could finish. "Carlos, we need to set up some incubators. Give me a hand with that. Some of you people are going to have to get out of the way."

Tom shook his head and smiled as Ki turned to him, saying, "Exciting times, Tom."

Everyone was flushed with the excitement of what they had just discovered, and Tom felt like he might start laughing at any moment from simple exhilaration. "You may have to lock Dr. Krazinsky in her room just to make her get some sleep tonight."

Ki laughed and rubbed his hands together. "I can't wait to see the Carbon 14 dating on these bugs. Knowing when they died will be a tremendous help in clarifying the geology of this planet."

Espanoza was pulling equipment from a cabinet under the expert supervision of Dr. Krazinsky who was still babbling questions to herself. "We need to figure out what they eat," she said. "I guess simple sugars would be the best place to start."

Tom raised his voice to carry across the lab. "Give them some of Melancon's grits. If they won't eat that, to hell with 'em."

It probably wasn't that funny, but the entire crew exploded with hysterical laughter. As the noise died down, Tom realized someone was missing. "Where is Cochran?" he asked, but the crew returned blank stares.

Tom left the lab, went through the kitchen and dining area, and walked down the hall of the living quarters. He knocked on the door to Cochran's room. There was no answer, but the door swung slowly open.

"What the hell?" Tom said. He stood in the doorway for a moment trying to make sense of what he was seeing.

Cochran sat wearing a full headset in front of his computer. His hands gripped some sort of control apparatus attached to the desk, and he twitched the handles left and right and up and down at seemingly random intervals.

Good God, he's playing a game. Tom walked into the room and tapped him on the shoulder.

Cochran jumped like he'd been shot and ripped the headset off. "Damn it!" he said, looking up at Tom. "You scared the hell out of me."

Tom knitted his brow and shook his head. "Video games, Mr. Cochran?"

Cochran switched off the game. "Yeah, video games."

"Aren't you a little old for that?"

"There's a lot of guys older than me still playing every day."

"It just seems like a colossal waste of time," said Tom.

"It keeps my reflexes up. It's what got me into the academy."

"Say what?"

Cochran stood up and laid the headset on the desk. "It's what got me into the academy. I was world champion of 'Jump Jet Squadron' two years in a row."

Tom scratched his head. "I remember something about that from your file, but what does it have to do with the academy?"

"You know how it works." He looked at Tom. "Hell, maybe you don't know how it works. My family wasn't military. We were nobodies as far as the academy was concerned. 'Jump Jet Squadron' is as close to flying as you can get without logging time in a simulator. The academy didn't know who I was, but they knew I was one in a million behind the controls of a fighter jet. Once I passed the physical, I was in."

Tom opened his mouth to speak but then shut it in a rare moment of diplomacy. "Whatever. I guess if you want to play games, that's your business, but get that damned helmet wired into the intercom system. You were paged over ten minutes ago."

"Yes, sir."

"We've got something in the lab you might want to see."

"Yes, sir. I'll be right there."

Tom left the room and walked back down the hall, shaking his head and thinking to himself, *So that's how he can be afraid of heights and yet not mind flying.* "Flying is different," he said. *Of course it's different to him. He thinks it's a game.*

Tom was still thinking about it when he returned to the controlled chaos of the lab. *That is some really spooky shit.*

Chapter Twenty-four
Surface of Mars
May 17, 2061

The crew was still giddy the next morning, and Tom had some difficulty getting them settled down for a staff meeting. Dr. Krazinsky was buttonholing anyone who would listen to explanations of her experiments. She was seated next to Mike Cochran who, although he was a biologist, seemed almost uninterested in the discovery that Mars had once harbored life. He had a bemused expression as Krazinsky waved a hand in his face.

"I finally decided," she said, "not to worry about the nutrient, so that I could concentrate on other things. There should already be enough nutrients in the water to sustain some kind of growth. We added some hydrogen sulfide to one of the incubators, some sodium sulfate to another, one of them we put in simulated Mars sunlight, and another we kept in the dark."

Commander Thon cleared his throat. "Dr. Krazinsky, we would like to begin."

Pamela Krazinsky turned with her most innocent smile. "Certainly, Commander."

"There have been some changes to the duty roster," Commander Thon said. "I have had several messages from NASA Central, and they are hungry for more news concerning our recent discovery. With that in mind, we will put off plans for the building of the greenhouse."

Tom sat impassively, he and Commander Thon had been over this already, but Espanoza nearly exploded. "What is this about? I can't believe it! Has growing plants on Mars suddenly become a trivial part of this mission? First, I am told Mr. Fielder needs my scaffold, and now you're telling me it doesn't matter anyway. Has Rick Jelton lost his mind?"

Commander Thon allowed him to run down a bit before he interrupted. "I understand your disappointment, Mr. Espanoza. Actually, I have had no direct communication with Rick Jelton since the Marler Phenomenon. I am a little surprised at NASA's disruption of our construction schedule, but we will follow their direction."

Ki frowned and picked up the duty roster in front of him. "Mr. Espanoza, Dr. Krazinsky, and Ms. Geller will remain in the lab and work with the core samples. Mr. Melancon, you will stay also. There are a few pieces of equipment not yet linked to the computer. We need that taken care of today. If you finish early, you are at the direction of Dr. Krazinsky.

"Mr. Fielder, Ms. Weiss, Mr. Cochran, and myself will travel to the drill site and set up the scaffold for the solar film. If there is time after that, we will carry the pump down the cave to the ice, and I will finally get a firsthand look at all the ice and quartz."

Commander Thon went on with one of his pep talks, mostly aimed at soothing Espanoza, but Tom quit listening. Ki had come to him earlier in the morning to discuss the situation with NASA. Changing the construction schedule was more than just a little strange, and it was hard to understand why Rick Jelton was suddenly too busy to talk to them. Ki had speculated a need for positive publicity but then decided it made no sense. The Mars expedition was still riding high in the public's mind from the discovery of the "Crystal Grotto" as it had come to be called, and the discovery of life on Mars was just now hitting the morning news on Earth.

Ki had told Tom the only logical conclusion was that NASA wanted to milk Dr. Krazinsky's discovery to distract the public from something else. The only thing occupying the public's mind these days, besides the Mars Expedition, was the Marler Phenomenon, and Ki had decided there was more to the incident than NASA was telling them or anyone else.

It seemed like weak logic to Tom, but he knew Ki was a master of reading between the lines. If Ki said something was up, then something was up. The trouble was, as Ki had said, "It's a little difficult to interpret the political nuances from the surface of Mars."

Commander Thon finished his speech and the crew-members stood up. Dr. Krazinsky was already half way through the kitchen on her way to the lab.

Tom signaled to Cochran. "We'll need the wagon hooked up to the rover, and Commander Thon wants to bring the field microscope. Ms. Weiss knows where it is. Commander Thon and I will load the scaffolding and the solar film. Make sure we've got all the tools we need."

Cochran was pulling his suit from his locker beside the front airlock. "Yes, sir."

They went through the now familiar routine of donning their suits and checking each other's fittings and were soon rolling easily across the boulder-strewn plane toward the hole they had drilled above the Crystal Grotto. Cochran was driving, and Tom rode shotgun. Commander Thon and Evelyn Weiss rode in the back seats. The poles of the scaffold stuck out on each side of the wagon behind them, and the solar film was folded up like a large bed-sheet under the scaffold.

Ki craned his neck back and forth like a tourist. "So familiar and yet so strange," he said.

Tom turned in his seat to look at him. "Hmm?"

Ki pointed off to the side. "It could almost be a desert in Nevada if you ignore the sky, but it has always been a planet of mystery—its red color, the early belief that canals covered its surface. The fiction of Edgar Rice Boroughs early in the twentieth century probably contributed to the sense of wonder, but his books simply exploited the existing hunger for understanding—a hunger present in mankind even before the planet was named for the Roman god of war. I began to wonder about that as the mission approached. Was it simply the red color that caused it to be named for a god of destruction, or was there something else? Is there some event lost in the depths of our prehistory that could account for our fascination with this planet?

"We haven't even begun our work here, and already we've found the remnants of life. I tell you I can't wait to get back in the lab and get some real work done."

Tom listened with affection to the ramblings of his friend. Ki was prone to such things in idle moments, whereas Tom was virtually incapable of it. And Tom would have denied it had anyone asked, but Ki's poetic approach to life had fascinated him since college. He smiled and shook his head. It was hard to believe that he now called "The Nerd" Commander Thon.

Cochran steered the rover in a meandering path around the various rocks but kept them moving to where the electronic map in the console indicated the drill site was located, and they soon came to a place almost directly on top of the Crystal Grotto. An incongruous piece of heavily insulated plastic pipe and a few wires projected from the sand. The pipe ran across the ground for a few feet and ended at the edge of a plastic-lined pit. The red sand was crisscrossed with the tracks of men and machines, and a few deep tracks went off in odd directions where small boulders had been pushed aside. Cochran pulled the rover next to the pipe and unbuckled his seatbelt.

Tom hit the ground first. "This really shouldn't take too long," he said. "I've already got the spikes in the ground. All we need to do is slip the scaffold over them and put it together. We don't want much tilt on the solar film, but then we really won't need much—the wind will keep the sand blown off."

Tom directed his crew with the expertise of a journeyman contractor, and in less than two hours they were unrolling the film over the scaffold and attaching it at the cross points. Tom picked up a heavy box from the rover and carried it to the pipe where he attached the wires from the ground to one outlet and the wires from the solar film to another. Cochran looked over his shoulder as Tom crimped the wires with specialized pliers.

"Just a few things to check," said Tom. He pulled a small meter from the pouch at his waist and clipped the leads to the wires between the solar film and the box. Evelyn came to look as he pushed a few buttons on the meter.

"Excellent numbers, Mr. Fielder," she said.

Tom looked at the sun and then at his watch. "Not bad at all. It's 11:00. I've set the timer to pump from 10:00 till 2:00. It looks like we'll have more than enough power."

Tom removed the leads and reattached them to the wires leading down into the ground from the other side of the box. "Let's see what this does," he said and pushed the single button on the side of the box.

"That's it?" asked Cochran.

Tom was reading numbers on the meter in his hand. "Yeah," he said. "It's really just a reset switch. The box has a simple mechanical timer and some batteries inside. We'll pump for four hours a day, but we have to keep the water in the pipe warm enough to stay liquid. The pipe is heat-traced under the insulation. In the morning and afternoon, the solar film will recharge the batteries and feed the heater. The batteries need to hold enough power to operate the heater during the night so the water won't freeze and break the pipe or the pump."

Tom pulled off the leads and wrapped them around the meter before stuffing it back into his pouch. "This looks good. I think we're ready to install the pump."

He stood up and looked around, brushing cold sand from the knees of his suit. Cochran and Evelyn were picking up stray tools, but Commander Thon was fifty feet away, looking through the field microscope at something on the ground. Tom bounced up behind him and saw a basketball-sized rock centered under the microscope. *I should have known.* He waited for a moment before speaking. "I believe it's a rock, Commander."

Ki turned and jumped slightly when he found Tom just two feet behind him. "Quite so," he said. "An absolutely fascinating rock in fact."

Tom looked down and deadpanned, "It *is* a rock, Commander."

"Yes," said Ki, "but if you look at these weathering marks, you can see the same thing we've seen on almost every other rock: it simply does not appear to have been sitting in this dry atmosphere for several billion years. The weathering associated with dry, wind-blown sand is quite characteristic. This rock has marks indicating erosion by water.

"This is one of the mysteries of Mars. What has happened to the water? Granted, we have found water underground, but where has all the surface water gone? Perhaps when I get a chance to run isotope dating on these rocks, we will begin to find some answers."

Tom started making soft, snoring noises in his helmet.

"Yes, yes, yes," Ki said. "I realize it doesn't have any gears or power supply, but it's one of the more important things we came here to do."

"It's one of the things *you* came here to do." Tom gestured at the desolate plane. "I came for the scenery. Commander, we have several tons of these rocks within 100 feet of our airlock door. I'm sure you can find something more interesting in the Crystal Grotto."

"Oh. Are we ready to go?"

"Waiting on you, Commander."

"Excellent." Ki picked up the microscope and turned to the rover. "This should be interesting indeed."

Cochran pulled the rover away from the drill site and reflexively checked the map even though they were only a little over a mile from the entrance to the cave. A little exploring had revealed a much easier path to the cave, and Cochran knew the way by heart.

Ki tapped Tom on the shoulder. "I believe Rick may have been right," he said.

"About what?" asked Tom.

"It looks as if we will be pumping water today after all."

Tom laughed. "We just might, if I can keep you from falling in love with every rock you meet."

Ki laughed with him. "It can truly be said, Tom. I never met a rock I didn't like."

The rover moved easily over the steadily rising ground, and they were soon at the base of the fractured slab that was the entrance to the cave. A winch had been installed above the split, and wires ran down the slope. Cochran pulled up and jumped out to attach the wires to the battery terminals on the rover.

Tom picked up the pump, and Ki grabbed the microscope while Evelyn Weiss shouldered a large bag of tools.

Evelyn looked at Cochran. "Mr. Cochran, you have not yet seen the cave. Perhaps you would like to go in my place?"

"No thanks, ma'am," he said. "I'll just stay here and guard the jeep."

Tom started to object but decided it was best to let it go. If there were wiring problems in the cave, he might need someone topside to reset the pump.

He turned without speaking and started up the slope. Ki and Evelyn followed, and one by one they strapped on the harness and lowered themselves to the top of the huge sand hill in the middle of the main cavern. Tom was the last to go, and his companions were already near the mouth of the old, underground river some 500 feet away when he reached the floor. They stood waiting, their suit lights bobbing against the gray and brown walls.

Tom hurried across the cavern to join them. "Let's roll," he said. "I don't want to make a liar out of Rick."

The relay antennas were still in place, and they stopped to turn each one on, testing the batteries and the signal by calling Cochran. There was no live video feed today, but all three of them carried recorders hooked to their helmets.

Ki tended to walk slower and slower as they approached the crawlway, stopping every few feet to examine a small outcropping or to pick up a piece of the ever-increasing rubble at their feet. "Just as the rocks you brought back from here seemed to indicate," he said. "This cave was filled with steam at some time. I can only speculate about the forces at work, but the river, perhaps miles farther downstream, contacted a source of intense heat. It caused the water to boil and blow backward up the slope. Undoubtedly, the water continued its attempt to flow downward and was repeatedly blown back in this direction. In effect, it formed a huge underground geyser. The distribution of the rubble clearly shows this uphill flow, and the huge geode we have come to call the Crystal Grotto was formed by exposure to superheated steam over a period of thousands if not millions of years.

"Eventually the planet cooled and the water condensed and turned to the ice we have found." He gestured around him as they approached the crawlway. "This must have all been full of ice at one time. The narrow outlet formed by the pile of rubble has helped to keep the ice in the Grotto from subliming.

"It's all rather troubling though. Mars is so cold now. This must have happened several billion years ago, but the scale of it is hard to imagine, and it seems likely that this cave should have shifted down and collapsed before now. I would guess Dr. Krazinsky's organisms drifted in with the air and found a home during the time between steam and ice."

Tom had gone ahead and was halfway through the crawlspace when Evelyn and Ki arrived at the entrance. "Give me just a few seconds," he called back, "and Commander Thon can get his first view of the famed Crystal Grotto." He pushed the pump ahead of him through the narrow space and soon stood on the ledge some twenty feet above the floor of the small cavern.

Though he had been here several times for the collection of core samples and setting up water pipe, it was still a breathtaking sight. "I'm through," he said. Ki and Evelyn had a short disagreement over who would go first—a disagreement Evelyn won—and Tom could hear Ki grunt quietly as he bent to enter the short tunnel. Tom played his lights across the jagged, crystalline walls and watched rainbows chase themselves in every direction.

The microscope slid out of the crawlway, followed closely by Ki's head as he emerged into the room.

"Welcome to the top tourist attraction on Mars, Commander Thon," Tom said.

Ki stood and moved his body back and forth, shining his suit lights in every direction. "Spectacular," he said breathlessly.

"We are through," Tom said.

"Coming," said Evelyn.

Tom stood without speaking while Evelyn moved through the tunnel. Ki appeared lost in the magnificent view before him and continued to rock back and forth silently. Evelyn crawled out of the hole, and Tom handed her the pump, saying, "Hold this while I get to the floor. I think our Commander is suffering from Crystalline Rapture."

She snickered. "I believe it is a temporary condition."

Tom grabbed the rope and began lowering himself over the side of the ledge. "I hope so, but you know how he is about rocks."

"It has not affected my hearing," said Commander Thon.

"Not yet," said Tom as he lowered himself to the floor, "but you never know how these things will go. I once had an uncle who became convinced he could read the future in cow patties and spent the last 20 years of his life roaming pastures in search of clues to fame and fortune."

"Somehow," Commander Thon said dryly, "that does not surprise me."

"Truly?" said Evelyn.

"Yep," said Tom, "it was a clear cut case of Pattie Rapture."

"Ah," laughed Evelyn, "you made this up."

"Yes," said Ki and Tom in unison. "But it makes a good story," added Tom.

Tom stood at the bottom of the ledge and looked up. "Okay. Pull up the rope and tie it to the pump. Once we get all the stuff down here, we can get to work."

Once the tools were down, Tom picked up the pump and walked to the edge of the ice. They had fashioned cleats from pieces of the Mars I, and Tom sat on a stiff piece of plastic as he attached them to the bottoms of his thick boots. The plastic protected Tom's suit from the sharp crystals, and the cleats would keep him from slipping on the ice. The ice, once perfectly smooth, was chipped and cracked in a narrow trail where they had walked while obtaining the core samples and setting up the water collection system.

Several feet to his left, the water pipe descended from the ceiling. Wires sprouted from a coupling where the pipe was joined to a section of flexible, insulated hose trailing out across the ice in a long coil. A metal ring, two feet in diameter and covered on one side with a wire mesh, sat in the middle of the ice near the end of the flexible section of hose. Four pieces of plastic projected upward from the ring, giving it the appearance of a large crown.

Tom carried the pump across the ice and set it down inside the metal ring. The wire mesh was on the underside of the ring, and a small electric current would soon warm the ring and the mesh, causing it to melt the underlying ice. The pump held a float switch and would not pump water unless the suction tube was submerged. The flexible hose allowed the pump to sink into the ice without losing its connection to the pipe, and the upward pointing plastic pieces would act as braces against the ice above the pump to keep the apparatus upright as it descended below the surface. If all went according to plan, the device would melt a circular hole in the ice and pump the water into the plastic lined pit above them. Eventually someone would need to return to the cave and move the pump or add another section to the flexible hose.

Evelyn walked up beside Tom, and he instructed her to clamp the pump to the ring and attach the hose while he checked the current on the wires.

"This looks good," he said. "Let's hook it up and see what happens.

Tom crimped the wires together at the pump, and immediately the ice under the mesh began to melt.

"Looking good," he said, and checked his watch. "Alright, it's 1:45. We'll need to hold this thing steady to keep it from sliding around till it melts a hole deep enough to get the plastic guides below the surface of the ice. It ought to take care of itself after that."

He looked at his watch again. "I want to stay till at least 2:00. The switches on the surface should turn off the pump at 2:00, but we need to make sure the current to the ring turns off at the same time. We don't want our pump melting down through the ice all night long."

"It would be a shame after all this work," said Evelyn.

They stood holding the plastic guides as water built up under the pump. The first bit of it spilled out and froze at the edges of the hole being created as the ring sank down into the ice, but soon they could feel a steady vibration as the pump caught suction and began moving water to the surface.

"Alright!" Tom exclaimed. He watched the water level drop in the hole. "We've got prime."

The pump stopped when the water dropped below the suction tube, and Tom continued to study the hole. "No backflow. Check valves are holding."

In less than a minute, the water level had again covered the pump suction and they could feel the vibration when the pump turned itself back on. "Excellent," said Tom. "I just love it when things work out the way calculations predict." He looked over at Evelyn who was beaming at him through her faceplate.

"It is a good design, Mr. Fielder," she said.

"With your help, Ms. Weiss."

Tom craned his neck and found Ki squatting near the wall of the cavern, staring through the microscope. "Commander, we've got water."

Commander Thon did not look up but muttered, "This is most troubling."

"What? You don't like water?" Tom said sarcastically.

"No, it's these crystals. The structure is extremely small and fine. Smaller crystals indicate faster growth. This quartz seems to have grown, not over a period of several thousand years, but perhaps just a few hundred years."

Ki looked up at the top of the cavern where the large growth hung down in what Evelyn had called a chandelier. "Most of the steam would have been directed straight up, causing this large outgrowth, but the volume of steam must have been huge. Even accounting for the relatively acidic water of Mars, this is perplexing."

Tom turned to Evelyn and crossed his eyes. Evelyn tried to muffle a laugh and failed. "I guess that's why I like engineering, Commander," Tom said. "If things are perplexing, it usually means I just slipped a decimal point someplace."

Ki didn't answer, and Tom and Evelyn stood holding the pump upright as it gradually carved its circular hole. "Did I ever tell you about my great aunt?" Tom asked after a time.

Evelyn laughed again. "Please, Mr. Fielder. No more stories about your family. I feel that I know too much already. And I believe we can now let go of the pump."

Tom looked down and saw that the plastic guides were indeed below the icy surface. He let go of the guide he had been holding and stepped back. "Ain't she beautiful," he said.

He checked his watch. "One forty eight and all is well," he announced in a booming voice. "Twelve minutes to kill. I should have brought a book to read."

"Why don't we look around," Evelyn said. "We have been so busy with the core samples and everything else that in all our trips we have not fully inspected this cave."

Tom looked to where Ki was still muttering to himself and moving the microscope from time to time. "Pestering the Commander would be better sport," he said.

"Mr. Fielder, come." She grabbed his hand and pointed across the ice. "We have never even looked closely at the far wall. Let us go see if we can find something interesting."

Tom looked at her and cocked his head to the side. "You're not developing rock fever like the Commander are you? I can't have my engineers developing rock fever."

"No, I am trying to keep you from disturbing Commander Thon in his work." She pulled his hand. "Now come. You are in much too good a mood and will get yourself in trouble if not properly supervised"

Tom laughed but looked longingly at Ki and then at the pump settling straight and true into the ice. "Okay," he said, "save me from myself."

They took off across the ice and were soon standing where the wall went down into the translucent green ice below them. Evelyn looked back over the chips made in the ice by their cleats. "It seems a shame to mar the perfect smoothness of this ice," she looked up to where the pipe emerged from the ceiling, "or even that small spot where the drill came through."

"All in the name of progress, I guess," said Tom. "The Literalist Church had a field day with it. 'Mankind treading where it has no right to be.' Yada, yada, yada. Those guys would have us in sackcloth and ashes, taking oxen into the fields, and dragging our women off to caves by the hair. Not a bad idea, that last one."

Evelyn struck him on the arm hard enough to rock him to the side. "Damn, woman! That hurt," Tom said.

Evelyn smiled the sweetest smile, and batted her eyes through her helmet. "I am certain you didn't mean that," she said.

Tom stood rubbing his arm. "No, seriously. It really did hurt." He dropped his voice and muttered under his breath, "I can see I'll need a bigger club with this one."

Evelyn pulled back her fist, and Tom stepped away, holding up both hands. "Just kidding. We don't have an official male chauvinist on the mission. I was just filling in."

Evelyn looked at him. "Let us declare the position vacant."

"No problem. It's not like I need the hazardous-duty pay."

"Good," she said and walked away, lightly rubbing her fingers against the quartz wall.

Tom watched her go and wondered, not for the first time, how she managed such an enticing sway while wearing a space suit. He looked away but found his eyes drawn back and realized there was a bit of a knot in his stomach. *Ah, this is not good.* Memories of past relationships flitted by, and he knew that all of them had just been a way to pass the time. Two of them had point-blank told him he had a fear of commitment, and he hadn't disagreed.

His eyes were glued to Evelyn. *Be careful here. This one is dangerous.*

Evelyn stopped and leaned forward, her faceplate nearly touching the wall, then backed up several steps and cast her lights back and forth. "Come see, Mr. Fielder. No. Stay where you are and look closely at the wall. Do you see the holes?"

Tom backed up and looked. There were small holes, six to eight inches in diameter, covering the wall directly in front of him. The rough crystals had encrusted the openings, making them difficult to see at first, but now that he had found the first one, he realized they were everywhere. He walked toward Evelyn, keeping an eye on the wall, and saw that they were evenly spaced every four to five feet both horizontally and vertically.

"Now this is strange," he said as he stopped next to Evelyn. His voice was even, but the engineer in him knew that it was more than strange. He could feel the hair on the back of his neck stand up.

He moved forward to look into one of the holes as Evelyn had done and realized the placement of his suit lights made it impossible to illuminate the hole and look inside at the same time.

"We've got a flashlight with the other tools," Evelyn said. "I'll go get it."

She headed back to where the tools lay next to the pump, but Tom turned and followed her. "It's after 2:00," he said, looking at his watch. "We need to check the pump."

Tom barely glanced at the pump, noting only that the water had begun to freeze around the wire mesh. "Just as it should," he said.

Evelyn was rummaging through the tools and produced the flashlight. She pointed at the ledge. "The same holes. Over there. We've been using them to climb the ledge."

"Right," Tom said and picked up the tools. "Let's take a look."

They walked to ledge, and Evelyn turned on the flashlight, leaning close while holding the light next to her helmet. "It's no good," she said. "I can't get a good angle. It's just darkness."

Tom took the flashlight but could do no better. He finally stepped away in disgust. Evelyn was looking where Ki squatted in front of the microscope.

"We need . . ." Tom said.

Evelyn turned quickly. "We need the probe."

"Right," he said, and they bounced the twenty feet or so to Ki's side.

Ki was totally oblivious to anything but the view through the microscope. He looked up, blinking in momentary confusion, when Tom touched his shoulder. "Is it time to go?" he asked.

"Not quite yet, Commander. I just need to borrow this." Tom bent forward and unclipped the probe from the side of the microscope.

"This site is incredible," Ki said. "I have no doubt at least one dissertation will be written on the photographs I have taken today alone."

"That's nice," Tom said, but he and Evelyn were already headed back to the ledge, and Ki's voice trailed off as his attention returned to the crystal formations.

The probe was a simple fiber optic tube, three feet long and the thickness of a pencil. It had been designed for use with the microscope, but the handle swelled to twice the size of the flash-light—containing not only batteries but a small video screen on the end for those cases when magnification was not necessary or use-ful.

Tom unwrapped the tube from around the handle and pushed a switch on the side. A small light came on at the tip of the tube. "Let's see what we can see," he said.

"Wait a minute," said Evelyn. She reached over and pushed another switch on the handle. "This may be worth record-ing."

"Good thinking," said Tom, and he selected one of the holes at random, snaking the tip of the fiber optic tube into the opening as he and Evelyn watched the screen on the butt of the handle.

The quartz crystals extended no more than a few inches in-to the hole, and they were soon looking at the bare stone walls of an oval cavity extending slightly upward into the rock.

"It is perfectly smooth," said Evelyn with wonder.

"And perfectly formed," said Tom. His voice was low, al-most a whisper. "This is impossible."

He pulled the tube out and moved to another hole in the wall. "Identical," he said and moved to yet another hole. "Com-mander, you may want to come look at this."

"Just a minute," said Ki.

"I think now would be good," said Tom. There was an edge to his voice.

Ki stood with a groan. "On my way."

Commander Thon came to stand between Evelyn and Tom. He was silent for a long time as he looked at the scene inside the hole. "This is impossible," he said.

Tom nodded. "My words exactly."

"They are everywhere," said Evelyn. "They cover the far wall. We have looked at three of them, and they are identical."

Ki took the probe from Tom and moved down to the next hole, repeating the procedure. Again, they found a perfectly formed, perfectly smooth, oval cavity just a few inches inside the opening.

"I know of no process that could account for this," Ki said. He began to thread the probe deeper and found a point less than two feet into the hole where it branched to the left and right. He twisted the probe to the right and pushed.

In a barely audible voice, Tom said, "What in God's name."

There were small openings leading deeper into the ledge on the left-hand side of the cavity. From one of them, a tiny metal framework resembling the top of the Eiffel Tower projected, as if it had fallen through a door—its I-beams no thicker than wires.

But it was the object in the middle of the oval hole that caught and held their attention. Ki's hand began to shake, and the end of the probe flipped around against the wall of the hole, coming to rest at the base of what looked vaguely like a shrimp carved in the stone of the hole's floor—a statue left behind when the oval tunnel was formed. On the base, in raised lettering, was an inscription that to Tom's untrained eye looked like a mixture of Egyptian Hieroglyphics and Arabic. The entire sculpture was less than one inch tall.

Evelyn gasped and reached out to Tom, clutching his arm tightly. Her voice shook with emotion. "Ce n'être pas possible."

"I'll be damned," said Tom. "Martians."

Gregg R. Overman

Chapter Twenty-five
Three Billion Miles from Earth
May 18, 2061

Space is slightly curved out near the orbital paths of Uranus and Neptune. The sun is merely a bright, cold star in the distance, but materials at rest in this region of space will not stay at rest. Lacking motion relative to the sun, an object will accelerate, slowly at first, but with ever-greater momentum—spiraling down the long curve of space-time—harvesting velocity from the gravitational bowl of the sun's mass.

Four cylinders, black as the spaces between stars, coast sunward here. They see the bowl of the sun's attraction without understanding, and they make no allowances for it. Their minds are simple—their guidance systems crude—but they have a singleness of purpose, and their detectors are accurate. The target is known, and it is in their sights.

But the target has moved. Rolling in the path it has known for millennia, delicately balancing centripetal force and gravity, the target flirts with the sun's call and dances an ellipse far from the fiery breath that sustains it.

The four cylinders do not know this, nor can they account for it—their minds are simple. Trajectory is computed. Target position is noted. The two are regularly updated and compared in a rhythmic pulsing of gated electrons.

Path and destination have diverged during their flight. Now, in this place of slightly curved space, a preset value is reached. Small attitude jets are fired, and main engines erupt in a shower of photons, radiation, and primary particles.

One by one, they adjust course. Trajectory and destination converge, and the engines are taken off line. Further adjustments will be necessary, but the cylinders do not know this—their minds are simple.

Space is curved here, and matter cannot rest. It must dance the elliptical dance, rimming the great gravitational bowl—or fall sunward and answer the beckoning, siren call of the sun's mass.

Chapter Twenty-six
NASA Central
May 18, 2061
2:54 PM CST

Rick Jelton sat shuffling paper across his desk and wished for perhaps the hundredth time in the last two weeks that he had stayed in operations. He leaned back in his chair, rubbed his face with both hands, and ran his fingers through his dark hair. *I could be sitting at a terminal right now instead of pushing paper around and trying to talk sense into thick-headed, single-minded military bureaucrats.*

Of course, if he was sitting at a terminal, he would be clueless concerning what he was doing or why. Morale was low at NASA these days. Only a handful of people knew why they were so carefully and continually surveying the region where the Marler Phenomenon had bloomed and died over two weeks ago, and that small group was none too happy about the situation. The rest of the staff was convinced that NASA management had gone finally and irrevocably insane.

Every piece of long-range observational equipment at NASA's command was now targeted on a small area of vacant space. Experiments that had been running for years had been unceremoniously interrupted, telescopes and radiation detectors of all types had been redirected—some of them suffering damage in the process—and work schedules were in a shambles. It wasn't so much that the staffers were angry. They had gotten over most of their irritation after the first week. The situation was worse than that—they were bored.

For 14 days, they had been monitoring a section of empty space in the shape of a thin cone with its tip on Earth and the open end over four billion miles away past the orbit of Pluto, and they had seen nothing. No planets, no comets, no peculiar sources of radiation, no asteroids worth noting—nothing. In three, eight-hour, rotating shifts, 24 hours a day for over two weeks, technicians had checked in and watched blank screens, unmoving gauges, dormant detectors, and the clock on the wall. Nerves were on edge, and obnoxious practical jokes were becoming all too common. Even the excitement of the discoveries on Mars had not lifted their spirits for long.

Nothing was simple anymore. Rick understood the military's concern over the Marler Phenomenon, but their thick-fingered approach to monitoring the area had generated exactly the sort of publicity they had hoped to avoid. It just wasn't possible to disrupt NASA to this extent without raising eyebrows. The press could put two and two together. There had even been speculation about possible Chinese involvement with the phenomenon and, by denying any interest in it, the Pentagon had simply left the scent of blood in the water. The press was in a feeding frenzy but had yet to find anything to chew on. At least so far, none of the articles had begun with the phrase: "Highly-placed, confidential sources at NASA have told us…"

He wondered sometimes just what Secretary Salness was thinking. If they had left him alone, he could have moved a few of the detectors and surveyed the area without causing even a ripple of speculation. As it was, he had fielded dozens of phone calls from universities and research institutes, all furious that NASA had commandeered their satellites. He couldn't even tell them it wasn't his idea—the Pentagon had forbidden mentioning their involvement.

Rick took a few deep breaths and rolled his head back and forth, making a conscious effort to relax the muscles of his back and neck.

And the Pentagon was sticking with the ridiculous idea that the Chinese were responsible for a tremendously energetic event over four billion miles from Earth. Rick had spent some time looking at the data and thinking about it over the last two weeks. *It seems clear to me that no government on Earth could have done it. It was too far away, and it was too much energy. No. It was either a previously unknown, natural phenomenon, or, if the wormhole theory was correct, it was . . .*

He shied away from the idea. It was just too big, too strange. He had too many other things to worry about. He picked up a communiqué from Commander Thon and scanned it quickly. Tom Fielder apparently wanted to blast open the face of the ledge in the Crystal Grotto to examine the interconnected tunnels in the rock. Well, that wasn't going to happen, and Thon undoubtedly knew it but felt he had to ask—probably to placate Fielder. Rick scrawled "No" across the memo and tossed it in his outbox. Somebody else could explain it.

Nothing is simple. Least of all politics and policy. The Literalist Church had been a growing force in politics for some time, but the Marler Phenomenon was the best thing that ever happened to them. They were masters at playing on the fears of the uninformed, and they had condemned the Mars Expedition from the very beginning. Of course, Literalists condemned almost all technology, though they seemed to have no problems with using satellite TV and the Internet to get their message across and collect their tithe.

It was plain as day to the Literalists that the Marler Phenomenon was a sign from God of His displeasure at man's transgressions against the natural order of creation. They had wasted no time or spared any expense explaining to their followers the dire consequences of continuing to ignore the will of God.

Rick exhaled in disgust. It galled him to have a group of religious zealots influencing policy, but he could see the headlines now: "NASA Desecrates Tomb of the Ancient Martians." Tom Fielder would just have to find another way to explore the tunnels.

Rick's computer chirped, and he looked at the screen. Marilyn Lindsay, his second in command, wanted him. "Yes," he said.

"Mr. Jelton, we've got something."

"Like what?" Rick said and immediately regretted his tone of voice.

"Like we don't know, sir, but every detector we've got is registering some kind of radiation, and the Sagan Scope is picking up faint visuals. I think you might want to get down to Mission Control."

Rick didn't answer but hit his door and sprinted down the hall. He yelled from 30 feet away, "Going down," and the elevator doors opened as he skidded to a stop in front of them. "Level C.

Close doors. Now." The elevator seemed to drop forever before opening on the right-hand side of Mission Control. Rick turned sideways to pass between the doors and jolted into a room full of calmly determined technicians who were busily calibrating and checking data feeds from more than a dozen sources.

The superficial appearance of this room had changed little in nearly 100 years. Five rows of desks and computers, curved like an amphitheater turned backward, faced a large wall taken up by three huge screens. Raw data tumbled down the screens, and a schematic of the Solar System turned slowly through three dimensions on the center screen while technicians coaxed computers into accurately recording and analyzing the flood of information. The soft click of keyboards could be heard, and a low murmuring noise filled the room from staff members quietly speaking to their computers or coworkers through headset microphones. Replies were received through an ear-piece, and the relative silence lent a surrealistic quality to the frantic activity as workers hunched unmoving over their consoles, eyes flicking from the small screens in front of them to the larger screens on the wall. Rick was the only person moving across the floor.

He walked quickly to his position on a slightly raised platform at the back of the room, and his computer blazed to life as he picked up a headset. Rick whispered, "Computer, duration of current event."

"Three minutes, 22 seconds."

General Laurence, dressed in civilian clothes, seemed to materialize from thin air and sat down at his private terminal to Rick's left. Rick nodded and turned back to his console just as every gauge and detector dropped to zero. There was a ripple through the room and a collective sigh, but few people moved while data continued streaming in from various satellites. General Laurence was mumbling to his computer in hushed tones and seemed not to notice.

"Computer," Rick said, "Chart approximate location of recent event. Tag to screen one."

A red "X" appeared near a circular line designating the orbit of Neptune on the slowly tumbling Solar System in the middle of the far wall. Rick hit a key and spoke directly to his second in command. "Ms. Lindsay, run a search on the pattern of this radiation. See if we can find a match in the database."

"We're working on it, Mr. Jelton," she replied, "but this is a real mish mash. We've got everything from beta particles to high energy photons."

Rick frowned. "See what you can do, and let me know."

He pushed the keyboard and spoke. "Computer, calculate approximate distance in miles of recent event to Earth and tag event on screen one with label, 'Distance to Earth.'"

The red "X" blinked and a caption appeared next to it. "Distance to Earth = 2,960,938,000 Miles."

Rick looked at it for a moment. *Almost three billion miles.*

"Computer," he said, "chart approximate position of Marler Phenomenon, tag screen one."

A blue "X" appeared outside the line indicating the orbit of Pluto.

"Computer, tag Marler Phenomenon, screen one, distance to Earth. Label 'Distance to Earth.'"

The blue "X" blinked and a caption reading "Distance to Earth = 4,092,000,000" appeared.

Rick knew the date and time by heart. "Computer, calculate velocity in miles per hour of object leaving Marler Phenomenon May 9, 2061 11:00 PM Central Standard Time and arriving at site of most recent event, at time of most recent event. Tag screen one equidistant between Marler Phenomenon and most recent event. Label 'Velocity.'"

Between the two "X's," a simple equation appeared. "Velocity = 3,141,000 Miles/Hour."

Rick let out a breath. "Holy shit," he whispered and realized the entire room was looking at the center screen. Even General Laurence had stopped what he was doing.

"Computer, extrapolate trajectory of object leaving Marler Phenomenon and passing through most recent event. Tag to screen one. White line. No label."

A white line popped into existence on the screen. It originated with the blue "X," passed through the red "X," and crossed the entirety of the displayed Solar System. It did not intersect the Earth as shown on the screen but made a nearly perfect tangent to the elliptical line indicating the Earth's orbital path.

Rick looked at the screen for a moment, and a sinking feeling came over him. He spoke again, but his voice was slow and hesitant. He knew what he was about to see. "Computer, display the position of the Earth at the time of the Marler Phenomenon. Tag to screen one. No label. Mark!"

A blue marble, a duplicate of the one representing Earth's current position, appeared on the ellipse of Earth's orbit. The white line of trajectory passed within what looked to be no more than a few thousand miles of the Earth's former position.

The room erupted as everyone turned and began talking to the person next to them. Rick hit a key for general broadcast and spoke, "Okay people, we've had some excitement, but there is a lot of work to be done. Let's take care of business."

Mission Control went silent, and Rick pushed a key for his private channel to Ms. Lindsay. "Ms. Lindsay, I will be in my office. Call me if you get a pattern match on the radiation."

Rick pulled off his headset and turned to General Laurence who sat staring at Rick with a grim expression. Rick's voice was calm but firm. "General Laurence, I believe we need to talk."

He stood without waiting for the General's reply and walked to the elevator. Neither of them spoke when the doors closed, and silence reigned all the way to Rick's office. His computer was steadily chiming when they walked in. Rick pushed a button to silence it and walked behind his desk to sit down. The General pulled a chair up close to the front. For perhaps ten seconds, they simply stared at each other.

"What," the General finally asked, "do you think you were doing in there?"

Rick leaned back and propped his feet on the desk. "I was making logical conclusions from the data at hand."

"In front of your entire staff?" The General's voice was clipped.

Rick shook his head and studiously cleaned one fingernail with another before looking sidelong across his desk. "General, I've got over fifty technicians down there. They didn't wind up in Mission Control because they lack the ability to think for themselves. Most of them are a lot smarter than I am and probably had it all figured out before I walked into the room. The rest of them would have figured it out before they left the building even if nobody drew them a picture."

"And you felt like you had to draw them a picture? You had to cram it down their throats?"

Rick pulled his feet off the desk and leaned forward. "No, General Laurence. I had to draw *you* a picture. I had to cram it down *your* throat. Do you still think the Chinese are behind this? Do you really think anyone on this planet has managed to assemble a vessel capable of covering over a billion miles in just 15 days?"

"These events may be unrelated," said the General.

Rick threw back his head and laughed sarcastically. "Christ Almighty! That's exactly what I'm talking about. Do you think it's just coincidence that the trajectory goes directly through where Earth was at the time of the Marler Phenomenon? I swear to God! If you people would get your heads out of your collective. . . "

Rick's computer chirped, stopping him in mid sentence, and he and the General glowered at each other for a moment before he turned to the screen. "What?"

"Uh, Mr. Jelton?"

"Yes, Ms. Lindsay."

"We have a match on the radiation pattern, but it's less than a 40 percent correlation. It's a pretty obscure reference. I guess that's why it took the computer so long to find it."

Rick engaged the projector from his computer so both he and the General could see it. "Computer, show the map in here, please."

Two jagged graphs appeared in three dimensional form on top of Rick's desk. They were roughly similar, having peaks and valleys at the same points, but the sizes of the peaks and valleys were considerably different, and there were a few small areas of the graphs that seemed to have nothing in common.

Rick studied it for a moment. "Not exactly a great match. What am I looking at?"

"These are charts," said Lindsay, "of radiation wavelength versus radiation strength. As you go from left to right, the wavelength decreases from radio waves on the left through microwaves and visible light, ending with gamma radiation on the far right. The height of the various peaks corresponds to the strength of radiation at that particular wavelength. The top graph is our most recent event. The bottom graph is from some experiments that were performed in the early part of this century with antimatter-catalyzed fusion engines."

Lindsay stopped, and Rick hesitated. "Okay, you're going to need to bring me up to speed on what an antimatter-catalyzed fusion engine is."

"Yes, sir. I had to look up the reference. Apparently, before the development of the current He_3 fusion process, there was an interest in using antimatter to drive a fusion reaction. There was a lot of promising work done, and what I'm reading indicates antimatter might be used to make an extremely efficient fusion engine—far better than anything we have today—but of course you need antimatter to keep it running. We can mine He_3 on the moon, but the only source for antimatter is particle accelerators."

"Sounds expensive," Rick interjected.

"Expensive in an energy sense for certain. It requires several terawatts of power to produce just a few nanograms of antimatter in a particle accelerator. In essence, you'd need to run a normal fusion generator for several hours to produce enough antimatter to keep your antimatter-catalyzed fusion engine running for just a few seconds. But none of this really makes any difference. There's not enough world-wide production of antimatter to, uh, matter."

"What are we talking about here?" asked Rick. "What's the production capacity for antimatter?"

"I looked that up too," said Lindsay, and Rick nodded with satisfaction. "We could make somewhere near 500 nanograms per year if all the accelerators in the world were dedicated to that process."

"500 billionths of a gram," said Rick.

"Yes, sir."

Rick had been studying the charts on his screen while listening to Lindsay. He waved his hand to place a cursor over the largest peak on the graph of the most recent event and tapped twice. A small circle appeared over the peak.

"What's this peak?" he asked. "It's present on both charts, but it must be 20 times larger on the recent event."

"That's especially interesting," said Lindsay. "The peak you're referring to represents photons of 500 million electron volts. That is the characteristic energy level of photons generated by matter/antimatter interaction. If this is a fusion engine, whoever built it had antimatter to spare."

Rick looked at General Laurence and held him in his gaze while he talked. "Is there any way to estimate the amount of power generated during this event or how much antimatter was used up?"

"No, sir. If this is a rocket, we have no way of knowing its orientation to our field of view. We might assume the rocket is pointed at the Earth, in which case the exhaust is pointed directly away from us. If that's true, then all we're seeing is backscatter. Ninety nine percent of the expended energy is probably hidden by the body of the rocket, but the size of the rocket's body and the exhaust design could have a tremendous impact on how much backscatter would be bounced forward in the rocket's direction of motion."

"What's your estimate of the antimatter consumption for this burn?" asked Rick.

"Oh, sir, there are too many variables. I don't have anything to go on."

"Guess," said Rick.

"Mr. Jelton, I really don't want to…"

Her voice was pleading, and Rick interrupted her. "Just a wild guess, Marilyn. Nobody is going to quote you on this."

"Yes, sir," she said, and Rick and the General could hear key clicks as she entered numbers into her computer. "If we assume 99.8 percent of the energy was hidden from view and comparing the peak heights for photons at 500 million electron volts. Let's see. The old antimatter experiment consumed 2 nanograms. Compensating for the duration of the burn . . . I come up with almost 4,000 nanograms of antimatter."

"About eight years supply," said Rick.

"Well, sir, that's assuming all of the accelerators were…"

"Yes, Ms. Lindsay, I understand. Is there anything else?"

"No, sir. We are continuing to collate data." Lindsay hesitated. "I'm assuming you'll want to speak to everyone before shift change."

"Yes. Don't let anyone in or out of Mission Control until you hear from me."

"Yes, sir."

Rick broke the connection and looked at General Laurence. "Comments, General?" he asked sarcastically.

"I cannot possibly comment on this wild speculation."

Rick's temper flared but just as quickly died. He suddenly felt tired, and his voice softened. "Well, General, somebody's going to have to comment on it, and soon. I don't think you really want to lock up all my technicians, and we're not the only people with telescopes and radiation detectors. The French, the British, not to mention the Chinese—they've all seen this. Like it or not, the cat is out of the bag, and this is going to be the lead story on the five o'clock news. Somebody needs to tell me what to say."

The General nodded. "I'm sure an appropriate press release is being prepared. You probably should turn your phone back on."

"Yeah," Rick said and reached to hit the button, but his computer chirped. "Yes, Ms. Lindsay."

"Mr. Jelton, we've got another one. Same place. Identical pattern."

Rick looked at his watch. "How long has it been since the first one?"

There was a moment's pause before Lindsay answered. "28 minutes 22 seconds."

"Thank you, Ms. Lindsay. Let me know if there are any differences between this one and the first one. Otherwise, you can handle it. I've got some calls to make."

"Yes, sir."

Rick looked at the General. "I'll give you ten to one we get two more before this is over."

General Laurence shook his head. "I'm not a gambling man."

"Well," said Rick, "Whatever they are, they seem to be spreading out. There was only a 20-minute lag between the first wormhole and the second. Now we have 28 minutes between what I would have to guess are course corrections. And speaking of that, why would they need a course correction? Whoever or whatever made these things seems to have implemented technologies we've only tinkered with. Why can't they just compute a course to where Earth will be when they arrive? Why this dogleg track?"

Rick rolled his head back and forth. He could feel a headache coming on. "And why haven't they tried to contact us?"

The General just shook his head and looked at the floor.

"I don't know about you, General, but I'm beginning to get a bad feeling about this."

The General looked up at Rick. "We've got a lot more questions than we have answers, but I'm beginning to get the same feeling. I'm afraid we may not like the answers." He paused. "Secretary Salness might not want me to tell you this, but it probably doesn't matter. The Alpha 2 has been hailing this general vicinity for over a week with no response. It detected today's radiation, and its course has been adjusted."

Rick pondered that for a moment. "You may want to adjust course for an intercept path somewhere between this event and Earth's current position instead of targeting the event itself."

"That has already been taken care of," said the General.

Rick chided himself for thinking of the military as stupid. They weren't stupid. They were just military.

General Laurence stood up. "I have some calls to make also."

Rick stood and offered his hand. "Sorry if I pissed you off earlier," he said.

The General shook his hand. "Nah. I work for Salness. It takes a lot more than that to ruffle my feathers."

Rick grunted. "Thanks. Let me know about the press release."

General Laurence looked down at Rick's computer. "You have messages," he said and left the room.

Rick sat down and hit a button on the keyboard. The computer immediately began chiming.

It was going to be a long day.

Chapter Twenty-seven
Surface of the Moon
Lexam Complex Barracks
May 20, 2061

The alarm chimed near his ear, and he rolled over, slapping at the off switch. The soft rustling of other men could be heard in the barracks as they quietly gathered their clothes and prepared for the day's work. There were different shifts, and the surest way to start a serious disturbance was to make a lot of noise at this hour of the morning.

Ben Allspot lay on his back for a moment—the broken strands of dreams clinging like cobwebs to his mind. He sorted through his memories. There was a vague recollection of Weasel getting irritated about something, and he slowly realized it might be a real memory. He frowned while he struggled with it and rolled to the edge of his bunk.

They had been in one of the larger clubs in the Consolidated Helium Complex, not far from the Cock and Ale, listening to the most popular rock and roll band on the Moon. The club was in one of the few rooms with a tall ceiling, and some of the crowd started jumping up and down. This wasn't exactly a recommended practice in a crowd with the Moon's low gravity, but that was part of the thrill. People were soon popping out of the throng like corks and landing at random in the midst of the audience. Weasel moved to the wall to avoid being the inevitable victim of a hurtling body. Ben followed but found himself caught up in the excitement. The music thundered through the room, echoing from the steel walls till he could feel the bass notes vibrating in his gut. Ben bent his knees, tensed his legs, and shot straight up in the air, nearly touching the ceiling twenty feet above.

It was exhilarating. He could see over the entire crowd at the top of his jump, and he fell slowly at first but gathered speed in his descent as people scrambled out his way. His feet slammed into the solid floor, and he launched himself again and again till he was sweating and breathing heavily.

Quite by accident, he landed near Weasel and pushed his way over, screaming to make himself heard above the booming drums and blaring guitar. "You've got to try this," he said. "It's a hoot."

Weasel frowned and shook his head.

Ben shouted, "Come on, man. Live a little."

Weasel shook his head again and clearly mouthed the word no.

In what seemed at the time to be a stroke of genius, Ben decided to help out his little buddy and grabbed him under the arms, flinging him wildly across the room. Weasel cart-wheeled over the crowd, landed roughly on the stage, bounced once, and skidded into the drummer, knocking him off his stool and sending a cymbal wheeling into the legs of the bass player who tripped and fell.

There was a stunned silence when the music abruptly stopped, and Weasel sprang up, standing close enough to a microphone that his words boomed through the speakers. "Goddamn it, Ben!"

Ben nearly collapsed with laughter, but few people appreciated the joke—least of all Weasel or the club's management. They were rudely escorted to the door while Weasel alternately protested his innocence and asked Ben questions like, "Are you out of your mind?" and "What the hell do you think you were doing?"

Ben sat on the edge of his bunk, unsure of the memory till he stood and felt the stiffness in his legs. *That would be from all the jumping around. Damn. I guess Weasel's pretty ticked.*

He stretched and scratched a bit. It was time to start his morning ritual, and he turned to the wall, pressing his thumb on a small plate on the front of his locker. There was a soft snick as the door opened. Reaching past his Lexam-issued jumpsuit, his hand went unerringly to the back corner where a small vial of white pills lay. He thumbed open the top with one hand, keeping his body close to the locker in case anyone was watching, and carefully palmed one of the pills into his mouth. He bit down, and a salty, bitter taste flooded over his tongue, almost gagging him. But he had found that Carbodine worked faster if it was chewed, and lately he had been craving its flavor. *I suppose it's an acquired taste.*

He shook out four more pills into the palm of his hand, counting them carefully in the dim light, hesitated, and shook out one more. The bottle went back into the locker, but he pushed the five pills into a small Velcro pocket at the waist of his jumpsuit.

Gathering up his jumpsuit and a few personal items, he walked quietly toward the communal shower, thinking about last night. Weasel was bound to be pretty upset, and Ben felt bad about it, but it was water under the bridge now. He decided he'd try to make it up somehow. Maybe he could buy something for his friend, sort of a peace offering.

Ben had plenty of money these days. Everybody on the Moon made good money, and tug pilots made more money than anybody but management or technical staff. He was still living in the Lexam barracks for just $400 a month, most of his meals were eaten at the Lexam cafeteria, and his Carbodine habit was barely costing $100 a week. Weasel had tried to talk him into getting his own little cubicle at Consolidated Helium, but Ben didn't mind living in the barracks, and the food wasn't all that bad. It just meant he had more money to send home to his children, and that is where all of his money went. Almost $20,000 had been transferred into his wife's account in the two months since he'd arrived on the Moon. He figured she was probably living pretty high on the hog with some of it, but she was a good woman and would see to it that the children were well cared for. She had e-mailed him a note just two weeks ago saying she'd started a college fund for the girls, and he didn't doubt it.

The shower felt wonderful sluicing over his body and Ben could have stayed in it forever, but he knew the water would automatically turn off in a few minutes. He soaped up quickly and then stood with his eyes closed, luxuriating in the feel of the hot water against his skin. It was perfect. The steam came up in clouds, filling his nostrils, the drum of the water against the stall and the low gravity made him feel as if he were floating in the belly of a hot thunderstorm. Even the stiffness in his legs began to feel right. His wife was going to see his children into college, and he was a tug pilot on the Moon.

All was well here. Everything was good.

The water shut off, and Ben bounded out of the shower, toweling himself off and saying to no one in particular, "Damn. There is nothing like a good, hot shower to start the day off right."

One of the other men from the barracks, Ben couldn't remember his name, stood looking at him strangely from the far end of the room. "Yeah, whatever," he said.

Ben dressed quickly, throwing his dirty clothes down a chute. "Laundry by Lexam," he said. "Ain't life grand."

He glided down the hallway to the cafeteria with a spring in his step and a smile on his face. Coffee would be waiting, and it would add a slight boost to the Carbodine. He grabbed a tray, moving forward as powdered eggs, oatmeal, and toast were piled on his plate. At the end of the line, coffee, strong and black, steamed from a large decanter. Ben filled his cup and went to sit down.

The cafeteria could have been in any university or elementary school on Earth except that every surface was metal, and the walls were the same cream white seen everywhere else on the Moon. Long tables were arranged in staggered rows across the windowless room, and there was a TV screen in one corner. Most of the men were clustered at tables near the TV, and Ben angled his way toward them. A handsome man with dark hair filled the screen. The men seemed glued to his every word.

Just a little too loudly, Ben said, "Wassup?" as he sat down.

"End of the fucking world," said one man. "That's what's up."

"Hmmm," Ben said, "sounds serious."

"Listen up," the man said.

Ben turned his attention to the screen where the handsome man continued speaking with a grim and serious tone. "The Chinese and other countries have confirmed our observations. The four objects are apparently headed toward Earth at a high rate of speed. There are indications these objects may be related to the Marler Phenomenon in some way, but we cannot substantiate this. NASA has recently determined a method of tracking the objects and has calculated they will arrive at Earth in 40 to 50 days.

"I would like to stress that there is no cause for immediate concern. It is possible that these four objects are some sort of natural phenomenon, but the United States, in conjunction with all of the other industrialized nations of the world, is developing contingency plans to cover any eventuality"

The scene changed to a woman at the network anchor desk. "That was Rick Jelton of NASA at a press conference yesterday. He did not accept questions following his announcements. And now, with sports news, we have Tim Slager."

Conversation at the table was brisk as every man expressed his opinion. Ben listened without speaking and noticed there were several variations on a few basic themes. There were those who leaned toward the Literalist belief that the expedition to Mars had triggered something, though only one man would say it was the wrath of God. There were those who believed it was some strange new kind of comet, and that the United States would have no problem blowing it out of the sky. Then there were the ones who quietly insisted that Aliens were coming to Earth. Out of this last group, half believed the Aliens would bring the Promised Land, and half believed they would either enslave mankind or destroy it.

The man next to Ben, the one who had spoken to him earlier, was solidly in the Aliens enslaving or destroying mankind camp, and he turned to Ben, "What do you think?"

Ben looked pensive as he took a bite of his eggs. "I think these eggs need some salt. Could you pass that down here?"

The man rolled his eyes and slid the salt to the end of the table. "Okay, but what do you think about these Aliens?"

Ben salted his eggs and took a huge bite. "Well," he said in a loud voice, talking around his food and pointing his fork in the air, "I think I don't know if it's Aliens, and I think *nobody* knows what it is. I think somebody besides this scruffy bunch of Moon rats is going to be who takes care of it—if it gets taken care of. I think if it gets taken care of, then I'll be fine, and if it doesn't, then it won't matter." He took another bite of his eggs and looked at his watch. "I think I'm *not* gonna be the one to fix it or figure it out, and I think if I don't get to work pretty soon, I'm gonna be in trouble."

Ben emptied his coffee cup and smiled at the men who had turned to listen. Some of them seemed irritated at his flippant attitude while others laughed. A few of them just nodded in agreement.

Ben carried his tray to the cafeteria exit and dumped the dishes in a hopper. It was almost an hour before he was due at the tug lift-station, but he truly loved flying the ugly little transports, and sometimes, if a tug was ready, he would start his shift early.

He moved through the transit tube station and onto the train with practiced moves, hardly thinking about it, and settled into a seat just as the train accelerated. Something was vaguely bothering him. *Was there something I was supposed to buy?*

Oh yeah, Weasel's present. He rolled the idea around in his head for awhile and finally decided to blow it off. *Screw it. Weasel's a big boy. He'll get over it, and if he doesn't, well, screw that too.* He didn't need Weasel anyway. He'd made lots of connections in the last few weeks. He fingered the five hard knots in the pocket at his waist where the Carbodine waited. The price might go up a little bit, but he could handle it. He was a tug pilot.

Ben walked into the pilot's room and went straight to his locker. A voice called out before he could open it.

"Allspot, get over here."

He turned and saw his supervisor, a pudgy balding man with a red face, standing in front of the office door. His face seemed especially red this morning, which usually indicated he was angry, but it was a little difficult to tell since he was almost always angry about something.

Ben muttered, "Shit," under his breath and covered the room in three long strides.

Offering his best smile, he said, "Yes, sir, Mr. Armstead. How are you this morning?"

Armstead turned and walked into the office. "Get in here and close the door."

Ooh, this is not going to be pretty,

He sat down, but Armstead remained standing in front of Ben's chair. "Let me get right to the point," he said,.

Ben thought, *I'd appreciate it*, and barely stopped himself from saying it out loud.

Armstead picked up a sheet of paper and waved it in Ben's face.

"This is yesterday's report. We've had this conversation before, and we're not going to have it again. If you come down into this base one more time dropping delta V the way you did yesterday afternoon, your ass is going to be welding beams in construction before you know what hit you."

He leaned down till his face was inches away from Ben's. "You're not flying a goddamn fighter jet, Allspot. You don't get any points for being the first one back to base. Do you understand that?"

Ben had a strangely vivid fantasy of laughing uproariously while smashing Armstead's face into a pulp, but he looked at the floor and mumbled, "Yes, sir."

Armstead straightened up and went to sit behind his desk. "I don't have any room for hotdogs in this outfit. People might get irritated when things don't get delivered on time, but they get downright pissed when tugs get smashed up."

Ben started to protest. "My safety record . . ."

Armstead jumped up and Ben flinched like the was expecting his supervisor was going to come over the desk. "Fuck your safety record! Here's the deal, Allspot. You might want to listen real careful. If you come into this base or approach a vessel with too much speed or do anything else that is not exactly what it says in the book, your ass is out of here."

Ben decided it was time to be contrite. "I'm sorry, Mr. Armstead. I guess I just love flying these things so much that I get carried away sometimes. It won't happen again."

Mr. Armstead sat down and cupped his chin in his hand. "I hope so," he said. "I really do." He sat looking at Ben and then bent his head, rubbing his eyes with both hands. "Look. I spent five minutes going over your file yesterday. That's about five minutes more than you deserve, but I need pilots."

Armstead shook his head. "You're kind of hard to figure. You've got the potential to be one of the best pilots I've ever had. They threw everything they could think of at you during training: busted jets, misaligned jets, wrong vectors on targets, even unbalanced loads. You slid through every bit of it without a hitch.

"But here's how it works. Things happen out there. We've lost a few tugs. Even lost a few pilots. As long as I'm taking care of business, nobody's going to bother me, but if you crack up a tug, and they come in here and find out you've been hot-dogging, then it's my ass, and I'll be the one welding beams or cooling my heels back on Earth.

"I like this job, Allspot. I plan on keeping it. If it comes down to my ass or yours, I'm not going to have any problems figuring out what to do."

"I understand, Mr. Armstead."

"That's good, but you're going to have to prove it every day for the rest of your tour. Now suit up and get the hell out of here."

"Yes, sir."

Ben walked out of the office and across the room to pull his suit out of the locker. There was a long daily checklist for the spacesuits, and he laid the suit down on a nearby table and went over each fitting and gauge before he was ready to put it on. Another part of the daily ritual was a last-minute stop in the bathroom. The suits had plumbing, but nobody wanted to use it if they didn't have to, and it was a common practice for pilots to make a pit stop just prior to suiting up. It fit into Ben's private ritual quite nicely.

He went into the bathroom and found an empty stall where he pulled down his jump suit and hooked one of the pills out of the waist pocket. Sitting down, he popped it in his mouth and chewed it with a grimace. Thoughtfully, he fished another pill out of the pocket and sat looking at it for a moment. He was going to be in the spacesuit for a long time, and there was no way to get another pill while he was wearing it. He rolled the pill between his thumb and forefinger. It wasn't like he'd never taken two at a time before, and if he swallowed this one whole, it would take effect slower. *Especially on a full stomach.*

With a thrill, he popped it in his mouth and swallowed. *It's done now*, he stood, remembering to flush the toilet before he opened the door.

Back in the pilot's room, he donned his suit quickly, and a technician looked over his seals one more time. "You're ready to airlock out, Allspot. We've got you in tug number 117. He_3 canisters going up." The technician looked at a clipboard. "Looks like you deadhead back. No cargo."

"Sounds like fun," Ben said and walked toward the airlock. "I never brought one back empty before."

The equivalent of a lunar dune buggy waited outside the airlock with a driver ready to take him out to tug 117. Ben slid into the passenger seat without speaking and sat back to admire the view. It was near the middle of the Moon's fourteen-day night, and the immediate vicinity was lit with floodlights. The black, sharp peaks of nearby mountains penetrated the gauzy fabric of a billion stars. Could one of them have sent something all the way to Earth? It didn't seem likely, but Ben figured stranger things had happened.

The cloud-streaked, blue crescent of Earth came into view from behind a mountain as they moved across the dusty plain, and Ben's heart swelled with the beauty of it. His children were there, Charlene and Connie. He wondered what they were doing at this moment. Was it night in Shreveport, Louisiana? He wasn't sure. Were they lying as he had seen them so many times before, tangled in the sheets, their mouths slightly open and those beautiful faces framed by dark, curly hair against a white pillow? He ached to see them again.

The buggy stopped and Ben stepped off, craning his neck to look up at cockpit of the tug. "These things sure are ugly," he said.

The driver said something as he pulled away, and Ben grunted in reply.

A tug was nothing more than a large, fusion engine with fuel tanks. Heavy, unpainted steel struts came down at the four corners of the exhaust cone, and the sand under the tug was fused into glass from its landing. The surrounding area was almost all fused sand from the many takeoffs and landings. Ben could feel it crunch under his boots. Except for shielding, the engine was uncovered. It made for easier maintenance, but Ben could see bare wires and conduit snaking over its surface. He would sit in an open cockpit just under a docking ring at the very top.

Tugs were designed to carry heavy loads into low, lunar orbit for docking with Earth-to-Moon transport vessels. The larger transport vessels were not designed for landing but would carry the cargo into orbit around Earth where it would be transferred to an Earth tug for the final descent into atmosphere.

This tug had four, fifty-foot, 20-ton canisters of He3 clamped to each side. Ben looked at it and giggled. "It looks like a pack of hot dogs with an erector set prize in the middle. Oh, yeah, no hot-dogging." He giggled again.

One of the landing struts was notched with handholds, and Ben scrambled up the side and into the cockpit. Strapping himself in, he flipped switches and watched as several screens came to life with information concerning everything from fuel status to cargo weight. He plugged his communication line into a jack on his suit and pushed a series of buttons to download the flight plan.

Another screen came to life with a blip indicating his destination ship moving in a slow glide above the Moon's surface.

Ben hit a few keys and contacted the tower. "This is Lexam tug 117. I show a possible window in two minutes 18 seconds. Requesting permission to lift."

The reply was almost immediate. "Tug 117, the lane is open, and you are cleared to lift."

"Roger that," said Ben.

"This must be my day," Ben whispered. It was not uncommon to sit in a tug for an hour or more waiting for the transport vessel to come overhead, but every now and then the timing was just right, and Ben wasn't in the mood to question good fortune. He tapped a few keys with his gloved hand and handed over control of the ascent to the computer. He hated doing it—it made for a boring ride—but with Armstead sure to be watching, it was best to play it safe.

The countdown rolled backward to zero, and the fusion engine slowly built up power till the tug lifted from the surface. It wasn't at all the way Ben would have done it, but it would have to do for now.

One hundred sixty tons was a moderately light load, and Ben noted the engine was at twenty-five percent thrust. His hands itched to bump the throttle, but he held back. It was still pretty exciting. The tug rumbled and shook as a nuclear fire lit the plane under him, and Ben looked over the edge of the open cockpit as first the lunar surface, then the mountains themselves dropped away.

"Twenty-five percent thrust to lift 160 tons of cargo off the moon," Ben spoke out loud to no one, "and I had a friend back in New Orleans who thought his Porsche was hot shit."

Tug 117 chased its destination ship around the Moon for twenty minutes of relative boredom while Ben looked at gauges and wished he could hurry things along. The docking was uneventful, and Ben sat feeling useless while mechanical arms lifted the cylinders from the tug and placed them in the cargo hold of the transport vessel. He was growing more restless by the minute.

A voice spoke in his helmet, startling him. "Tug 117, this is transport vessel. You are cleared for break."

"Roger that, transport," Ben said. "We'll see you next time."

With that, he flipped a switch and allowed the computer to disengage the docking ring and fire small retrorockets to push the tug away from the much larger transport ship. He looked up and watched as the transport vessel seemed to rise up and away from him and then waited for the computer to turn the tug over and fire the main engine to slow the tug for descent to the Moon's surface.

A few minutes later he was still waiting, and a memory floated up from his days in the simulator. Empty tugs didn't use the main engine for braking. An empty tug weighed only 70 tons, and the retros had plenty of power for the job. The main engine would only be engaged during the last few minutes of flight.

"*Man, this has got to be one hot baby with no cargo.*"

He stared at his display, clenching and unclenching his hands. In a few minutes, he would pass on the far side of the moon from Lexam Complex. He knew Lexam didn't have a tracking station on that side of the Moon, and tugs didn't carry flight recorders. No doubt, somebody would be watching, but they wouldn't care as long as he didn't endanger any of their vessels.

Ben sat with his hands poised over the controls and his eyes focused on the console. He would be hidden by the moon in just a few seconds. He was thinking furiously. The tug was slowly losing speed and altitude from the action of the retrorockets. His current path would leave him lower and slower when he came back around the Moon. He tapped the computer and quickly memorized a few numbers. His heart was racing, and he could feel sweat forming in his gloves.

The sun's rays moved steadily across his suit from the motion of the tug, and the cockpit was suddenly plunged into darkness. A ghost of his reflection rose up on the backside of his faceplate through the lights of the console. He was startled by the crazed look in his eyes and the savage grin on his face but then nodded to himself and grinned broadly, showing teeth. "Yeah," he said breathlessly.

The tug slipped around the backside of the Moon, and the light indicating radar contact with Lexam Tower winked out. There was no way he could resist it. "Alright, 117, we're gonna see what you'll do." He reached out to turn off the autopilot.

It was a complex maneuver, but he could see it with crystal clarity in his mind. The tug would shoot off at a tangent to the Moon and gain altitude when he engaged the main thruster, but

Lexam was expecting to find him on his current path and would not be happy to see him several miles higher. He would need to flip the tug end for end at the top of his flight and burn the thruster at just the right angle to reinsert himself into the proper orbit—all of this before he came back into range of Lexam's radar. After that, he could flip the tug back over, engage the autopilot, and enjoy the ride home. His flight path would look like an upside-down "V" instead of a low, smooth curve, but Lexam would never know.

He flashed the docking radar overhead and forward. The path was clear, and he gritted his teeth while one hand gripped the throttle and the other hovered over the autopilot switch. The difficult part was the angle of the burn on his trip back down, and he hesitated for a moment, but he could see it perfectly—like leaning over a pool table when you just knew the ball was going to fall in the hole.

"Eight ball, side pocket," he whispered, simultaneously turning off the autopilot and slamming the throttle forward.

The effect was instantaneous, and he managed to push the throttle to only seventy percent before the force of the engine slapped him back. It probably saved his life. Tugs were not expected to accelerate at high gravities, and the pilot's seat was not designed for it.

His body slammed against the seat, knocking the wind out of him, and his head cracked against the back of his helmet. The tug didn't so much shake—it screamed. A shrill, vibrating whistle transmitted itself through his suit and into the bones of his legs and arms. His skin tingled with it, and his chest hummed like a tuning fork. He could feel his cheeks pulling back in an involuntary grimace from the force of the acceleration, and his eyes became lead balls, dropping into his skull.

With every bit of strength he could muster, Ben reached out, straining to bring his hand forward, and cut the engine.

He sat struggling for breath as black spots swam in his vision. Blinking them away, he looked at the speed indicator. "Zero to 800 in less than four seconds," he crowed and finally managed a gulp of air. "Goddamn, that was cool!"

"Now comes the tricky part." His hand shook slightly as he fired the attitude jets to tumble the tug through a little less than 180 degrees. The craft needed to point slightly into the Moon's surface before the burn, and he let it rotate slowly till something clicked in his mind, and he knew it was right.

Gently this time, he pushed the throttle forward and felt himself sink back into the scant padding as the engine noise filled his suit and grew till he could once again feel it in his bones and teeth. He could hardly breathe at fifty percent throttle, and he held it there while watching numbers on the console tumble back down. In just six seconds, he was almost back on his old flight path. Cutting the main engine, he tumbled the tug forward and sat back to take stock of his position.

There was still almost ten minutes till he came into view of Lexam Tower, and Ben hummed softly one of the tunes he had heard last night while he made a few small adjustments and polished his orbit to match Lexam's expectations.

Every fiber of his being rang with energy. He could feel it in the tips of his fingers. He could taste it in his mouth. Even the pain in his back, the ache across his face, and the sharp throbbing of his eyes were reasons for exultation. He replayed the last few minutes in his mind and had to choke back laughter.

"*Damn, what a ride*," he thought and clicked on the autopilot just seconds before Lexam's radar flashed the tug.

Ben unbuckled his harness and scrambled down the side of tug 117 as soon as it landed. One of the buggies was pulling up to take him back to the pilot's room, and he slipped into the passenger seat.

"You got another load for me?" he asked as they pulled away.

The driver hesitated. "I don't think so. Mr. Armstead wants to see you."

Ben contemplated this while the buggy rolled toward the airlock entrance. *What could Armstead want?* He was certain the tug had been perfect in the orbital slot when Lexam's radar found him. Had somebody at another tracking station called Armstead and ratted him out? It was a possibility, but companies didn't generally share tracking information for free.

Ben shifted in his seat, trying to find a comfortable position. His back ached and his eyes hurt, and he was beginning to worry. *Did I miss something?*

The buggy pulled up, and Ben cycled through the airlock into the pilot's room. With every step, a new pain came to his attention. He craved the taste of Carbodine and wanted nothing more than to run for the bathroom and the pills in his pocket, but Armstead stood in front of the office, motioning him over before he could even get to his locker.

Ben popped the seal on his helmet and placed it on the table as Armstead turned away. One of the other pilots looked at him with a peculiar expression and then averted his eyes.

What in the hell is going on? Ben puzzled as he trudged slowly to the office.

Armstead was looking at a piece of paper when Ben walked in. He lifted it up as if to hand it over, started to say something as he looked up at Ben, then closed his mouth in obvious surprise. Ben sat stiffly in the chair while Armstead simply stared at him for what seemed like minutes.

Finally, Armstead laughed and shook his head. "Boy, you are one big, dumb sonofabitch, Allspot."

"What are you talking about? I didn't do . . . "

Armstead raised one hand and laughed again. "Save it. These are your walking papers." He slid the sheet across the desk. "You can report for construction detail on Monday."

Ben felt anger well up. "You can't do this to me."

"Of course I can do this to you. Now take your paper and get out."

Ben stood up too quickly and bounced a foot in the air. "I don't deserve this. I'm a good pilot."

"You're a goddamned idiot."

Ben clenched his fists and took a step toward the desk.

Armstead stood up and leaned forward on the desk without blinking. "Come on, big boy. You want a piece of me? Give it your best shot, and I hope you enjoy it, because two hours later you'll be heading back to Earth."

Armstead slapped the table with his palm. "Come on! End your tour now. Here's a chance to go right back to what you were doing before you came to the Moon."

Ben stood with his fists at his side. "I don't deserve this."

Armstead relaxed a bit. "Of course you do. I gave you that deadhead load on purpose." He looked at Ben and laughed. "I guess you figured out that an empty tug packs a pretty good punch."

"My orbit was perfect," Ben protested.

Armstead raised both hands. "Agreed, and it was a damn good trick. I'm almost tempted to ask how you did it."

He sat back down. "If you hadn't shown up on this side of the Moon ten minutes too early, you might have gotten away with it. That is, if I hadn't gotten a look at your face before shift change."

Ben opened his mouth to protest but "Ten minutes?" was all that came out.

Armstead waved Ben to the door. "Now pick up your paper and get out. And before I hear any more about your innocence, you might want to go look in a mirror."

Ben was shocked into silence at the realization of his mistake. He picked up the sheet of paper, leaving Armstead's office without another word.

Ben stripped out of his suit, dropped it on the floor, and walked straight into the bathroom. It was empty, and he pulled out a Carbodine tablet, biting into it as he turned to the mirror. The sight confused him at first. Who was this frightening hulk of a man? "Holy shit," he said.

The skin of his cheeks was reddened as if from windburn, and there was a small, crusty patch of dried blood under one of his nostrils.

But it was his eyes that held his attention. It was his eyes that were going to cause people to turn and stare as he walked by. The flesh, in a circle around each one, was puffy and already turning dark—the pupils dilated as always—but the whites were bright red with ruptured vessels. He looked as if he could cry tears of blood.

He palmed another pill and swallowed it whole without turning from the mirror. Grimacing with pain, he bent to wash the blood from his face and used his hands against the sink to push himself back up. Now that all the excitement was over, he hurt from head to toe. It was, he decided, time to go to the infirmary for some anti-inflammatories and some pain medicine.

Chapter Twenty-eight
Surface of the Moon
Lexam Complex Infirmary
May 20, 2061

Ben hobbled out of the clinic but increased his pace as soon as he was around a corner. Things weren't all that bad. He was going to take a big pay cut to work construction, but it was still more than twice as much money as he could have made on Earth. It was Friday night, and he had pockets full of pain pills and Carbodine.

He took the transit tube to his barracks and regaled all the men with his story about the tug and how he had decided it was too dangerous to fly them. "Construction work is the life for me," he said. "It might not be as much money, but at least I'll get home in one piece."

The men took one look at his eyes and could only agree.

Ben had plans. Consolidated Helium would be jumping tonight, and he didn't want to miss it. He took a shower, ate dinner in the cafeteria, and then swallowed an anti-inflammatory, a Carbodine, and three pain pills in one gulp.

By the time he arrived at dome three, level four, he was floating. The early crowd had yet to fill the hallway, and he skated around and through the small groups, waving and smiling at the expressions of surprise when people turned to look at him. The Carbodine and pain medication was a pleasant combination. The pain pills left him dreamy and relaxed. The frenetic energy of the Carbodine high was sometimes exhausting. Right now, he felt just about right.

Believing that even a good thing could be improved upon, he stopped and crunched another Carbodine. Three people standing in the doorway of a nearby shop looked on with interest. Ben grinned at them. "Breath mint," he said.

They all laughed, and one of them raised his drink in a toast as Ben continued on his way to the Cock and Ale.

Spiral was in his usual place behind the bar, his earrings bouncing and glittering as he wiped down the counter, and Ben threaded his way through the tables with what he was sure must be an extraordinary example of poise and grace. "How about a beer," he said.

Spiral didn't so much as raise an eyebrow at Ben's appearance but poured the beer and placed it on the counter. "That's a new look for you," he said mildly.

Ben launched into the story of his near death experience—he was getting quite good at it—while Spiral quietly polished glasses and arranged bottles of liquor for the night's crowd.

". . . And I just decided to work construction instead. It's a whole lot safer." Ben drained his glass and set it down. "How about another beer."

Spiral put up another beer and took the empty glass. "So they kicked you out," he said.

Ben's laugh was a little too shrill and a little too loud. "Yeah, I guess they did. Bummer, huh."

"I guess," said Spiral, eyeing Ben carefully.

Ben was still laughing. "You're alright, Spiral."

The light of the hallway spilled into the bar as someone opened the door, and Ben turned to see Weasel walking in. "Weasel, my man," he called.

"Screw you," said Weasel and sat on a stool all the way at the other end of the bar.

Ben grinned in the dim light. "Ah now, buddy. This wouldn't be about last night, would it?"

"You're damned right it's about last night." Weasel stopped when he got his first look at Ben. "What in the hell happened to you?"

"I had a little run in with a tug."

Weasel waved him off. "I don't even care. Spiral, could I have a beer?"

Weasel pointed across the bar at Ben and asked Spiral, "Did you hear what this asshole did last night?"

Spiral served up the beer. "I heard," he said impassively.

Ben got up and walked over to where Weasel sat with his hands around the cold glass. "Come on, Weasel. Let me buy you a beer."

"I can buy my own damned beer," Weasel said. "I don't need nothin' you got."

Ben laid his hand on Weasel's shoulder, but Weasel shrugged it off.

"Lighten up, Weasel. I was just having a little fun."

"A little fun! I could have been killed. Not to mention all the business I used to do in that club. Notice I said, 'used to do.'"

Ben stood there with the smile fading from his face. "Jeez, Weasel, take it easy. It's Friday night. Let's party."

Weasel took a sip of his beer and spoke without looking at Ben. "I ain't partyin' with you no more, Ben. You're too god-damned wild. Why don't you go someplace and party with your Carb-head buddies."

There was silence for a few seconds, and everyone in the bar turned to watch the exchange. Ben felt anger boiling up like a black tide. He reached out and spun Weasel off the barstool. "You're going to take that back," he said in a low voice.

Weasel stood there, dwarfed by his old friend. "I ain't ta-kin' back shit," he answered. "You used to be a nice guy, Ben. It used to be fun hangin' around with you. We've had some good times. But you are way too deep into the stuff. You're actin' crazy, and you don't even know it. Fun is fun, but you don't know when to quit, and you need to quit."

"You're going to take that back, or I'm going to kick your ass."

Spiral stood, still as a rock, both hands on the bar.

"You're too screwed up to kick anybody's ass," Weasel said. "Look at you. You're standing there swayin' back and forth, and you don't even know it.

"How long you been on the stuff, Ben? You were strung out before you got to the Moon, weren't you? I should have known it. You were too damned eager. Is that why you came up here? Is that why your wife and kids moved to Shreveport?"

Ben let out a bellow and launched his best punch. Weasel blocked it with his arm, but the force sent him sliding on his back across the barroom floor. The combination of drugs and the Moon's gravity caused Ben to bounce backward against the wall.

Spiral eyed Ben and spoke with a smooth, even voice. "Fighting on the Moon is an altogether different sport, Mr. Allspot."

Weasel scrambled to his feet and looked at Spiral who nodded once. "He's yours, Weasel."

Weasel kept his body close to the floor and took one long step before pushing himself into the air. He turned halfway around in mid-flight, and his heel caught Ben squarely in the forehead.

It wasn't the worst shot Ben had ever taken, but his head bounced back and cracked solidly against the metal wall. He slumped to the floor, and Spiral bounded over the bar, picking him up by the back of his pants and carrying him like a rag doll to the door.

"Make way," Spiral shouted, and the crowd parted in front of the door. "If you like seeing people fly around," he grabbed Ben's shirt, and using both hands, heaved Ben hard enough to throw him in an arc across the hallway, "you ought to love this." Ben slammed into the far wall and landed in a heap.

Spiral looked at him as the crowd gawked. "Don't come back till you're clean," he said and walked back into the bar.

The crowd gathered around to watch as Ben tried with little success to regain his feet. He was stunned. "Goddamn," he grunted, "Weasel just kicked my ass."

Chapter Twenty-nine
One Billion Miles from Earth
June 10, 2061
8:42 AM CST

Space is stretched and warped here—each bit of mass making a dimple in the fabric of space-time. The dimples vary in size and depth according to the amount and density of the mass, and they interlock. In complex dances, bowls of gravity great and small extend into each other, pock marking the taut skin of space into a dented ruin.

Nor can these bowls rest, or the mass at their center, for that is the rule here. Relative motion is mandatory. Two pieces of matter may slide together and become one—forming a larger bowl, or they can dance—borrowing angular momentum from the time of the system's creation to move in great elliptical waltzes.

Four black cylinders glide silently through this region of tortured space. Some time ago, they blended normal matter with its opposite in a brief but violent marriage and translated the resulting energy into velocity. Momentum, the daughter of their velocity and their mass, has rendered them largely immune to the twists and turns of space-time. Their paths are relatively straight—even here.

The cylinders, with beautifully crafted eyes, can see the smooth rolls of interlocking depressions formed by the presence of matter. They have been told to watch the larger ones and to listen. A ball of matter, large enough to have pulled smaller masses into orbit around it, is nearly directly in their path, but it has no song and is ignored.

In all of this system, only one ball of matter sings in the proper key with the long electromagnetic waves of radio. In all of this system, only one of the many gravitational bowls is of interest.

Clamped around each cylinder, four smaller cylinders sit and watch, but they cannot see the folds of space-time, and they have no ears for listening. Beautifully crafted, but narrow of vision, their eyes see only the smallest slice of radiation. It is the slice emitted by objects with excess thermal energy.

This place is cold in its distance from the sun, and the smaller cylinders have been carried billions of miles through a silent darkness. Having nothing to look at, they have had no thoughts—till now.

Two brilliant points of heat bloom into being one after the other. The large cylinders, with their equally narrow vision, cannot see them, but the smaller cylinders are instantly aware. The points are tracked, and calculations are made. The distance is measured.

One of the small cylinders detaches itself from its mother and accelerates away at nearly 100 gravities. The other small cylinders watch and wait.

The lone small cylinder burns almost all of its available fuel—it has no intention of returning—and activates small jets along its side. The jets impart a spin to the cylinder, and they burn till the cylinder is rotating at nearly 80,000 revolutions per minute.

The cylinder, moving rapidly and spinning furiously, checks its alignment with the nearest of the hot points and carefully marks the distance. The point changes direction and speed several times, and the small cylinder tracks with it, burning more fuel reserves to maintain alignment. At just over one hundred thousand miles from the target, the front of the small cylinder opens, releasing a net with weights around its edge.

The net, responding to the rotation, spreads out across nearly 200 miles of space. It is made of extremely strong material. It is moving very fast.

Space is indifferent to all of this. The mass of even the large cylinders is hardly enough to make the smallest dip in its fabric. But there is someone watching intently. And though they will have to wait a few hours for the photons of this encounter to reach them, their attention does not waver.

Chapter Thirty
NASA Central
June 10, 2061
10:20 AM CST

Mission Control was tense. The long-awaited rendezvous of the Alpha 2 with the four "alien objects" was at hand, and technicians were busily calibrating data feeds from every satellite and detector at their disposal. Adding to the tension was the presence of the military personnel, conspicuous in their uniforms, manning several of the workstations. These men and women with their close-cropped hair and stiff demeanor had displaced eight regular NASA workers, and a certain amount of culture clash was inevitable. Neither group was comfortable.

The military technicians focused their efforts on two sources of information: The Alpha 2 and a Chinese probe called something that roughly translated as "The Defender of the People." NASA personnel, when they were being polite, simply called it "The Chinese Probe."

A lot had happened in the 23 days since the alien objects had changed course. Close analysis of the data received after the course correction had revealed a small and quickly diminishing heat signature from each of the four objects. It had been enough to verify the objects' velocity and trajectory and had confirmed the speed at over three million miles per hour and the target as Earth.

Armed with this information, NASA could compute with precision the exact location of the alien objects at any given time. It had drastically narrowed the area of space they needed to survey and allowed them to focus their detectors and telescopes on the needle in the haystack. Disappointingly, the exact speed, location, and direction of the objects was, as yet, all they knew.

The heat signature had faded below detectable limits within a few hours, and tightly focused radar scans had proven only that the objects were invisible to radar. They seemed, in fact, to be invisible to everything, absorbing all incident radiation and reflecting back nothing. NASA was reduced to watching with high-powered telescopes for the brief flickering of the background as the objects eclipsed one star after another in their blind rush toward Earth.

The United States government, needing to reassure the people that something was being done, had admitted the presence and current mission of the Alpha 2. The Chinese government, not to be outdone, had admitted the existence of their own similar probe. In a gesture that would have seemed unthinkable just 24 days ago, the two governments had agreed to share data from the two probes in real time. Somewhere on the other side of the world, Chinese technicians were pouring over information from the Alpha 2 just as the military personnel at Mission Control were interpreting a direct feed from the Chinese Probe.

The two probes had left Earth at almost identical times and with nearly identical accelerations. They were now at rest relative to Earth and approximately three million miles from the closest alien object. At current speeds, the objects would pass the probes in about one hour, but the probes had been programmed to turn and accelerate back toward Earth at maximum thrust before the objects arrived. This would give the probes more time to view the objects as they flashed by since their velocities would more nearly match that of the objects, but 30 minutes of acceleration at 10 gravities was all that either of the probes could handle, and they would nearly be out of fuel when it was over. The two probes would achieve a velocity of nearly 400,000 miles per hour relative to Earth after the engine burn, but the objects would still flash by at a relative speed of over two and one half million miles per hour. There was not going to be much time for close observation.

So the atmosphere in Mission Control was tense, and in the back of everyone's mind was the knowledge that the alien objects would arrive at Earth in just 16 days.

The three large screens on the wall of Mission Control were almost completely blank but for a background of stars. The middle screen was a view from the Sagan Telescope, high in orbit above Earth and targeted precisely on the position of the two probes and the four alien objects. The center of the middle screen revealed the presence of the objects in the form of stars winking out and reappearing as the telescope moved around the Earth.

The left-hand screen was a view from the telescope aboard the Alpha 2. It too was blank except for a small area to one side, which rendered the radar from the Alpha 2 as a "picture in a picture." The Alpha 2's radar showed one blip to the right, indicating the Chinese probe's position nearly 1,000 miles away.

The right-hand screen was the view from the Chinese probe's telescope and radar, and it was identical to the view from the Alpha 2 except that the radar blip recording the Alpha 2's position was on the left side of the picture in a picture. Neither the American nor the Chinese radar showed any sign of the alien objects.

A large box with glowing, block numbers was in a countdown above the middle screen. It showed just four minutes 37 seconds and clicked down to 04:36 as Rick looked up. In less than five minutes, Mission Control would watch the two probes initiate their burn, and if all went well, they would see the four alien objects pass between the probes one hour and ten minutes later.

General Laurence sat at his usual workstation to Rick's left and leaned back to pull the headset off and rub the back of his head. "This is amazing," he said.

Rick looked over. "Hmm?"

The General gestured at the radar views in the left and right-hand screens. "Look at that. I can't believe there are four objects less than three million miles from the Alpha 2 and we can't see the smallest blip. I don't know about the Chinese, but we've got some damned fine radar these days. We should be able to see a basketball at this distance." He settled into his chair and scowled at the screens.

Rick cupped his microphone with his hand. "Maybe they're smaller than a basketball."

"You don't believe that anymore than I do." The General drummed his fingers on the desk. "I guess I don't sit and watch very well."

"Feeling a little helpless, General?"

The General glared at the screens without turning. "Damned right I am. No action to be taken. Nothing to be done. It's like watching a movie."

"Except that we've all got a stake in how it turns out," said Rick. "But unless we can figure out a way to speed up light, all we can do is look into the past at something this far away. Whatever happened has already happened, and what we're about to see is over and done.

Rick pushed a few keys on his computer, in effect looking over the shoulders of some of the technicians. "I hope the Alpha 2 is well programmed for contingencies," he said, "because there's not a whole lot that can be done about events that occurred two hours ago."

"She's got the finest artificial intelligence in the world," said the General, "and I'm sure the Chinese Probe is reasonably good," he paused, "but this is a hell of a way to fight a war."

"Who said we were at war?" asked Rick.

"Nobody, yet."

Rick nodded and turned his attention to the information on his terminal. General Laurence's statement summed up the feelings of almost everyone familiar with the scant facts concerning the alien objects, and public opinion was swinging strongly in the same direction.

For over three weeks, Rick had been pummeled with questions for which he had no good answers.

"Would asteroids be visible at this distance?"

"Yes."

"Would comets be visible at this distance?"

"Yes."

"Are these objects of natural origin?"

"We don't know."

"What are these objects made of?"

"We don't know."

"Are these objects of extraterrestrial origin?"

"We don't know."

"What is the mass of one of these objects?"

"We don't know."

"What would be the effect of an object weighing 100,000 pounds impacting the Earth at this speed?"

Unthinkable.

The stock market was in a downward spiral from which it would not quickly recover even if the objects disappeared overnight. Industrial productivity had dropped drastically worldwide, and many businesses had failed or were in the business of doing so. There had been a run on banks in the U.S. and elsewhere, and the United States, along with several other countries, had found it necessary to step in and regulate withdrawals.

Travel was up, as people went to visit relatives and long-lost friends; consumer debt was exploding with a sense that it didn't matter; the price of gold and other heavy metals was through the roof; crime was sharply on the rise; and food shortages were beginning to appear even in the affluent countries, as people hoarded canned goods and other nonperishable items.

And in all of this chaos, people found religion in droves. Churches were swelling with new members and new money. It had been said the alien objects were the best things to happen to organized religion since the appearance of Moses, Buddha, Jesus, or Mohammed.

The Third United Literalist Church, with a well established network and a gospel of retribution and damnation, seemed to have been planning for it all along and was well positioned to be the prime beneficiary of world-wide fear. There were Literalist flyers in the windows of almost every building in Houston, proclaiming the arrival of the Rapture, and there was no escaping their presence on radio or TV while commercials and talk-show appearances of the more prominent Literalist ministers peppered the airwaves. Many Literalist congregations had taken to meeting in stadiums or on hillsides to accommodate the huge crowds, and their coffers were swelling with the billions of dollars for which some people felt they would soon have no need.

In a little over two weeks, the alien objects would arrive at Earth unless they could be stopped, and no one knew what they were bringing. Very few still believed it was going to be good news.

Rick keyed his computer and looked at the clock. It read 00:45. "Ms. Lindsay."

"Sir?"

"I've got all green here. Are we finished with the calibrations?"

"Yes, sir. We are right on schedule."

He could see her across the room, scurrying back and forth like a mother hen. "You might as well sit down and relax, Ms. Lindsay. This should be an interesting show."

She continued moving from one technician to another. "I've got just a few more things I want to check."

Rick let her go. There was no stopping her anyway. "I guess she can catch the reruns," he mumbled to himself.

The clock hit 00:30 and Rick set his headset for general broadcast. "Heads up, ladies and gentleman. We have 30 seconds and counting. Remember, the countdown is only an estimate of when our probes should begin their acceleration. It could be off by a few seconds either way."

Rick cleared his microphone and slouched down in his chair, chin in hand. All eyes were on the clock above the middle screen, and as it ticked off the final seconds, Mission Control became ever more still and quiet till only the soft hum of computer fans could be heard. Even Ms. Lindsay stopped and stood like a statue near the right-hand screen.

The clock hit 00:00, and for perhaps two seconds nothing happened while every person in the room held their breath.

A bloom of light popped into being on the middle screen. Simultaneously, the right-hand screen, with its view from the Chinese Probe, showed a large plume of fire erupting from the back of the Alpha 2. The background of stars on the left-hand screen began to shake as the Alpha 2's camera vibrated from the acceleration.

A cheer went up, and before it could die down, another bloom came to life on the middle screen as the Chinese Probe fired its engines. Now the right hand screen shook from the Chinese Probe's acceleration, and the left-hand screen, from the vantage point of the Alpha 2, showed the flame of the Chinese engine spearing back into space. The cheer redoubled in the control room. Both of the probes were now headed toward Earth at their maximum thrust of 10 gravities. The alien objects were rapidly gaining on them and would sail by in just over an hour.

The cheer subsided quickly as technicians hunched over consoles to check calibrations against the new incoming signals. Ms. Lindsay resumed her frenetic hunt-and-peck search for someone or something that might not be exactly right. General Laurence stroked his keyboard and mumbled in a singsong voice, "She's looking good. She's looking very good."

Rick settled back and watched it happen. Nobody was going to need him unless something went wrong, and his eyes roved back and forth across the large wall. Twin points of light were visible on the middle screen from the flames of the two probes' engines, and the two side screens were almost perfect mirror images, each one a vibrating background of stars broken only by the long, thin light of fusion exhaust from the Chinese and American probes as they watched each other race neck and neck toward Earth.

For almost ten minutes nothing happened. It was just enough time for everyone to relax, and the entire room jumped when there was a soft chime through the headsets. "Unidentified radiation source," the computer announced.

There were now three spots of light on the center screen. The new one, dim and visible against the stars only by its strange, blue color, was directly between the two probes. The two side screens echoed the phenomenon with a better view of a pale blue light, nearly out of the camera angle at the very edge of each screen. The clock read + 11:17

Rick stabbed his keyboard. "Ms. Lindsay, I want an energy level and a comparison of the radiation fingerprint to the course correction recording ASAP."

"Yes, sir."

Rick covered his microphone and leaned toward General Laurence. "General, you've got a better chance of getting an accurate speed and trajectory by triangulating the data from the two probes. We'll concentrate on identifying the source."

"We're on it now," said the General.

"It might just be another course correction," said Rick.

The General hands moved across his keyboard, and he looked anxiously at the terminal in front of him. "I don't believe in coincidence of that magnitude, Mr. Jelton."

There was nothing Rick could say. He didn't believe it either.

"Mr. Jelton."

"Yes, Ms. Lindsay."

"We are refining the data with multiple scans, and the radiation from our two probes is complicating matters tremendously, but this is definitely a different engine than the ones we saw three weeks ago."

Rick gritted his teeth for a moment. "You're sure this is not the lead object."

"Not unless it has changed engines or modified its engine in some way. The radiation fingerprint shows a huge spike at 500 million electron volts. Whatever this is, it's burning almost straight antimatter."

Rick digested that and then turned to the General. "It's not the lead object."

General Laurence frowned. "You're certain."

"Completely. It's a different engine fingerprint."

The General shook his head. "I don't get it. It originated at the precise point where the closest alien object . . ." He stopped in mid sentence, stared off into space for perhaps a second, then jumped to his feet. "Oh crap! It's a missile!"

"Right," said Rick, hitting his computer once again. "Ms. Lindsay, fine tune that radiation signature. We need to be certain this isn't one of the objects."

"Working on it, sir, but this fingerprint looks completely different. I really do believe it's object number five."

Rick heard the General snort in disgust and turned to listen.

General Laurence stood over his desk, holding his earpiece and glaring at the tight group of his personnel near the center of the room. "Not possible," he said. "Recalibrate, recheck, I don't care what you have to do, but I want the right numbers, and I want them now."

"We don't think the lead object has moved," said Rick. "Do you have a speed on the missile yet?"

"It's accelerating," said the General, "but they're trying to tell me it's already jumped ahead some 10,000 miles."

Rick looked at the clock above the center screen. It read + 14:21. "General, if you'll send that data to my console, I'll have Ms. Lindsay take a look at it."

The General hit several keys. "Done."

A new window full of numbers popped up on Rick's screen, and he called to his second in command. "Ms. Lindsay, I've got some data on the fifth object from our two probes. We need velocity, acceleration, and trajectory, and we need them now."

"Yes, sir. We've confirmed the difference in engine emission, and the total energy output appears to be slightly lower than what we saw three weeks ago."

"Have someone else work on the energy calculations. I want you on the speed and trajectory problem."

He could see her across the room, looking at the numbers from the two probes as it spilled across her screen. "This looks unlikely," she said.

"Hard numbers, Ms. Lindsay. I need hard numbers."

"Yes, sir."

Rick turned to the large wall screens, and as he watched, the fifth object became perceptibly brighter. He had to restrain himself from calling Ms. Lindsay. She had enough to keep her busy as it was.

"Mr. Jelton," it was the General, and he looked shocked. "We are showing the fifth object as accelerating at 100 gravities plus or minus ten gravities. The trajectory is directly at the Alpha 2, and its current speed relative to the Alpha 2 is approximately four million miles per hour."

Rick didn't know how to respond. It seemed impossible that any object could accelerate at such a pace. He looked up and saw the clock clicking through + 17:58. He rolled the numbers around in his head for a moment. The alien objects were traveling at three million miles per hour. If the fifth object had started at that speed, then it had gained one million miles per hour in a little under seven minutes.

The General stood helplessly clenching his fists while his eyes flicked from the wall screens to his terminal to his personnel.

"It's already happened, General Laurence," Rick said. "This information took almost two hours to get to us. Like I said before, there's not a whole lot we can do about events that occurred two hours ago."

The clocked blinked off nearly 15 seconds while the General simply stood with his fists at his sides. Barely audible, he whispered, "I just wish I was there."

Well that's one of the differences between us, Rick silently wondered. It didn't seem to Rick that the near vicinity of the Alpha 2 would be a particularly healthy neighborhood right now.

"Mr. Jelton?" Ms. Lindsay's voice was hesitant and soft in his ear.

He looked across the room and saw her standing with a calculator in one hand, looking back over her shoulder at him. Her eyes were wide. "What do you have?" Rick asked.

"I show 100 gravities of acceleration, target is the Alpha 2, and current speed," she looked at her computer and punched the calculator, "is four and one half million miles per hour. Distance to the Alpha 2 is just over two million miles"

"Thank you, Ms. Lindsay. That confirms the General's numbers. See if you can figure out why it brightened up a few minutes ago."

"Yes, sir."

"We confirm your numbers, General. It is closing fast on the Alpha 2."

The General nodded and pointed at the left screen. "We're finally picking up something on this high dollar radar."

Rick could see a faint smudge in the radar window from the Alpha 2.

The General continued, "And it looks like our radar is better than the Chinese." There was nothing showing on the right screen from the Chinese Probe. He pushed at his earpiece and listened intently with a steady frown. "They're telling me the radar is picking up ions from the fifth object's exhaust. The object itself is still not visible."

Rick pointed to the screen on the right, where a hazy dot had formed on the Chinese radar. "We've got a weak echo from the Chinese," he said.

There was a voice in Rick's ear. "Mr. Jelton."

"Yes, Ms. Lindsay."

"We have no explanation for the increase in brightness. There was a corresponding increase in energy across a large band of frequencies that closely resembles the radiation fingerprint of the fifth object, but it is not a perfect match. The fifth object has not increased its acceleration as a result of the increase in energy output."

Rick looked across the room at her and raised both his hands to his sides with the palms up, clearly asking for more information or some kind of explanation as to what the object was doing with the extra energy. Lindsay shrugged her shoulders and returned the gesture.

Rick muttered, "Damn," and sat back down, tapping his hand on the desk and feeling helpless. The General paced back and forth behind his own desk with a snap and turn that made Rick think of marching bands, and everything remained the same for several minutes—the General pacing with a military precision, and Rick tapping his desk while he wondered idly about the average blood pressure in Mission Control.

There was a sharp intake of breath in the room, and Rick looked up to see the view on the left screen shifting wildly. The General stopped and looked. "She's taking evasive action," he said. "The Alpha 2 is running." He listened for a moment. "The Alpha 2 has turned directly away from the Chinese Probe and is now accelerating at a right angle to its previous course."

Before Rick could ask the question, Lindsay's voice came through his earpiece. "The Alpha 2 has turned away from the Chinese Probe. We have the fifth object at nearly six million miles per hour and less than one million miles from the Alpha 2."

The clock read + 27:18.

"Anything else?" asked Rick.

"The fifth object decreased its energy output to previous levels," she paused, "there was no change in acceleration."

There was another pause. "Just a minute, sir."

Rick sat sitting on his hands and rocking back and forth with frustration.

"Sir, the fifth object has adjusted course. It is chasing the Alpha 2. We will have impact in less than ten minutes."

There was a roar from Rick's left. "Damn it!" The General had just been advised of the fifth object's course correction.

The radar images from the two probes now showed a large smudge from the ion trail of the fifth object, and the camera on the Chinese Probe clearly demonstrated the Alpha 2 in full retreat as a bright circle of fusion exhaust. As Rick watched, the radar images of the ion trail faded. On the center screen, the view from the Sagan Telescope now showed only two spots of light—one from the Alpha 2 and one from the Chinese Probe.

"Sir, the fifth object has cut its engines."

"What the hell is this?" Rick said to no one in particular. He looked at the General, who stood with his arms crossed on his chest.

"This," said the General, "is a perfect strategy."

"I don't get it," said Rick.

"The fifth object is on an intercept course. The Alpha 2 won't be able to see it now except with the infrared detectors. An offensive missile without infrared detectors would be receiving an all clear signal. The Alpha 2 will see it and will continue to dodge."

The left screen shifted again.

"Sir, the Alpha 2 has changed course downward into the plane of the ecliptic."

There was a brief burst of light from the fifth object.

"The fifth object is still giving chase."

The left screen shifted again, and Lindsay's voice was in his ear. "The Alpha 2 is moving off at a 45 degree angle," she paused as a burst of light came from the fifth object, "the fifth object is tracking."

Suddenly, the vibration ceased on the left screen, the view from the Sagan telescope showed only the exhaust of the Chinese Probe, and the camera on the Chinese Probe confirmed the silence of the Alpha 2's engine.

"She's cut her engine," said the General. "She's got to be almost out of fuel." He pursed his lips and considered the situation. "The Alpha 2 will probably coast along her current path till the missile is right on top of her and then accelerate at full thrust along a new heading. The missile will miss her on the first pass, but she's going to be dead in the water pretty soon." He shook his head. "The Alpha 2 is going to be space-junk unless the missile runs out of fuel before she does."

The clock read + 31:03, and the Chinese Probe cut its engine in accordance with its program as it too ran low of fuel. The three screens in Mission Control now looked much as they had before any of this had started. There was no light but the background of stars, and the only thing showing on radar was the mirror image of blips as the American and Chinese probes scanned each other. But now, somewhere unseen, the fifth object was closing on the Alpha 2 at over five million miles per hour.

The radar screen from the Alpha 2 went black just before the entire left screen blinked and turned to the random snow of a blank TV station.

"The Alpha 2 has ceased all transmission."

"She's gone to stealth mode," said the General. "If the missile can't see the residual heat from her engines, she may get out of this yet."

"Time to impact, Ms Lindsay?"

"Approximately one minute. Distance should be about 100,000 miles."

Rick and the General stood behind their desks. All chatter ceased as technicians froze into position while the clock ticked off the seconds. Once again, the only noise in the room came from the soft hum of computer fans.

With thirty seconds to impact, a bright spot appeared from nowhere on the Chinese radar. It was closing with incredible speed on the Alpha 2.

"What the hell is that?" Rick blurted.

Even Ms. Lindsay had no answer, and the room began to fill with the muttering of people as the spot grew rapidly. It now had the form of an oval and continued to spread out as they watched. Rick could even see the gauzy, spreading oval on the view from the Chinese Probe's camera. Smaller, but still visible, was a rapidly growing, hazy circle on the center screen as the Sagan telescope recorded the unfolding events.

There was a flare of light as the Alpha 2 fired her engines, and the Chinese radar showed several small spots in her wake as she accelerated.

"She's jettisoned everything she's got," said the General. "Her maximum thrust should be around twelve gravities."

Lindsay spoke. "We've got the Alpha 2 headed back along her previous trajectory at emergency speed."

The oval continued to spread.

"She's not going to make it, sir. Whatever that thing is, it's expanding too fast. We're going to have impact," she paused, "now."

Light splintered across both of the active screens as the force of an unknown object traveling five million miles per hour shredded the Alpha 2. On the Chinese radar, the blip of the Alpha 2 changed from a sharp point in front of the oval to a diffuse fog of matter behind the oval. All of it now moved rapidly along the path of the expanding circle, and it was soon carried off screen.

The General stood without moving, and Rick was about to say something when the computer chimed in his ear. "Unidentified radiation source."

A new spot of blue light bloomed on the center screen and on the camera of the Chinese Probe.

"Sir, it is identical to the fifth object. Trajectory appears to be the Chinese Probe."

The General simply nodded. "I never would have believed I'd find myself cheering for a piece of Chinese hardware—but Godspeed. I hope she does better than we did."

"Distance to the Chinese Probe, Ms. Lindsay?"

"Barely over one million miles. It's going to happen a lot faster this time. I show eight minutes to impact."

The right-hand screen died as they watched.

"The Chinese Probe has ended transmission."

Mission Control went silent once again as everyone watched the center screen. A lone spot of blue flame across an unwavering backdrop of stars was the only indication of the sixth object.

For several minutes, no one moved or spoke as the sixth object brightened and dimmed just as the fifth object had. Finally, a plume of light could be seen as the Chinese Probe fired her engines.

A subdued cheer spread around the room, but the game of cat and mouse was only beginning.

"The sixth object is tracking as expected."

Twice more the probe turned, only to be followed by the sixth object, and then, without warning, four smaller sources of light split off from the Chinese Probe, heading directly back toward the sixth object.

"We have four objects separating from the Chinese Probe and accelerating toward the sixth alien object."

"Those goddamned bastard Chinese have fired missiles!" exclaimed the General, but there was a wild grin on his face. "Come on, baby."

A gossamer circle began to grow in front of the sixth object, and Lindsay's voice continued the commentary. "The spreading object has been launched. We will have impact in less than five seconds."

Four flashes of light indicated contact of the Chinese missiles with the spreading object as they were reduced to scrap metal and a cloud of dispersing vapor. Less than two seconds later, a fifth and final flash indicated the destruction of the Chinese Probe.

Silence, broken only by a few muffled sobs, settled slowly over Mission Control. Rick could see the hunched shoulders of several of his technicians shaking as they wept. Lindsay was already consoling one of them, and Rick should have done something, but he was stunned into immobility. Should he stand up and tell them not to worry, it's just the end of the world?

The General had his hand pressed firmly to his earpiece and was listening closely. "Yes, sir," he said. "I understand, sir. We will be there within a few hours."

He turned to Rick with a grim expression. "I hope you've got a bag packed, because we're leaving."

"Who?"

"You, Mr. Jelton. We're going to Washington."

Rick threw his hands in the air. "No way. Do you realize how much data we've collected over the last 45 minutes? It's got to be checked, rechecked, enhanced…"

"You're wanted in Washington."

"I don't give a damn who wants me in Washington. I've got a job to do in Houston."

"Fine," said the General. "I just got off the phone with the President of the United States. Maybe you'd like for me to try and get him back on the phone. That way you can explain why you can't make it to this meeting."

"The President?"

"Of the United States," finished the General.

"I'd like to bring Ms. Lindsay."

"No problem. We leave the building in ten minutes. There is a military jet waiting at the airport, and a police escort has been arranged."

Rick hit his keyboard. "Ms. Lindsay, You and I are leaving for Washington right now."

"Sir?"

"Right now, Ms. Lindsay. Get Mosley and Rogers to form up teams for the enhancement of the data. Bring your laptop. I want that data encrypted and sent directly to your computer." He turned to the General. "We'll need Internet access while we're aboard the plane."

The General was speaking in a low voice into his microphone and simply nodded in Rick's direction.

Lindsay looked bewildered. "Right now?"

"We leave in nine minutes."

Chapter Thirty-one
The Planet Harmony
Exact Time Unknown

The dreams of Trees are complex and vivid. The fusion of three young to form a single adult produces a large, multi-lobed brain, and the need for motor neurons is reduced considerably by the rooting of the mature Tree. The areas of the brain once concerned with walking are subsumed by the new structure and given new functions.

And the Trees may sleep—when they sleep—for weeks or months. It is not an idle time. As with many species, the dreams of Trees are a time for correlation and tabulation of recent input. Many breakthroughs in Mathematics and Physics have sprung from ideas generated while a Tree slept, and they have a saying that "A dream may extend the reach of even the firmly rooted."

So the old Tree slept and dreamt, but his dreams were troubled, for they recalled, in the manner of Tree dreams, his last conversation with the young Koombar.

He stood in the dream, as he had for over 400 years, in his glade. Not a breath of wind stirred the grass or the brush around him. None of the young were present, and not even an insect moved. Time, as he watched, began to march forward rapidly. Hours blinked forward in the twinkling of an eye, and seasons advanced with ever-greater speed till he saw thousands of years pass while he stood without moving. Still, nothing moved in this dream.

Each blade of grass, each leaf, was frozen in place, and the old Tree felt a horror descending upon him.

He struggled to move his arms and could not. Something was coming, perhaps the end of all time, and he stood like a rock, powerless before it. The glade remained as it was, nothing changed, and the sun flickered like a strobe light.

He looked down and saw a large red crystal in his forward hands. The crystal shown with the light of the racing sun, throwing crimson rays all around, and he could see into its heart. There were small lines inside the crystal and flat planes intersecting and splitting apart, growing ever smaller as he looked deeper, and he knew they went on forever. He knew there was no end to them.

A voice came from nowhere. "What color is this crystal?" it asked.

"It is red," he said.

"Are you certain?"

"Yes."

"Then turn it over."

The Tree struggled to turn the crystal to no avail. Although it was large, as large as one of his children, it felt weightless in his hands, but no amount of twisting or turning would allow him to move it and see the other side.

"I cannot turn it," said the Tree.

"Of course not," said the voice with a tone of disdain.

"How then can I see the other side?"

"If the gem cannot be turned, then the Tree must move to see it fully."

Tree pleaded. "But Trees cannot move."

"And others have paid your price," said the voice. "Behold."

Suddenly the old Tree found himself looking with his forward eyes at the back of his glade. It was terrifying. For four hundred years, his forward eyes had looked east down the hill to where the road passed by in front of him. The road was now visible only with his other eyes, and his forward eyes looked toward the back of his glade where the mountains rose to the west. He had been turned around 180 degrees, and nothing was the same.

The Tree screamed in fear. "No! This cannot be."

"Behold the gem."

Tree looked down and saw that the gem was blue. His fear left him as he looked in wonder.

"What color," asked the Tree, "is this crystal?"

"Can you not see that it is blue?"

"But it was red before."

"It is red still."

The Tree stood looking at the intricacies within the crystal for some time, and the years continued to flash by while nothing moved. "How then can a Tree know the color of a crystal?"

"The Trees cannot," said the voice, "unless they are willing to teach their children to look where they have not dared look before."

There was a flash of movement, and the Tree saw that a wind had sprung up. The grass bent before it, slowly at first, but vibrating with energy as the wind grew into a gale and began to strip the glade bare. Brush was ripped from the ground, and the world thundered with the raw power of a primeval force. He felt himself spinning, looking first east then south and west and north and east again, and the crystal flashed as he turned—red, then blue, then green, then every color of the rainbow in a scintillating dance of light.

The wind stopped and Tree saw the glade naked but for the bare ground. New growth began to spring from the earth, and the Crystal turned in his hand. He rolled it over with his forward hands and saw that it was white but with large black imperfections.

The dream ended, then began again in slightly different form, and for almost a year, as the Tree slept, the dream replayed itself.

The Tree awoke in the twilight of the day and stretched his arms over his head. His deep root shook violently—the equivalent of a yawn—sending vibrations through the ground that could be heard for hundreds of miles around by other Trees. Within a radius of five miles, even the young could feel the noise in their feet, and they came running.

The old Tree was alone for a short time, and he looked about his glade, half expecting to see it frozen in place. *A tiresome and troubling dream.*

The first of the young burst from the foliage to his right and came charging full tilt up the hill. The Tree wrinkled his noses with pleasure and braced himself as the child leapt through the air to land spread eagle in the Trees forward face. Tree caught the child and threw him high in the air with a laugh and a shout. "Hello, little one."

The youngster chirped with delight. "Father, father, you have come back to us," he squealed. "You were asleep for so long."

The woods rustled with the movement of young Trees, and soon the old Tree was covered with children as they climbed up his arms and sat on his head, tickling his noses with their tails.

A game ensued, and for over an hour, as the sun set, the young scrambled up one after another to hold the highest position while the rest pushed and pulled to bring them down. The old Tree caught them as they fell and placed each one gently on the ground. The dream faded into a background of childish laughter and warm fur against his face.

He shook them off. "That's enough for now. What news is there? What has happened as I slept?"

"We fixed the harvester," said one.

"Skrin has asked to be notified when you awake," said another.

"Humph," said the Tree, "Let it wait till morning. He will not venture out tonight. Anything else?"

One of the older children at the back side of the glade spoke. "You are pregnant again."

"What!" Tree looked at the area of his trunk directly opposite his mouth. There was a small bulge approximately two feet above the ground.

He was surprised. It had been some time since he had given birth, and although it was not unknown for Trees of his age to bear children, it was unusual.

The dream came back to him. "…unless they are willing to teach their children to look where they have not dared look before." What did this mean? Was he to teach this child differently, and if so, how?

His pregnancy *did* mean he was going to live a bit longer. Trees never found their final dream while they had young children to attend.

"Well, well," he said. "You are all going to have a new brother."

"New brother," said one of his children. It was echoed across the glade by another child. "New brother." Yet another child caught the words and repeated them. "New brother." The words bounced back and forth across the glade and then fell into a chant as all the children cried out in unison, "New brother. New brother. New brother."

Tree held up his arms to quiet them. "It is getting late. Children should sleep each night."

There were groans of displeasure, and several of the children flopped down on the ground in disgust.

"I will tell you a new story in the morning, and we can play. Is there anything else that has happened?"

"Just one thing, father," said one of the children as he picked himself up off the ground. "A probe has come from the antimatter generator and sent information to the Koombar."

Tree wrinkled his eyes with dismay. Children simply had no sense of proportion. "Run along, all of you. I have business to take care of."

"What kind of business?"

"It is not for you to understand."

The children scattered, and Tree listened with his deep root. As usual, there was a lively discussion in progress—it went on all the time—but he usually tuned it out.

An adult Tree could not normally be found any closer than a half mile from its nearest neighbor. The young, when they came together to form an adult, had a strong inclination to find a quiet place away from other adults. This served to insure that the root-bound adults would not crowd out the available food supply, but it also meant that they could only communicate by vibrating their deep root. The resulting sound waves carried for miles through the ground and would be heard by neighboring Trees in a rough circle around the speaker.

Trees had a near reflex tendency to repeat whatever they heard, and ideas would spread across the land in ripples of underground vibration, through soil and rock formations from one Tree to the next like the circles from raindrops on a still pond till an entire continent might hear the single thought. Good ideas traveled far, while bad ideas tended to damp out quickly.

And the roots of Trees grew ever longer with age. The older Trees could be heard for hundreds of miles as their long roots boomed out their opinions. The younger Trees could not speak as loudly or hear as well.

Tree listened. The probe had sent the information only a few days ago. It was meant for the Koombar, but of course the Trees had monitored it.

He sighed with the news. The Koombar had found another one. It was the third such in his lifetime, and he knew how the Tree discussion would go: expressions of dismay, followed by questions of what to do, ending with a decision to do nothing.

Tree pulled up the raw data from the probe on a holographic display in front of him. The glade flickered with its light as he scanned through the information, but something struck him as strange about the coordinates of the find, and another display bloomed into life on his left. He wrinkled his eyes at the numbers and performed a few simple calculations.

The results caused him to draw in a sharp breath. He double-checked the numbers. There could be no doubt.

"I have news," he boomed with all his might.

He rarely engaged in discussions with other adults anymore, but he was well known for his age and insight. They would be a little surprised to hear him speak, but they would know his voice.

He heard his name repeated by the nearby adults first then by those farther away in a slowly diminishing echo. "Kismayan has news. Kismayan has news. Kismayan has news."

There was near silence for a moment, and the old Tree savored it before he spoke. What he was about to say would rock the Tree world.

Chapter Thirty-two
NASA Central
June 10, 2061
11:00 AM CST

The next thirty minutes was a whirlwind of activity as Rick and Lindsay were hustled from the building and rushed to the airport amidst flashing lights and screaming sirens. Rick slumped in the back seat of the staff car and looked out the window as buildings flashed by. The streets seemed oddly quiet for lunchtime on a Friday, and they twice passed small groups carrying signs warning of the coming of the Rapture.

They don't even know the half of it, he thought.

They boarded a small jet that began taxiing down the runway before they could get their seatbelts buckled, and they were airborne within seconds. Lindsay sat next to the window and plugged her computer into a socket in the armrest. Rick looked over her shoulder, watching as she logged on to NASA's database and verified the encryption. He wondered, not for the first time, what he would do without her.

Marilyn Lindsay was a small woman with thin, straight brown hair and had never been seen without a pair of wire-framed glasses balanced precariously near the end of her nose. She might have been cute in a mousy sort of way if she had taken the effort, but Ms. Lindsay, as Rick called her except when he was wheedling something out of her, seemed to go out of her way to appear completely sexless. The glasses were a part of her persona, and when Rick had suggested she have her vision corrected, she had looked over her glasses and politely but firmly informed him that she would never undergo surgery for the sake of vanity.

She dressed in starkly simple pantsuits and had a habit of pulling her hair back in a small bun. Rick had never heard her speak of a boyfriend or a girlfriend, and for all he knew, she had no social life whatsoever. Her office was empty of any clues except for two small pictures of a niece and nephew on her desk alongside a slightly larger picture of a nondescript dog. She had graduated cum laude from a prestigious university and immediately gone to work for Rick. It was the only job she had ever had.

When he remembered her, Rick saw her sitting at a desk in a white lab coat, hair pulled back and a pencil behind one ear, peering over the top of her glasses at him. She was a genius, a tireless worker, and totally devoted to Rick Jelton.

He found it tiresome at times, but she had saved his ass on so many occasions he had lost count, and after eight years of working together, their relationship had become symbiotic. The question of who needed who was now meaningless.

Rick leaned his seat back as the plane made a banking turn, closed his eyes for a moment, and went to sleep without a warning of any kind.

He awoke with a start and lunged against his seatbelt.

"Are you okay?" asked Ms. Lindsay.

Rick rubbed his face with both hands and looked around the plane with his eyes wide. "I feel a little disoriented," he said. "I can't believe I went to sleep like that. What time is it?"

Unconsciously, Lindsay answered his real question. "You've been asleep over an hour. We'll be in Washington soon."

He stretched and rolled his head back and forth. "Hmmm. I wonder if this thing has coffee."

"Soft drinks only. Should I get one for you?"

"Nah, I'll wait till later."

Lindsay's laptop was open in front of her, and Rick could see a schematic of the latest encounter on the screen. "What have we got?" he asked.

"It's interesting. I assumed you were going to make a presentation of some kind and concentrated the efforts of the team on enhancing the video and radar images. I then had Mosley put together a computer-generated version of what we believe happened. The graphics are a little crude, but we haven't had much time." She looked at her watch. "We need to go over this now if you feel up to it."

"No time like the present," Rick said. "Let's see what it looks like."

Lindsay started from the beginning and was still going over the reports and conclusions when the plane landed in Washington. They were hustled onto a helicopter, and Rick hardly noticed any of it as he and Lindsay continued their back-and-forth, question-and-answer brainstorming of the data till they landed on the White House lawn.

When they emerged from the helicopter, blinking in the heat and sunlight, Rick could see a crowd of people milling about just outside the White House grounds. Signs with Literalist slogans bobbed and moved above the iron-barred walls as they were escorted directly into a side entrance, and a shout floated across the compound. "Are you ready, brother?"

They were scanned and searched after a brief argument concerning Lindsay's computer—an argument General Laurence won by brute force—and guided through a maze of hallways, down an elevator, and into a large room with an oval table at its center. It was twice the size of the meeting room at NASA and included a large computer screen on the left wall. President Bremmer sat leaning to the side at one end of the table as Secretary Salness spoke in his ear, and what appeared to be the entire Cabinet along with the Joint Chiefs of Staff filled most of the available chairs. Muttered conversation echoed back and forth through an air of urgency and gloom, and not a smile could be seen. Several of those present displayed the pale complexions and hollow eyes of lost sleep.

The President saw Rick enter the room and stood up, beaming with the boyish grin that had cost the Democrats an election. "Mr. Jelton, it's a pleasure to see you. I'm glad you could make it on such short notice."

The power of the man was such that Rick felt for an instant he'd actually had a choice in the matter. "Thank you, Mr. President." He gestured to Lindsay. "This is my associate, Ms. Lindsay. I have asked her to accompany me here."

The President turned the spotlight of his attention on Lindsay. "Ah, yes. Marilyn, is it not? I have heard about your work at NASA. Excellent, truly excellent."

Lindsay turned bright red and stammered a reply. "Thank you, sir, but we just follow Mr. Jelton's lead."

The President laughed. "Of course you do." He winked at Rick. "She's a good one, Rick. I hope you pay her well."

"As well as I'm able, sir."

The President chuckled and sat down. "Nice point, but we're not here to negotiate budgets." He looked at the General. "General Laurence, it's good to see you. I believe we are all here. If you could find a seat, we will begin."

Rick pulled out a chair and leaned over to Lindsay, whispering as they sat down, "I need to know the muzzle velocity of a high-powered rifle in miles per hour," he said.

She opened her laptop and began tapping at the keys. "Yes, sir."

There was a scuffing of chairs, and the President waited till everyone had settled down. "Mr. Jelton, you are the one with the information. I think we would all like to know what caused us to lose a 20 billion dollar, military probe this morning."

Rick cleared his throat and stood. "Yes, sir. It would help to explain things if Ms. Lindsay could broadcast graphics from her computer to the wall screen."

Lindsay was typing rapidly. "I believe I've found the connection, Mr. Jelton. This should do it." She hit one final key, and NASA's logo, rotating against a background of stars, bloomed into life on the side wall.

Rick wondered, *How does she do that*, but continued without a hitch. "As I'm sure you are all aware, we have been tracking four objects of undetermined origin for the last three weeks. These objects are currently on a course that would take them behind Earth as we travel in our orbit, but we expect a course correction in the next week or so. This course correction will adjust for the movement of the Earth and retarget the objects on Earth's current position. They are traveling at over three million miles per hour."

Lindsay tapped her keyboard, and the screen on the wall changed to a tightly focused view of the Solar System. Mars and Earth were the only visible planets, but four white "X's," labeled one through four, indicated the location of the alien objects.

"These four objects are becoming more separated in space as they near us. The lead object, designated by the number one, is moving slightly faster than the other three and is now several million miles ahead of the next two. The last object is several million miles behind two and three.

"Within hours of the first course correction some three weeks ago, the United States directed the Alpha 2 to an intercept position. We now know the Chinese sent a similar probe at the same time. Coordination with the Chinese government allowed us to post the two probes so that the four objects would pass between them."

With a few taps, Lindsay showed the Alpha 2 as a blue "X," and the Chinese Probe as a red "X." A white line, indicating the trajectory of the four objects, materialized between them.

"Since the objects are traveling at such a high velocity, they would pass between the two probes very quickly, and there would not be much time for close-up observation. With that in mind, we planned to have the Alpha 2 and the Chinese Probe accelerate toward Earth at maximum thrust for thirty minutes. This would deplete their fuel but would give them a speed of 400,000 miles per hour relative to Earth. The velocity of the probes would make the speed of the four objects roughly two and one half million miles per hour relative to our probes and would give us a little more time for gathering data as the objects passed by."

The President interrupted. "It sounds like running down a race track to get a better look at a dragster."

"Somewhat, sir. It increased our viewing time by only 16 percent, but it was considered significant."

"Continue, Mr. Jelton."

"All was going according to plan till about eleven minutes after the engine burns. At that time, we detected an unknown source of radiation. This source proved to be a fifth object accelerating at 100 gravities away from the number one object."

"Wait a minute," said the President. "I'm not up on all this gravity business. How does that compare to our current technology?"

Rick considered it for a moment. "Well, sir. The Alpha 2 was capable of twelve gravities acceleration under emergency conditions with all extra cargo jettisoned. The real problem is the weight of the fuel and the weight of the engine. It would take a very large fusion engine to generate that kind of thrust, but an engine that large would be very heavy. The heavier the craft, the more fuel it would take to achieve a specific acceleration rate. I'm not sure if it is theoretically possible to make a fusion-powered rocket that could pull 100 gravities, but even if it could be done, the thing would run out of fuel in a few minutes. And the more fuel you carry, the more the craft would weigh."

Rick looked around the table. "Perhaps the military has done some experiments in this area."

Secretary Salness coughed discreetly. "We have reason to believe it is not possible."

Rick shrugged his shoulders. "We have data indicating these objects are using some kind of antimatter drive. One of the beauties of an antimatter drive is the efficiency of the fuel source. Rather than carrying hundreds or even thousands of pounds of He_3, an antimatter rocket needs only a few grams of fuel to carry it long distances or to achieve high accelerations.

"At any rate, the fifth object achieved a velocity of nearly five million miles per hour over a very short period of time and tracked the Alpha 2 through several course changes. The Alpha 2 ceased all transmission and cut its engine, waiting for the object to approach, then accelerated at emergency thrust when the object was very close. It's an excellent strategy to avoid a conventional missile, but the object cast out what we believe was some sort of expanding web."

There were grumbles from around the table, and Rick held up his hands. "Please bear with me. I know this sounds strange, but I will show you some video later that will back up this idea."

The room settled down, and he continued. "This web expanded quickly to a diameter of some 200 miles, and the Alpha 2 was destroyed on contact."

The President looked skeptically at Rick. "You're telling me the Alpha 2 got tangled up in some kind of web?"

"Not tangled up, sir, pulverized. The Alpha 2 was torn into small pieces."

"Wait a minute." The President looked at Secretary Salness and then at General Laurence. "I was told this Alpha 2 had some kind of Titanium alloy skin and could survive a direct shot from a small missile. Now I'm being told she was torn to bits by some kind of outer space web."

Salness squirmed a bit in his seat, and Rick considered letting him try to field the question. "Yes, Mr. President," said Rick. "You have to consider the speed this web was traveling. For example, a bullet from a high-powered rifle weighs only a few grams, but it can do a tremendous amount of damage by virtue of its velocity. This web was traveling nearly five million miles per hour when it hit the Alpha 2. By contrast, the muzzle velocity of a good hunting rifle is more like," he looked down at Lindsay's laptop where a single number blazed across the entire screen, "2,300 miles per hour. Sir, even a net made of fishing line, traveling at five million miles an hour, would have destroyed the Alpha 2."

There were a few nods of assent around the table, but most of the audience looked skeptical. The President seemed unconvinced, but he watched the group carefully and finally leaned back in his chair with his elbow on the armrest and his chin resting on his fist. "Okay. Go on."

"The Chinese Probe came to the end of its burn and cut its engines just prior to the destruction of the Alpha 2. Within seconds of the Alpha 2's destruction, a sixth object was launched. It too accelerated at 100 gravities, but its target was the Chinese Probe.

"The chase was not nearly so long this time because the number one object was over one million miles closer to the Chinese Probe when it launched the sixth object, but the particulars of the chase were similar. The Chinese Probe dodged and turned, went into stealth mode, and was eventually destroyed by another expanding net. Before she was destroyed, the Chinese Probe launched four missiles at the sixth object."

There was pandemonium at the table. The President and several of his closest advisers had obviously been briefed on the Chinese missile attack, but most of those present were shocked by the information, and outrage echoed in the room for several seconds while the President sat quietly with his fingertips forming a steeple in front of him.

President Bremmer rapped his knuckles on the table. "That's enough, ladies and gentleman. We can express our displeasure at the actions of the Chinese through diplomatic channels at a later time. Right now we need information.

"And what, Mr. Jelton, was the effect of the Chinese missiles?"

"There was no effect, Mr. President. The Chinese missiles struck the net and were destroyed just seconds before the net destroyed the Chinese Probe."

The meeting once again erupted with expressions of disbelief and anger, but the President quieted the group by frowning and looking daggers around the table. He turned to General Laurence. "Tell me a little bit about this Chinese Probe. Did the Chinese instruct it to attack?"

General Laurence hesitated. "Yes and no, Mr. President. It is important to understand that the event took place over one billion miles from Earth. Both light and radio waves take almost two hours to travel this distance. With a two-hour lag time, it was impossible for the Chinese or us to give any meaningful instructions to our probes. We were both relying on the Artificial Intelligence of the probes to respond to unforeseen circumstances.

"Having said that, I should point out that the Artificial Intelligence aboard a probe must be programmed with certain criteria for action. Something, or a combination of things, triggered the Chinese Probe to attack. The Chinese Probe had seen the Alpha 2 destroyed, and was being pursued by an identical object. It is likely, and perhaps understandable, that this set of circumstances brought the Chinese Probe to an attack decision."

"Very well," said the President. "Now, Mr. Jelton, if you could explain the reasoning behind this expanding net idea."

"Yes, sir. There were two observations for which we had no immediate answer."

The screen on the wall changed to a recording from the Chinese probe. A pale, blue flame showed the fifth object during the early part of its pursuit of the Alpha 2. A digital display in one corner was ticking through + 15:01.

"The time indicated is minutes from the initiation of the Alpha 2's engine burn. The fifth object did not appear until eleven minutes after the Alpha 2 began accelerating.

"If you'll watch closely, you'll see a distinct brightening of the fifth object about … now."

On cue, the object brightened.

"This brightening was recorded by the Alpha 2 as well as the Sagan telescope. Several other detectors registered an increase in energy output from the fifth object. What puzzled us was the lack of change in acceleration of the fifth object. We now believe this energy was used to spin the fifth object."

Lindsay tapped away, and the screen on the wall changed to a crude graphic of a black missile with a fountain of blue flame at its tail. As they watched, small jets of blue light sprouted along the sides of the missile, and it began to spin.

"This leads us to another thing that puzzled us. The fifth and sixth objects both released what appeared to be a net of some kind. This net quickly expanded to cover a circle 200 miles in diameter. It was, at first, difficult to understand why the net would spread so quickly, but if we assume the objects were rotating at several thousand revolutions per minute, the centrifugal force would be sufficient to cause the net to open in the same way that a cowboy might keep a lasso open by spinning it in the air."

On the screen, a small hatch opened in the front of the missile, and a rotating net expanded as they watched.

"We have some enhanced video clearly showing stars faintly visible through the opening net. These stars were more easily seen as the net expanded. Although we cannot see the individual strands of the net from this distance, it seems likely that whatever destroyed our two probes and the Chinese missiles was an open structure of some kind.

"I can show you that video if you would like."

"That won't be necessary," said the President.

The rotating net remained on the screen and there was silence around the table as everyone stared at it in fascination. Rick gestured to Lindsay, and the picture was replaced by the original view of the Solar System with Mars, Earth, and the white "X's," labeled one through four.

It broke the spell, and President Bremmer surveyed the table. He spoke slowly and bit his words. "And now, ladies and gentlemen, what, pray tell, are we going to do? We have just sixteen days to figure it out."

Rick sat down as everyone clamored for the President's attention. He listened for awhile, but it was a depressing business. No one had a clue what they should do next, or if anything could be done, and what was going on around the table was mostly posturing and dominance games. Rick found his mind wandering, and his gaze came to rest on the computer screen occupying the wall to his left. The spheres of Mars and Earth floated against the stars. He could see the Southern Cross, and the white line of trajectory slicing through and between the orbits of the two planets. His vision blurred, and his mind was far away.

It was in this dreamy state that something began to bother him about the line of trajectory. He came around slowly and frowned at the screen. He was missing something.

Lindsay was in rapt attention to the conversation around the table, and Rick tapped her on the shoulder.

"Yes, sir."

"Can you bring up this view," he pointed to the wall screen, "on your laptop?"

"Certainly."

With one click, it was done, and Rick leaned sideways to get a better look at it. His eyes went from the wall to the smaller screen in front of Lindsay. He wasn't sure why two views of the same scene should have made a difference, but an idea began to form.

He touched the laptop screen. "Bring this forward in time. I want to see how things will line up a few days from now."

Lindsay clicked away, and everything began to move as Mars and the Earth rolled slowly around their orbits and the four "X's" streaked across the system in a straight line. A small box in one corner displayed the date. June 12, June 13, June 14 rolled by, and Rick reached out a hand. He could feel the small bones of Lindsay's shoulder through the fabric of her coat.

"That's it! Hold it right there." He studied the computer display for a short while. "Okay, I'm going to need you to roll the main screen forward in the same way when I give the signal."

Lindsay studied the screen. She was beginning to see it too. "Yes, sir."

Rick stood and raised his voice, nearly shouting above the bedlam. "Mr. President, I may have an idea."

All heads turned, some of them with angry expressions, and the President raised both his hands. "It would be nice if somebody did. Proceed, Mr. Jelton."

"Thank you, sir. One of the problems we are faced with is a complete lack of knowledge concerning the motives of these objects. We don't know what they want or what they are going to do."

There were derisive snorts from around the table, and someone spat out, "It looks pretty goddamned obvious to me."

"That's enough," said the President, "let's hear him out."

"I understand the sentiment. I watched this morning as two probes and four missiles were destroyed by the actions of the number one object alone, but it's possible these objects viewed our probes as a threat."

There was more noise around the table, but Rick continued. "We need something to test the intentions of these four objects. We need a decoy."

Rick pointed at the wall screen. "What you see is a representation of the position of the Earth, Mars and the four objects as they are now. In sixteen days, the objects will arrive at Earth. They will pass very close to Mars in just fifteen days."

Rick nodded to Lindsay, and everything on the screen began to move. "We are now looking forward in time from today. The box in the lower right hand corner displays the date."

Mars and the Earth crawled around their orbits while the four objects raced through the Solar System. The box in the corner changed to June 14th and stopped. Mars was almost touching the white trajectory line.

"Here is the interesting opportunity," said Rick. "If the objects do not make a course correction, Mars will come between the objects and the Earth four days from now, partially eclipsing their view of us."

He stopped for a count of three to let that sink in. "I believe we should have the expedition on Mars turn their satellites outward and begin hailing the four objects before this happens."

Half the room nodded while half the room shouted. The President sat expressionless, but his eyes darted around the table.

Secretary Salness raised his voice. "We hailed these things from the Alpha 2 for three weeks with no results."

"The Alpha 2 was not a planet," Rick responded.

The undersecretary of the Navy shouted loudly in a sarcastic tone. "You are willing to sacrifice the Mars expedition?"

Rick felt anger rise in him. He leaned forward and put both hands on the table. "I am not willing to sacrifice anybody. I count several members of the Mars crew as my friends. Sacrificing personnel is a military prerogative."

The President rapped on the table to restore order. "Enough," he said.

The raucous debate ebbed, but slowly, and the President slammed his fist on the table. "Enough!"

There was instant silence, and President Bremmer turned to Rick. "This is an interesting idea, Mr. Jelton. What do you foresee happening if we pursue this?"

"I see three possibilities, sir. The objects may ignore the hail and simply continue to Earth—in which case we have lost nothing. If they turn to Mars, we will learn what they want. If it is good news, then all will be well regardless.

"But if they intend the destruction of this planet, we may see them expend all of their resources on Mars. At the very least, sir, we will have gained a little time and learned a little about how they operate."

The President spoke quickly, cutting off comment. "Does anyone see a downside to this?" He stopped and frowned. "Other than the possible loss of the Mars crew?"

Everyone at the table seemed to be looking back and forth to see who would speak, but there was silence except for the rustling of clothing as people shifted in their seats.

"Very well then," said the President. "Let it be done." He looked at Rick. "Thank you Mr. Jelton." There was a hesitation as he looked at the screen on the wall. "And may God show mercy to your friends on Mars."

Chapter Thirty-three
Surface of Mars
June 13, 2061

Tom would have trudged down the hall to Ki's room, but the light gravity of Mars made trudging almost impossible, and he bounced lightly despite his mood. He stopped at the open door and watched Ki scribbling in a notebook. Everything in the room was, as always, perfectly in place, and the joyful Buddha looked down from the bookcase to where Ki worked at his desk.

Tom tapped the doorframe. "Knock, knock."

Ki turned in his chair and attempted a smile. The result was anything but cheery. "Come in, my friend." He gestured to the bed. "Have a seat."

Tom stepped across the room and slumped to the bed where he sat with his shoulders hunched and his hands on his knees.

"It has been a long day," Ki said. "I'm sure you must be tired."

"Yeah, kind of."

It was obvious Tom had something on his mind, but Tom couldn't easily be pushed into action even when it was something Tom wanted. Ki had learned from experience that it was usually best to sit and wait for his friend to make the first move.

Tom picked at the cover on the bed for a while and then looked up. "Why don't you use the word processor?"

"Excuse me?"

"Why don't you use the word processor for your notes?"

Ki looked at his notepad. "Oh. I do. This is a personal journal. Most of what goes in here is not for publication."

"Too personal?"

"Too personal and too . . . " he searched for the word. "Too poetic I guess. Very little of it would make sense to anyone but me."

Tom nodded. "Maybe I should keep a journal."

"I find it helpful," said Ki.

Tom changed the subject. "I'm getting a little worried about Cochran. He seems to be isolating himself from the rest of the crew, and he shows no real interest in his work. In fact, he doesn't seem to be interested in anything except video games."

Ki pursed his lips. "I've noticed it too, but we're under a great deal of pressure. He may simply be going through a period of adjustment. It's hard to realize we've only been here a little over two months with everything that's happened. He may come out of this on his own."

"Maybe," Tom said, "but I want to switch some of his duty assignments. He's been working with Dr. Krazinsky for the last three weeks straight. I'd like to put him with Melancon, but Melancon is a computer and equipment guy—there's no reasonable way to get them together."

Ki considered it. "I suppose it won't do any harm. Why don't you place Cochran with Melancon as much as possible. Talk to Melancon about it. We can trust him to be discrete. You don't have to go into too much detail. Just tell him to start asking Cochran for help when he needs it. We may find that Mr. Cochran is not a bad cook."

"That might work," said Tom, "and I can get him to help Espanoza part of the time."

"Carlos will not like it."

Tom grimaced. "Carlos Espanoza doesn't like anything I do."

Ki chuckled. "True."

They sat in a silence that grew weightier as the seconds clicked by, and finally Ki gently asked, "And how are you feeling, Tom?"

Tom let himself fall back across the bed till his head bumped against the wall. His chin came down on his chest, and his arms fell limply at his sides. "Like I don't want to get out of bed in the morning," he said. "It's hard to see the point of what we're doing anymore."

"The alien objects?"

Tom stared dully across the room and took a deep breath, letting it out slowly. "You've seen the reports. Two probes snuffed out and the objects didn't even slow down. The best technology mankind has to offer—destroyed by defensive weapons capable of 100 gravities acceleration, and they're headed straight for Earth."

"We may yet find a way to stop them," said Ki.

Tom snorted. "Come on, Ki, it's not like I'm a complete idiot about this sort of thing. I've spent way too much time thinking about it, and I don't see a way out. Their mission is the destruction of Earth, and we don't have the science to stop them."

"We have no proof of their intentions."

Tom shook his head. "Give me a break. I don't need any more proof than what I've already seen, and neither does anyone else. Have you looked at the stock market figures lately?"

"There have been significant economic repercussions," replied Ki mildly.

"Significant economic repercussions," Tom spat out. "You make it sound so clinical. It's a goddamned panic. Take a look at consumer debt. Take a look at productivity. People are staying home from work and buying luxury cars just because they've always wanted one, and nobody's worried about paying for it."

Tom sat up straight and slapped the neatly made bed with his open palm. "It's worldwide panic, Ki. And what are we supposed to do? We can't get off of Mars on what's left of the Mars I. We're stuck here!"

He paused and then blurted without thinking, "And Mars is probably a whole lot safer than Earth."

His eyes flicked to the pictures of Ki's wife and children on the bookcase. Ki sat stone faced in his chair without speaking—he was the only member of the crew with immediate family on Earth.

Tom flushed red and stammered, "Ah, jeez. I'm sorry, man. I . . . I just . . . I didn't mean . . . Look, I'm sorry. I wasn't thinking."

Ki blinked hard and looked at the pictures. "It's okay, Tom. This has affected all of us. I know it's difficult to understand why we should continue our work, but what else can we do? The

Mars Expedition can do nothing to save Earth, and although I will admit it doesn't look good, we may yet survive and so may the Earth."

Ki brushed his left eye with one hand. "Consider this. Any reasonable, objective observer would have written off humankind not once but on a number of occasions. Plagues, famine, war—even the Mid-East Nuclear Conflict of 2010—we survived them all and became stronger."

He gestured to the Buddha above his desk. "It is in times like these that a man's faith can sustain him. I know you don't share my views in this, but I have a belief that mankind was meant for something more. Something I don't understand. We seem to pull ourselves out of the most impossible situations with an almost unconscious resilience. I don't know how we will avoid destruction from the alien objects, but I believe we will, and so should you."

Tom shook his head and looked at the floor.

"Oh, Tom," Ki said, "of all people, you, the engineer with nine career lives, should believe in the impossible."

Tom smiled in spite of himself. "I *have* survived some pretty horrendous mistakes," he said.

"Remember the time you told NASA's chief engineer to shove it up his fat . . . "

"Ass," finished Tom with a grin. "And the next day he gets caught for selling technology to the Chinese." He shook his head again and looked up at Ki with a wry expression. "It was pretty amazing."

"It was impossible," said Ki. "It should have ended your career at NASA, and yet you are here on Mars."

"Only with your help," Tom said.

Ki shrugged his shoulders. "You are here because you are the best, and because, as your friend, I can sometimes overlook the fact that you're a jerk."

Tom laughed. "Okay, I deserved that."

Ki reached out and briefly touched Tom's shoulder. "Tom, you are my friend. Your friendship is important to me, and I know that deep down it is important to you too. Let us not forget that."

Tom made a face and shivered in mock disgust. "You know I hate all that mushy crap."

"That's why I do it," Ki said with his most innocent smile.

"Alright, I give up," said Tom. "I'll put on a good face for the troops."

"Good," said Ki. "You'll be fine. You're just suffering from that…" he struggled with the memory, "that snaky thing."

Tom looked puzzled for a moment. "Oh," he said, "snake bit."

"Yes. You fear we are snake bit."

"Yeah," Tom said, "but before all this, I thought it was just the Mars crew."

Ki looked at his watch and slid his notebook into a desk drawer. "It is time for our staff meeting."

Tom rose slowly from the bed. "This should be fun."

"Tom," Ki said with a frown.

Tom raised his hands in surrender. "I know. Stiff upper lip, good face in front of the troops and all that."

Commander Thon and Tom Fielder walked down the hall to the dining area without speaking further. The rest of the crew was seated around the table, and the conversation died as they entered.

The Commander put on his best smile and walked around the table to his customary chair with Pamela Krazinsky and Carlos Espanoza to his left and Kaitlin Geller to his right. Tom sat across from them between Evelyn Weiss and Adrian Melancon. Mike Cochran was a discrete but noticeable distance down the table to their right.

"I know you are all tired from the day's work," Commander Thon began "I don't want to take a great deal of time with this. However, we have been working very hard in our separate areas for over three weeks now. There has been a lot of talk back and forth across the dinner table, but we have not taken the time to sit down and tell each other about what we've found. Let us begin by having a member of each team give a very brief synopsis of the important findings to date. I want to encourage each of you to speculate freely. We can go into more detail and weed out the bad ideas later."

He looked to his left. "Dr. Krazinsky, you have been doing some excellent work with the core drillings from the ice cave. I'm sure we would all be interested in hearing why we are in no danger of catching the Martian Flu."

Dr. Krazinsky cleared her throat and spoke without standing. "Thank you, Commander. It has been fascinating work, and I want to thank Mr. Cochran for his help and Car… Mr. Espanoza for the time he has been able to divert from the greenhouse project."

Espanoza smiled, but Cochran was leaning back in his chair and staring at the ceiling. It was impossible to tell if he heard what was being said.

"As you all know, we have been able to isolate and grow some primitive, one-celled organisms from the ice-core samples. As yet, we know almost nothing about these organisms except that their respiratory cycle is strongly anaerobic. In fact, one of the difficulties in obtaining viable cultures has been the need to eliminate all oxygen from the growing medium. Trial and error has proven that even a few parts per million of oxygen are deadly to Martian bacteria.

"And this is not surprising. Everything we know about Mars tells us that gaseous oxygen was never present in abundance. Free oxygen is highly reactive and very useful if you have evolved the means to take advantage of it, but it is deadly to those organisms that cannot use it. Anaerobic bacteria on Earth are killed by oxygen. On Mars, we believe all life was anaerobic.

"This is why we are in no danger of being infected by these bugs. They are extremely sensitive to oxygen and will die instantly if mammals such as ourselves were to drink them, inhale them, or even inject them directly into our bloodstream.

"The Martian bacteria appear to be using Iron and Sulfur to extract energy by oxidizing Sulfides to Sulfates. Changing the valence states of Sulfur for respiration isn't unknown on Earth and is well represented by Thiotrix bacteria and other genera. Undoubtedly there was something in the ecosystem of Mars to reverse this oxidation just as algae and trees use up carbon dioxide and renew the oxygen in Earth's atmosphere. We haven't yet found what did this on Mars."

Dr. Krazinsky looked around the table to see if anyone had questions. Cochran was still staring at the ceiling, and she frowned in his direction. "Are you still with us, Mr. Cochran?" she asked.

"I was there when we did the work," he said without changing position.

Tom shot a glance at Commander Thon who shook his head no in an almost imperceptible move. This was not the time or place to take care of the problem.

"Very well," said Dr. Krazinsky. "Moving into the area of speculation, it's interesting to consider how this method of respiration might have shaped the lives of the intelligent, shrimp-like creatures who fashioned the tunnels in the ice cave.

"Although we have no evidence to support it, we can assume the shrimp used a similar respiratory system, and the ramifications for larger organisms are profound."

Krazinsky spoke slowly for emphasis. "Anaerobic respiration is simply not very efficient.

"If you think about life on Earth, you will realize that all large, mobile organisms use oxygen for respiration. Anaerobic bacteria are small. Plants can be large but are incapable of movement. Some plants, such as the Venus Flytrap, can move, but this movement is a once in a while activity. They must store energy for days to enable them to snap shut just once. Mammals, reptiles, crustaceans, and even flatworms use oxygen because it allows the animal to burn large amounts of energy over extended periods of time.

"Have you ever wondered why we don't have insects the size of… oh, say, a Cocker Spaniel?" Krazinsky stopped and surveyed her audience.

The crew stared back, apparently unconcerned that cockroaches could not retrieve tennis balls, and she continued. "Insects use oxygen, but they have spiracles instead of lungs or gills. Spiracles are inefficient compared to lungs and cannot move the volume of air necessary to fuel a large body. Insects weighing more than a few grams would have difficulty obtaining enough oxygen to move around.

"Our intelligent shrimp had much the same problem. Even with gills, the fundamental inefficiency of anaerobic respiration would have severely limited the maximum size of all animal life on Mars, and we can therefore be sure there was nothing on Mars comparable to an elephant or a whale. The shrimp could well have been the largest animal on Mars.

"And we can also be sure that all animal life on Mars had gills instead of lungs."

Krazinsky paused for the effect of her last statement to sink in, but it was clear she was far more excited about it than anyone else. Even Commander Thon was having difficulty feigning enthusiasm.

"You see," she said with a flourish, "neither iron nor sulfur exists in a gaseous state at anything near room temperature. We can breathe air because oxygen is a gas. Our little shrimp-like friends did not have that option, and although hydrogen sulfide is a gas, the corresponding sulfates are not. It is clear to me that all life on Mars was small and lived in the water."

Dr. Krazinsky put her hands flat on the table and smiled her perky little smile. Tom Fielder felt an urge to throttle her.

"Thank you, Dr. Krazinsky," said Commander Thon. "That was most interesting." He was beginning to get the feeling this had been a bad idea, but there was nothing to do but plow forward.

"Mr. Fielder, perhaps you could tell us what you have found concerning our cave-dwelling shrimp."

"Why I'd be happy to, Commander," said Tom. He tried with little success to keep the sarcasm out of his voice, and Commander Thon raised an eyebrow in his direction.

"Of course," said Tom, "I'd know a lot more if Rick Jelton would let me chip a few pieces of rock out of the way, but we don't want to activate the Curse of the Ancient Martians."

Ki interrupted. "If we could concentrate on the achievements instead of the obstacles, Mr. Fielder."

"Right," said Tom, and he began speaking quickly. He wanted to get this over with as fast as possible. "We stripped some fiber optic cable out of the Mars I and made extensions on the field microscope. The tunnels created by the shrimp extend into the rock face to a distance of twenty feet in some areas. If you put together the depth of the tunnels, the size of the shrimp, and the area of the walls covered with tunnel entrances; you come up with the equivalent of a good sized city.

"We found small wires imbedded in the walls of the tunnels everywhere we looked. After a little experimentation, we were able to send a small radio signal through these wires and map them by moving a detector across the rock face. This gave us a three-dimensional view of the tunnels and confirmed that they are interconnected in many places. The shrimp could have moved around the entire ice cave without leaving the tunnels.

"We also found that there are at least two separate, unconnected wiring systems. It seems to me we are looking at a power grid and a communication grid side by side. We would see the same thing if we performed a similar test on houses on Earth. One set carries electricity, and the other carries communication.

"We found several wires leading to the surface. Tracing these wires back, brought us to a room containing electronics. We salvaged this equipment and brought it back to the Lab for examination. Although the design is a little peculiar, it is obviously radio equipment.

Tom scratched at his cheek and looked thoughtful. A bit of wonder crept through his mood and into his voice. "Now that was pretty amazing. When you look at this stuff under the microscope, you can see an entire broadcasting radio in a space about half the size of a pea. Tuner, microphone, modulators, capacitors—all right there. Ms. Weiss called our shrimp 'Magicians of the Miniature.' It would have been great if they could have built computers for us.

"But anyway, we haven't found anything terribly sophisticated. The equipment looks like it might have come out of late Twentieth-Century Earth except for the design and size.

"The wire itself is kind of interesting. In fact, all the metal we found was interesting. Our shrimp seem to have found a way to cause iron to grow crystals in a particular shape. I guess it's not surprising, since they lived under water, but X-ray diffraction and crystallography doesn't show the typical patterns found by forming and forging. No doubt, they could have taught us some pretty good tricks about alloys and corrosion resistance. Every piece of wire and metal we've seen is spotless. I expect to spend a lot of time during the next few weeks trying to figure out how they did it."

Cochran made a noise at the end of the table, and several of the crew turned to look in his direction. He remained leaned back in his chair, staring at the ceiling. Tom and Ki exchanged another glance, and there was a short silence.

Tom resumed his speech but with an edge in his voice, and he spoke a little bit louder than was necessary. "Another interesting find has been the statues. It wasn't just luck that allowed us to find one on our first look into the tunnels—they are sprinkled all over the place. Each one of them has some kind of inscription at the bottom in raised letters. We've found raised letters on the walls at almost every intersection and inside many of the rooms.

"The shrimp lived in darkness, and examining the statues shows nothing that might be an eye. They don't really look that much like shrimp when you get up close. They have a large round head, completely smooth, on what I guess is the front end. Ms. Weiss pointed out that they look kind of like Beluga whales with no snout and legs along the sides instead of flippers. It's tempting to think the head was filled with shrimp brains, but it resembles an underwater sonar sensor, and I'm betting they used sonar to see.

"There is a kind of segmented structure to them. We see between seven and ten legs on each side. The three front legs are always much longer and have well-developed pincers at the end. These must be the hands. The other legs get smaller as you go back toward the tail, so maybe they grew more legs as they got older. The tail is a simple fan-shaped flipper. They aren't curved over like Earth shrimp, and the angle of the tail flipper indicates they traveled forward through the water.

"And that's all I've got." Tom ended abruptly and looked at Ki.

Commander Thon was caught a bit off guard. "Uh, thank you, Mr. Fielder. I guess I'll go next."

He remained seated, as had the others. "I wish I could tell you the geological work had gone well and that I had solved some of the mysteries of Mars. In fact, all I've been able to do is amass a large amount of confusing data.

"For example, the quartz in the ice cave has a particularly small crystal structure. The water on Mars was fairly acidic from the carbon dioxide in the atmosphere, and it is known that acidic water tends to grow smaller crystals due to the formation of silicic acid, but it is still puzzling."

Tom gritted his teeth. He wasn't sure how much of this he could stand.

"Calculations have shown that tremendous amounts of steam moving through the ice cave might have resulted in a similar crystal structure, but the numbers are not reasonable. The temperatures required are quite high, and the volume of steam equates to the total discharge of a moderate aquifer on Earth.

"The situation is not much better when we begin examining the other minerals in the cave and some of the rocks we have retrieved from various places on the surface. Although some of the rocks are quite normal, for others the standard radiometric dating processes seem to be useless. Rubidium-Strontium dating is generally useful for rocks that are around 30 million years old. This process produced no useful results with some of the specimens. The same was true for the Uranium-Thorium-Lead methods used on rocks that are about 100 million years old. I finally tried the Potassium-Argon process in desperation, and I got data, but it makes no sense.

"The Potassium-Argon method deploys the decay of Potassium 40 to Argon 40 and is used for igneous and metamorphic rocks of one million years or older." He shook his head and frowned. "The result of these tests on some rocks indicates an age of five million years or less. This is, of course, impossible, since Mars has been geologically dead for billions of years.

"I am coming to the conclusion…"

Tom was near to praying. Please come to a conclusion.

"…that something was at work here we have never seen before. Perhaps Mars had a radioactive core at some point in its past. This might have reset the radioactive clocks we use to determine the age of various rocks, but if that were the case, we would show all the rocks as having similar ages, and this is not what we have found.

"I was attracted to one rock which I found on the surface due its peculiar fracture lines. An analysis of its magnetic characteristics proved a different orientation on the surface than in the interior. This also seems impossible. And it was not the only rock I found bearing this phenomenon.

"Of course, we have no knowledge at this point of the paleomagnetic history of Mars."

Commander Thon looked at the faces around the table, and Tom realized that Ki was actually losing interest in talking about his favorite subject. The Commander was usually oblivious to the pain of his audience once he began talking about Geology, but the mood was tense, and Tom watched Ki decide that it was time to wrap things up.

"At any rate," Ki said, "there is much yet to learn. I look forward to the field trip to Olympus Mons and the many things we can accomplish before the end of our mission."

Ki very obviously immediately regretted his choice of words, and a loud clunk came from the end of the table as Cochran rocked forward and the front legs of his chair hit the floor.

"H-o-o, boy! That's rich," said Cochran loudly. There was a wild grin on his face, and his eyes were luminous under the fluorescent lights.

A stunned silence followed until Tom gritted out the words, "You got somethin' to say, Cochran."

"I don't know. Maybe I do, maybe I do." His teeth shined white between the thin lips of a mirthless smile. "I mean, what is this talk about the end of our mission. This mission isn't going to end. Am I the only one here who understands that? We're all really smart people. Hasn't it occurred to anyone else that we can't get home on what's left of the Mars I? Hasn't anyone here considered the fact that in less than two weeks there won't be a home to go to?"

His grin seemed frozen in place, but a quaver entered his voice, and he shook his head. "Earth is going to be destroyed, people. They aren't going to send a ship to bring us home. They aren't sending anymore supplies. We're going to be here till we run out of food or He_3. We're either going to starve or freeze to death. This mission will end when the last one of us dies."

A sob escaped Dr. Krazinsky, and tears ran down her face.

Tom spoke through clenched teeth. "Shut the fuck up, Cochran."

"Gentleman!" said Commander Thon, coming to his feet. "We are all adults here, and we are all professionals." His face was red. Some of the crew had never before seen him angry, and most of them dropped their heads in shock as the Commander stared them down one by one. Cochran continued to grin like an idiot.

"Mr. Cochran," the Commander said, chopping each word with a deliberate emphasis, "I am pleased to see we have a psychic among us. Since you seem so adept at reading the future, perhaps you would like to tell us exactly where these things came from, why they want to destroy the Earth, and how they are going to accomplish this feat."

The grin began to fade slowly from Cochran's face. "Well, I don't know . . . "

"Exactly!" said Commander Thon. "You don't know! You don't know what they are, where they came from, or what they're going to do, and until you do know, you can keep your speculations to yourself. Is that clear?"

Cochran seemed to deflate as they watched. As if all the air was slowly released from a balloon, he dwindled into his chair and became all but lifeless before their eyes. "Yes, sir."

Commander Thon turned to Tom. "And you, Mr. Fielder, will address Mr. Cochran in a polite and proper manner, or you will not address him at all. Is that clear?"

One of Tom's eyebrows inched fractionally upward, and he looked across the table for the smallest part of a second before responding. "Yes, sir, Commander Thon."

"Good. This is good," said the Commander, and his voice modulated downward just slightly. He straightened up and locked eyes once again with each member of the crew as he talked. "We have been sent to Mars to investigate, explore, and analyze. We will continue that mission.

"I do not share Mr. Cochran's views concerning the imminent demise of Earth. There are four objects of apparent Alien construction headed toward Earth. At this time," he slapped the table with open palm for emphasis, "that is all we know. If their intent is Earth's destruction, and I would remind you that we don't know their intent, then the Earth will deal with it. Let us keep in mind—there are only four of them."

He paused, and his voice returned to near normal. "I can assure you the entire resources of Earth are even now being brought to bear on this problem. This includes the Chinese, the Russians, all of Europe and the Americas, Africa, Australia, and Asia.

"Mankind is a rugged and resilient species." His head turned as he scanned the crew. "We are a rugged and resilient group. We were sent here because we are the kind of people who would not give up quickly or die easily, and mankind has survived to this century because of similar traits.

"I do not know who or what sent these four objects, and I don't know what they will do when they reach Earth, but my strong belief is that, if their intent is destruction, they have badly underestimated the resourcefulness of humankind.

"I, for one, believe it will take far more than four small missiles to end the history of our home planet. Whoever or whatever sent these four objects to Earth is in for a surprise, and they may find themselves wishing they had sent forty or four hundred.

"*Of course* the financial markets are upset, and of course people are running around predicting the end of the world. The sudden appearance of these objects has changed our view of the universe—we now know we are not alone. But there have always been people predicting the end of the world, and they have always been wrong. They are wrong now.

"This mission will continue to follow its mandate. Mankind will continue to do as it has always done, struggling in the face of all odds for survival—and winning."

Commander Thon sat down, grimly staring about as if daring someone to contradict him, but even Cochran seemed to be sitting up a little straighter, and after a short pause, Evelyn Weiss began to clap. The rest of the crew joined in, and a slow smile came across Ki's face as the applause continued. He held up his hands.

"Please. I had hoped to end this meeting with a report from Mr. Espanoza regarding progress on the greenhouse, but it has been a long day. Mr. Espanoza, with your indulgence, if we could cover that at some other time."

Espanoza nodded. "The work goes well. We can go over the details later."

"Very well then," said the Commander.

There was the sound of chairs scraping on the composite floor as people stood up, and Ki walked around the table to talk to Tom. "Your instincts were good," he said in a low voice.

Tom shrugged and turned his hands palm up without answering.

"Let us take a little time to read through his file again. Come to my room in the morning, and we'll go over it."

Just as Tom was about to reply, there was a soft tone over the intercom, and the computer, in its sterile voice, announced, "There is a priority one message. Download and decryption are in progress. Initial instructions read, 'Mandatory viewing. All personnel.'"

Everyone froze. Tom looked around the room. "Melancon," he called, "get Cochran back in here."

Melancon bounced quickly out of the room and down the hall of the living quarters as the rest of the crew gathered back around the table and moved chairs to face the large screen on the wall to the left of the kitchen door.

Cochran and Melancon reentered the room, and Commander Thon spoke into the air. "Computer, roll recording of most recent priority one video to screen one."

The larger-than-life image of Rick Jelton blinked into being on the wall screen. He was talking to someone off camera as the video began. His head turned, and he looked directly into the lens, giving the impression that he was staring intently at each member of the crew.

"Mon Dieu," said Evelyn, "he looks terrible."

Tom nodded his head in agreement. It had been weeks since they had heard directly from the head of NASA, and Rick seemed to have aged years. There was a gray pallor to his skin and bags under his eyes. His hair, normally groomed to perfection, had grown over the tops of his ears, and his moustache needed trimming. He sat with his tie loosened and the top button of his shirt open. He did not attempt a smile.

"This is not encouraging," muttered Tom under his breath.

"Ladies and gentlemen," began Rick, "members of the Mars expedition. I must first begin this with an apology. Commander Thon, we have no intention of usurping your authority over the mission. There was a great deal of debate concerning the question of speaking to you first. It was decided that, given the gravity of this message, we should release the information to the entire crew at the same time.

"I should also apologize for interrupting your meeting, but we are sending it now to ensure that you are all together."

Rick took a deep breath and seemed to struggle with what he was about to say. "As you all know, the American and Chinese probes were destroyed in an encounter with the alien objects just three days ago. These probes had been hailing the four objects for several weeks with no obvious results. We don't know why the objects failed to respond, but we have speculated they may only be interested in planets."

Rick knit his hands together in front of him. His elbows were on the desk and his eyes looked down and then straight back up and into the camera lens. "I want all of you to know that I take full responsibility for the orders I am about to give you. It was my idea, and I am the one who worked to see it implemented."

Rick stared in silence for a moment, and the muscles of his jaw bunched with effort as he fought to control his emotions. "In roughly 16 hours, Mars will, for a short time, come between the Earth and the alien objects. From the standpoint of the objects, Mars will partially eclipse Earth. Before that occurs, you will turn all three of your communication satellites on the position of the alien objects and begin broadcasting to them at the highest possible gain. A broadcast message is attached to this video.

"My apologies also for not giving you more warning of this order. Yours is a multinational expedition, and it took some time to obtain the consent of all the parties involved. A separate attachment to this video contains the actual order. Commander Thon can decrypt the order at his leisure. The position and tracking data for the alien objects is contained in another attachment. Mr. Melancon will need that information to properly align your broadcast satellites."

Rick seemed to relax a bit with the worst of his message behind him. "We will not be able to contact you, nor will you be able to contact us till this is over. Any broadcast from Earth to Mars would be a broadcast in the same general direction of the alien objects. An agreement was signed at the United Nations this afternoon to sequentially shut down any and all radio transmission that would be pointing from Earth toward Mars or the alien objects.

"As the Earth rotates, this process will disable twenty five percent of Earth's communication satellites at any given time. It will begin in twelve hours. All communication between Earth and Mars will cease at 0800 hours tomorrow, and any letters or videos that you wish to prepare must be sent before that time."

Rick nervously moved some papers around on the desk in front of him and spoke for a while without looking up. "I have no words to comfort you. It is our obvious hope that the objects will be drawn to Mars and will reveal their plans when they arrive there. At their current speed, their nearest approach to Mars will occur ten days from now." He looked back into the camera. "If they don't stop, they will arrive at Earth just one day later."

Rick swallowed and once again looked on the verge of tears. "Know that the thoughts and prayers of the entire world are with you. May God look upon you, and good luck."

The screen blinked to gray and a monstrous silence descended on the dining area of the Mars Expedition.

"Fucking decoy," said Cochran. "We're sitting ducks!"

No one answered, and Tom stared numbly at the empty screen for a time. "So the snake strikes here after all," he said softly.

Chapter Thirty-four
750 Million Miles from Earth
June 14, 2061

The blanket of space becomes steeply curved near a massive object such as a star, and the fabric of time curves with it. Planets, if present, tend to huddle near the star—not for warmth or light, but from the circumstances of their creation. The compaction of hydrogen that forms a star is the result of a huge gravitational depression—a sink down which all nearby matter must tumble. The basin of the sink deepens as the young sun devours the dust of its conception, and the fury of a star's fusion-driven life is sparked into being by the simplicity of a relentless compression. Hydrogen is brought closer and closer together in the throat of the basin, and finally, it gives way. Voicing its objection by ejecting high-energy photons, it sheds the identity it has known since the beginning of time. The hydrogen fuses to itself and gives birth to helium. And the process continues.

Such is the lineage of all matter.

The star will gather hydrogen, helium, dust and debris for billions of miles around, crushing it into light within its heart. But some of the dust will escape. Some of the dust and debris, in a near miss, will roll forever near the bottom of the star's basin, and other, smaller basins will form as the orbits are swept clean and planets are born.

Four, black cylinders speed down the sun's slope and into the inner system. They see the stretched and warped space extending from the planetary masses, but they do not see the planets. Their eyes, so wonderfully constructed, see with clarity the curved threads of space-time, yet they are blind to the balls of mass that have pulled the fabric into shape.

They watch, and they listen. One basin—one small depression—sings to them. Another, closer but silent, is a potential obstruction. They will move around it if the need arises, but they do not know this. Their minds are but a set of values given to them long ago—if this, then that. It is a simple statement, and it is executed simply. They do not anticipate action, they do not appreciate completion, and they cannot remember if theirs was ever a different position or a different state. Existence, to the four cylinders, consists of a series of microsecond slices of time unconnected by any common theme. No past, no future. They awaken thousands of times each second into an unknown present. Thousands of times each second, they sleep, and in sleeping, they forget.

The song of the farther bowl, the basin in space-time that has held their flickering attention since they arrived here, grows suddenly quiet—not silent, but quiet. Simultaneously, a song erupts from another, closer gravitational bowl. The new song is louder but simpler. The stuttering attention of the cylinders changes. No decision is made; no thoughts pass through their electronic brains. The position of the nearer bowl is compared to a set of numbers indicating their trajectory and speed. No action is necessary, and they sleep. Awakening again, they hear the song from the center of the nearest concavity in the blanket of space. Trajectory is checked, action negated, and they sleep. They do not remember that once they tracked a different bowl—a bowl with a song of lower volume and greater complexity. It was milliseconds ago, and they have slept.

Planets huddle close near the inner part of a star's domain. They have missed its crushing grip by the slimmest of margins. For that simple feat, they are rewarded and may bask in the sun's light for billions of years. But when the hydrogen is gone and the sun has nothing left to burn, it will expand rapidly, exploding outward with a wrath it has never shown before. Helium will be crushed together and will in turn shed its identity, and the sun, reaching out in the throes of death, will claim its wayward children for its own.

Chapter Thirty-five
Surface of the Moon
Lexam Complex Barracks
June 20, 2061

The mess hall was nearly deserted. Less than a month ago there would have been thirty to forty men sitting around the cream-colored tables eating breakfast and drinking coffee. Ben Allspot sat with six others at the table nearest the television. He shoveled down food with a fierce determination and kept his eyes on the screen, but his mind wandered. He was contemplating change.

The television displayed the morning news in a real-time video feed from Earth, and the men savored every report and picture—it would be their last word from home for some time to come.

The theme of the current story was social unrest in America. Helicopter and satellite views of several major cities showed plumes of smoke rising slowly in the wind as rioting had broken out from sporadic food shortages and a worldwide apprehension growing daily with the countdown of the objects' arrival. The announcer talked over footage of gangs roaming New Orleans and looting a deserted French Quarter, and Ben was glad his wife had taken the children to her mother's house in Shreveport.

It's a different world here and a different world there, he contemplated the changes, men and women all across the Moon stopped what they were doing to watch what might be the final Earth-to-Moon broadcast as their workplace swung into alignment with Mars. All satellite and groundside broadcasting was being shut down in a wave across the continents of Earth as it rotated, and the Earth now kept a mostly silent side turned always toward Mars. The Moon was spinning into that area of silence and would not emerge till after the missiles arrived.

The effect for those on Earth was a complete loss of all telephone, television, radio, and Internet service for six hours out of every twenty-four. Many satellites, not having been designed for intermittent use, had failed completely, rendering computers and telephones all but useless over much of the world.

But the habits of a lifetime were hard to break, and like people without electricity who constantly find themselves flicking dead light switches, the populace reached into purses or pockets millions of times each day to push numbers into inactive cellular phones.

"Out of Service" messages flashed on everything from ATM's to gas pumps, and computers, woven so tightly into the day-to-day life of industrialized nations, were quite likely to report "Server not found." Emergency functions had broken down for the lack of a dial tone, and police could only patrol the streets, looking for fires or people in need of help. A myriad of details and services, so much taken for granted for so long, had abruptly disappeared. The television announcer said that a man in Los Angeles, infuriated because he could not order a pizza, had walked out of his house and shot four people at random before being gunned down by police. Those who were not inspired to rage felt cast loose from all they had known and sat huddled in their homes with the worst of all terrors—fear of the unknown.

The loss of global communication was a cruel shock to those cultures that had for over three generations relied upon it to conduct business. Battered beyond recognition by the panic of the last four weeks, the economic markets had withered and died. In the words of one economist, "We believe that the world stock markets have collapsed, but there is currently no way to verify our suspicions."

Ben didn't care. He didn't own any stocks, and it was just fine with him if a bunch of rich assholes had suddenly become poor assholes. He took a bite of toast and washed it down with the last of his second cup of coffee. The newscast blinked several shots of various cities across the screen—I-75 in Atlanta all but deserted at 8:00 in the morning, ships waiting to be unloaded in Seattle with no workers in sight, factories in Detroit abandoned. The aggressive purchasing of luxury goods had stopped. The frenetic traveling of a month ago was now a thing of the past. People sat in their houses, praying for deliverance or trying to console each other and only occasionally parting the curtains to peer out at the empty streets.

The men in the cafeteria watched a short interview with an older woman standing outside her apartment in Orlando. The wind blew her hair into her face, and she held it back with one hand as the palm trees swayed and rustled along the street behind her. Four lanes wide, and not a single car passed while she talked.

"I'm Lucille," she said, "and I've lived in Orlando almost 15 years." She gestured at the scene behind her. "I've never seen anything like this. I used to complain all the time about the traffic noise. It kept me awake at night, you know? But now I can't sleep because it's too quiet. I'd give anything to hear the cars go by again. It's just spooky, and I can't get in touch with my children or grandchildren to see if they're okay."

Her weathered face crumbled as she fought back tears. "It was different at first. It was almost like a holiday. Now..." She sobbed, and the tears rolled down. "I'm scared. I'm so scared. I just want it to be over."

Some of the men fought back their own tears of sympathy, and Ben watched them while he ate. *I guess facing Armageddon in four weeks is different from facing Armageddon in four days.*

The announcer was saying that the situation was better in some places and worse in others. The United States, so well informed and for so long dependent on the electronic transfer of money, was among the nations hardest hit by social unrest. Sections of Chicago, Memphis, Houston, and other cities were in ruins where the thin veneer of civilized behavior had cracked under the pressures of a primal fear and a need for food, and distribution channels had collapsed rather suddenly when the news of food shortages hit the airwaves. The large corporate farms of America—so efficient at producing milk, meat, and vegetables yet so far from the industrialized centers—were now a logistical problem, but the shortages were mostly a media driven phenomenon. Cows still grazed on the plains, and wheat still grew, but those people who had not yet begun to hoard canned goods, rice, and pasta rushed out on the news of food shortages to empty the store shelves and made a truly horrifying discovery—their credit and bank cards no longer worked.

Spontaneous rioting erupted as people took what they could not buy, and the rough, raw texture of humanity's animal past was exposed. Viewing the mayhem laid bare the fear and anger of the onlookers, and disorder, fed by the increasing dread of the objects' approach, began to spread like a cancer in small pockets through the inner cities.

A truck carrying food was hijacked and overwhelmed by crowds in Chicago—the food disappearing in minutes as throngs of wild-eyed people clawed, stomped, and shot each other over boxes of cereal or crates of canned vegetables. Freight companies could no longer find drivers willing to accept shipments into North Memphis, and even the relief agencies temporarily pulled out of downtown New Orleans when attempts to distribute food incited riots where both the distributors and the needy were killed.

Martial law was becoming all too commonplace. The image on the screen switched to a recent report from Washington D.C. where soldiers in groups of no less than three could be found sprinkled throughout the streets. They stood in front of empty stores and at intersections, weighted down with full body armor and holding machine guns at the ready. They were natural targets for the rage fueling the mass psychosis of a riot, and some of them had been killed in places where carrying a bag of groceries across the street was tantamount to a death sentence. The guns were kept off safety, and fingers hovered over the triggers. The troops were young, edgy, and inexperienced. Their expressions were grim, but their bellies were full.

And so Ben shoveled his food, and watched the news, and contemplated change.

He was making more money now than he had as a tug pilot. The Moon was dependent on a constant influx of food and other goods. As the situation on Earth had deteriorated, the shipments became less dependable. Faced with declining revenues and resources, most of the companies with lunar operations closed down their businesses and sent everyone home. Everyone who was left. At the beginning of the panic, most of the people on the Moon quit their jobs or took leaves of absence to go home to their families. During the last four weeks, the population of the Moon had dropped 90 percent to below 100,000. The companies remaining had taken over various maintenance duties for those who had gone. The net result was a labor shortage, and large bonuses were paid to keep the remaining workers.

These workers, as they watched the last, live video from Earth, were beginning to wonder if it was worth it, but it was too late. All traffic had been suspended till the end of the crisis because the tracking radar used during launches might shine toward Mars.

Ben scraped the last bite of eggs from his plate and got up to get more. He could feel the muscles rippling across his back, and his legs felt as solid as oak trees. The four Carbodine tablets he had chewed this morning were kicking in, and he felt almost normal—whatever normal was.

He had seen the exodus from the Moon starting and had taken care of his supply. His locker in the barracks contained 4,000 tablets, and his locker at the construction site held almost as many. Even at his current consumption of nearly twenty pills a day, he figured he wouldn't run out anytime soon, and he had recently solved the problem of access to his medication while wearing a spacesuit for six hours at a time.

All spacesuits held a small supply of water attached to a straw in the helmet. Ben glued a Pez dispenser next to the straw after discovering that Carbodine tablets fit nicely into the slot once the candy was removed. He now needed only to reach out with his tongue and push Mickey's head back to retrieve a bitter, salty pill while he worked in hard vacuum.

And work was pretty much all he had left. Consolidated Helium's complex had been shut down. The music and the smell of food in the air, the crowds and the raucous delight of nights spent drinking and drugging were gone. He was once again isolated from those around him with nothing but his thoughts and the voices in his head for company.

He'd managed to infuriate the supervisor of the construction crew within two hours of his arrival on the job. The supervisor, being a vindictive man by nature, made a conscious decision to make Ben's life as unpleasant as possible. From that point on, Ben got every difficult and labor intensive job that came along, and there were plenty of them.

Ben responded by requesting overtime and by working harder and faster than anyone could reasonably expect, and they remained at that impasse—the supervisor determined to break him, Ben determined not to be broken.

The first week had been the worst. Ben had rolled out of bed every morning in agony from muscles and joints swollen with overuse, but Carbodine was a decent anesthetic when taken in high enough dosage. He told himself it was the reason his usage had increased, but he knew better, and it really didn't matter. For the last month, he had pushed, pulled, dragged, and carried heavy objects from point A to point B for six hours at a stretch, twelve hours a day, six and seven days a week while wearing a spacesuit. It was a mindless and repetitive existence that he had come to perversely enjoy for those times when hours could go by without a single coherent thought.

Coherent thoughts were now unpleasant and difficult to come by. He knew that changes were occurring in his brain chemistry—some reversible, some not—just as changes were occurring in his body. He rolled his shoulders, feeling the rock-hard muscles and sinews moving easily with an unfamiliar strength and vaguely remembered reading that Carbodine had a strong anabolic effect. His body was like granite, but his mind was a jumbled mess of fleeting emotions and vagrant ideas. *I'll be okay as long as I can ignore the voices.*

He had noticed one day that his ears were ringing. It didn't really bother him even though his only previous experience with it had been during withdrawal. For a week, he ignored the constant high-pitched whistling in his ears, but one morning it was accompanied by a low rustling noise. The low rustling hadn't changed in volume since then, but it had grown in definition till he could hear distinct phrases and sentences. He ignored them too.

He returned to his place at the table and began once again to methodically shovel food into his mouth. The television was replaying video footage of the evacuation of NASA Central, and a helicopter camera showed thousands of people battering through the gates while tear gas canisters and stun grenades exploded among them.

Three hundred people had died, most of them trampled in the riot, and NASA's building was now a smoking ruin. The announcer was saying that investigators discovered the crowd had spilled from the Twenty-first Century Literalist Church after being whipped into a frenzy by their minister. The mob then stormed through the streets of Houston, growing quickly in numbers and in the power of its anger as it approached NASA, and authorities estimated that as many as 30,000 people may have been involved. NASA personnel were evacuated by military helicopters and armored personnel carriers. Twenty-first Century Literalist Church leaders could not be reached for comment.

The scene on the television shifted to that of a tall man in flowing robes marching energetically back and forth across a broad stage with a single lectern at its center. A frayed bible with a soft cover flopped back and forth in his left hand as he gesticulated wildly, and his long, white hair flew into the air with each turn and movement. A choir of perhaps 100 people stood in robes behind him, moving nothing but their eyes as he walked, stopped, raised the bible over his head, shouted at the crowd, and walked again. His voice boomed out in a deep and resonant bass.

"And the wrath of God has come, brothers and sisters. The angels of the lamb are seen in the heavens, and the signs of the Rapture are everywhere about us. For who can deny that man has sinned? Who among you can say they have not sinned and angered God with willful acts and deeds born of arrogance?"

The camera tracked him as he paced the stage. "Arrogance, brothers and sisters, arrogance. The arrogance of Adam, who was given the Garden of Eden but needed more. The arrogance of mankind, who was given the Earth but found it lacking. The arrogance of a people given dominion over the lands and the seas, dominion over the beasts of the fields, dominion over all that swims or walks or flies. And have we been satisfied with these gifts from God?"

"No!" thundered the crowd.

"Have we fallen to our knees in gratitude?"

"No!"

"Have we found our blessings complete?"

"No!" screamed the crowd in a rising crescendo.

He stopped and let his arms fall to his sides. His head fell forward till his shoulder-length hair hung down, and he stood without moving just long enough for the crowd to become slightly restless. When he looked up, a single tear rolled down his cheek.

"No," he said in a near whisper that filled the auditorium. "No, we have not."

He walked to the lectern as if the recent tirade had taken all his energy. The camera zoomed in for a close up, and a light, perfectly aligned behind his head, cast streamers of gold through his white hair, surrounding his face with a diffuse glow. "Brothers and sisters, Adam, in the midst of the perfection of the Garden of Eden, reached out to take the apple, the fruit of the Tree of Knowledge, the one thing he was not to touch, saying to God, 'Lord, all that you have given me is not enough. I must have this one thing which you have forbidden,' and mankind was cast from the Garden for all eternity.

"But we were not abandoned by God." He gestured with his arms. "We were given all of this, an entire world of our own, a world containing everything we could need."

He shook his head and looked into the crowd. "And what have we done?"

He began to walk again, slowly at first, but gaining speed and energy as his voice grew in strength and volume till it echoed from the walls and reverberated in the hearts and minds of those who watched. "We have put before Him a false God. And we have called that God 'Technology.' And we have sacrificed everything before it. Exterminating the beasts of the land, sea, and air that were brought to life by His hand. Polluting the water and the earth of His creation. And when we were finished with that, when we could do no more without exterminating ourselves, we began to look around.

"'What about these other planets?' we asked. 'What about the Moon hanging in the sky? Should that not be ours also? Should we not take it? Should we not take the very stars from the heavens to be our own?'

"Brothers, sisters," he bellowed, "Adam was thrown from the Garden for taking that which was not his. Mankind will be cast from this world for exactly the same sin!"

The crowd howled, and the preacher held his up hands to quiet them. "Do you doubt it? Do you want to hear the proof?" He raised his bible high but spoke without opening it. "Follow with me in Revelations near the end of the sixth chapter." His voice went out over the crowd with an almost hypnotic rhythm.

And every mountain and island were moved out of their places. And the kings of the earth, and the great men, and the rich men, and the chief cap-

tains, and the mighty men, and every bondman, and every free man, hid themselves in the dens and in the rocks of the mountains; And said to the mountains and rocks, Fall on us, and hide us from the face of him that sitteth on the throne, and from the wrath of the Lamb: For the great day of his wrath is come; and who shall be able to stand?

And after these things I saw four angels standing on the four corners of the earth, holding the four winds of the earth, that the wind should not blow on the earth, nor on the sea, nor on any tree. And I saw another angel ascending from the east, having the seal of the living God: and he cried with a loud voice to the four angels, to whom it was given to hurt the earth and the sea.

"The four angels come, my brethren. The four angels to whom it was given to hurt the earth and the sea. We have seen them. Their destruction of the false God has already begun.

"And the men who have brought this upon us, the great high priests of technology, where do you suppose they can be found?" He pointed with one hand. "In the belly of the mountain in Colorado at NORAD of course!" The crowd moaned a long, wailing cry.

"The prophecy is being fulfilled. The kings of earth, and the great men, and the rich men, and the chief captains, and the mighty men have gone to hide themselves in the rocks of the mountain, but the great day of His wrath will come in just four days, and who among us shall be able to stand before it?"

The television blinked once, and static filled the room as the screen turned to snow. Within a few seconds, it was replaced by a blue screen with a simple statement: "Live broadcast from Earth will resume in seven days."

The men seemed frozen in their chairs, and Ben took his last bite of breakfast, scraping the fork loudly across the plate. "We'll see about that shit," he said and looked at his watch. They turned and looked at him with anguished expressions. Most of them had not touched a bite of their food.

"Time to go to work, boys," Ben said and stood up to leave the room. His attention switched effortlessly to his supervisor, and he clenched his jaw as hatred welled up within him.

Kill him, said the voice clearly.

"Shut up," mumbled Ben.

Four days, said the voice.

"Shut up."

You'll be dead in four days.
"Whatever."

Chapter Thirty-six
20 Million Miles from Mars
June 24, 2061

The great, gravitational bowl of Mars extends for millions of miles. Mars is but a speck at its center. It is in the nature of massive objects that their reach should far exceed their grasp. In this one respect, Mars reflects in a material way the spiritual landscape of the tiny, nearby creatures who have only in the last few thousand years begun to ponder such things. Mars knows nothing of the forces that act upon it, nor does it appreciate or understand the force it exerts on the fabric of space.

The tiny creatures on the nearby planetary mass are different. They are dimly aware that they can effect change, and beyond that, they have become aware of their awareness. But it is not by their doing. The cruel and indifferent chaos of evolutionary pressure has molded these beings, robbing them of claws, sharp teeth, strength, and speed but granting them thought, and finally, abstract thought.

They have, without will or effort, been blessed with a fragmentary knowledge of their place in the universe and cursed with an obscure understanding of their present predicament. For nothing is without cost, and the delightful repast of thoughtful abstract exploration may, at times, be overwhelmed by the bitter taste of genuine fear.

Four cylinders, black as space itself, move with great speed within the bowl of a planetary mass that sings loudly but with a simple song. Soon, one of them, the one in front, must slow down and adjust its course or slide by and rim out of this depression in space-time.

A preset value has nearly been reached, but the cylinder does not know this—its mind is simple, and though the goal is near at hand, the cylinder cannot see it. Its eyes, narrow of vision and perceiving only the warping of space, do not detect the solid mass that has twisted this region into a broad, shallow basin.

A planet is but a small speck near the center of the basin it has pulled in the fabric of space, and the guidance system of the cylinder is crude. Soon, the preset value will be reached, and a program, previously unknown, will be enacted. The program is effective if not elegant, and the cylinder will flip end for end before slowing so that it might spiral down into the well of the planet's gravity. Contact with the goal is thereby made indeterminate but inevitable.

Eight sentient beings occupy a space that is but a dot on the speck of Mars. They are cut off from their billions of kindred, and they are aware of their isolation. In pain, they labor to survive and to understand.

Such is the price of self-knowledge.

The kindred watch with dread from the seeming safety of 80 million miles as the cylinders approach their eight cousins. They have all but forgotten the beauty of their flawed ability to know the essence of existence and can now only lament that the world, as they know it, will soon end. Destruction is but one of many disturbing possibilities, and their minds seethe with ideas and potentialities.

Such is the price of intelligence.

The dawn of their intelligence has been lost to the memories of those that watch and wait. It bloomed long ago in the heart of a continent they now call Africa, and though their minds are agile and quick, they are now trapped by the sheer simplicity of the scene before them—four objects of unknown origin moving through space.

With agility and speed their minds process one possible ending after another and begin again. They are transfixed by the unfolding drama—held prisoner by the fear of an unknown abstraction.

Such is the price of abstract thinking.

Chapter Thirty-seven
Surface of Mars
June 24, 2061

Adrian Melancon picked up a pen and waved it at the keyboard on the table in front of him. "Be gone, demons of antiquity."

Tom Fielder was coming through the airlock and had just popped the seals on his helmet. He called across the room, "Have you lost your mind?"

Melancon turned with a sheepish grin. "A long time ago. Her name was Denise."

Tom shook his head as he peeled out of his suit. Of everyone on the team, only Melancon seemed unfazed by their status as decoys and the loss of contact with Earth.

"You seemed to have gotten over it," said Tom. "Are you relapsing?"

"I didn't get over it. I just got used to it."

"Well you've done a pretty good job of hiding your insanity so far. Why are you banishing demons?"

"It's the weather satellite. I'm not sure it's working."

Tom opened his locker to hang up his suit and looked over his shoulder at the screen on the wall. It showed a slowly moving field of stars with a series of numbers scrolling rapidly upward in the bottom left-hand corner. He was amazed that Melancon had managed to resurrect some of the old satellites. The view on the wall screen was from an orbital surveyor that had been decommissioned over ten years ago. Using nothing but a keyboard on the ground, a satellite uplink, and some computer magic that Tom didn't begin to understand, Melancon had activated the surveyor and turned its camera toward the alien objects.

It was a laborious process, and the crew had taken turns in the kitchen, offering up several varieties of tasteless canned soup and numerous cold meals while nervously watching their cook pull up old protocols from an old database as he tried one avenue after another to raise the electronically dead hardware in orbit around Mars.

The orbital surveyor was left over from the early planning days of the Mars Expedition and had been used to help determine a landing site. Melancon had struggled for half a day to activate its long-unused solar panels from what little bit of power was left in the battery. The payoff was the discovery that the telescope was still in good condition, giving clear, crisp images in real time. Three days later, Melancon had tricked the onboard tracking computer into reporting data he could use to determine the angle of flight and the speed of a moving object.

The only other potentially useful piece of equipment was an old weather satellite in a polar orbit. It too carried a telescope, but Melancon had been frustrated in his efforts to retrieve the images it seemed to be recording. Fortunately, the infrared detector was another matter.

The weather satellite had originally been designed to, among other things, record and transmit very precise temperature readings from the surface of Mars. It was perfectly suited for detection of an engine burn in nearby space, and Melancon had turned it away from the planet. It now tracked the computed position of the closest alien object.

The most difficult part was making use of whatever information the satellites might transmit. The crew would be concerned when and if one of the objects fired its main engine, but there would be a deadly interest with where the object was going and at what speed.

For that, they needed data in three dimensions. With two satellites transmitting information, the data was there, but the satellites were moving in different orbits. The motion of each had to be accounted for and canceled out relative to the motion of the object being tracked. It was a complex problem, but Melancon finally pieced together a program that would collate the data; subtract the motion of the two satellites; compute the speed, direction, and acceleration of the tracked object; and extrapolate the object's target and time of arrival.

Tom closed his locker door and stood scratching the various itchy spots on his skin. For a time the crew had kept to their normal work schedules while Melancon tapped away at his keyboard and whispered arcane commands to the computer, but Tom had finally convinced Ki to take some protective measures.

Of course this raised the question of what sort of protective measures were appropriate, and the crew had been gathered together to discuss it. It had been a tough meeting. Tom replayed it in his head while he walked across the room to look over Melancon's shoulder.

Ki had stood up at the meeting and looked carefully around the table before speaking. "I am not averse to taking protective measures, but I will insist that we stay in the living quarters until we are certain the object's do not intend to communicate with us."

Cochran snorted, "It's not like we have anywhere else to go."

Tom looked down the table and leaned forward, hunching his shoulders. "Actually, that's not true." He had already outlined his plan for Ki, but the rest of the crew had no idea what he was talking about. Even Cochran raised an eyebrow in Tom's direction.

"We can go to the cave," Tom said.

"And do what?" from Espanoza.

"And live for a time if we have to," replied Tom.

"In our suits?" asked Espanoza.

"Not necessarily," said Tom. "We have two spare temporary shelters just like the ones we lived in while we were building the permanent living quarters. We have electricity already run to the cave from the solar film on the surface. We can move some of the solar panels over there to boost the power. We'll have plenty of water. We can set up the two shelters in the Crystal Grotto and use the electricity to run the air scrubbers and heat the shelters. If it ends up being a long term arrangement, we can put together a hydrolysis unit to make Oxygen from the water."

There had been silence around the table as the crew digested the idea. Several of them nodded dutifully while Cochran looked on with his now trademark idiot grin.

Ki explained further. "There is nothing to be lost by preparing for the worst. We will drop whatever gear we might need down the crack and move it to the Crystal Grotto. It's only a few hours' work to assemble the shelters, and we can set them up when and if the need arises."

Ki cleared his throat and looked at the upturned faces of the crew. The strain of the last few days was evident in his face and even in his mannerisms—he was softer somehow—almost hesitant. Tom was seriously frustrated with the situation and had become even more abrasive and belligerent than usual.

There was an uncomfortable silence as everyone waited, clearly expecting Commander Thon to continue.

Tom broke the silence. "We need to think about how to prepare for the worst. It's reasonable to assume some sort of blast with radiation. We'll need to firmly anchor the Mars I. We will also need to bring any critical, radiation-sensitive equipment with us to the cave. If anybody has any other ideas, the floor is open."

"We should put the seed supplies in the cave," said Espanoza. "The seeds would be killed by radiation."

"Good," said Tom.

"I want to bring my video games," said Cochran.

Tom snapped his head to the right, gritting his teeth and trying his best to silence the man with a glare. "Get real, Cochran."

"Get real?" said Cochran. "Get real? Why don't we all get real? Protect our equipment from the blast? Anchor the Mars I? Do you think these Alien missiles are going to be lobbing hand grenades or something? This whole planet is going to be fused into radioactive glass."

"Cochran," said Tom, "If you don't shut up…"

Cochran continued to grin. "What, Tom? I can call you Tom can't I? You gonna fire me? You gonna send me home?" He laughed and raised his hands, shaking his head. "What, Tom?"

"You can be confined to quarters."

"Ooh," said Cochran. "Slip my meals under the door. I don't care. Going down into the cave is ridiculous. We'll be lucky if it falls in on top of us, 'cause otherwise we'll be sitting around waiting for the food to run out. Now if that happens, I'd really like to have my games handy to pass the time while I starve."

Once again, there was an uncomfortable silence, and Tom sat, trying to restrain himself. "Are you finished?"

"Yeah," said Cochran with a tip of his head. "Sure."

The meeting had ended with little further discussion, and they had gone out to bury numerous boxes of tools and supplies in the sand behind the living quarters. Cables were tied around the Mars I and anchored to metal rods driven deep in the sand. They had taken down the reflective sheeting used to concentrate sunlight on the greenhouse and tied it securely over the fusion engine on the Mars I. Espanoza had thrown a fit, and it hadn't helped that Tom could only come up with a lame excuse about shielding the electronic relays from radiation. It wasn't likely to do much good, but Tom had insisted, and they had covered part of the living quarters with the last of the reflective sheeting.

Another scaffold had been erected on the surface above the Crystal Grotto, and a second sheet of solar film now fed power to the cave. The seeds, temporary shelters and associated tools, air tanks, air scrubbers, and several tanks of cherry-flavored, nutrient broth had all been dropped by the hoist into the large cavern and carried through the long, winding passage to the place where the shrimp-like Martians had once lived.

The only problem had been the crawlway into the Grotto, and they were delayed for a day as Tom, Evelyn Weiss, and Carlos Espanoza worked to enlarge the opening and shore it up.

Cochran had been mostly silent after his outburst at the meeting and had worked hard at almost everything Tom suggested, but he'd refused a direct order to help with the work on the crawlway. Tom finally backed away from it and assigned him to other work. Other than beating the crap out of him—a constant temptation—there wasn't a whole lot Tom could do about it, and he was thankful Cochran was, for the most part, keeping his mouth shut.

The air lock cycled open, and Espanoza came through the door with Dr. Krazinsky and Evelyn. The work outside was finished, and the remainder of the crew would be coming in to wait for whatever was about to happen. They had buried the last box and fastened the last cable. The equipment and stores they would need for living in the cave were in place. The entire inventory of nutrient broth was now resting in the rubble-filled passageway outside the Crystal Grotto. Dr. Krazinsky estimated they might live for four months on starvation rations.

Tom looked at the small screen in front of Melancon. Simple text scrolled slowly upward with an occasional "Status

Okay" displayed in the midst of commands written in a computer language Tom could not read. "It seems to think it's okay," he said.

"Yeah," said Melancon "All the diagnostics report active systems, but I don't have any way to calibrate the damned thing."

"It was working when it was pointed at the surface."

"Doesn't mean it's working now," said Melancon.

The airlock cycled once more and Commander Thon, Mike Cochran, and Kaitlin Geller walked into the room and began removing their suits. Tom listened to the seals popping and was about to remind Kaitlin that it was her turn for kitchen duty when he realized he could smell something.

He turned to Melancon. "Are you cooking something?"

Melancon tapped on the keyboard and replied without looking up. "Just a little jambalaya."

"I thought you were busy."

"It's just a chicken and sausage jambalaya. You sort of throw it together and let it cook. Y'all were out working, and I'd pretty much banished all the demons I could find. It'll be ready in about 45 minutes."

Tom nodded. "Sounds good. I was getting tired of soup and sandwiches."

Melancon chuckled. "You're not the only one."

"Right," said Tom, and he turned to the crew. "Listen up. Mr. Melancon has found time to cook us a decent meal. Let's all get a shower and get back here for dinner. It's going to be a long night."

There were murmurs of appreciation from the crew, but Tom frowned as he watched them move slowly down the hall. The hard manual labor of the last few days had physically exhausted everyone, and the emotional strain of the situation was wearing them down to their individual worst possible states. Evelyn, Kaitlin, and Carlos were snappish and edgy with fear. Dr. Krazinsky and Commander Thon seemed to have slipped into some kind of depression. Cochran was too weird to talk to, and most of the crew tried to avoid him. Melancon, solid as a rock, had changed little if any, although his Cajun accent seemed stronger than before.

And Tom knew that he had been affected along with everyone else. He was becoming increasingly mean and spiteful and had twice caught himself publicly berating his Commander's recent indecisiveness. He decided to wait till everyone else had showered before he took his turn, and he ambled off to his room to lie down for awhile.

It was nearly an hour later when Tom returned to the dining area and followed his nose into the kitchen. Melancon was serving up steaming plates of chicken with disks of sliced sausage in a fragrant, reddish-brown mixture of rice and aromatic vegetables. Tom's mouth watered from the smell of the spices. "What do you put in a jambalaya?" he asked.

Melancon smiled as he took the towel from his left shoulder to wipe his hands. "There ain't no strong rules on how to make it. You brown the meat and sauté the Holy Trinity of Cajun cooking."

"Excuse me?"

"The Holy Trinity of Cajun cooking—onion, bell pepper and garlic. You might want to add some celery. You got to add some tomato paste or sauce. Add the rice, the seasoning, some chicken stock and water and cook till the rice is done. Dat's a jambalaya."

"It sounds easy enough."

"Ain't nothin' to it,"

Tom took his plate into the dining area and sat down. Someone had changed the picture on the wall screen, and a high-definition, three-dimensional view of a wooded area with mountains in the background played on a taped loop. It was so real Tom felt he could reach out and touch the leaves of the nearby bushes as they gently moved in a slight breeze, but he couldn't decide if it made him feel better or worse to look at it.

Despite the good food—the jambalaya was delicious—this meal, like every other meal for the past few days, was quiet—the crewmembers too self absorbed to offer much in the way of small talk.

After ten minutes of listening to plates being scraped by forks and Espanoza smacking his food, Tom felt like he might explode. He looked at his watch somewhat dramatically and said, "I'm saying the objects are going to pass by without a visit to Mars."

Heads bobbed and swiveled with his words, but no one spoke.

"When is the closest approach to Mars?" Tom asked.

Melancon looked at his own watch and talked around a mouthful of rice. "Just about three hours."

"Okay," said Tom, "the objects are traveling at three million miles per hour. They have not adjusted course, and they have not begun to decelerate. If they were planning on plowing into Mars, they would have changed course by now. If they were going into orbit around Mars, they would have begun a deceleration burn."

He looked around the table, challenging them to debate his position. "I'm saying the objects are going to pass by without a visit to Mars," he repeated.

Commander Thon nodded agreeably. "You may have a point, Mr. Fielder."

Just then, a soft-toned gong sounded. "Unknown infra-red source in nearby space," announced the computer.

"Damn," said Tom.

"You were saying . . . ?" asked Cochran.

"I was saying I don't know a thing about Aliens. Melancon, let's see what we have."

Melancon spoke into the air. "Computer, surveyor view to main screen. Execute."

The fluffy clouds and blue sky disappeared from over the mountaintops, and the wall screen blinked into a multitude of hard, bright pinpoints—the signature of stars when seen in a vacuum. In the exact center of the picture was a perfectly formed, blue flame.

Melancon pulled his small computer from under the table, flipped it open with a practiced movement, and began typing rapidly. He studied the screen in front of him for a moment. "We got signals from both satellites. It's gonna take about thirty minutes to get enough data to figure trajectory."

"Right," said Tom. He gazed at the blue spot on the wall screen for a short time and then turned to find Ki looking at him. "Commander?" he said.

Ki stared back and then blinked as if coming out of a daze. "Let's get the dishes cleaned up," he said. "I want a thorough check of those suits while we wait for the trajectory, and I want everybody, including you, Mr. Fielder, wearing video recorders."

Tom looked at his commander and breathed a sigh of relief. *Good.*

Chapter Thirty-eight
NASA Central
June 24, 2061

Rick Jelton snapped to attention when the alarm sounded. "I'll be damned," he said. "There it is."

He looked across the darkened room to where Marilyn Lindsay was leaning over a console. Before he could speak, she glanced over her shoulder and pushed her glasses up from the tip of her nose.

"We're working on it," she said, "but these computer systems are still not happy with each other."

Rick keyed his microphone to a different number and spoke without preamble. "We've got contact, General Laurence. There's an engine burn just off of Mars."

"Be there in two minutes," replied the General.

Rick clicked off without further conversation. The stress of the last few days had begun with the nightmare of their forced evacuation from NASA Central and had continued with the long, tedious work of trying to get NASA's data-recovery systems to interface with the military hardware and software at NORAD. To a certain extent, it was still a work in progress. The reticence of the military computer experts to divulge particulars of their proprietary operating system had not helped matters, and Rick had talked himself blue in the face concerning the need to meld NASA's software with theirs.

It was a typical turf battle, and it had gotten ugly more than once. The President finally stepped in and declared it a matter of national security, but precious time had been lost, and nobody felt good about it. The military felt invaded; NASA felt slighted.

The room was smaller and darker than the one they had used in Houston—the one that was now a twisted mess of melted plastic and burnt wires—but there were fewer NASA personnel here. Almost one third of NASA's technicians had simply disappeared after the evacuation, and no one knew if they had died in the riot or decided it was better not to be associated with their old jobs. Rick hadn't yet found the time to worry about it.

There were five large computer screens on the far wall instead of the three they were used to, but the middle one was by far the larger, and the other four were stacked two to each side, one on top of the other. A large oval table took up most of the space in the center of the room. Rick could visualize the table overlaid by a map with small plastic ships and tanks spread out in strategic positions, but the NASA personnel mostly used it as a large trash can. It was covered with wadded up paper and discarded computer printouts, and it was driving the military technicians nearly insane.

The computer stations, five or six to a bunch, were grouped around smaller tables arranged in roughly the same semicircular shape as NASA Central. Several steps above everything else was a dais with ten consoles looking out over the room. Rick manned one of these stations to the right of the middle position. The consoles to his left and right began to fill up with military brass while Ms. Lindsay scurried around below him.

General Laurence sat down to his left and picked up his headset. "Jesus Christ," he said, "can't your people clean up that table."

"We're a little busy right now," said Rick.

Lindsay's voice spoke in his ear. "Mr. Jelton?"

"What have we got?"

"It is not one of the smaller objects that destroyed the two probes. The radiation signature is identical to what we saw during the course corrections several weeks ago, but it is significantly stronger. Initial readings indicate the object is decelerating. This would be consistent with the engine being pointed at us instead of away from us. We should have the trajectory in just a few minutes."

The middle screen on the wall was receiving a transmission from the Sagan telescope and showed the pale, blue exhaust of the closest alien object in fine detail. Rick studied the picture for a moment. It could have been a still photograph except for the shifting of stars in the background as the telescope moved through its orbit around Earth. The fire from the object projected sideways, filling half the screen with the shape of a long, thin chandelier light, and like a candle flame in perfectly still air, it did not flicker or move.

Rick had to admit the military computers had the best video-enhancement technology he had ever seen. When and if the objects impacted or landed on Mars, they should be able to see anything larger than a coffee table.

He hit a few keys and whispered a command to run a program designed to compute the size of objects seen at an angle and then whistled softly when it showed him the dimensions of the object's exhaust.

"I've got to hand it to you, Mr. Jelton," said General Laurence. "This was a good call."

"Thanks, but we haven't saved the world yet. Let's congratulate ourselves when the last Alien object is on Mars."

Rick gestured at the screen. "They've got some damned fine rocketry, General. That plume is almost a mile long, and there's not a hint of turbulence."

The General looked at the screen and scowled as Ms. Lindsay's voice returned in Rick's ear.

"We've got a trajectory, Mr. Jelton, but it's a strange one."

"Put it up on the top, left-hand screen. What is that, screen one?"

"Yes, sir."

A red sphere depicting Mars came into being on the screen. A blinking "X" showed the position of the decelerating Alien object, and a white line indicated its current destination.

"What the hell is that about?" said General Laurence.

Chapter Thirty-nine
Surface of Mars
June 24, 2061

"I don't think I believe this," Melancon said softly. Tom's suit was spread out on the table next to Evelyn's, and they were checking each seam and seal for wear or damage. He made a mental note to bring extra fittings and patch kits to the cave, and raised his head to look at Melancon. "Believe what?" he asked.

Melancon frowned and scratched his head. "Well, according to this, the object will be moving at nearly 100,000 miles per hour at its nearest approach. Now that's about a dead stop compared to how fast it's going now, but it's still damn fast, and this thing is gonna pass close."

"How close?"

Melancon had a pained expression on his face. "Twenty miles." He made it sound like a question.

"Twenty miles from the surface?" said Tom incredulously. "Plus or minus what?"

Melancon glanced at the small screen. "Twenty miles?"

Tom closed his eyes and shook his head. "Shit." He called out to Ki across the room. "Commander, we've got some information."

Commander Thon stood up and placed his suit gently on the chair. "What is it?"

Tom looked at Melancon and tilted his head in Ki's direction. "You tell him."

With the same pained expression, Melancon told his story to Commander Thon. "My program is telling me the Alien object will pass within 20 miles of the surface of Mars at a speed of 100,000 miles per hour. That's plus or minus 20 miles, so it might disintegrate in the atmosphere just before it slams into the surface, or hit the atmosphere and bounce off, or pass way too close for comfort." A lopsided grin came over his face. "I don't know who's drivin' that thing, but I'd be tempted to get out and walk."

"You're sure it's not going to dead center the planet?" asked Tom.

Melancon shook his head. "Oh yeah. There's no way I could be that far off. I wasn't sure the weather satellite was working, but when I took the visual readings from the surveyor and compared it to the infrared signal, everything checked. She's gonna skim by with a near miss or a near hit at nearly 100,000 miles per hour."

Ki glanced from the wall screen to Melancon and then to Tom. "I don't think we are going to figure this out right now. If they were going to hit Mars, they would be headed straight at us, but if they were going into orbit, they would not approach this close at that speed."

The rest of the crew had gathered around to listen to the conversation, and Ki listened considerately to them before he spoke. "Any ideas?"

No one responded and Tom finally said, "I think we should go to the cave."

Ki shook his head no. "Not now." He turned to Melancon. "How much longer till closest approach?"

Melancon checked his computer. "Just over two hours."

"If it actually hits the planet, how far from us would it be?"

Melancon hesitated, then consulted his computer. "It's passing on the sunny side of Mars just north of the equator. It will be about 10:00 PM when it comes by. That puts it over one fourth the way around the planet, 20 miles or so above a point 4,000 to our west."

"Good," said Ki. "Will we be able to see what happens at closest approach?"

"Yes, sir. The surveyor satellite will be right on top of it."

"Okay then. We wait."

Tom was fuming. "Commander, we need to be in the goddamned cave."

Ki looked at Tom with an arched brow. "Understood, Mr. Fielder, but we are in a position to make observations that may mean the difference between life or death for Earth. Our orders are to record whatever information we can and to turn our broadcast satellites back toward Earth only after all four objects have landed or passed us by. We will not leave till we have learned everything we can learn, or until we are certain this area is in imminent danger of attack." Ki paused. "And perhaps not even then."

Tom paced back and forth for a few turns then stopped. "How about this? We can't carry everyone in the rover even with the wagon attached. That means two trips to transport all of us to the cave. Why don't we send Weiss, Espanoza, Geller and Krazinsky to the cave right now? Ms. Weiss can bring a computer and check out the relay antennas we laid down when we found the ice. With Melancon's help from here, she may be able to link up with the two satellites from the Crystal Grotto."

Ki's mouth twisted as he chewed the inside of his lip.

"It gets half the crew into the cave right now," Tom said, "and if we get the computers linked up, we can gather the data from there."

Tom watched Ki turn and look at Melancon.

Melancon raised his eyebrows. "I don't see any reason it won't work. We need to make sure the batteries on the relays are still good."

"We've got extra batteries," said Tom. "Weiss can replace them if she has to."

Ki nodded. "It's a good plan. We can record data here as well as on the computer in the cave. Even if this site is destroyed, we may be able to save the information."

"Then it's a go?"

"Yes," said Ki.

Tom looked around. "Ms. Weiss, would you go drag Cochran away from his games and tell him we require his services."

Weiss turned and walked down the hall, and Tom began pacing again. "Okay," he said, "it'll take a little over thirty minutes to get to the cave. Cochran will need to stand by and help with the winch. Figure thirty minutes to get everybody down the hole and another thirty minutes for Weiss to check the relay batteries and get to the Crystal Grotto." He looked at his watch. "It's 8:07 now. She should be in place by 9:30."

He practically pounced on Melancon. "How long to establish the computer link?"

Melancon shrugged. "Fifteen minutes tops."

Tom rubbed his hands together. "That leaves fifteen minutes to closest approach. Perfect."

There was a flurry of activity while the designated crewmembers donned their suits and cycled through the lock, and Tom, Ki, and Melancon found themselves staring at each other when the door closed.

An excited voice came over the intercom. "Commander." It was Evelyn.

"Yes, Ms. Weiss, what is it?" Commander Thon asked.

"You can see it! In the western sky. It is clearly visible."

"I didn't think about that," said Tom.

"Interesting," said Ki. "Let us see if we can capture the video from your suit camera."

Melancon bent over his computer, and within a few minutes, the wall screen blinked to a view of the back of Cochran's head. The scene bounced and jiggled from the movement of the rover.

"Ms. Weiss," said Ki, "if you could lean back a bit, we should be able to see the object with your suit camera."

The view panned upward and there, amid the stars, was a bright, oblong, blue flame. It shifted slowly against the stars even as they watched.

"Thank you, Ms. Weiss," said Ki.

She leaned forward to a more comfortable position and the scene returned to the back of Cochran's head. The sand of Mars, caught in the headlights, rolled toward them and dipped left and right as the wheels of the rover moved across the uneven surface.

Melancon tapped a key and restored the video from the surveyor satellite. "That was making me seasick," he said.

Tom was still standing at the table next to Melancon. Ki was sitting with his chin in the palm of his hand, staring almost dreamily at the wall screen. "Angel of death, angel of mercy, what will it be?" he said.

"It's going to be the angel of my death if we don't find something to do for the next hour and a half," said Tom.

"Relax, Tom," said Ki. "We've done all we can do for now."

Tom started pacing again. "This is driving me nuts. Do you guys want to play cards or something?"

Melancon brightened. "Y'all know how to play bourré?" he asked.

Tom and Ki stared blankly. "What is a bourré?" asked Ki.

"Well," said Melancon, "it's kind of like Cajun poker. We could play a nice little friendly game. Say, a dollar ante and a dollar to stay."

Tom considered for a moment. "I don't play cards very much," said Ki.

"It's easy to learn," said Melancon. "Most of the rules are the same as draw poker. I've got some cards in the kitchen."

"I don't know," said Ki, hesitating.

"Just a dollar to ante and a dollar to stay. We could use dried beans for chips."

"What do you think, Tom?"

"If I don't find something to do, I'll throw a blood clot," said Tom. "Let's give it a try."

"Great," said Melancon. "It'll be just like home." He jumped up and headed toward the kitchen. "I'm gonna get some ice cream too."

"Ice cream?" said Tom.

"Yeah, I got some chocolate chip hid in the back of the freezer. Y'all come on if you want some."

Tom and Ki looked at each other, shrugged, and stood up to follow Melancon into the kitchen.

~

"You mean I have to match the pot again?" exclaimed Tom.

"I'm afraid so, Mr. Fielder," said Melancon. He was looking over the huge pile of beans in front of him. Tom and Ki had much smaller piles in front of them, and they had already found it necessary to go back to the "bank" several times.

Tom looked at a piece of paper on the table. "I already owe you $235," he said.

Ki looked at a similar piece of paper. "I too seem to have suffered some losses. This game is deceptively simple."

The sound of the outside, airlock door stopped them, and Melancon looked at his watch as he started gathering up beans and cards. "Closest approach is in 13 minutes, and Ms. Weiss should be ready for the link pretty soon," he said.

Cochran cycled into the room and released the catches on his helmet, twisting it to the left till he could lift off of his head. "Cochran's delivery service. We aim to please."

"How's the rover?" asked Tom.

"It's fine," said Cochran. "I hooked up the battery and set it for quick charge. The headlights put a pretty good drain on it, but it was still over three quarter when I got back."

Evelyn Weiss' voice materialized in the room. "Mr. Melancon?"

"Yes."

"I am ready to make the link if you could guide me through it."

Melancon pulled his computer in front of him. "No problem."

Tom and Ki cleaned up the table while Cochran removed his suit and Melancon talked Evelyn through the link up.

Cochran chattered as they worked. "You ought to see that damned thing now. It looks like a big, blue cigar or something, and it's bright enough to cast a shadow, but it's about to disappear over the horizon."

Tom looked at the wall screen and nodded his head. The object was much bigger than it had appeared earlier.

"Okay," said Melancon, "you should have the view from the surveyor on your screen now."

"Oh, yes," said Evelyn. "I can see the edge of Mars on the left-hand side."

"Good," said Melancon. "Now, if you'll press F1 you should get a screen that has a bunch of numbers scrolling up. In the top, right-hand corner it should say 'Satellite MW832.'"

"Satellite MW832," said Evelyn. "I have it."

"We're done then," said Melancon. "You can toggle back and forth between the two screens by hitting F1. The data for both satellites is being recorded on your hard drive." He looked at his watch and checked his computer. "I'm showing closest approach in ten minutes at a distance of 27 miles from the surface."

Tom could not take his eyes from the wall screen where the plume from the alien object could now be seen moving ever closer to the disk of Mars. The surveyor satellite tracked the object, giving the impression that Mars was moving while the object held its position. "What can we expect to see from an object moving by at 100,000 miles per hour and a distance of 27 miles from the surface," he asked of no one in particular.

"It's cutting it pretty thin," said Cochran. "Whoever made that rocket is way ahead of anything we can do. The light from it doesn't even shimmer. Everything we make has a certain turbulence in the exhaust. Turbulence means inefficiency." He too was caught up in the scene on the wall. "That is one beautiful piece of machinery, but there's not enough air at 27 miles to make much difference as far as heating or anything like that even at 100,000 miles per hour. We'll see a little shaking on the exhaust plume is all, and it will sail on by."

"Which begs the question of what it will do after that," said Tom.

"And why it is following this course," said Ki.

"They're just hot pilots with big cajones," said Cochran. "They're going to skim by, continue to decelerate into a tight orbit, and then nuke this planet into a ball of glass."

Tom glanced over to where Cochran sat gazing at the screen. He hoped it wasn't true, but he wasn't betting on it. He'd lost enough money today already.

As they watched, the blue flame slowly intersected the disk of Mars and slid forward till the object itself could finally be seen against the backdrop of the Martian surface.

"Good God," Tom said, "that doesn't *even* look right."

Gregg R. Overman

Chapter Forty
NASA Central
June 24, 2061

Rick watched the middle screen with keen interest. The Sagan Telescope, with the help of the military image enhancement system, rendered a near perfect picture, and the pale, blue exhaust plume could be seen in fine detail. There just wasn't much detail to be seen. From where Rick sat, the flame could have been an exquisitely made glass vase sliding across the heavens.

But in a few seconds, when it passed across the sunlit face of Mars, Rick and everyone else at NORAD would finally see one of the missiles. After weeks of charting their course and guessing their intentions, he would know the size and shape of the objects that had turned the world upside down and his life with it.

All eyes were glued to the screen as the front of the blue fire edged closer to the disk of Mars. Technicians were poised over keyboards to issue the commands that would compute the dimensions of the first alien object ever seen by mankind. Rick gave a signal to Ms. Lindsay, and the picture zoomed in till all that could be seen was the far edge of the exhaust where it exited the unseen missile.

Slowly, slowly the body of the rocket slid between the bright disk of Mars and Earth, but even before it was completely revealed, the people in NORAD were looking at each other with puzzled expressions.

It was black of course, and so efficient at absorbing light that it looked as if a section had been cut from the screen, but no one would have predicted the size and shape.

"It looks like a toothpick," said Rick. His voice was full of wonder.

"The ends are flat," said General Laurence.

"Okay, a pencil, a long, thin pencil."

"Mr. Jelton?" It was Lindsay. "We have a diameter of just under six feet and a length of," she waited while the number came up, "between 1,000 and 1,100 feet."

Rick had Lindsay zoom the main picture out till the entire object and its fiery tail could be seen. The Alien object almost disappeared as it shrank down to a thin, black line, and the exhaust plume, five times longer and ten times wider, dwarfed the object.

"The object seems to be rotating, Mr. Jelton."

Rick looked at Lindsay. "Speed of rotation?" he asked.

"There's no way to tell. We are picking up a slight change in diameter just above the exhaust. There appears to be something bulging from the side of the object in that area, but whatever it is, it's too small to resolve at this distance, and we don't know if it's one bulge or several, so we can't compute the revolutions per minute."

General Laurence was listening in. "You'd probably want to spin something that long and thin just for stability," he said.

"Time to closest approach," asked Rick.

"Less than ten seconds," replied Lindsay. "We're already getting some interference in the plume."

The plume started to sparkle with sharp, yellow lights from contact with the few, errant molecules of the Martian atmosphere, and the sparkling grew till it covered the blue flame while everyone in the room held their breath. The plume itself, still as blown glass till now, began to waver as shock waves rebounded across its surface.

"She's going to explode right there," said General Laurence, but just as he spoke, the fire began to resume its shape and stability, the sparkling decreased and disappeared, and the object was soon, once again, sliding serenely across Mars.

"You've got to be nuts to pull a stunt like that," said the General.

Rick turned in his seat to look at the General and noticed President Bremmer standing off to one side. The President's hands were clasped behind his back, and he rocked forward on his toes and back again on his heels while he watched the activity around him.

Rick looked at General Laurence. "Should we be glad it didn't explode?" he asked.

Before he could reply, Lindsay's voice shouted in Rick's ear. "Mr. Jelton!"

Rick saw Lindsay standing with a finger pushed against her earpiece. "Sir, we have an engine burn on the second object." Rick was about to say something, but she held up her hand. "And number three. We now have an engine burn on number three."

"Damn!" said Rick.

"Isn't this what we wanted?" asked the General.

"I don't know. I guess."

The first object had moved clear of Mars and once more appeared as a disembodied blue flame against the stars.

"Let's keep the telescope on object number one. I need the coordinates on object two and three. Is this the same place the first object fired its engines?"

"Almost exactly, sir."

"And where is the fourth object?"

Lindsay leaned over a console for a few seconds. "It is currently lagging about four hours behind number two and three, but it will catch up quickly."

Several minutes went by while Rick tried to think of something to do, and more out of frustration than anything else, he decided to put some information on the screen. His hands pecked at the keyboard, and he whispered a few commands to the computer, then mumbled a curse when nothing happened.

"Ms. Lindsay," he said, "can we get the velocity of object number one relative to Mars displayed on the middle screen?"

"I'll try, sir."

Lindsay went over and talked rapidly to one of the lieutenants. The conversation dragged on while Rick fretted, but the number finally materialized in white letters against a black background. It was dropping rapidly through 3,000 miles per hour.

"Look at that," said General Laurence. "Four hours of deceleration at ten gravities. Do you realize how much fuel that represents?"

The number dropped to zero and began to move back up, climbing past 1,000 in less than five seconds.

"Object number one is now accelerating toward Mars," Lindsay said. "Distance to the surface is just over 2,500 miles. Trajectory would have it impact this side of Mars."

With a change that made everyone in the room draw in a sharp breath, the long, blue exhaust flame winked out.

"Object is now in free fall." Lindsay was furiously banging away at her keyboard. "It will impact the surface at a speed of 3,250 miles per hour including acceleration due to gravity in," she hesitated, "one hour and six minutes." She looked over her shoulder at Rick and pushed her glasses up with one finger. "Unless something happens."

Chapter Forty-one
Surface of Mars
June 24, 2061

"Where the hell did it go," exclaimed Tom when the exhaust disappeared.

Melancon was looking at the screen on his small computer. "It's there. It just shut down the engine, and it's still hot. The weather satellite is having no trouble tracking it with infrared."

"Where is it going?" asked Tom.

Cochran giggled. "I shot an arrow into the air. It came to Mars I know not where."

"Shut up."

Melancon was frowning at his computer. "I don't know about your arrow, Cochran, but we know exactly where this is coming down." He leaned back in the chair. "Unless it makes another engine burn, she's gonna fall on the daylight side right near the terminator line. That would be 4,500 miles east of here in a little over an hour."

"We should have a really spectacular sunrise, don't you think?" said Cochran.

Tom looked at Ki. "It is time to go to the cave, Commander. If we leave now, we'll be there before the object comes down."

Ki frowned and shook his head. "We should stay here."

Tom threw his hands in the air. "Commander, there is nothing to be gained by staying here. We'll be safer in the cave, and we can broadcast the data to Earth after this is over."

"Our duty is to remain here."

With a suddenness that surprised everyone, Tom almost screamed, "Our duty, your duty, is to preserve the mission personnel. Staying here will get us nothing and will put us all in danger."

"Danger's bad," said Cochran with a grin.

Ki glanced at Cochran and then turned toward Melancon.

Melancon nodded his head yes and spoke softly. "The data is safe, Commander. We should leave now."

"And there is nothing else we can do here?" asked Ki.

"Nothing," replied Melancon in a quiet, even tone.

Ki looked for a moment at the satellite picture of Mars. Somewhere in near space was a small, unseen object falling toward the surface. He nodded slowly. "Yes. To the cave then."

"Okay, let's move it," Tom said with relief.

"The cave?" said Cochran. "But I don't want to go to the cave. Don't you guys realize we're in for some really great weather? Predictions are for a substantial warming trend with temperatures climbing into the mid to upper 900's by noon tomorrow."

"Goddamn it, Cochran," said Tom. "Shut up and get into your suit."

Cochran jumped up and saluted. "Aye, aye, Captain Tom. Cochran's delivery service will take you where you," he pointed at Tom with both hands, "want to go."

"Cochran, if you don't calm down, I'll have you sedated."

"Nope. I don't do drugs. Slows the reflexes and all that. 'Don't dope and drive,' you know the saying."

Ki looked at Tom and pursed his lips, shaking his head no.

The suits were a familiar drill, and they were through the lock within minutes. Tom went to shut down the reactor while Melancon drained the water from the lines in the living quarters, and they were soon seated in the rover and rolling toward the cave. Melancon carried his computer and kept the screen open, looking for any change in the object. Ki sat quietly watching Phobos race across the night sky while Cochran sang pop songs, softly and off key. Tom sat gritting his teeth and trying his best not to think too much about reaching over to detach Cochran's airline.

The headlights caught the sharply rising slab of rock that led up to the cave entrance, and Cochran wheeled the rover into a tight turn at its base. "Last stop, everybody out," he said.

They scrambled up the face of the rock to where the winch was anchored, and Tom checked the battery. "It looks good," he said, gesturing to Commander Thon. "After you, Commander."

Ki strapped himself into the harness and was quickly lost from sight as he lowered himself down through the crack and into the cavern below them.

"I'm down," he said. ""I'm sending the harness back up."

Melancon was next to go, and when the harness returned, Tom looked at Cochran. "Your turn," he said.

Cochran took a step back and held up his hands. Tom could see a wild grin on his face in the suit lights. "Oh no, Mr. Fielder, I wouldn't dream of it. After you."

"Come on, Cochran, let's go. We don't have all night."

"Oh but I insist."

"Damn it, Cochran, get in the harness!" Tom was screaming.

"I don't think so."

Tom lowered his voice but chopped his words. "In the harness now. That is a direct order."

Cochran mocked the tone and cadence of Tom's voice. "Not going there. That is a direct no."

Tom took a step toward Cochran, and Cochran immediately took off down the rocky slope in great leaping strides. "Catch me if you can, Tommy," he cried over his shoulder. He stopped at the rover and turned to look back up the slope. "Tag, you're it."

Commander Thon spoke from the cavern. "Mr. Cochran, you will be much safer in the cave with us. I suggest you get into the harness as Mr. Fielder has directed."

"Gee whiz, Commander, I'd really like to, but I don't like caves, and I don't like heights. To be honest, the idea of eating a nuke out here in the open is a lot more appealing than dangling from a wire in the middle of some big hole in the ground. Why don't you guys go on? We'll keep in touch. Maybe a postcard from time to time?"

Commander Thon pleaded, "Mr. Cochran, please, we need all of the crew to stay together. I will come back up and help you down if you'd like."

Cochran jumped into the rover and pulled it about fifty feet away from the base of the rock. "I would not like," he said.

"Commander," said Tom, "he's in the rover. We'll never catch him."

"Times a-wastin'," Cochran said. "The sun rises pretty damned early this time of year in these parts, or so I've heard."

There was silence for some time while Tom and Commander Thon weighed their options. "Very well," said Ki. "We cannot force you into the cave against your will, but I would ask of you one thing."

"By your command," said Cochran.

"I want you to stay at the base of the rock slab. Keep your radio on, and keep in touch with us. If you change your mind, we will come back and help you into the cave."

"Not a problem," said Cochran.

"Very well then," said Ki. "You can join us in the cavern, Mr. Fielder."

Tom looked down the tilted rock to where Cochran sat in the driver's seat of the rover. Despite everything that had happened, a wave of sadness passed over him, and he raised a hand in farewell.

Cochran waved back. "See you later, Tommy."

"I hope so, Mike. I really hope so."

Tom strapped into the harness and lowered himself over the side. He was soon traveling down the winding cave of the old underground river with Melancon and Commander Thon at his side. None of them spoke till they were through the narrow passage and inside the Crystal Grotto.

Several lamps had been set up, and the three late arrivals shut off their suit lights when they emerged onto the narrow ledge overlooking their new camp. Tools and supplies were scattered everywhere on the floor of the cave, and a large sheet of stiff plastic had been laid down to protect the crew from the sharp and jagged quartz. Tom made a mental note to get the tools arranged against one wall, but even with that thought, he was impressed by the beauty of the room from his vantage point on the ledge. Rainbows scattered and split against the walls, and moving halos of multicolored light slid and jumped with each turn of his head. The sculptured, gray-green ice caught the dim reflection from the ceiling and glowed in fractured reds and blues as if jewels were hidden just below the surface.

Is this a good place to die? he asked himself as he scrambled down the short ladder to join the rest of the crew.

Evelyn had started laying down the foam insulation for one of temporary dwellings on a rough but level surface next to the plastic, and she placed the applicator on the floor of the cave when they walked in.

Commander Thon looked about. "Mr. Cochran will not be joining us just yet," he said.

"We heard," said Evelyn. "Do you think he will be alright?"

Cochran broke through. "I can hear you," he said in a singsong voice.

Tom motioned them to turn down their radios.

"He would be safer here with us," said Ki, "but there was little we could do."

"We should have sedated him," said Tom.

Dr. Krazinsky spoke up. "Moving a sedated patient in a space suit is not a recommended procedure. It would have been a danger to him and to the rest of you."

"She is right, Mr. Fielder," said Ki. "I hate to think what he would have done if he had awakened in this cave. He could not be allowed to endanger the rest of us."

"I just hope he's got sense enough to come into the cave if..." Evelyn stopped without finishing.

"Speaking of which," said Melancon. He was sitting on the plastic next to where Evelyn had sprayed the foam. "We've got just three minutes till this thing hits. If it doesn't slow down real soon, it's gonna make a mighty big splash."

The crew crowded around behind Melancon to look at the screen on his computer. Evelyn picked up the computer she had brought with her and placed it next to Melancon's. The two screens showed an identical crescent of Mars, half in sun and half in darkness.

"Why can't we see it?" asked Espanoza.

"We're looking at it from the wrong angle," replied Melancon. "It's like trying to see a pencil at fifty yards from the pointed end. If you look real close, you can see a little dot right here." He pointed to a tiny spot near the line marking dawn from night. "That's the object."

Tom turned up his radio. "Mr. Cochran."

"Yes, Tom."

"We have less than two minutes till the object hits. Are you sure you won't come into the cave?"

"It's such a beautiful night. I really do appreciate the offer, but I think I'll stay out here. That is, if you don't mind."

"Suit yourself," said Tom.

Melancon checked his watch. "My numbers could be a little off so don't be surprised if she's a little early or a little late."

There was a tiny puff on the screen, like a pebble landing in fine dust.

"It's down," said Tom.

Blue light began to shine in a small spot at the point where the object impacted the surface. The light grew then dimmed, grew then dimmed, growing quickly larger and oscillating faster as they watched. Dust and sand blew in clouds that Tom knew must be hundreds if not thousands of feet tall.

"This ain't good," said Melancon. "That's a lot bigger splash than. . ."

They were plunged into darkness as the lights failed. Only the screens from the computers with internal batteries still glowed—not with the pictures of Mars, but with the snow of random static.

Chapter Forty-two
NASA Central
June 24, 2061

The Sagan telescope was zoomed in tight on the spot where the alien object was coming down. Some of the larger boulders were clearly visible on the surface, and the object was a small, black circle in the exact center of the screen.

Lindsay counted it down. "Impact in five, four, three, two, one."

Sand billowed out and the black circle disappeared to be replaced with a blue light. Rick miscalculated at first that the object had fired its engine at the last second, but the light quickly grew, scattering sand and boulders before it, till it almost filled the screen. Just as quickly, it dimmed slightly, then brightened and grew again.

"Zoom out," Rick yelled.

The light went through several cycles before Lindsay could change the setting—each cycle faster and brighter than the last. The picture moved back, and Rick could see sand, dust, and large boulders hurtling away from the point of impact in clouds thousands of feet tall as shock waves pounded the Martian plane.

Lindsay panned the telescope back further as the area of blue light grew in size and violence. The cycle of bright and dim climbed up in speed till it strobed the entire room, and still it increased in speed and brightness till everyone present was bathed in a harsh, blue glare. Lindsay panned back even further just as the light flared brilliantly and began to die.

Rick tried to blink away the spots before his eyes. The shock waves continued to ripple across the plane in an expanding circle already hundreds of miles wide, and he could see rocks and dust rushing upward from the explosion. The blue light still shone—but dimly now—and it spread in an almost leisurely fashion behind the outwardly expanding wall of dust and sand.

Rick had lost track of the scale of things from the shifts in magnification. He keyed his microphone. "Lindsay, are some of those rocks headed into outer space?"

"Yes, sir, but I wouldn't call them rocks. We are tracking one that is nearly the size of Gibraltar."

Rick leaned back in his chair and reassessed the size of what he was seeing. "Good God," he whispered. The shock of it was almost too much. He felt the blood drain from his face and a wave of nausea and dizziness came over him. The magnitude of the devastation was difficult to comprehend. He looked back at the screen and tried to bring it into a perspective he could understand, but he could only sit and watch as wave after wave rippled outward in a grotesque semblance of a raindrop on a still pond.

"So if this thing had hit Houston, New Orleans would be leveled by now."

"Yes, sir." Rick jumped slightly. He hadn't realized he was speaking aloud. "As well as Dallas, Austin, and San Antonio," replied Lindsay. "The shock wave is beginning to dampen slightly, but we are less than ten minutes post impact."

The blue light, pale and dim compared to its previous splendor, continued to spread outward. "Why are we still getting light from the explosion, and why is it spreading out like that?" Rick asked.

"We are apparently seeing antimatter continuing to react with the dust and atmosphere of Mars. The radiation signature is unlike the objects' engines but contains the strong spike at 500 million electron volts."

Rick saw that General Laurence was staring grimly at the screen but nodding his head. He seemed unsurprised. "Your input, General?"

"One of our models predicted an almost identical explosion," said the General, "but I'm surprised at the size of it."

"What?" Rick exclaimed. "You knew this would happen?"

The General turned toward Rick. "We knew it might happen. The objects obviously use antimatter for propulsion. It seemed reasonable to assume they would use antimatter for a bomb. One of the models suggested that quickly releasing a large amount of antimatter would begin a fusion reaction."

"A fusion reaction?"

"Yes. Antimatter reacts with normal matter to generate huge amounts of heat and light. As the reaction begins, the outer layer of antimatter explodes as it contacts the normal matter around it. It was explained to me as being similar to the shell of an egg exploding. The shell blows inward as well as outward. The inward blast will compress the antimatter at the center. If the antimatter at the center is Hydrogen or some other fusible element, then a fusion reaction takes place. This fusion reaction blows the antimatter outward again to contact more normal matter, and the process continues till the antimatter at the edge of the expanding egg is too diffuse to cause enough compression to sustain another fusion reaction."

"You're telling me that not one but several Hydrogen bombs just exploded at exactly the same point on Mars?"

General Laurence gestured at the screen. "Several hundred, from the looks of it. Every blink was another bomb. They got bigger and more violent as the outer shell expanded."

Rick's stomach churned as another wave of nausea swept over him. "And this?" he pointed to the slowly spreading cloud of blue light. "What did your model say about this?"

"That is the leftover antimatter. What you're looking at is a mushroom cloud tall enough to project into outer space. It might be two or three hundred miles wide at the base."

Rick was struck speechless. He simply could not conceive of destruction on such a scale.

Ms. Lindsay spoke in his ear. "Mr. Jelton."

"Yes."

"Object two and three have cut their engines."

"What now!" exclaimed Rick. "What's their distance to Mars?"

"Several million miles, sir. We are getting some very faint readings similar to the objects' main engines. I believe they are realigning themselves."

"Realigning themselves for what?" Rick asked.

Lindsay held up one hand and used the other to press her earpiece firmly against her head. She then leaned down and looked at something on the computer display in front of her. "The objects have fired their main engines. Initial readings indicate the engines are once again pointed away from us and that the objects are accelerating relative to Mars."

Rick shook his head and rubbed his face with both hands, trying desperately to make sense of what was happening. "Maybe the first one was just a range finder. Maybe the other three will hit Mars at full velocity."

Lindsay was still leaning over the computer. She straightened slowly and turned to look directly at Rick. Her face was white. "The target appears to be Earth."

Chapter Forty-three
Below the Surface of Mars
June 24, 2061

The dreadful fear and monstrous tension of the Mars' crew, so well hidden for the last ten days behind a façade of professional behavior, flared up in the sudden darkness of the failed lamps, catching them unaware. Screams filled the radio, and even Tom yelped involuntarily. Kaitlin Geller ran without sight, headlong into Carlos Espanoza, and Carlos screamed that he was being attacked as he and Kaitlin fell on top of Melancon.

Melancon uttered a single, "Oomph," but managed to turn on his suit lights amid the tangle of too many arms and legs. Ki was next to click on his lights, and he bent to lift Kaitlin from the ground. She was sobbing uncontrollably and trying without success to wipe away the tears streaming down her face. Her gloved hand pawed ineffectively against the glass of her suit's faceplate in a strange parody of a woman crying. Ki gathered her tightly in his arms and cooed softly. "It's alright. It's alright now. We just lost power. You're alright." The room began to brighten as one by one the crewmembers activated their lights.

Carlos choked back his own sobs while struggling to stand, and Pamela Krazinsky began to cry with him. Carlos held out his arms, and she flowed across the space between them. He wrapped her tightly in an embrace as she wept.

Tom squinted and looked at Evelyn. She was standing still as a statue almost directly in front of him, and although she made not a sound, her lashes glistened in the light from his suit with tears barely held in check. She looked at Tom.

"Now don't you start," he said.

A single tear rolled down her cheek and her eyes flashed. With conviction she said, "Sometimes I hate you."

Without thinking, Tom reached out and gathered her to him. She stiffened at first but then melted into his arms. Tom leaned back so she could see his face and mouthed the words, "I'm sorry."

She looked up, blinked, and stared a hole right through him. "Can you say that out loud?"

He almost laughed, but Evelyn's expression was serious, and she was not looking away. A light-headed feeling came over him, and he found himself whispering, "I'm sorry," before he even knew what happened.

"Hey," said Melancon. He was still sitting on the plastic. "Ain't nobody gonna love a poor boy from Louisiana?"

They were in serious need of an icebreaker, and the laughter was almost hysterical as Melancon stood up to be hugged by Dr. Krazinsky, Carlos, and Kaitlin in turn. Tom took a step back. "Don't start that big-hug crap with me," he said. "I can't stand it."

Commander Thon turned his radio up to full power. "Mr. Cochran, do you read me?"

There was no answer, and he repeated the call several times without result.

Tom unclipped a meter from his belt and walked over to attach it to the wires trailing across the cavern floor from the surface above. "We've got no power at all," he said.

"I don't understand," said Evelyn. "The object exploded over 4,000 miles from here."

Kaitlin Geller sniffled and cleared her throat. "It was an EM pulse."

Everyone turned to look at her. "An Electromagnetic pulse," she said. "An EM pulse can be generated by a nuclear bomb. It's just like the communication problems we get from solar flares but much worse because it's closer."

Tom dimly recalled reading about problems with electronic devices all over the world caused by nuclear explosions during the Mid-East War of 2010. "So this EM pulse knocked out, what?"

"Depending on the force of the explosion," said Kaitlin, "it could have knocked out everything but the simplest switches." She pointed to the snow-covered screens of the computers. "It apparently overloaded the satellites, and," she pointed to the dark lights, "our power supply. If we hadn't been protected by all the rock above us, it probably would have shut down our suits and these computers."

"But if I remember correctly," said Tom, "it's unlikely the circuits have suffered any real damage."

"That's right. The devices will need to be reset."

"Hello." In a singsong voice. It was Cochran. "Is anybody home?"

"Mr. Cochran," said Ki, "are you alright?"

"Oh, I'm fine, but we need to return this suit for a refund. I was sitting here minding my own business when, bang, out of nowhere, it just decides to turn itself off. Now I don't know mind telling you I'm used to getting better merchandise than that. Did we get these at some kind of discount house? Are they still under warranty?"

Ki ignored his rambling. "We have experienced an Electromagnetic pulse from the explosion of the object. Are you sure your suit is functioning normally?"

"Well it is for now, but with shoddy workmanship like this, who knows…"

"I'm sure your suit will be fine. Did you see anything out of the ordinary."

"What? Like the blue light that lit up the sky for a few minutes?"

Tom considered Ki to be showing remarkable patience in dealing with a madman, but Ki continued without a trace of anger. "Yes, like that," Ki said.

"That's been about it," said Cochran, "but I've seen a couple of really nice shooting stars. Say, did this Electromagnetic pulse thingy knock out your suits too?"

"Our suits are fine," said Ki, "but we have lost power from the surface. You said you have seen some shooting stars?"

"Yeah, and there goes another one, and another one. Are we due for a meteor shower?"

Tom waved to Melancon and pointed to the computer and then jerked his thumb toward the surface. Melancon sat down and began searching for Cochran's video feed.

"Do you feel something?" Cochran asked.

Even as Cochran said it, Tom felt a vibration from the floor, and then he heard the noise. It was far away at first, like a distant roll of thunder, but steady and unrelenting. Quickly it grew and changed tone, sliding upward on the scale as it gained power, sounding more and more like the rasping scream of some giant insect.

"Down!" Ki screamed. "Everybody down! Get down!"

"What's going on," yelled Cochran above the noise.

"Get down on the ground now!" screamed Ki.

Tom grabbed Evelyn and pulled her down next to him, and the noise grew. He could feel it moving through his hands and feet where they touched the plastic and resonating behind his eyes and in his chest. The floor of the cavern disappeared beneath him, and he and Evelyn fell less than a foot before the floor slammed upward. Evelyn's elbow caught him in the stomach, and he struggled for air as the floor slid violently sideways. They grabbed at each other and fought to stay on the protective sheet. Tom's boots caught a jagged piece of quartz at the edge, and they stopped sliding just as the floor bucked up. Tom found himself in a kneeling position with Evelyn on her side to his left. The floor jerked sideways again but in the opposite direction, and Tom pitched forward headfirst as they slid into the spread-eagled form of Melancon, nearly pushing him off the opposite side of the plastic.

There was another drop in the floor but milder, and a pitch to Tom's left but smaller, and the quake began to subside with small tics and spasms. Tom sat up, pulled Evelyn close, and reached out a hand to Melancon who pulled himself over to huddle with them. Commander Thon crawled across the plastic with Kaitlin at his side, and the cavern shook once more and stopped.

"Status check," yelled Tom.

"Help me." It was Dr. Krazinsky. She sat at the edge of the plastic trying to pull the prostrate form of Carlos Espanoza toward her. He was flat on his back and did not move. The steam of his escaping air supply billowed from underneath him. "I fell on top of him. His suit is cut. Help me!" she screamed.

Tom jumped up.

"Be careful," said Ki. "There will be aftershocks."

"Melancon," Tom yelled. "Get him back on the plastic sheet. I'll get the patch kit."

Tom bounced across the jagged quartz, and another shock sent him stumbling. He heard Evelyn scream. "I'm okay," he said.

"What the hell was that?" It was Cochran. "I didn't sign on for this shit. Mars is geologically dead. That's what they told us. Over and over again, they said Mars is geologically dead."

"Mr. Cochran," said Ki.

"Yes, Commander."

"Are you unharmed?"

"Yeah, I guess so."

"Then shut up."

Melancon rolled Espanoza over on his stomach, and Tom looked down on a forest of small slits and pinholes on the back of Espanoza's suit starting just below his flat, square air tank and ending just above his knees. Each one spewed warm, wet air in a tiny jet.

"Oh man," said Tom, "this is not good. Somebody get another air tank."

He knelt down and ripped open the repair kit, throwing half of it toward Evelyn. "Get on his other side. We've got to get this patched up as quickly as possible."

"I have a small hole on my knee," said Pamela.

Tom looked up. "And one on your right elbow. Kaitlin, can you take care of that?"

Kaitlin picked up some of the scattered patches and sat down, patting the plastic for Pamela to sit down next to her. Commander Thon and Melancon sat nearby, helplessly watching the repairs.

Espanoza began to stir. "Whoa, buddy," said Tom, "just stay as still as you can."

"What happened?" Espanoza asked.

His speech was slurred, and Pamela shot an agonized glance at Tom. "There was a quake, Carlos," she said and reached over to lay a hand on his arm. "You have some holes in the back of your suit. Tom and Evelyn are repairing them now."

Tom leaned down to look at the air gauge on the side of Espanoza's helmet and waved to Melancon. "We've got to change your air tank, Carlos. You've got quite a few holes back here, so you're going to feel a pretty severe drop in air pressure for just a second."

Carlos mumbled something that was lost as the ground shook and groaned. "Carlos," said the Doctor sharply. "You must stay awake."

His voice was weak and he was lisping. "Okay, Pam, if you say so, but I'm tired. Why is it so cold?"

"Keep talking to him," Tom said. "He's losing heat because of the air loss. We've got to get him patched up, and I mean fast."

Pamela Krazinsky kept up a mostly one-sided conversation with her patient as Tom and Evelyn poised themselves over Carlos' air tank. With a nod they moved together. Tom uncoupled the airline with a smooth movement, a slight puff of air was released, and Evelyn snapped in the new tank. Carlos stiffened and moaned from the popping in his ears and the brief but intense tingling of his skin as his suit collapsed and re-inflated, and Tom and Evelyn went back to patching the holes.

Ten minutes, another air tank, and several aftershocks later, Tom sat back on his heels and looked over at Evelyn, shaking his head. Several small areas of steam still escaped from the back of Carlos' suit. "This is the best we can do without taking his suit off," he said.

"We need to get the temporary housing assembled or he'll freeze to death," said Evelyn.

"Right," Tom said and stood up stiffly, his knees and back complaining from the time he had spent kneeling at Carlos' side.

Evelyn's face was bleak. "We have no power," she said.

Tom cursed and stomped back and forth across the plastic. "We can't finish the foam application without power, and we can't heat the damned thing even if we had that part finished." The ground trembled, and he sat down quickly.

Pamela began to cry again. "I have to give him medication. He has a concussion."

The forgotten member of the crew spoke. "You guys sound like you could use some help," said Cochran.

"He can reset the power on the surface," said Tom.

"I can do that," said Cochran, "but I want you to know I was right about the sunrise."

Melancon pulled his computer closer and resumed his interrupted search for Cochran's video feed.

"What about the sunrise?" asked Ki.

"It is spectacular and early. Just like I said it would be. I've got a bright, blue sun rising in the east behind clouds of red dust that look like they go all the way into outer space. It's just now midnight, and when you add in the meteorites coming down every second or so, even my friend Tommy would have to agree it's spectacular. Just like I said—spectacular and early."

Ki had a peculiar look on his face. "Mr. Cochran, has anything changed about the meteorites in the last thirty minutes?"

"As a matter of fact, the angle of descent has changed. The first ones were coming down almost horizontal and all from the east. Lately they've been more straight into the ground, and there have been some big ones. You guys may have felt the ground shake from the last one. It was beautiful. I could see red-hot sand exploding out of the crater about forty miles south of here."

Ki put both hands up to his helmet and shook his head. "It can't be true," he said.

Melancon turned his computer toward Tom and Ki. "Check this out," he said.

It was the video from Cochran's camera and it showed the front of the rover moving forward across the rolling sand of Mars as he threaded the vehicle past small boulders and rocks. But it was the color of the sand and the look of the sky that made everyone stop and blink. The sand was now brown from the strange light, and half the sky was covered with a glowing, blue cloud. Almost every second, a shooting star fell down in a long streak of bright white and yellow.

Kaitlin Geller drew in a sharp breath. "It's the antimatter," she said softly.

Everyone turned.

"The antimatter from the object is spreading out and reacting with the upper atmosphere. Mr. Cochran must find shelter immediately."

"To late for that," said Cochran cheerily. "My radiation dosimeter pegged out about fifteen minutes ago."

Commander Thon seemed lost in some sort of daze, and Tom spoke. "Cochran, you've got to get into the cave now."

"Gee, I thought you wanted me to turn on the power."

"Cochran, this is no time to play games. You've got to find shelter. We'll help you into the cave."

"Now, Tommy," Cochran said with an almost affectionate tone, "you know I like my games, and I'd have to say the graphics on this one are the best I've ever seen, but the plot kind of sucks. It looks like the only way to win is to die."

The solar-film covered scaffolds came into view on Melancon's computer.

"Come on, Mike," Tom pleaded. "Just reset the switch and come back to the cave."

"I don't think so, Tom. To tell you the truth, I'm not feeling too good, and there's not much point anymore. Ask our good doctor. She'll tell you I'm dead already."

Dr. Pamela Krazinsky looked at Kaitlin. "What kind of radiation is he being exposed to?"

"It's high-energy gamma," said Kaitlin. "Like they use to irradiate food. It's not going to leave any residual radiation in the soil, but exposure to it is. . ."

Pamela's face crinkled up as tears once again came down her face. She looked at Tom and shook her head.

"Is real bad," Cochran finished. "I'm a rocket pilot, remember? I know all about radiation."

The scene on the computer showed that Cochran was walking slowly toward the box containing the timer for the batteries and solar film.

"Just reset the switch and get back to the cave," said Tom. "We can treat you once we get the shelter up."

"Not gonna happen, Tom. All that rocking back and forth in the rover has left me with a seriously upset stomach, and I'm really tired."

They watched as he reached down and pushed the red button on the side of the box. The lights in the cave blazed to life, and Tom signaled Evelyn to finish the work of laying down the foam for the base of the temporary shelter.

"You got power?" asked Cochran.

"Yes," said Tom. He pleaded once more, but he knew it was past hope. "Come on, Mike. Come back to the cave."

Cochran trudged toward the rover and tripped as a minor tremor shook the ground. The picture on the computer pitched violently forward, and they could hear Cochran grunt. He rolled over on his back, revealing a glowing, blue sky full of quick, yellow streaks. "No, this is good. I think I like it right here."

Tom didn't know what to say, and he looked at Ki, but the Commander didn't seem to be paying attention.

"You guys never really liked me anyway," Cochran said wearily. "I'm going to turn my radio off now. According to the books, I'm supposed to start throwing up and gagging in a little bit. There's no reason you should have to listen to all that. If you ever get a chance to tell my Mom about this, tell her I did the best I could."

"I'll tell her, Mike, and thanks," said Tom, but Cochran never heard it. The radio was silent but for the sobs of those who had just listened to the last request of the first man to die on Mars.

Ki stood rock still with his hands out in front of him. Tom could see that Ki's mouth was open and his eyes had a wild look. "Are you okay, commander?"

Ki reached out and gripped Tom's arm hard enough to cause pain through the fabric of his suit. "This has happened before," he said in a near whisper.

"What?" said Tom. "What has happened before?"

"The strange distribution of craters on Mars. The disappearance of the atmosphere and all the water. The two strange moons. The problems dating the rocks. All those places where water seems to have gushed from the ground and then disappeared. The formation of all this quartz. It's all happened before."

Tom feared for his Commander's sanity. "What are you talking about."

"The bombs, Tom. It was the bombs. One million, two million years ago. I don't know, but Mars has been bombed before."

~

And on the slopes of Cheyenne Mountain above NORAD, in parks and in backyards across half the Earth, in the streets and from windows with the curtains barely parted, people raised their eyes and trembled at the sight of Mars burning with a pale, blue flame in the sky above them.

Gregg R. Overman

Chapter Forty-four
The Planet Harmony
Exact Time Unknown

The old Tree watched Skrin climb the grassy slope in front of him. There were two cars this time, one of them containing nothing but guards, and Tree could see the armed Koombar as they fanned out in the woods around him. Skrin approached to the usual twenty feet and stretched to his full height with an air of casual impatience while Tree looked him over quickly. Having a life span of only 60 years, the Koombar grew rapidly to maturity, and Skrin was visibly taller than when they had last met. He had in fact grown into a fine specimen of Koombar adulthood and was now larger than most of the guards coming to positions of readiness in a broad circle around the clearing.

Tree bent forward as far as he was able, and lowered all three of his arms, placing his six hands on the ground. "This one is greatly honored to be in the presence of such a fine specimen of the Koombar heritage."

"Yes, yes," said Skrin, dismissing the obligatory obeisance with a wag of his head.

"You have grown since we last met."

"Your sleep was long, and I approach adulthood. In two days, I will celebrate the Feast of Ascendance."

"And you will be an adult," said Tree. "Excellent. This would explain the extra guards."

"Yes."

"Yet I understand the Koombar discourage the murder of children."

"The murder of children is discouraged but not unknown. The eldest son of the Supreme Watcher is exposed to greater danger than most."

"And is more dangerous than most," said Tree.

Skrin's ears shivered with amusement as he dropped to the ground. "Yes."

The old Tree watched Skrin snuggle into the grass in front of him. The nearly adult Koombar had been an interesting pupil, and despite their differences, Tree was glad to see him. "What should we speak of today?"

"A probe transmitted a message of contact four days ago. It is an omen of good fortune for my Feast of Ascendance, and there has been much rejoicing among the Koombar, but I am curious, what do the Trees think of this matter?"

"The Trees consider the actions of the Koombar toward other intelligent races to be the most despicable part of the Koombar paranoiac insanity."

Skrin rolled on to his side and blew a tuft of grass into the air. "Really?"

"Really."

"And what do you intend to do about our depravity?"

"The Trees will do nothing."

"Because you cannot?"

"Because we will not."

Skrin rolled over on his back to let the sun warm his belly. "Thought without action. Outrage without outlet. Tell me, old Tree, is this philosophy?"

"It is a result of our philosophy."

"Then it is good that the Koombar do not understand or study it."

"The Koombar would do well to expand their view of things."

"As the Trees have done?"

"The Tree vision is broad and long."

Skrin wiggled back and forth with his legs in the air, scratching his back against the ground. "The Tree eyes see all, but the Tree hands do nothing. I have no doubt the Trees have talked endlessly about the message of contact, but to what end? What does it matter? Nothing will be done, and our practices will continue as they have for thousands of years."

"There is a small minority among the Trees who believe action should be taken."

"But will they act?" asked Skrin.

"They will not act alone."

"The Koombar would band together in a conspiracy and accomplish whatever needed to be done."

Tree considered this. "You are familiar with the adult Tree's method of communication?"

"Shouting at each other through the ground? Yes."

"It is not a situation conducive to learning the art of subterfuge."

"So they will not act?"

"No."

"Then I remain unimpressed." Skrin rolled over on his stomach and plucked more grass from the ground. "Our ways seem to cause the Trees some degree of pain and discomfort, yet you will not act to relieve yourselves of the distress. And you have the temerity to call the Koombar insane—it is beyond me."

"The needless extermination of intelligent life is an abomination. They have done nothing to you."

"Not yet."

"You have no evidence they would harm you."

"And you cannot prove they will not harm us. The Koombar prefer safety to speculation."

"It is a genetic insanity," said Tree, "and you cannot escape it. The Koombar simply are what they are."

"And the Trees are what they are?"

"Yes."

"I have been thinking about some of the things you have told me," said Skrin. "All of this nonsense about evolution. You said the Trees evolved intelligence from a need to communicate. Is that true?"

The old Tree sensed a verbal trap but could only respond in the affirmative.

"And that need has been fulfilled?" asked Skrin.

"Yes."

"Then there is no more evolutionary pressure on the Trees."

"The Trees have not changed in millions of years."

"As I thought," said Skrin. "But what of the Koombar?"

Tree wasn't sure how to respond. The thrust of Skrin's questions was making him nervous. "What of the Koombar?"

"You have pointed out that accession to the position of Supreme Watcher is a highly selective process, and only the most intelligent and resourceful Koombar could succeed."

"This is true."

"And who among the Koombar will have the largest harem and sire the most children?"

The trap was sprung, but far from feeling irritation, Tree was intrigued. "The Supreme Watcher," he answered.

"Then evolution is still at work on the Koombar race."

"I suppose it is."

"But the Trees continue to view us as the simple people who were so badly in need of rescue from the planet they had destroyed. The Trees believed the intelligence of Cheswan Swi Geberak to be an aberration. Perhaps at the time he was, but we have changed, and we continue to grow. The day approaches when we will understand all of the secrets of the Trees, and we will have no further use for you."

"What nonsense is this?" said the Tree. "The Koombar cannot even build a guidance system capable of hitting a planet with one of your bombs."

Skrin's ears shivered with a laugh. "You find this aesthetically displeasing? This offends the Tree sensibility?"

Tree rattled his hands together in frustration. What had ever made him glad to see this insolent and irritating Koombar? "We find the entire practice to be disgusting."

"Well, my old Tree friend, we are different, you and I. The Koombar will continue to protect themselves from the dangers of other intelligent life by the most practical means at our disposal. Our guidance systems are not up to the Tree standards, that is true, but even the Trees would have to agree they are up to the task before them. Elegant, no. Efficient, yes."

"Your guidance systems and your bombs may not be as efficient as you suppose."

Skrin rolled over on his back again. He was clearly enjoying himself. "And how is that?"

"The system reported by your probe has been struck before."

Skrin flipped back over and raised his head. "Truly?"

"Yes. It was one of the first systems the Koombar destroyed."

Skrin seemed puzzled. "How long ago was that?"

"Approximately one million years."

Skrin's ears began to shake so hard they blurred in the Tree's vision. The young Koombar rolled to his back and waved his feet in the air. "One million years? Now that is reason for concern. I shall make a note to send a surveillance probe to the area in, oh, what do you think, a million years or so?"

Tree was furious. "Arrogant Koombar."

Skrin's ears shook even harder. "Impotent Tree."

"Remember my words, Skrin. The Koombar will one day anger a race that will seek you out and destroy you. Your bombs will one day miss their mark, or you will find a race that has grown so quickly as to achieve space flight before you find them. They will not take kindly to being attacked without reason."

"Let's see," said Skrin. "From the Tree records: 'The average time from the advent of simple radio to the colonization of other planets would then appear to be no less than 400 years.' I believe one of your historians said that."

Tree was shocked beyond reckoning as he recalled the passage. "The words of Letsmyan, but where did you learn this?"

Skrin ignored the question. "Our actions have kept us alive for over two million years. You argue that the Koombar will be found by a race advanced to the point of space flight. That they will be angered by what we have done. That they will destroy us all. But the Tree records refute this. According to your own texts, the Trees were the first long-lived intelligence in this region of space. Your Cosmologists speculate that a galaxy must reach maturity before it can bear life, and the galactic core is too energetic to support organic life.

"We have thousands of probes, and they patrol only this spiral arm. It is a great deal of space to be sure, but the probes need only travel two hundred light years, listen for a moment, and travel on. No, the extermination of threats to the Koombar existence will not stop. Not now, not ever."

Skrin stretched his legs and rolled to his side. "Old Tree, who do you think you have been talking to? I am the eldest son of the Supreme Watcher—the best of the best by your own reasoning, but I am more than that. Cheswan Swi Geberak was twisted in body but brilliant of mind. Because of his body, he could not lead. I have no such restrictions."

Skrin sat up and held the Tree in his gaze. "Perhaps there is a genius born to every generation. I don't know. I only know that I was bored by concepts with which my classmates struggled for weeks. I only know that I see things around me that others do not understand.

"I had one of your children translate some of the Tree records, and I have spent a great deal of time in the months of your sleep reading those records, looking for patterns, looking for changes. It is clear the Koombar are more intelligent in this age than when they first came to Harmony. The process is slow but inexorable. The day will come, my friend, when the Trees will not be needed to repair the antimatter generators or for any other purpose, and we will act as we always have. We will destroy the potential threat the Trees represent.

"Today we need the Trees, but I will do everything in my power as Supreme Watcher to hasten the day when the Koombar will stand on their own. On that day, Harmony will stink with the smell of burning Trees."

Skrin pulled more grass from the ground and chewed absently on the end of one stalk. "I personally wish you no injury. I understand the Trees well enough to know you are harmless. You are frozen in time, rooted in ancient opinions and perceptions, and stranded by your own inability to act. I will be long dead when the day of the Tree destruction comes, but I know the Koombar as you never will, and though it might be a thousand years or ten thousand, they will obliterate you, and they will remember the name of Skrin—the Supreme Watcher who set the Koombar on the path to freedom."

"You seem assured of becoming Supreme Watcher," said the Tree. He was horrified by what he had heard and wanted desperately to change the subject.

"There is danger in all things," said Skrin, "but I will be Supreme Watcher, and I have you to thank for it."

"I don't understand."

"My father was right. There are many useful things to be learned from Trees. From Trees, we learned to destroy planets, and from you, I learned how to murder my father."

"I know nothing of murder."

Skrin's ears vibrated once again. "True enough, and Trees know nothing of genocide, yet your technology has been most helpful in the Koombar campaigns. My father's days are numbered, and that number is two. I will come back and tell you about it when it is done."

"I do not care to hear it."

"Dear Tree, that is not the point. I will enjoy the telling of it."

Skrin stood up and signaled his guards. "I must be going. There is much to prepare."

Tree bowed low. "By your leave," he said, and Skrin began to walk back to the car as guards streamed out of the woods and down the hill.

"Perhaps you are right about our guidance systems," Skrin said as he walked away. "As you have been right in some things and wrong in others. I may undertake to have them improved when I am Supreme Watcher."

Tree watched as Skrin and the guards entered the cars and drove away. He was devastated by what Skrin had said and shocked at the changes in his young pupil, but he'd had very little first-hand experience with the Koombar, and this was true of all Trees. The Koombar simply told the nearest young Tree when something critical was in need of repair. The young Tree would find the nearest adult who would then see that the work was done. The two species, for different reasons, lived in separate worlds on a single planet.

The Trees maintained equipment through the efforts of their young. The Trees constantly debated the finest points of any subject imaginable. The Trees told stories and taught their children, and the Trees were content.

We are content," he scoffed to himself, and the words had the undeniable, bitter taste of self-revelation. *We have become custodians of machinery and custodians of our own heritage, and our heritage is crumbling to dust as we chat with each other over the minutiae of ancient philosophies.*

A question came to him, and he approached its answer with dread. *When last had a Tree promulgated a truly new idea, something revolutionary and fresh?* He rifled through his prodigious memory and found nothing.

Slowly and with difficulty, he came to see himself and his brothers as little more than highly skilled mechanics. Did anyone now among them understand the subtleties of the physics that had allowed them to build the antimatter generator? It was not his area of expertise, but whose area was it? There were those who enjoyed debating the topic, but did they truly understand it?

On reflection, he believed they did not, and he was forced to the conclusion that the Tree intelligence was in decline. It seemed likely that the decline had begun even before they had found the Koombar.

And Skrin was right. The Trees had first seen the Koombar huddled at the poles of their dying planet—a pitiful race of beings caught in the trap of their own self-destructive behavior—but the Koombar race had grown to adulthood while the Trees had become nothing more than talented children preferring endless word games to an honest assessment or further exploration of the world around them.

Their perception of the Koombar had remained unchanged for two million years, and they would one day be destroyed by the solidity of their outlook.

Tree let his arms drop to the ground, and he wept in the manner of Trees, his skin exuding a thin version of the secretions found on mature children. His ancestors had taught the Koombar the skills necessary for extinguishing the rare light of intelligence across half the galaxy and had then allowed it to happen. His progeny would die as a result, and in his present state, it seemed a fitting end.

Skrin had learned well from the Trees. He had taken what the Trees knew best and would use it to his own purposes while rejecting the useless and inane ramblings of thousands of philosophers and pseudo scientists. Tree found himself admiring the strategy. It was pragmatic rather than theoretical, and it would succeed.

Tree felt his unborn son quicken within him—the first movement of perhaps his last child—and the words of his dream came back to him: "Unless you are willing to teach your children to look where you have not dared look before."

The dream seemed prophetic now, and he wondered at its meaning, but where could they look? Skrin had turned to the Trees for knowledge, but where might the Trees turn for inspiration?

An idea flashed into his mind with such speed and power that he trembled with its force. Had he gone insane, or was this the stuff of genius? Was he grasping at a ridiculous concept in the hope of saving his unknown great grandchildren, or had a Tree finally, after two million years, produced a fresh and revolutionary idea? He decided he didn't care.

Tree raised his hands to the sky and called his children with a deep, booming laugh. His thoughts raced ahead. There was much to be done.

Where indeed might the Trees look for enlightenment, unless it would be to the Koombar?

Gregg R. Overman

Chapter Forty-five
NORAD
June 24, 2061

Rick had hoped for something different, but the meeting room at NORAD was a carbon copy of the rooms at NASA and the White House. A large, oval table took up most of the space, and a computer screen covered one wall.

Rick and Marilyn pulled out chairs on one side of the table and sat down, watching the people in uniforms, gray suits, and the occasional white lab coat file through the door. President Bremmer, flanked by Secretary Salness and General Walker, was already seated at one end. General Laurence sat down to Rick's left, and most of the other available chairs filled up with high-ranking, military personnel.

"Christ," said Rick, "there's enough brass in here to start up a goddamned jazz band."

Marilyn giggled a little hysterically and held her hand in front of her mouth. General Laurence simply raised his eyebrows and nodded.

President Bremmer looked around, and even though people were still entering the room, he tapped the table with his knuckles and said, "Let's get started. We don't have a whole lot of time. Can anyone tell me why one object hit Mars and the other three seem to be headed toward Earth?"

"We believe it was due to an Electromagnetic Pulse," said General Laurence.

"Explain," said the President.

General Laurence placed his elbows on the table and interlaced his fingers in front of him. "The alien object that struck Mars released a large amount of antimatter. This antimatter began to react with the air and soil of Mars in such a way as to make a fusion bomb. Fusion bombs generate a very strong pulse of electromagnetic radiation during the first few milliseconds of the blast. This radiation pulse affects electronic hardware of all sorts. It is our belief that the broadcast satellites around Mars were overloaded by this pulse and shut themselves down. Mars ceased broadcasting, and Earth became the only thing in the sky with a radio frequency signature."

The President frowned with displeasure and shook his head. "We have jumped through hoops to shut down all the satellites on the side of Earth that faces Mars. What radio are you talking about?"

Secretary Salness fielded the question. "Sir, we have done the best we could to eliminate all broadcasts from Earth toward Mars, and our efforts were apparently good enough to divert the objects to Mars as long as Mars was broadcasting. However, there are still many sources of radio transmission on Earth. Even in the United States, there are several television and radio stations that have continued to broadcast to local audiences during the blackout period. These stations have been, uh, strongly encouraged to shut down, but as soon as one of them stops, another one starts up. There are simply too many of them for us to effectively police, and for all we know, even a cellular phone might be strong enough to attract the objects to Earth."

The President was drumming his fingers on the table. "Okay, we have three of these damned things heading our way with an E.T.A. of what, twenty-four hours? We can't seem to maintain the radio silence we need to make them forget about us, we have no way of shooting them out of the sky because the United Nations banned all research into space-based offensive and defensive weapons, and the only two probes that had a prayer of stopping them have already been destroyed. Is that about it?"

There was a chilling silence around the table as the president looked back and forth across the group. Finally, he leaned back in his chair and laced his fingers behind his head. " And what can we expect when they hit?"

Nobody moved till a small, thin man standing against the wall cleared his throat and spoke. "I believe I can answer that."

All heads turned in the direction of a pale man wearing a white lab coat. He was perhaps forty-five with thin, sandy hair. The NORAD insignia on his left lapel showed him to be a civilian worker with permanent status.

"And you would be?" asked the President.

He seemed overwhelmed by the attention and tried to stammer a reply before General Walker spoke out. "This is Professor Wilson Jenkins," said the General. "He is our Chief of Physics Research and an expert on nuclear weapons."

"Very well, Dr. Jenkins," said President Bremmer. "What are we looking at?"

Jenkins swallowed hard, and his Adam's apple bobbed in his throat. "Well, sir, Mr. President, sir, um, it will…be…bad."

Rick could almost see the President gritting his teeth from where he sat. "We sort of figured it would be bad," said the President. "If you could give us a few specifics?"

The man took a deep breath and swallowed again. "Uh, well, what we've seen from the impact on, uh, Mars indicates a blast of several hundred thousand and perhaps several, uh, million megatons. There are, uh, a number of things to consider. The first of these is the, uh, blast itself. The initial force of one of these objects would level everything within a radius of about one thousand miles, but, uh, as bad as that seems, it's probably not the worst part.

"The blue cloud we saw spreading away from the blast site on Mars was antimatter reacting with the atmosphere on Mars. The atmosphere of Earth is much more dense than that of Mars, and we could expect to see an accordingly more violent reaction, although it would not spread out as far."

Jenkins was picking up speed as he warmed to his subject, and his hands barely shook when he raised them to indicate the slowly spreading cloud. "That's not to say the cloud from one of these objects wouldn't cover a large portion of the globe. As a guess, I would estimate 15 to 20 percent of the Earth might be covered by a cloud of antimatter from the explosion of just one object. All life under that cloud will die unless it is protected by massive amounts of shielding. Antimatter reactions produce large amounts of high-energy gamma radiation. This radiation does not linger in the environment, but it is capable of penetrating most conventional radiation shields."

President Bremmer interrupted. "You're saying three of these objects would wipe out 60 percent of all the life on Earth?"

Dr. Jenkins made a face and picked nervously at the back of one hand. "I wish the news were that good. There are several other things we can expect. The explosion will release a significant amount of heat. If the other three objects strike the Earth, we will see a rise in global temperature that will wipe out existing farmlands and partially melt the polar ice caps. Sea levels will rise across the Earth, but the Ice Age that follows will be like nothing this planet has ever seen."

"Ice Age?" asked the President.

"Yes, sir. The water vapor and dust blown into our upper atmosphere would be enough to cause an Ice Age by itself, but the force of the blast on Mars was such that much of the surface near the impact point was actually blown into space. Some of that debris is now in orbit around Mars. We can expect a similar occurrence on Earth, and the Earth will be surrounded by an orbiting cloud of dust. This dust will take thousands of years to clear off. Before that happens, the world's oceans will be covered with ice down to the equator."

Dr. Jenkins swallowed once more and looked up at the President for a second before dropping his eyes to the floor. "Sir, I, uh, don't think civilization or Mankind could…survive such a thing."

President Bremmer leaned back in his chair and stared at the ceiling. "Thank you, Dr. Jenkins."

It was as if all the blood had been drained from the room. They had lived for weeks with "The end of the world as we know it," but the phrase had just been shortened to read "The end of the world," and no one could speak or make eye contact while their minds choked on the idea and their thoughts spiraled downward into contemplation of shattered dreams and the choice between quick death by radiation or a slow but inevitable starvation for them and their children.

The President's head remained tilted back, and he had not moved except to close his eyes. "What if we hit one with a surface-to-air missile on its way down?"

"Um, that might be worse. It's hard to tell. It would lessen the shock wave, but the antimatter cloud would spread out farther—probably a lot farther."

"Well we can't just sit here. We have to do something."

"We need to shut down all the radios," said Secretary Salness.

"Obviously," said the President, "How do you propose to do it?"

General Walker spoke up. "We put troops on the ground and mobilize the Air Force. If we have to, we blow up the goddamned transmitters."

President Bremmer sat up and looked at the General with one eyebrow raised. "All over the world? You've got a lot of planes and a lot of real smart bombs. I'm sure you could teach them to target any radio transmitter in operation, but every university has one or two radio stations. A lot of churches have radio stations. Are we going to blow them up?"

"If we have to."

The President shook his head. "You don't have enough bombs to cover the United States and no time to deploy on that scale. It just won't work, and I can't see us dropping bombs on transmitters in England or France, much less in China or the Middle East."

"Drastic situations call for drastic measures."

The President spoke slowly through clenched teeth. "It won't work. If I thought it would do any good. . ." He stopped and brought both hands up to his face. "God Almighty, I can't believe we're even considering such a thing."

General Walker continued to push his idea. "We can't sit here and do nothing, and we don't know how sensitive the objects' detectors are. We might at least keep them from coming down in Iowa or New York City. The rest of the world will have to see to their own damned transmitters.

General Laurence spoke up to Rick's left. "I agree with the President. We will never silence every broadcast station in the United States by knocking them off the air one by one."

General Walker's expression shot daggers across the table, and a vein throbbed at his temple. "Do you have any better ideas?" he asked in clipped tones.

General Laurence pursed his lips and rocked back and forth in his chair. His hands were clasped tightly between his knees, and his head was bowed forward. His eyes scanned back and forth across the surface of the table as if there was a book open in front of him. "I don't like this," he said slowly. "It isn't any less drastic than General Walker's proposal. The only advantage is that it should work."

"Let's hear it," said the President.

General Laurence wiped his palms on the legs of his uniform and placed his hands in front of him. "A fusion burst on Mars caused an Electromagnetic Pulse that knocked out their satellites. A fusion burst here, or several of them, would do the same thing to satellites and ground-based transmitters on Earth."

Secretary Salness practically screamed, "General Laurence, do I need to remind you that in accordance with the Nuclear Disarmament Treaty of 2015 the United States has dismantled its nuclear warheads?"

General Laurence nodded slowly. Rick could see the pain in the man's eyes, but the General spoke clearly and with precision. "I am well aware of the provisions of that treaty, Mr. Secretary. I am also aware, as are you, that the United States has never fully complied with it."

It was instant pandemonium, and the reactions ranged from shock and dismay to incredulity and anger. Secretary Salness jumped up from his chair, shaking a finger at General Laurence. His voice could be heard over everyone. "I will have you arrested for public disclosure of top-secret information. What in the hell do you think you're doing?"

President Bremmer sat stoned faced for a moment and then, almost casually, reached up and grabbed the Secretary's tie. With a sharp jerk he pulled the Secretary's face down to within inches of his own. "You are not going to have anybody arrested, and if you don't shut up right now, I will have you disappear completely."

It was like flipping a switch. The room was plunged into silence. Those who had come to their feet sat down quickly and became very still. For a moment, you could have heard a pin drop.

The President released the tie in his hand, and the Secretary slowly straightened up. "This is insanity," said the Secretary. His face was bright red.

President Bremmer didn't even look at him. "Sit down and shut up. These are insane times. Perhaps insanity is called for." He looked over at General Laurence. "This would work?"

General Laurence nodded. "It would probably take several high-altitude bursts. They could be placed so as to minimize any…collateral damage. Dr. Jenkins is better qualified to tell us where to put them and how many we'd need."

"Dr. Jenkins," asked the President, "will this work?"

Jenkins cleared his throat. "Oh, well, yes, sir. The timing of the bursts would have to be precise."

"Not a problem," said General Laurence. "We can broadcast a trigger signal to activate all the bombs at the same instant."

"Okay," the President looked at Dr. Jenkins, "how many do we need and where do we put them?"

"I would need to run some, uh, simulations. It is difficult to…"

President Bremmer slammed his palm on the table. Several people jumped, and Dr. Jenkins would have stepped back, but he was standing next to the wall and succeeded only in thumping his head against the computer screen. "Make a guess, Dr. Jenkins. Just make a damned guess."

Jenkins stood rubbing the back of his head, but the words flowed freely. "Between five and seven. We can put one each over the North and South Poles, one over the southeastern Atlantic Ocean, one over the southwestern Pacific Ocean, and two more somewhere over water in the Southern Hemisphere. That might do it."

"And what would be the projected casualties?"

"That would be very difficult to say, sir." The President raised his hand above the table, and Jenkins hastily continued. "Make a guess. Yes, sir. Make a guess. Uh, well, it probably won't be that bad. These would be high-altitude bursts, somewhere in the range of 250 to 300 miles above the surface. The shock wave will be minimal, and radiation would not be a problem except for people out in the open directly under the burst. If we can do this without placing one of them over a populated land mass, then casualties as a direct result of the blasts might be less than a thousand."

"How does that compare to the casualties we could expect if just one of the objects hits Earth?"

Jenkins brushed his thin hair back from his forehead. "Um, there is really no comparison, sir. Even if one of the Alien objects comes down in, uh… the Australian Outback for instance, the shock wave would probably level Sidney, and the radiation cloud might spread as far north as Cambodia or even Japan. The death toll would be in the billions, not counting the fact that we'd still get a small Ice Age."

The President had been stroking his chin with one hand while he listened, and he waved his other hand in the air. "So we set off the nukes in outer space, every radio in the world blinks off, the Alien objects fly on by, and we're back in business?"

"Uh, not exactly, sir. Radios are not the only things that will be affected by the EM pulse." Jenkins grinned self-consciously. "Uh, that's what we call an Electromagnetic Pulse."

The President waved in Jenkins' direction. "Whatever."

"The results of an EM pulse of this magnitude would be far reaching and long lasting. The Van Allen belt will be pumped full of excess, high-energy electrons. It will take years for these electrons to dissipate. While military satellites are hardened against such a possibility, most civilian satellites are not. The civilian satellites that survive the initial pulse will fail in a matter of days or weeks.

"But that's probably not the worst part of it. Not only will cellular phones and transmitters be rendered inoperable, but every power grid on Earth will go down as well. A lot of computers will be fried, and…"

"Hold it," said the President.

"Sir?"

"Back to the power grid thing. Are you telling me this EM pulse will turn off every light and electrical motor in the world?"

Jenkins bobbed his head and grinned as if he had just taught calculus to an idiot son. "Yes, sir. Absolutely."

The President leaned back in his chair, closed his eyes once more, and rubbed his forehead. "Christ Almighty, is there anything else I need to know?"

"Nothing I can really think of. Most of the military hardware on the ground will survive the pulse. Um, if that makes any difference."

"Very well then, Dr. Jenkins. I want a full report in two hours. I want to know how many, where, and what the full effects will be."

"I can't possibly…"

"Two hours, Dr. Jenkins."

"I, uh, yes. Could I, uh, be excused from the remainder of this meeting, Mr. President."

President Bremmer waved him to the door, and Jenkins scurried out with one final look over his shoulder.

"This is nuts," said Secretary Salness. "The Chinese will retaliate by launching nukes at us. They didn't comply with the treaty anymore than we did. You're talking about starting a World War—a real one this time."

The President nodded his head, and when he spoke, his voice was slow and soft. "Well, Mr. Secretary, it seems to me that global thermonuclear war might be preferable to getting hit by one of the objects, but I don't really think it will turn out that way. We can tell the Chinese we're going to do it. We can tell them exactly where, exactly when, and exactly why. They will respond publicly by denouncing our actions, but my gut tells me they'll be glad to see somebody trying something, and they'll be very glad that it's us and not them."

"Mr. President," pleaded the Secretary.

"I would be very happy to consider any other viable alternatives."

There was a long silence around the table, and Secretary Salness spoke again. "We don't even know if this will work."

Rick had been waiting for the right time. "It worked before," he said.

Both Secretary Salness and President Bremmer looked in his direction, but it was the Secretary who spoke first. "It worked before because we had Mars broadcast to the objects. If you will recall, they didn't respond to the hails from the two probes."

Rick nodded. "I remember it quite clearly, Mr. Secretary. Our conclusion was that the Alien objects are programmed to respond only to radio signals from a planetary-sized mass."

The Secretary's voice dripped with sarcasm. "In case you haven't noticed, Mr. Jelton, we have run out of planets with broadcast capabilities."

"Planets yes, but not planetary-sized masses. Our moon is almost as large as Mars."

Excited murmurs and the rustling of clothes filled the room as people shifted in their seats and talked to each other. The Secretary's mouth dropped open, and he stared at Rick for a moment. "There are over 100,000 people on the Moon."

"And multiple billions on Earth," Rick said.

The President was nearly at attention in his chair. "So we set off these nukes, generate an EM pulse to shut down all the radios on Earth, and begin broadcasting to the Alien objects from the Moon at the same time."

Rick nodded without speaking.

The murmurs rose to a crescendo of discussion. Secretary Salness stuck to his opinion that it was insanity, but General Walker seemed to have come around to considering it, and President Bremmer was obviously ready to try anything no matter how insane it might sound.

Rick looked at Lindsay, and their eyes met. He could see deep distress in the slight tightness of her mouth and the small crease of a frown just above the bridge of her nose. He knew she could see much the same in him. "They'll do this," he whispered. "They'll do this because there's nothing else we can do."

Chapter Forty-six
Surface of the Moon
Lexam Barracks
June 26, 2061

Ben was feeling pretty good about things in general. This put him directly at odds with the other 100,000 people on the Moon, but that was okay.

All non-essential work had been canceled on this, the big day, but it had started out like any other. Ben had rolled out of bed, crunched down four Carbodine tablets, taken a shower, and walked to the cafeteria—it seemed like he was always hungry lately. Just as he sat down to eat, the television in the corner emitted a strange series of tones and flashed into life for the first time in four days. The President of the United States, Haywood Bremmer, stood staring into the camera. Even with stage makeup, he looked a bit hollow eyed.

"People of the Moon, my friends, I'm sure you must be surprised to hear a message from Earth. Believe me, we would not have broken our radio silence if the situation were not desperate."

Everyone in the cafeteria moved to the corner of the room where the television was placed high on the wall, and Ben picked up his plate to join them as they clustered together at a single table.

The President shuffled some notes on the podium and continued with a bit of hesitance in his voice. "As I am sure you are all aware, the United States, together with all of the other governments on Earth, has been shutting down radio broadcasts in the direction of the four Alien objects. At the same time, Mars turned their transmitters toward these objects. It was our hope that we might divert the objects to Mars and learn of their intentions.

"We were successful in this, and some of you may have been in a position to see the effects of the first object's impact on Mars."

The President took a deep breath and did the near impossible by appearing even more serious than before. "We now understand that the objects carry bombs of a size and of a destructive force we could have only imagined just a few short hours ago, and it is likely that the entire Mars crew lost their lives in giving us this information."

The President gazed into the camera, and even through the television, he seemed to hold each man personally with his eyes. "This is the stuff of heroes. These men and women, far from home and isolated from the ones they love, gave their lives so that their families and friends—their loved ones on Earth—might live. Through the efforts of this courageous group, we now know the intentions and the capabilities of the remaining three Alien objects," he paused for the length of short breath, "and we now know how to stop them."

With the mastery of a world-class politician, President Bremmer tightened the muscles slightly around his eyes, and his voice took on a tremulous quality. It was impossible to believe he wasn't holding back tears. "What you may not know is that the remaining three objects are now targeted on Earth and are moving in this direction at nearly three million miles per hour. We expect first impact in less than six hours."

The President waited for his audience to absorb what he had just said, and there were exclamations from around the table while Ben finished the last of his toast.

"Our scientists," continued the President, "have determined that the Earth cannot survive the impact of even two of these objects and might not survive the impact of just one object. Obviously, we cannot allow this to happen."

President Bremmer looked at his notes and then laid them face down on the podium. "We have but one hope," he said and paused, "and that hope lies with you, our brothers and sisters on the Moon."

He paused again before continuing. "Our previous strategy was to silence the radios on Earth and draw the objects to Mars.

Eight men and women, the heroes of the Mars Expedition, risked and may have lost their lives so that we on Earth might live. It is with deep regret and profound misgiving that I must ask you to do the same."

Several of the men at the table cried out, and one of them jumped up. His chair fell backward to the floor with a loud clatter. Ben sipped his coffee and wondered if he should refill his plate now or wait till the speech had ended. He decided to wait.

"In one hour and twenty five minutes, six fusion bombs will be exploded at various points high above Earth's surface. This will disrupt all communications from Earth and will enforce a worldwide radio blackout. At the same time, all stations on the Moon will begin broadcasting to the position of the Alien objects. It is our belief that the objects will turn away from Earth and toward the Moon."

The table erupted with expletives, and two men screamed together, "They can't do this!"

"Shut up," Ben roared over all of them. "I put off the rest of my breakfast to hear this speech, and I will rip an arm from the next man who talks and beat him to death with the bloody stump."

Ben was half again as big as the largest of the other men and well known for his violent and abrupt mood swings. The vision of Ben Allspot standing in a rage with a bloody arm held high above his head was easily rendered, and the silence was immediate.

"What effect the Alien bombs will have on the Moon is not completely known," said the President, "but our scientists are certain that, because the Moon lacks an atmosphere, it will not be as devastating as what we have seen on Mars or could expect on Earth.

"I am not trying to minimize the danger. The situation, for all of mankind, is extremely serious and could be deadly for those of you on the Moon. Our military personnel on the Moon have been instructed to pass out medications to help alleviate the effects of any radiation exposure that might occur. They will also explain other measures that should be taken for your protection.

The President placed his elbows on the podium and clasped his hands together. There was a long pause while he bowed his head as if in prayer, and when he looked up, his eyes were bright with unshed tears. "There is little that I can say or do to comfort you. Some of you may experience the supreme sacrifice.

You may be asked to lay down your life so that your neighbor might live, but do not doubt the nature of our plight. Nothing less than the continued existence of the human race is at stake."

The President held up an official-looking piece of paper. "I signed an executive order this morning granting life insurance policies in the amount of one million dollars, payable to the next of kin of any man, woman, or child who might die as a result of the Alien objects' impact on the Moon."

Ben's eyes snapped to the screen, and a joyful smile came over his face. "Well I'll be damned," he said softly.

President Bremmer placed the paper back on the podium and shook his head. "It is little enough that I can do for those whose names will go down in history as the greatest servicemen the world has ever known.

"Though you may not hold rank, you are soldiers. Though you may know fear, you are heroes. Though you may have doubt and even anger, you are our saviors—the saviors of mankind. God be with you all."

The screen slowly faded to black, and the face of the President was replaced by that of a young and obviously scared Corporal. Ben got up to get seconds and a loud buzz of conversation rose up from the men at the table.

Ben returned with his plate piled high while the Corporal told them that anti-radiation medication had already been placed at all transit substations. The talk died to a whisper when Ben sat down.

"The medication should be taken immediately," said the Corporal. "Instructions are on the back of the package. Taking more than one dose is not recommended and could cause unpleasant side effects. All personnel should don spacesuits and move to the interior, ground floor of whatever structure or building you are in before the objects arrive. Please stay close to a television monitor for further updates."

The screen went to solid blue, and Ben found himself laughing around a mouthful of food. "Unpleasant side effects? Whew, sounds kind of scary. Maybe we shouldn't take that stuff. It might be bad for you."

The men around Ben were in various stages of anger and denial. Some of them wanted to kill him for making light of the horror they were being forced into. Some of them couldn't even hear what he was saying.

"Oh, come on gang," Ben cajoled them. "This is life, remember? Nobody gets out alive. Why all the sad faces?"

One of the men shook his head and stared at the floor. "This is nuts," he said and looked up at Ben with undisguised hatred. "You must be nuts."

Ben seriously considered the statement, and one of the voices—the thin, reedy one—spoke up for the first time that morning. *Definitely, clinically insane*, it said.

Ben nodded. "Yeah, probably clinically insane. At least that's what I'm being told. But blessed are the clinically insane for they shall inherit one million bucks. You all heard it. One million bucks for every man, woman, and child, and all I have to do is manage to die sometime today. I got a feeling that's gonna be no problem at all."

"Do you want to die?" asked the man. "Is that it?"

All God's chillun' gotta die sometime, said the voice.

"Um, uh, well, I don't know," said Ben. "All God's chillun' gotta die sometime, and if I die today, my kids get one million dollars. Now that's a bargain, and I didn't have anything else planned for later on this afternoon, so sure, why not?"

The man shook his head and looked away.

"Say, are you going to eat that sausage?" Ben asked.

Without looking, the man pushed the plate at Ben and stood up to leave. The rest of the table left with him, and Ben found himself alone with the scattered silverware and coffee cups and the voices in his head. He was immensely cheered by the idea that his children would soon be rich.

You're going to be dead soon, said a mild baritone voice.

"Yeah," said Ben, speaking aloud. "Ain't life grand. I'm gonna be dead, and you guys are gonna die with me, and my kids will go to college. I couldn't have planned it better myself."

Charlene and Connie, said the thin voice.

"That's the ones."

But they will be dead soon.

Ben's mind slid away from the possibility. He couldn't even think about it.

You need another dose, said the thin voice.

Ben swilled down the rest of his coffee. "I reckon you're right," he said and left the cafeteria.

Chapter Forty-seven
NORAD
June 26, 2061

One of the lieutenants, Rick couldn't tell one from the other, was solemnly intoning a countdown. "Fusion generator is coming on line in five, four, three, two, one." A new, barely perceptible hum joined the low chorus of computer fans and electrical equipment.

The NASA personnel stood huddled against the right-hand wall of the darkened room, waiting for NORAD's technicians to seal them off from the outside world. Rick was in his assigned seat to the right of center on the dais above the room with General Laurence to his left. A small table and chairs had been set up behind them, and President Bremmer listened carefully to something Secretary Salness was saying while General Walker looked on. Aides bustled back and forth in the cramped space behind the ten forward-facing consoles on the raised platform, and a few previously unseen men and women in white lab coats stood in front of computers at seemingly random positions throughout the room, giving a patchwork appearance to the assemblage.

General Laurence cupped his microphone and leaned over to Rick. "You might want to have your people take a break. There's nothing they can do for the next hour or so."

Rick nodded and keyed Lindsay's headset. "Ms. Lindsay, you might as well take everyone down to the lounge for now. Tell them to get spruced up and take care of any personal needs. We need you all back here in 45 minutes, and it's going to be a long haul after that."

"Generator is within acceptable limits," said the lieutenant. "Switching to internal power on my mark. Three, two, one, mark."

There was not even a glimmer in the lights when NORAD became dependent on the generator deep in the bowels of the mountain, and the crowd of NASA personnel shrank like a deflating balloon as they exited the side door.

"Beginning outside door closure sequence on my mark. Three, two, one, mark."

The brassy honk of a siren came from the halls surrounding the control room, and a computer-generated voice spoke in soft feminine tones. "All outer doors will be sealed in sixty seconds. Internal personnel must return to stations immediately." The voice repeated the message at ten-second intervals in a periodic countdown for the next minute.

"Door closure commencing now," said the computer, and a thin, squealing sound was quickly replaced by a low rumble as the main doors, several tons each, slid into place. They closed with a solid thunk that Rick could feel in the soles of his feet. The siren fell silent.

"Transition to internal air supply on my mark," said the lieutenant. "Three, two, one, mark."

Rick couldn't see or hear anything different, but several technicians flipped switches and monitored various dials and gauges for the next several minutes.

The lieutenant turned and spoke to someone off to Rick's left. "General Slater, transition to internal air supply is complete, sir. We are at attack readiness stage one."

A voice, presumably that of General Slater, came from somewhere on the other side of General Laurence. "Run diagnostics on all internal bulkheads and doors, and maintain an alert status for stage two."

The lieutenant responded, "Yes, sir," and turned back to his console.

"I guess this thing is like a submarine right now," said Rick.

"Pretty much," replied General Laurence.

"What is stage two?"

The General opened his mouth and then shut it. "That would be classified."

"Will we use it?"

"Not if everything goes according to plan."

Rick looked at his watch and then remembered that the countdown for launching the fusion bombs was reeling off on the left-hand, top screen against the far wall. There was less than ten minutes remaining, and General Laurence had told him the bombs would explode less than twenty minutes after that.

He leaned back in his chair and ran his hands over his forehead and then through his hair till they rested at the back of his head. He couldn't really grasp the magnitude of what they were about to do. Perhaps he didn't want to.

In just under thirty minutes, every power-generating facility on Earth would be knocked offline. The United States had already shut down electricity across much of the nation to minimize damage from the EM pulse, but every unprotected telephone and computer would soon be rendered useless—some of them permanently. All planes had been grounded, and woe be unto those who found themselves in the air when the sky exploded above them. Instructions had been issued for all ships to move at full steam to the nearest port, but some of them would not arrive in time. Police sat at roadblocks, pulling aside and hustling into makeshift shelters anyone foolish enough to be driving a car, but within minutes even the police would abandon the roads for the relative safety of a church basement or a National Guard Armory.

Stores had been stripped bare of anything resembling camping gear, batteries could not be purchased at any price, and, somewhat strangely, aluminum foil had all but disappeared from commerce. Rick could imagine it wallpapering the cellars and covering the ceilings of interior rooms throughout America. It wouldn't do any real good, certainly not if the Alien objects hit the Earth, and it wouldn't be needed if the U.S. strategy was successful, but Rick had to admit that, if he was at home and had some foil, he would probably be lying on his bed and staring up at it.

Light flashed from the back of the room, and Rick turned around to see what appeared to be elevator doors opening. He hadn't noticed the doors before and was surprised to see three very serious looking men walk out of what he'd thought was a blank wall. Each man carried a small black box. They walked to the table at the rear and distributed the boxes in front of President Bremmer, Secretary Salness, and General Walker.

The President and General Walker took keys from their pockets and opened the boxes without preamble. Secretary Salness hesitated, and there was a sharp exchange in whispered tones that Rick could not quite hear, but the last box was finally opened.

There was not much to see inside. A red light shined brightly just below a covered switch set in the exact center of a nearly featureless black panel. A small square in the bottom right corner glowed a dull yellow, and a microphone grill was barely visible in the upper left corner.

Each of the three men took out another key and unlocked the cover from the switch, flipping it back and out of the way.

Rick suddenly realized it had become preternaturally still in the control room. He turned to see the countdown rolling down past two minutes. Every eye was on the hands of the three men at the table, and the hum of the equipment became louder and louder till it packed Rick's ears with an ominous tone.

Strange shadows flickered from the wall screens and computers, casting brief fingers of light across the faces of the three men and their boxes. The numbers on the wall screen clicked down, and the room filled with a soundless, swelling pressure. Rick struggled to breathe, forcing himself to empty his lungs, but the air seemed to climb down his throat of its own accord, stretching his chest till he feared he might explode.

The countdown went below a minute, and President Bremmer nodded to his colleagues. In a strangely choreographed dance of death, the three men simultaneously pressed their right thumbs on the glowing grid and bent their heads to whisper long phrases into the microphone grill. Straightening up, they looked at each other and reached out to flip the switches up. With three soft snicks, the lights turned green. The countdown rolled to zero.

"Missile number one is away," announced a lieutenant.

"Missile number two is away," from across the room.

The large screen flicked to a map of the world. Two slowly lengthening arcs, one going north and one going south, sprouted from the Atlantic and Pacific oceans.

A deafening boom rattled the coffee cup on Rick's console, and a roar loud as thunder filled the room. Rick jumped up to run or hide and then realized no one else was moving. The roar quickly died. One of the lieutenants said something, but Rick was not patched into the command link, and the sound was lost as another boom shook the floor. The quickly dying thunder trailed off. Rick sat down and tried to concentrate on breathing out.

"Missiles three and four are away," said a lieutenant.

Two new lines grew on the map from a point Rick recognized as Cheyenne Mountain. One of them went west toward the Pacific, and the other arced to the east and the Atlantic.

"Those damned things were here?" exclaimed Rick.

General Laurence gave him a look normally reserved for difficult schoolchildren but said nothing.

"You could have at least warned me."

General Laurence turned back to his work without a word, and for the space of about a minute, nothing happened while technicians poured over telemetry data.

"Missile five is away," said the lieutenant.

From a point in the Indian Ocean, a new arc stretched upward and toward the southeast.

"Missile six is away, sir."

From the same point, the last missile angled down and away to the southwest.

The lieutenants and technicians busied themselves with checking the massive amounts of data coming from the six missiles, and there was relative silence in the control room for the next several minutes.

Finally, one of the lieutenants turned to the Generals lined up at their consoles above the working area. "All six birds are in the air and on target. Detonation signal will be executed in three minutes and thirty four seconds."

General Laurence pulled off his headset and scratched above his ear. Rick could see an imprint of the earpiece in the General's hair.

"This better work," said the General.

"Why wouldn't it?" asked Rick.

The General shook his head. "We haven't actually tested one of these things in over sixty years. It's all computer mock ups." He pointed across to where Dr. Wilson Jenkins stood watching the lines spread across the map. "If you think you're uptight, just think about what he's going through. If we get a dud, he's going to have a hell of a lot of explaining to do."

Rick hadn't considered that scenario. If even one of the fusion bombs failed to go off, the entire strategy would be ruined. Rick felt sympathy for the quirky, little Doctor. It wasn't often that the fate of the entire world rested on one man's faith in his—so far—theoretical calculations.

Rick watched the countdown to detonation roll past two minutes, muttered "crap" a few times under his breath, and waited.

"All telemetry is within acceptable limits," said a lieutenant. "The birds are solid in the slots. Detonation in 45 seconds. All computer data is being moved to hard storage."

Dr. Jenkins stood motionless in front of the large screen while the numbers ticked down toward zero. With less than ten seconds left, he crossed himself. Rick wondered if the Doctor had been praying the entire time and wondered if he shouldn't have been praying also.

"Five, four, three, two, one. Detonation signal has been..."

The screen exploded in a bright glare and turned to snow.

"What the hell?" Rick shouted.

"Calm down," said General Laurence. "Our satellites are hardened against an EM pulse, but they'll have to reset themselves. They should come back online in a few seconds."

The screen blinked back to life, and the map of the world shimmied for a second while the image stabilized. Six red "X's" marked the final destination of the missiles.

"We have positive detonation on all six birds."

The control room erupted with a cheer. Dr. Jenkins had collapsed in a chair. His head was on the desk in front of him, and Rick could see the man's shoulders shaking. Was he crying because he had succeeded or from relief that he hadn't failed?

General Laurence was speaking rapidly into his microphone. "I want an inventory of operable satellites both here and on the Moon, and I want it now."

"I need to get my people back in," said Rick.

A voice spoke from behind him. "That won't be necessary." It was General Walker.

Rick wheeled around in his chair. "What!"

"This is our show now. We don't need a bunch of NASA Techies cluttering up the place."

Rick looked at General Laurence who barely moved his shoulders in a shrug.

He spoke without thinking. "You can't do this."

General Walker sneered. "Of course I can. You are here as a courtesy, Mr. Jelton, and nothing more. We will handle it from here."

"This is outrageous." Rick was trying to think of an angle, and he looked over at General Laurence who had a deep scowl on his face as he watched data floating across his screen. He seemed oblivious to the argument.

"How is your satellite inventory going, General Laurence?" Rick asked.

General Laurence glanced at Rick, and then turned his eyes to General Walker. "Not good. Over seventy percent of our satellites in Earth orbit have not yet reset themselves and may be permanently offline. We also seem to have lost several satellites near the Moon. We are trying to reactivate some of them with tight radio beams from the ground.

"Doesn't that defeat the purpose of the EM pulse?" General Walker asked.

General Laurence took a deep breath. "I don't like it any more than you do. The objects were attracted to Mars when the Earth was making a lot more noise than it is now, so our little radio bursts probably won't make any difference, but we've got to get more lunar broadcast capability and soon. Frankly, I was hoping we could get through this part of the operation in better shape."

Rick looked back and forth at the two Generals. "I'm sure we can all agree that civilian satellite broadcasts would be useful."

"I'll take any data and broadcast capability I can get," said General Laurence.

General Walker's voice was full of sarcasm. "And what makes you think any civilian craft could have survived?"

"I'm sure very few of them did," said Rick, "but some of them were on the far side of the Moon when the nukes went off. Others were built for longevity and have multiple safeguards against solar flares and continual bombardment by gamma radiation. The Sagan telescope, for example, has a projected life span of over 100 years. I'll be very surprised if we can't make it operational."

General Laurence spoke while he watched his computer. "We could use some help, General Walker. The Sagan Telescope will give us a front row seat, but what we really need is broadcast signal strength from the Moon. This does not look good. The transmitters on Mars were powerful because of the distance involved. Everything on the Moon was designed to broadcast to Earth. We've got only seven functioning units in lunar orbit."

"Seven?" asked General Walker incredulously.

"Seven. We thought the lunar satellites would be safe because of the distance, but three of the fusion bombs were on the side of Earth facing the moon, and two other bombs were in a position such that part of their pulse was felt on the Moon. It all added up, and we lost a lot of satellites. The problem is broadcast strength. Nobody knows how sensitive the Alien objects are."

"NASA understands civilian space systems better than anyone," said Rick. "We've been working with industry for years."

General Walker frowned and stood up straight. "Very well. You can have three people."

"I need four plus Ms. Lindsay."

"Three plus Ms. Lindsay."

"I need four plus Ms. Lindsay," Rick repeated.

General Walker threw his hands in the air. "Whatever. I don't have time to argue about it. Four plus Ms. Lindsay."

"Thank you, sir," Rick said and keyed his microphone.

"Your microphone is not working," said General Walker as he walked away. "Give the names to General Laurence."

Rick turned to his left. "I want Lindsay, Mosley, Rogers, McCrae, and Bishop."

Laurence echoed the names into his headset, and the door to the right of the work area opened almost immediately. Lindsay walked through the door in a state of high rage, followed by the other four.

Rick stood up and walked quickly down the steps. He grabbed Lindsay's elbow and spoke before she could open her mouth. "It's okay, Marilyn. There's been a little bit of a misunderstanding. We can talk about it later."

He guided her across part of the room to a workstation. "We have a problem. The EM pulse has knocked out most of the military satellites around the Moon. Our first priority is to resurrect the lunar, civilian communication satellites and get them broadcasting to the Alien objects."

Lindsay sat down and adjusted her headset. "How many do we want?"

"All of them. It doesn't matter. Do what you can."

"What is the second priority?"

"I'd like to see the Sagan back on line, but don't worry about that till we know the objects are heading toward the Moon."

Lindsay bent to her work with a curt, "Yes, sir," and Rick hurried back up the steps to his station beside General Laurence.

"How is it going?" asked Rick.

"We've got two more up and running for a total of nine, but I'm beginning to wonder about bandwidth. All of our satellites are designed for encrypted communication on a tight band. What if the objects can't hear it?"

Rick didn't have an answer to that, but Lindsay spoke in his ear. "We have three AT&T satellites operative and," she pushed a button in front of her and waited for a response, "broadcasting. Mosley has found a whole group of Consolidated Helium satellites that were put on standby just six months ago. They are coming online one by one and should be broadcasting within five minutes."

Rick raised a fist in the air. "Yes!" He turned to General Laurence. "There's your bandwidth. When do we expect first burn from the Alien objects?"

"Any minute now. We're lucky the objects are closer to the Moon than Earth, but the longer we go without a burn, the more likely it is that they are still targeting Earth."

Rick fretted. There wasn't much he could do, so he sat back and listened to the chatter around him. Most of it concerned the scrambling of planes into the sky above North America. That had been part of the compromise. Salness finally agreed to the use of the fusion bombs but had insisted on air cover in case someone with a generator repaired a transmitter and decided the people at home needed a few game shows to take their minds off their troubles. It was agreed to with the proviso that the planes maintain strict radio silence.

"Mr. Jelton."

"Yes, Lindsay."

"Mosley has four Consolidated Helium satellites broadcasting, and we have two British telecommunications satellites online and," she waited for a signal from Rogers, "broadcasting. There is a group of three French satellites that show promise, but we can't do anything with the Chinese hardware. I don't know if it's burned up or if we have a protocol problem."

"Don't worry about the Chinese stuff. Concentrate on what you know."

"Yes, sir."

"Ms. Lindsay."

"Sir?"

"I want you to know I'm proud of you and the rest of the team. This is great work under a lot of pressure."

Lindsay actually sighed. "Yes, sir," she said, but it sounded more like, "Yeah, whatever."

An alarm sounded, and General Laurence put one hand over his earpiece. "There they are," he said. "We've got a burn on the first alien object. No trajectory yet."

Rick caught himself before he asked Lindsay for a trajectory. NASA currently had no operative surveillance satellites. Lindsay shot him an agonized glance across the room.

Laurence still had his hand against the side of his head. "We've got a burn on another object. That's numbers two and three. Number four probably won't fire its engines for another 30 minutes."

Rick started to ask a question, but General Laurence held up his hand and looked at his console.

"Trajectory is coming up," said the General. He turned to Rick with a grin and held out his hand. "It's the Moon Mr. Jelton. They're going to the moon."

The control room exploded with a cheer that rivaled the noise level of the missile launch just 45 minutes earlier. Grown men with high rank could be seen hugging each other. Dr. Wilson Jenkins stood to the side, grinning like an idiot. Rick jumped down the steps and grabbed Lindsay, spinning her around. President Bremmer worked the crowd, shaking everyone's hand.

And in that moment, for just that moment, the reluctant heroes—their brothers and sisters on the Moon—were far away and forgotten.

Chapter Forty-eight
Surface of the Moon
Lexam Barracks
June 26, 2061

Ben was lying on his bunk with his hands behind his head, staring upward without seeing. He had been there for a while. The barracks was now empty and silent except for his occasional muttering or exclamations, and he hadn't moved for the last two hours except to reach down into the pocket of his jumpsuit from time to time to retrieve a small, white pill. The pillow on either side of his head was soaked through with tears.

He missed them terribly, and his mind replayed over and over the beautiful, joyous moments he'd had with his children—cool, sunny days in the spring of the year at Audubon Park—baloney sandwiches eaten on a simple quilt alongside Lake Pontchartrain with sailboats gliding past and the warm, humid breeze blowing the girls' hair in their eyes—rides on the trolley down St. Charles Avenue—sitting in the Café du Monde and laughing with his wife at the sight of Connie and Charlene looking up at them, their little noses white with powdered sugar and their faces wide eyed with the first taste of a beignet—Christmas morning and the two girls all agog at the meager presents in the living room.

And memories of his wife—making love in the afternoon with slow and tender care while the babies slept in the next room—smiles and brief touches as they planned their lives across the wobbly kitchen table—late nights spent snuggled deep into the old couch where she might shed tears into the popcorn over some silly movie.

They had been so proud of that dingy little apartment, spending days scrubbing floors and cabinets, painting walls and shelves, putting up the cheap, plastic venetian blinds that were all they could afford. The throw rugs came from the Good Will store. The furniture, cast off by relatives and friends, was frayed and worn. The cinder block and plank bookcase was made from pieces Ben found at the construction site where he worked.

And it had been all they needed. The children knew nothing of their relative poverty, and his wife had not cared, seeing only the bright future before them.

She believed in you, said the baritone.

Ben moaned, and great sobs wracked his body. Why was it, he wondered, that the good of his past should bring such aching pain in this present? He wept and mourned the loss of all he loved—inconsolable in the knowledge that he would never see his children again.

It's for the best, said the reedy voice. *They're better off without you.*

Ben couldn't argue with that, and he rolled to his side, curling his legs up to his chest and wrapping his arms around his knees. He felt as if he was all cried out. There was nothing left to do but wait for death and comfort himself with the reassurance that his children would never want for anything.

The girls need a father, said the baritone.

"I can't do it," said Ben. "Someone else will have to be their father."

They need you.

"I'm no good to them now."

True. The baritone was clear as a bell in the silence of the barracks. *They need you the way you used to be. They need you clean and sober.*

"I can't be clean and sober. I don't know how."

You need help.

"What kind of help?"

You know where to go," said the baritone. *You're too proud for your own good.*

Pride goeth before a fall, said the thin voice. *Endless pride goeth before an endless fall*"

Ben pondered the ideas and decided it was all true. There were government agencies, private programs, self-help groups.

There were people who knew how to deal with addiction. He knew where they were or how to find them, but it wasn't natural to him. He wanted to be rid of this demon that lived within him, but he wanted to do it the way he had always done everything else—by himself and without outside interference.

There are some things over which even Ben Allspot has no power, said the baritone.

"Yes," said Ben.

Your children love you, and in the manner of children, they will love you no matter what you do. Your wife too, perhaps a better woman than you deserve, continues to love you and would welcome you, clean and sober, into her arms and back into her life"

"You don't know that."

I know only what you know.

You're worth a million bucks dead, said the thin voice.

And you're priceless to your family sober, said the baritone. *Make the effort to live, and if you live, then find the help you need to continue.*

Ben rolled off the edge of the bunk and came to his feet. A wave of dizziness washed over him. *Too much Carbodine.*

Not enough, said the reedy voice.

He made his way through the empty halls and down to the transit tube only to find the terminal blinking an "Out of service till further notice" sign.

"A problem," Ben said. He needed to go to the construction site to retrieve his suit, but the only way to get there was on the transit. There was a box on the floor half full of plastic packages containing oddly shaped pills, and he ripped the top from one and tossed the pills into his mouth while he considered what to do. He had to stop himself from reflexively chewing them up.

"Okay, we walk." He bounced over the turnstile and jumped off the platform to the tracks below. It was only a few miles to where his suit waited in its locker, and he was soon enjoying the smooth flow of his muscles as he took great leaping bounds down the tunnel, nearly brushing his head on the ceiling at the top of each jump. The surface of the floor was smooth between the tracks, and the tunnel curved ever so slightly to his left as it made its way in a broad circle around the Lexam complex. He was quickly lost in a rhythmic trance and was surprised to see the tug-hangar platform coming up on his right. He was even more surprised to see a crowd of about 20 men and women gathered together in the far corner of the pilots' locker room.

He jumped up to the platform and bounced into the room. Several people turned to look at him strangely, and someone called out, "Where the hell is your suit, man?"

Ben saw that he was the only person not wearing a spacesuit—there were helmets scattered over the floor and on tables all around—and he suddenly felt naked in front of the group. "I'm on my way to get it. What are y'all doing?"

One of the men jerked a thumb toward the corner. "Some guy hacked into the military communication lines through a cable in the wall over there. He's got it rigged up where we can listen in to what's happening."

"So what's happening?"

"All according to the President's plan. And to think I voted for that asshole. We die, and he lives. All three of the alien bombs are heading this way, but we're in better shape than a lot of folks. Power is out over half the moon. We're right on the edge of it. Everything east of here is dark."

Ben nodded. "I'll be back," he said and bounced out of the room to continue his trek down the tube.

The construction locker room was the next stop, and he took the time to go through the checklist on his suit before he put it on.

Dead or sober in a few days, said the thin voice. *Take the Carbodine with you.*

The baritone was silent, and Ben chewed two of the pills before sliding the bottle into a Velcro pouch on the hip of his suit.

It was a much slower trip back down the tunnel in the bulk of his spacesuit with his helmet tucked under one arm, and over an hour had gone by before he walked back into the pilots' locker room. A tall, thin man stood watching the screen of a laptop computer, and Ben recognized him as one of the tug pilots. A vague memory of seeing the man with a book across his knees in the waiting room of a training session came to him.

Ben collared one of the men at the edge of the crowd and pointed at the man. "Who is that guy?"

"He says he was a hacker back in the states. He's been hiding out on the Moon and flying tugs because things got a little too hot back home."

Ben nodded. An access plate had been removed from the wall, and several wires now ran into the back of the tall man's computer. A grainy, two-dimensional picture of the Earth floated by, and the speakers blared out a conversation that was clearly from the lunar military base.

"Anything new," asked Ben.

"No. We're still sitting ducks. Our computer geek says we've got less than 45 minutes before the first one hits. If you want to find a safer place, you probably need to leave now."

Ben looked at the group milling about in front of the computer and then peered through the small portal at the dark, cratered landscape of the lunar night just through the wall on his right. "I reckon this is as good a place as any."

Chapter Forty-nine
NORAD
June 26, 2061

The top, left-hand wall screen came to life with a perfect close-up of the Moon in half crescent.

Rick muttered, "Damn, finally."

"The Sagan telescope is now online," said Ms. Lindsay.

"And just in time," said General Laurence. "All broadcasting is being shut down as of now. We're going to have to make do with the satellites we've already got. Zoom the Sagan out so we can see the objects, and leave it tracking the Moon. I need you to patch the positional data on the objects into NORAD's database. We're having trouble getting a precise trajectory."

"I'm on it," said Lindsay. "Switching to wide-field optics." The picture blinked back from the Moon, and three blue flames could be seen on the far, left side of the screen. Two of them were so close together they might have been a single bright light, and the third trailed behind, dimmer and smaller. "Changing broadcast mode to dish only," she flipped a switch, "and disconnecting. The Sagan is now tight-beamed into NORAD. Positional data is flowing." Lindsay checked her computer and pursed her lips. "It's a little slow because of the constraints on the radio transmission, but as long as the gyros keep it lined up, we'll be okay."

Rick looked at the screen on the wall. "I'd feel a lot better about this if the objects were in a bunch. We're bound to lose some lunar satellites when the first two hit."

"Nothing we can do about it," said the General, "but be quiet as a mouse. We've got eleven operative military satellites around the Moon. At least a few of them should be on the far side of the Moon from wherever the first two objects impact."

"We've got fifteen civilian craft in operation," said Rick. He tried not to sound like he was bragging. "I hope it's enough. We're going to lose every one of them that's not shielded by the Moon from the first two blasts."

"We have a trajectory solution from the Sagan," said Lindsay.

"Let's hear it," Rick said.

"Objects two and three are at virtually the same speed and distance from the Moon. Number three will pass about 50 miles from the Moon and will cross the Moon's axis at 100,000 miles per hour in a path pretty much identical to what we saw from number one when it went by Mars. Number two, however, is a little strange. The trajectory solution is fairly precise, but it's anybody's guess whether it will hit a glancing blow or skim by less than a mile from the Moon's surface."

General Laurence and Rick looked at each other, and Rick spoke into his microphone, "Say again."

"The number two object is on a course that makes an apparent perfect tangent to the Moon's surface. Whether or not it strikes the Moon as it goes by will depend on its exact path and the presence of any mountain peaks along that path."

"This is nuts," said Rick.

"I don't know," said the General. "If it was coming down through our atmosphere at 100,000 miles per hour, the shock wave would be huge, and the radiation cloud would spread halfway around the globe. I guess precision doesn't matter when you carry that much firepower."

Rick thought about it for a while. Perhaps the General was right, but it seemed strange that the objects didn't appear to have the ability to precisely locate a planet. "Ms. Lindsay, what's the time to closest approach on object number two, and when can we expect object number four?"

"Closest approach for both number two and number three is ten minutes twenty five seconds and will occur on the far side of the Moon. Object number four is just twenty minutes behind them, and it will also pass on the other side of the Moon."

"So we're going to miss the show if number two hits on the first pass."

"Yes, sir."

General Laurence leaned back in his chair. "Jenkins is running simulations for the trajectory of any debris that might be generated if number two hits a glancing blow. It depends on a lot of things, but there appears to be no danger to Earth—just a big cloud of antimatter and wreckage speeding out of the system at about 100, 000 miles per hour."

The video feed from the Sagan showed the first two objects moving slowly to the right and edging closer to the dark half of the Moon. The two perfect tubes of blue light were more obviously separate now and oriented ahead of the objects as monstrous amounts of energy were expended in a deceleration that would have rendered a human being unconscious in a matter of minutes. The last object, its motion less noticeable from the distance, trailed in the path of its two companions.

Rick let his head fall back against the chair. *More high-tension waiting.* He wondered for the second time in as many weeks what the average blood pressure of his colleagues might be. *Or the average blood pressure across the world. Or on the Moon.* For the next several minutes, he concentrated on his breathing and stared at the ceiling.

"Objects being eclipsed by the Moon," said Lindsay. "Emergence from the bright half of the Moon will occur in two minutes."

Rick looked up to see the blue flames disappearing behind the dark side of the nearly perfect half moon. "See if you can't use the computer to enhance the point of emergence, Ms. Lindsay."

The picture clicked forward in several jumps and moved to the right hand side of the crescent and then smoothed out till every crater and mountain was crystal clear.

Rick leaned forward and tapped his foot on the floor. "Come on, baby," he whispered. With a start, he realized he could see domes and mining equipment clustered in the center of Mare Nectaris. He closed his eyes and turned away. For a moment, he was afraid he would throw up.

That would be Raxon Manufacturing. We're lucky the Moon is half in darkness.

Almost all of the mining enterprises had settled in the flat plains of Oceanus Procellarum and were now hidden in the deep, lunar night to the west.

A lieutenant started a countdown. "Emergence in five, four…"

A sparkling, diffuse cloud edged out from behind the bright disk of the Moon.

"What the hell is that?" exclaimed Rick

"She hit!" yelled General Laurence. "The number two object hit the far side of the Moon."

A small cheer rose up just as the blue exhaust of the third object came into view.

"Why is the debris in front?"

"The debris isn't decelerating anymore," said the General. "Number three is still decelerating."

"That's two down and two to go," said Rick.

Lindsay chimed in his ear. "Trajectory on number three and number four remains unchanged, sir. They have not changed course to Earth." Rick looked over to give her the thumbs up, but she was staring intently at the readout in front of her. A deep frown grew across her face while Rick watched.

"We've lost a… No, we've lost two… No, three." Lindsay turned and looked at Rick over the top of her glasses. "Mr. Jelton, we're losing the lunar satellites."

"What's going on?"

"Unknown. We now have four that we should be able to hear, but they were dead when they came back around from the other side of the Moon."

The screen showed the twinkling cloud now far ahead of the third object and well clear of the Moon.

"Make that six, sir,"

General Laurence was busily tapping at his keyboard. "We're losing them too."

"What the hell is going on?"

The General frowned and shook his head.

Dr. Jenkins grabbed a headset from one of the lieutenants. "I may be able to explain. All of our, uh, simulations showed the bulk of the debris and antimatter heading out of the, um, system, but some simulations showed a cloud of dust and antimatter bouncing off the surface and going straight up from the point of impact. Any satellite that passes through that cloud will be, uh, ruined."

"Goddamn it, Jenkins." It was General Walker. "You could have told us about it."

"Well, uh, it didn't seem to matter. There's nothing we could have, uh, done. I really didn't, uh, think about the satellites. We were mostly trying to see what would happen to Earth."

"Shit! How many are we going to lose?"

"Uh, well, probably not all of them, but probably a lot of them. It kind of depends on their, uh, exact path and the size of the, um, cloud."

"And what happens when number three comes down? Are we going to lose more satellites then?" asked General Walker.

"Oh, well, yes, of course."

Rick glanced at Lindsay, and she spoke before he could ask the questions. "We have six known dead, five still broadcasting, and four whose status will not be known till they come around to this side of the Moon. The trajectory of objects three and four remains unchanged. Projected time to impact of the number three object is one hour and thirty-five minutes."

"We're doing a little better than you percentage wise," said General Laurence. "Probably because our satellites tend to be in a higher orbit. We've got three known dead, six broadcasting, and two of unknown status."

"Will that be enough?" Rick asked.

General Laurence looked at the screen and scratched at the stubble on his cheek. "I guess it depends on how many we lose when number three comes down." He turned and held his chin with a thumb and forefinger. "But I've got a feeling it doesn't matter. My gut tells me these things will continue to target the Moon even if we lose all the satellites. As long as Earth stays quiet."

Rick watched the two flames sliding across the background of stars with the bright, crescent moon between them. "I hope you're right."

~

Earth's Moon

Ben was lying on the floor with his helmet under his head. He hadn't moved in almost two hours. There'd been some kind of hubbub a while back—one of the objects bouncing off the Moon or something, and the floor shook a little—but he'd hardly paid attention. A strange calm covered him like a warm blanket, and he hadn't taken any Carbodine since he'd picked up his suit. Perhaps this was how it might end. Perhaps the screaming need for the painless existence he could sometimes find in the middle of a Carbodine high would just fade away, and he would be clean.

You'll never be free of it, said the thin voice.

It will be with you always, said the baritone, *but action need not follow desire.*

"I wish y'all would shut up," Ben said. "I'm feeling like I could take a nap."

Some of the people in the room looked in Ben's direction, but after listening to him mumble for the last two hours, they were convinced he was harmlessly insane and just needed to be left alone. It suited Ben just fine.

The squawk of military voices from the tall man's computer floated over to him. "Number three object should impact in less than ten minutes near the location of Mare Crisium."

"Where is Mare Crisium?" asked someone.

"It's a couple thousand miles east of here. There's a mountain range in between. I guess there might be a moon quake or something, but we should be alright unless the radiation gets bad."

"What about number four? Where is it going to hit?"

"Shut up. That's what they're talking about."

The room quieted, and the tall man's computer pronounced sentence on them all.

"The last object is in free fall and will impact in approximately 45 minutes. Trajectory shows the contact point to be near the center of Oceanus Procellarum."

"Oh shit!"

"Isn't that where we are?"

"Oh shit."

Death it is, thought Ben and closed his eyes.

~

NORAD

"Impact of object number three is in five, four, three, two, one."

A brilliant ball of blue light spread quickly for half a second. The light flashed brightly enough to dazzle the onlookers then just as quickly dwindled to a small area of blue on the south side of Mare Crisium, but a sparkling cloud promptly obscured even that. A single shock wave spread across the Moon, tossing boulders and dust before it.

"What the hell is that?" shouted General Walker.

Dr. Jenkins was studying the screen. "Uh, General, we need to get a trajectory on that cloud."

"What's going on? This doesn't look anything like what happened on Mars."

"No atmosphere," said Jenkins. "We need a trajectory on that cloud. There's no air on the Moon to compress the antimatter and hold it to the, uh, surface. The first contact with normal matter, uh, blew all of the antimatter out of the, uh, crater and straight up. Well, maybe not straight up. It kind of depends on the, uh, slope of the ground where it landed."

"Are you saying this cloud is headed to Earth?" General Walker was practically screaming.

"That is a, uh, possibility, sir."

General Walker exploded in a string of profanity while Dr. Jenkins cringed and Lindsay coaxed data out of the Sagan.

"We've lost some more satellites," said General Laurence.

Rick pecked at his keyboard. "I think we've lost all of ours. How many do you have left?"

"Four. No, make that three. They're dying when they get anywhere close to the impact point."

"What do the orbits look like? Are all of them going to pass near Mare Crisium?"

General Laurence whispered a command to his computer and briefly looked at the screen. "We've got one in polar orbit that should make it."

"We have a solution on the cloud," said Lindsay. "It is angling slightly to the north and should pass over Earth's northern pole. It looks like minimal contact with Earth's upper atmosphere."

"Effects, Dr. Jenkins?" asked General Walker.

"Uh, minimal actually, except I'm not sure about how all that dust will affect Earth's weather, and we're going to have satellite problems for a long time."

General Walker was standing directly behind Rick, and the sound of the General's teeth grinding together was clearly audible.

"Could you explain that?" the General asked.

"The dust may cause some, uh, cooling of the Earth as it filters the sunlight. We'll have to run some simulations, and the, uh, Van Allen belts are going to be charged up for a long time," said Jenkins. "We've already made a mess of them with the EM pulse. This is going to make it a lot worse, and we're probably going to have to change the way we construct our communications satellites for the next ten years, but it's not anything we can't, uh, live with."

"Very well," said General Walker.

Lindsay spoke up. "Trajectory on number four is unchanged. The object is in free fall and should impact the Moon in a little over 25 minutes. It is coming down southwest of the cloud and will not pass through it."

"That's kind of a pity," said Rick.

One of the lieutenants turned toward the back of the room. His hand was held to his earpiece, and his face was white. "General Walker, sir, we have an incoming message from the AWACS plane over Texas."

"What the fuck! Have they gone insane?" screamed General Walker. "This had by God better be good."

"I think you'll want to hear it, sir."

~

Earth's Moon

Ben couldn't quite go to sleep. He drifted in and out, and the moans and sobs of misery from those around him ebbed and flowed with his attention.

With a background like this, said the thin voice, *you might wake up in hell and never notice the difference*"

"With a life like this," said Ben, "you might be right."

Oh, poor boy.

Ben opened his eyes and looked at the ceiling. "Yeah, I know. Things are tough all over."

The recent flash of blue lightning from the fall of object number three had brought screams of fear from those around him, and Ben had cracked his eyes to watch as some of them put on their helmets.

Put on your helmet, said the baritone.

Ben stared at the ceiling. His mind was blessedly blank.

Make the effort to live, said the baritone.

"Oh, bother," Ben said and sat up, grabbing his helmet.

A television monitor on the far side of the room blinked into life, and a man with long white hair and wild eyes screamed into the camera. "The forces of God cannot be denied! Those who would thwart His will shall find that they seek a terrible vengeance." Ben recognized him as the Literalist preacher from the last regular TV broadcast he'd seen.

An excited babble filled the room. The tall man leaned over his computer in an effort to hear what the lunar military base was saying. He turned and screamed at the small crowd. "Shut up! This is important."

Ben stood up. "This is getting stranger and stranger," he said, but he couldn't hear what was going on between the cries of those in the room and the screaming of the man on the television. He waded through the crowd and grabbed the tall man's shoulder, spinning him around. "What the hell's going on?" Ben asked.

The man was near shock in his disbelief. "It's a television broadcast from Earth. The military guys say it might cause the fourth object to turn away from the Moon and target Earth."

Just then, a rumble filled the room, and the shock wave from the third object hit the Lexam Complex. The floor popped upward, and everyone went with it, smashing into the ceiling in a tangle of arms and legs.

Yee haa, said the thin voice. *All we need now is some music.*

The group bounced off the ceiling and fell. Ben viciously kicked people away in mid air and landed on his shoulders, rolling on his back and coming to his feet. Miraculously, his helmet was still in his hand. The floor shifted sideways, dropping out from under him, and he fell to the side, cushioned by the body of a man who was either unconscious or dead. Ben rolled over and sat up.

The lights went off, and the hangar lit up with the dim glow of emergency strips along the base of the walls. Thankfully, the television had died with the loss of regular power, but there was a loud hiss in the room, and a computer voice spoke in dispassionate tones. "Emergency. A pressure drop has been detected. All patch teams report immediately to your assigned posts. Bulkheads will be sealed in three minutes. Emergency."

The floor shifted slightly once more and a sound like thunder faded slowly into the distance.

Ben realized he could feel a breeze on his face and looked around at the scattered bodies. Some of them stood, and some of them tried to stand, but several lay twisted and still as death. Wails and groans once again filled the air but with the sharp, high notes of pain rather than fear.

He felt confused. "Number four is going to Earth?"

You will live, said the baritone.

But your children will die, said the thin voice.

"No," said Ben.

Oh yes.

Ben was stunned by the thought, and then something happened that made him jump to his feet and look wildly around the dim room. A new voice was speaking—singing—and it brought memories of a time when his father was away and the days were sane and secure. It was a female voice, and the pure tones of a lustrous contralto filled his head as his skin crawled with fear and a cold sweat broke out over his body. It was the voice of his mother.

Ben bent double and moaned. "No. No. Not this."

The voice crooned sweetly an ancient rhyme:

"Ladybug, ladybug
Fl-y away home
Your house is on fi-re
And your children
They will burn
They will burn"

Ben threw his head back and screamed. "No, no, no!"

They're gonna burn, Ben, said the thin voice. *They're gonna burn in a big, blue fire.*

"No," said Ben, and he reached into the pocket at his waist to remove the bottle of Carbodine. He shook out a handful without bothering to count and shoveled them into his mouth.

That's a trooper, said the thin voice. *Go out in style.*

"Shut up," Ben snarled. He fumbled in the darkness to load up the candy dispenser in his helmet and then slapped the helmet onto his head, latching it down tight.

"Emergency," repeated the computer, "bulkheads will be sealed in one minute."

Ben bounced to the airlock and slapped the switch. The doors opened slowly under the emergency power and Ben tugged at the edges, slipping sideways into the lock. Someone was screaming at him to get back inside, but the doors closed and the sound dwindled as the airlock cycled the small space into vacuum.

He squeezed through the outer doors and ran in great leaps to the nearest buggy. The dull glow of a strange blue sunrise could be seen in a cloud of dust that towered over the mountains to the East, and the landscape was lit with unfamiliar shades of turquoise and magenta. Ben saw none of it and hopped into the nearest buggy, gunning its electric motor and heading off at full speed toward the tugs. A meteorite fell in front of him and he swerved recklessly—the buggy going up on two wheels. Ben threw his weight to the side and brought it down. His foot never left the accelerator.

This will never work, said the thin, reedy voice.

"Just shut up."

He turned the buggy, sliding on four wheels toward the first tug he saw and leapt out, nearly losing his footing on the hard, fused glass of the landing field. The buggy rolled on without him and crashed into the next tug in line.

Tensing his legs, Ben thrust himself upward and slammed into the ladder fifteen feet above the ground. His hands clawed for a grip, and he slipped down several feet before catching himself.

You want to die right here? asked the thin voice.

Ben didn't answer but pulled himself up with quick snatches at the rungs and powerful thrusts from his legs. Within seconds, he was strapping himself into the seat and firing up the engine.

Gauges came to life on the console, and he plugged the communication jack into his suit with a reflexive move that didn't register in his conscious mind. "Fueled up and ready to go," he said.

Reaching up, Ben slapped a switch to release the cargo held on the sides of the tug. There was a sharp clank and then a series of dull thuds as the tanks hit the ground and scattered, rolling over each other in the slow motion of objects falling through the Moon's airless gravity, but each of them carried the full power and inertia of their 20 ton weight, and one tank bounced into a landing strut with the sound of rending metal. The tug shuddered and began to tilt as the strut bent from the impact. Ben slammed the throttle to thirty percent, and the tug jumped away from the surface at an angle.

He was pushed back in his seat and fought for a moment to bring the tug up in a straight line.

And how do you expect to land this thing? said the voice.

"Not really worried about it," Ben replied.

The tug shot up into the lunar night and soon cleared the mountains to the east. A great ball of blue fire still burned in Mare Crisium under a column of dust that seemed to stretch to infinity in the stars above, and lightning-like flickers lit the plane below him while hot, yellow sparks, as if from Roman Candles, flew up into the sky.

Ben leaned his head back and looked up out of the open cockpit.

"Alright you son of a bitch. Where are you?"

~

NORAD

"It's what?" exclaimed President Bremmer.

"It's the Literalist Church," said General Walker. "They have a transmitter up and running somewhere in downtown Houston and are broadcasting directly at the Moon."

"What's the last object doing."

"Course is unchanged," said Lindsay. "The fourth object is in free fall and should impact the western side of Oceanus Procellarum in fifteen minutes."

"We've got to take out that transmitter," said General Walker.

The president frowned. "That's a lot of damned civilians, General. If the object is still heading to the Moon, then all we need to do is wait.

General Laurence spun around in his seat. "We've got another problem. There's only one lunar satellite still in operation, and it will disappear over the horizon relative to object number four in less than five minutes. There are a few surface-based transmitters in operation, but they have no ability to track something moving at the speed of the Alien object."

"Meaning what?" asked the President.

"Meaning, sir, that the transmission from the Literalist Church will soon be the only thing the last object can hear. It is my belief that it will turn toward Earth at that time."

"We've got to take out that damned transmitter," repeated General Walker.

President Bremmer looked around. Practically everyone in the room was watching the exchange. "It's civilians," he said.

"And it's civilians that will die if the object turns to Earth," said General Walker.

The President took a step forward and stared at the screen where the fire burned under a haze of dust in Mare Crisium. He turned to Secretary Salness.

"Take it out," said the Secretary.

He looked over at General Laurence.

General Laurence hesitated only a moment. "We've got to take it out."

The President nodded. "Very well, by my order then—destroy the transmitter."

General Walker turned away and spoke in a hurried whisper into his microphone.

Lindsay's voice was breathless with surprise. "I don't know what to make of this," she said. "We've got a launch from the Moon."

The room turned as a group toward the wall screens where a small blip of yellow light could be seen rising above the eastern side of Oceanus Procellarum.

"Let's get a radiation signature," said Rick, "and a trajectory."

Lindsay bent over her console for a few seconds. "It appears to be a lunar tug, sir." She waited while numbers streamed across her computer. "It originated near the Lexam complex, but I can't get a clear trajectory. It seems to be wandering."

"Someone trying to escape," said Rick.

General Laurence sat hunched over his console. "I wish the bastard luck. But not at our expense. We're going to lose the lunar satellite over the horizon in less than two minutes."

~

Above Texas

Captain James Driscoll was not enjoying his current mission. It just seemed stupid. Flying an F–60 fighter by visual flight rules was not something he or anybody else had really trained for, and the restrictions of this assignment—no radar, no transponder, no radio contact of any kind—had him edgy and nervous.

He banked the jet in a sharp turn and looked down over his shoulder for the ribbon of Interstate 10. *Let's see, I've got a compass, an altimeter, and an Interstate highway. I'll be low on fuel in about one more hour, and I'm not sure I can even find the base. Once I get there, I've got to land without radar assistance and just pray to God that nobody else has picked the same runway I have.*

He spied the highway and set off almost due west. Houston was just a few miles in front of him. *Not that I have any way of knowing exactly where Houston is.* He stabbed at a button for perhaps the hundredth time in the last three hours and listened to the computer whisper in his ear. "Global Positioning System is offline."

This is one hell of a way to run an Air Force..

His radio crackled, and the unexpected noise made him jump in his seat. "This is AWACS A259. Fighter AE438, please respond."

Driscoll keyed his mike. "AE438 responding."

"Proceed at full speed on a heading of 265 degrees west. Dial two birds to 84.3 megahertz, and await our command to fire."

Driscoll pulled the throttles back and corrected his direction as the acceleration pressed him into the seat. With the flip of a switch, a small keypad popped open, and he punched in the frequency requested.

"Heading is now 265 degrees west," he said. "Two birds are set for 84.3 megahertz."

"Hold for our command to fire."

"Holding."

Driscoll's mind was whirling. "What is this about?"

As he watched, the outskirts of Houston came over the horizon.

"Fighter AE438, release birds now and return to radio silence," came the command.

Driscoll swallowed hard. "I have Houston Texas directly in front of me, sir."

"The situation is known. Fire immediately. That is a direct order."

Driscoll thumbed the cover from the stick in his right hand and pressed the red button underneath. The jet bucked, and two rapidly accelerating, air-to-ground missiles drilled parallel spears of smoke into the air above Houston.

He watched as they began to curve toward the ground. "God almighty. I hope we know what we're doing."

~

NORAD

"Our satellite is over the horizon," yelled General Laurence. "Where are those missiles?"

General Walker stood listening to something the rest of them could not hear. "Birds are in the air above Houston," he said.

Lindsay broke in. "Object number four has begun emitting a small amount of radiation."

General Walker bobbed his head once in a quick yes. "The Houston transmitter has been disabled."

Lindsay stood up from her chair as numbers flew across her computer screen. She looked at Rick. "I think it's too late. I think the object is correcting its orientation for a burn toward Earth."

"We don't know that yet," said General Laurence, but as the words fell from his mouth, a glowing, blue tube popped into being above the dark half of the Moon.

~

Earth's Moon

Ben felt positively electric, but the voices were louder than ever. He was floating the tug a few miles above the surface, and every move of the controls—every turn and dip—made him feel more and more a part of the machine as he waltzed the tug through a zigzag ballet above the flat plains of Oceanus Procellarum. The clouded crescent of Earth twirled over his head in perfect synchrony.

The baritone half-heartedly pleaded with him. *You've taken too much Carbodine. Find shelter. Make the effort to live.*

Take some more, said the thin voice. *Be strong. Be alert.*

Ben licked another pill from his dispenser and crunched it down. "I've got business to take care of, and y'all aren't helping one bit."

A harsh, blue glare lit the cockpit, and Ben wheeled the tug in a tight turn. His hands moved over the controls without deliberate thought, and he felt nothing but excitement as he accelerated toward the flame and the seatbelt straps bit into his chest.

Nothing could have prepared him for the sight of the alien object in full thrust, slowing its plunge toward the moon. "Whoa," he said softly.

He looked at his range indicator and took a deep breath.

"Oh man."

The range finder was having difficulty getting a reading and was wavering between 100 and 200 miles, but the long plume of blue fire looked close enough to touch and covered half the sky. The object dropped closer to the Moon as if it was coming down for a landing.

Ben squinted into the light. "Where the hell is the rocket? I can't see the rocket. He continued accelerating toward the object as he searched the area in front of the plume.

"It's got to be on top of the exhaust. Why can't I see it?"

This is not a good idea, said the baritone.

Maybe not, said the reedy voice, *but it damn sure is fun.*

The object stopped its downward plunge and began to lift upward with what looked like a slow and graceful change in direction.

Ben checked the range and ran it through his mind. "The distance makes it look slow," he mumbled. "That thing has got some legs under it."

He nudged the throttle and felt himself sink into the seat as the blue flame climbed upward till the pencil-thin blackness of the object was silhouetted against the blue and white crescent of Earth.

"There. There it is," Ben said.

Your destiny, said the baritone.

God, what a pompous prick, Ben moped.

He braced himself, and his hand gripped the throttle.

"Hold on, boys. This is gonna hurt."

~

NORAD

Lindsay held up a hand and watched her display as Rick leaned forward. "The object appears to be slowing its fall to the Moon." She sat down and tapped a few keys. The video picture on the wall screen zoomed in on the blue fire with three quick steps then smoothed out as image-enhancement software did its work. The body of the object was almost invisible against the black backdrop of the shadowed Moon, but the fiery exhaust was clearly pointed away from the Sagan telescope.

Lindsay turned in her chair and squinted over her glasses. "It's coming this way."

"We need to scramble the jets to high altitude," said General Walker. "Maybe we can knock it out on the way in."

"That's going to make an awful lot of radio noise," said Rick.

General Laurence turned to the back of the room where President Bremmer stood listening. "I don't think it matters anymore. The object is headed toward us. We need a decision, Mr. President."

The President looked across the room at Dr. Jenkins. "I thought exploding the thing at high altitude was a bad idea. What can we expect, Dr. Jenkins."

"Uh, well a high altitude explosion will spread the radiation cloud farther than a ground explosion, but we're still probably, uh, better off if it doesn't hit the ground." He turned to where Lindsay was trying desperately to work with the slow stream of data from the Sagan. "Do we, uh, have a trajectory?"

Lindsay remained bent over her desk, and, for a moment, Rick thought she might not have heard the question. She looked at her screen for a second and cursed. "Damn it!" Rick blinked. In all the time he'd known her, she had never uttered even the mildest curse word.

She continued to stare at her computer and spoke without looking up. "No near miss this time. It looks like it will come straight down somewhere in the middle of the Pacific Ocean."

"Oh, uh, well that would be extremely bad. The, uh, density of the water will accelerate the fusion reaction, and the resulting cloud of steam will, uh…"

"We need to scramble those fighters," said General Walker.

The President nodded. "Let's do it."

General Walker turned on his heel and paced back and forth while he whispered commands that only he could hear.

"Can I change the broadcast mode on the Sagan?" asked Lindsay.

"Might as well," replied General Laurence.

The video from the Sagan telescope immediately brightened, and the resolution went up considerably. If Rick squinted, he could almost see the figure of a man in the cockpit of the Lunar Tug. He shook his head and frowned. "What the hell is that guy doing? Why is he so close to the object?"

"He appears to be giving chase," said Lindsay.

"Chasing it? Can he catch it?"

"I don't know. He's maintaining 12 gravities right now, and he's got an angle on the object, but nobody can take that kind of acceleration without passing out after a few minutes. He may already be unconscious."

Several people looked at each other with puzzled expressions. Rick raised an eyebrow and rubbed his chin. "General Laurence, permission for an attempt to hail the Lunar Tug."

General Laurence waved his hands in frustration. "Why not. We might as well find out what that idiot thinks he's doing."

Near Earth's Moon

Yee h-a-a! screamed the thin voice.

You must return to the surface and save your life, said the baritone.

Ben could hear them clearly over the screaming whistle of the tug's engine, and he wanted to tell them to shut up, but all the air was gone from his lungs. The acceleration had slammed him back into the seat and compressed his chest so brutally that he could feel the pain through all the adrenaline and Carbodine. In one great "whoof" his air had gone and no amount of straining would allow him to take a breath.

His eyes were sunk deep into the sockets, and he could feel the skin of his face peeling back in a hideous grin. The tug shrieked with the force of its engine and vibrated like a tuning fork. Ben felt the oscillations tearing at the joints of his arms and legs, and he began to fear that the tug would fly apart from the shaking.

But none of it really bothered him till he realized he was going blind. His sight was collapsing from the outside edges as darkness spread from the boundaries of his vision toward the center till he seemed to be looking down a long pipe. The gauges disappeared and then the object itself.

He pulled the throttle back to fifty percent and drew a huge draft of air into his lungs.

Do it again. Do it again.

Ben took another breath, and his eyesight began to clear. "Shut up." He coughed, and flecks of blood covered the inside of his faceplate.

This is killing you. Return to Lexam.

"Lunar Tug in pursuit of Alien object, this is Rick Jelton at NORAD. Please respond."

Slam it. Take some more Carbodine.

Return to Lexam.

"Lunar Tug, please respond."

"Shut up!" Ben screamed. "Everybody just shut up!"

"Lunar Tug, this is NORAD. What is your intention?"

More Carbodine. More Carbodine.

Ben's vision was rapidly returning to normal as he panted under the six G acceleration of the fifty percent throttle, and he looked up to find himself bathed in blue light. The object was a mere thirty miles away—the blue fire, still and solid in the vacuum of space, warmed his suit, and Ben could feel sweat running down his back.

Cooking on blue flame now, Ben, said the thin voice.

You will die from the radiation if you don't return to Lexam, said the baritone.

"Lunar Tug, please respond. This is NORAD. What is your intention?"

Ben blinked at the object and squinted to see his gauges. "My eyes hurt," he said.

Of course your eyes hurt. They weighed twelve pounds apiece just a few seconds ago. Carbodine will make it go away.

Make the effort to live.

"This is NORAD hailing Lunar Tug in pursuit of Alien object. What is your intention?"

Ben could see the object pulling away from him, and he screamed at it. "You bastard. You're not gonna do this." He frantically scanned his console and scrunched his eyes against the glare of the object. There was a targeting solution somewhere—it should be right in front of him—but he couldn't find it.

"I can't see it," Ben yelled and slammed his fist into the armrest. "Where is the line that will intersect."

Take some more and let's fly around the Moon. This is getting boring.

Ben made an animal noise in his throat. "There's no time! I need to know where it's going. I need to know its acceleration."

Screw this. Take some more stuff.

The radiation is killing you. Return to the surface.

"Lunar Tug, the object is expected to impact in the Pacific Ocean near Hawaii. It is accelerating at ten gravities. What is your intention?"

Ben looked up at the crescent of Earth. The Pacific Ocean, mostly covered by the white tufts of clouds, was directly above him. He could see the flecks of the Hawaiian Islands. He checked his docking radar. The object itself was not there, but a large fuzzy reading showed the blue exhaust plainly. "Ten gravities," he mumbled.

And it came together. It popped into his mind as if it had always been there. He suddenly knew exactly where he needed to be.

"Lunar Tug, this is NORAD. What is your intention?"

Ben took a few strong breaths, trimmed the orientation of the tug, and gripped the throttle. "My intention is to save my children."

He screamed as the air was jerked from his lungs and the tug howled with him when he slammed the throttle full open. Straining every fiber and sinew to its limit, he watched the object, checked his radar, and trimmed the tug. His vision began to close in, and he made another adjustment.

That's it.

You're starting to scare me, said the thin voice. *Let's stop this nonsense.*

Go back to Lexam.

Dimly, dimly, someone was asking him about what he was doing, and something like a proximity alarm started honking, but his vision was gone, and his hearing faded as a sweet darkness came over him. Somewhere in the distance, his mother was singing a lullaby.

~

NORAD

"What the hell is he doing?" Rick was confused and frustrated by his efforts to talk to the man in the tug. "He sounds like he's lost his mind."

"Mr. Jelton!" Rick looked up to see Lindsay staring at him with a shocked expression. "He may be crazy, but he seems to be on an intercept course for the object."

"What?"

"He's got an angle on it. If he doesn't run out of fuel or throttle back, he might ram the object."

Rick shook his head. "I don't get it. The first object took out two sophisticated probes without slowing down. Why doesn't this one launch one of those web things?"

"I don't know," said Lindsay. "The tug is between the last object and Mare Crisium where the third object came down, and

Mare Crisium is still burning. Maybe the object can't see the tug against all that radiation."

General Laurence suddenly laughed. "No that's not it." He was grinning. "These damn things came zipping in here at nearly three million miles per hour. Now if you can move that fast, you generally don't have to worry about something catching up with you. I'm betting they can't see anything behind them."

"It looks like impact in less than twenty seconds along the back half of the object," said Lindsay. She frowned at her display. "It's going to be close. He might miss it."

General Laurence leaned forward. "Come on you crazy bastard. Let's see you save everybody's kids."

"I don't know," said Lindsay. "It's going to be real close."

Everyone in the room was standing and watching the wall screen. The blue flame from the object dwarfed the bright yellow of the tug's exhaust as the tug slowly decreased the distance and closed from the side on a line that would take it just above the blue light or straight through it.

"Possible impact in five, four three, two, one."

The yellow light from the tug winked out, and the tug went spinning wildly away at an angle.

"He hit it!" screamed Rick. "He hit the damned thing right in the ass."

"Sir," said Lindsay. "The object is turning."

The blue flame winked out as they watched.

"What's going on?"

"I don't know," said Lindsay. "The object has cut its engine and is on a new course. It looks like one of those near-miss orbits."

The object fired its engine, and blue fire once again lit the control room.

"It's turning again."

The fire died once more.

"The object is now on a course that will take it about 3,000 miles above Earth's surface at closest approach."

The seconds dragged on, and nobody moved a muscle, waiting for the object to come back to life.

"He broke it," said General Laurence.

"What?" asked Rick.

"He bent some kind of steering mechanism at the back of the object. It can't aim. I think it's going to shut itself down."

Lindsay plunked into her chair, and the only sound in the room was the clack of her computer keys. "The object is in a long, elliptical orbit around the Earth. If it doesn't make another engine burn." She pushed her glasses up and blinked back tears. Her voice shook with emotion, "then I guess it's over."

"What about the tug?" asked Rick.

"It's in a rapidly decaying Earth orbit."

General Laurence ran some data on his screen and shook his head. "If he's not dead already, he's going to burn up on entry. We don't have anything that can reach him."

~

Near Earth's Moon

Ben drifted back to a semblance of consciousness and found himself hanging lightly but apparently upside down from his harness. His arms hung out to his sides, and pain ruled his universe. Every surface from his feet to his hands, from his legs to his arms, from his back to his head screamed in agony. His face felt puffy and seemed to be covered with hot needles. Each breath sent knives through his chest and he wondered idly how many ribs he'd cracked or broken.

This is a fine mess you've gotten us into. It was the thin, reedy voice, but far away and weak.

He struggled to open eyes swollen nearly shut and cried out with the effort. The stars swung by in lazy arcs. "We're tumbling," he slurred. "I wonder if we hit it."

Unknown, said the baritone.

You need a dose real bad.

Ben considered it and cracked open his eyes again. The inside of his faceplate was almost completely covered with a brown stain, and he could taste blood. His tongue was so thick it filled his mouth nearly to the point of choking him, and he ran it over split and swollen lips. Trying to curse his fate, he could only croak.

Take some Carbodine. You'll feel better.

Ben looked at the dispenser. The small, white pill was just within reach of his swollen tongue.

You are alive, said the baritone. *We have a deal.*

"Yeah," Ben croaked, "a deal."

Panting with pain and effort, he fought to bring his right hand down to his side and roared when something popped in his shoulder.

Don't do this, said the thin voice. *You'll regret it.*

Ben fumbled at the pouch on his side and finally extracted the bottle. He let his arm fall above his head and screamed again as the shoulder made a snapping noise. The bottle was held loosely in his gloved hand—the pills clearly visible through his slitted eyes.

You just don't get it, do you? said the thin, reedy voice. *If you quit taking Carbodine, we'll go away and die.*

"Sucks for you I guess," Ben said and let the bottle slip through his fingers. It twirled away into the stars, and something like warm, black velvet wrapped Ben with folds of tranquility as he sank into a sweet and pain-free unconsciousness.

~

NORAD

It took them a long time to believe it was over, but as minutes grew to hours and the last Alien object drifted past Earth, one by one they found themselves smiling and, in some cases, dropping off to sleep at their consoles. Finally, even General Walker was laughing and congratulating everyone.

Rick was leaned back in his chair with his hands laced behind his head when a lieutenant cried out. "We've got something accelerating out of Earth orbit."

The entire room snapped to attention and Lindsay nearly dove at her computer. She wheeled the Sagan telescope around till a thin, yellow light shown on the screen. "It's a Chinese transport vessel."

"What are those bastards up to?" asked General Walker.

Lindsay watched for a while and then turned with a smile. "It's on an intercept course for the tug."

"Well I'll be damned," said President Bremmer. "If that crazy son of a bitch is alive, I'd sure as hell like to shake his hand."

Chapter Fifty
Surface of Mars
July 2, 2061

The weather on Mars was radically altered by the explosion of the first alien object, and the remaining seven members of the Mars' Expedition, though deep underground in the Crystal Grotto, had suffered greatly as a result.

Millions of tons of dust and rock were propelled high into the Martian atmosphere by the force of the alien object. The majority of the dust, gathering frozen carbon dioxide and small bits of water vapor from the air, returned slowly to the surface as a glittery, red snow; but Mars, where planet-wide dust storms are not uncommon, has often experienced similar if less drastic circumstances. It might recover quickly if no other factors were at work—if the Alien bomb had not burned with such incredible heat or detonated with such unimaginable intensity.

A portion of Mars' surface was ejected from the point of impact with such power and to such a distance that it was compelled to achieve orbit. This dust now rims the gravitic bowl of Mars like billions of microscopic moonlets—reflecting and refracting light away from a planet already grown cold and lifeless from its first cataclysmic defeat. Free of atmospheric interference—the dust will affect the Martian climate for thousands of years to come.

But first, Mars must grow warm. Far to the east of the Crystal Grotto is a rough circle where molten rock flows like water. It is ten days since the impact, and still, several hundred square miles of surface glows red in the Martian night as it ever so slowly relinquishes the fervor of the recent conflagration. Even from Earth, Mars can be seen giving a long slow wink as it rotates, hiding then revealing the angry new eye on its face—the larger twin of the one on Earth's moon.

The cold, thin air rushes hungrily to this place and is blown high above the plane to spread out in a great umbrella of warmth stretching thousands of miles in every direction. Like a vast, stationary hurricane, this place gives birth to storms that move off in a diaspora of thermal energy. The storms deliver their burden of heat and gradually decay as their warmth and their fury deserts them.

The temperature of Mars will soon drop below anything it has known before, but it must first submit to its warmest season in a million years and endure the storms that go with it, and though the days on Mars are warming, they have become windswept, dark, and gritty. The sun, always pale and distant, now hides behind a veil of red dust, and those who would rely, however briefly, on its rays for life have found life to be difficult indeed.

Chapter Fifty-one
Surface of Mars
July 2, 2061

Tom realized just how bad morale had become when Melancon snapped at Carlos for constantly whining and complaining. Carlos deserved it, and Tom had not-too-politely asked him to shut up on several occasions, but to hear Melancon utter an unkind opinion was something new and troubling.

They were making preparations to return to the permanent living quarters and it would all be over soon, but the last ten days had taken its toll. Nobody had considered what a dust storm would do to their plans for life in the Crystal Grotto. The electricity that should have been present in abundance for heat and air scrubbers gradually slowed to a trickle. Instead of using two warm temporary shelters, the seven crewmembers were reduced to living in one unheated space that had been designed as a tight fit for four people. The lack of power for heat meant that suits were mandatory at all times, and except for the brief and bitterly cold moments necessary for sanitary reasons, they had lived in their suits for the last week and a half.

Everyone had developed raw patches in the armpits, groin, and around the neck collar. Dr. Krazinsky did the best she could with the salves and ointments at her disposal, but the suits weren't intended for this kind of unrelenting use, and painful skin sores were the inevitable result.

Perhaps worst of all was the lack of anything constructive to do. Forcing seven, highly motivated and strong-willed people to live in a small area with nothing to do but talk to each other might have been an interesting psychological experiment—so long as you weren't a subject—but, to put it mildly, they had seen way too much of each other. They needed space, they needed a hot shower, they needed something constructive to do, and they needed real food.

Tom was willing to believe NASA was correct in stating that human beings could live for extended periods of time on the cherry-flavored, nutrient broth. He just wasn't sure he could drink enough of it to stay alive. The taste of it made him gag, the smell of it made him nauseous, and by now, even the thought of it was enough to turn his stomach.

And before any of these problems surfaced they had moved like zombies through the long days of living with the horrible, grinding unknown of what had happened to Earth. For twelve hours after the first object struck Mars, they sat cross-legged and still on the thick plastic, waiting for the rumble and the quake that would signal the distant impact of the second object. Or the quick blink of a hot death that would be the result a closer detonation.

Commander Thon had been adamant that they would have felt or heard something from the explosions of the other objects even if the objects had fallen on the opposite side of Mars. It was Melancon who eventually pointed out the possible loss of all broadcast capability from the effects of the first explosion. If the objects were not going to Mars, it seemed reasonable to assume they had continued their trek to Earth.

For five days, Melancon had done nothing but peck at his computer as he struggled with the satellites around Mars, hoping to coax at least one of them into life. When he finally succeeded, the news was both excellent and awful. The Earth had been spared, but, although radiation from the fusion bombs had been inconsequential, tens of thousands had died from complications related to the loss of power. Missiles from the United States Air Force had killed over 2,000 people in downtown Houston, most of them Literalist Church members, and President Bremmer was desperately trying to defend the action on strategic grounds. And on the Moon, almost 80,000 were dead—40,000 at Raxon Manufacturing as a direct result of object number three—the rest from combinations of power loss, air loss, and the massive quake object number three had spawned. On Mars, there had been only one casualty.

Power had yet to be restored to most of the Earth or the Moon, communications satellites were down by a factor of ten or more, and it would take years to restore the infrastructure to its pre-object condition, but some things would apparently never be the same again. Weather scientists were frantically trying to convene a worldwide conference to discuss the significance of the dust now in orbit around the Moon and around Earth. The sun could be seen through a high, thin haze, and temperatures around Earth were already growing unseasonably cool. Everyone agreed it would get worse before it got better. The only question was how bad it would be and how long it would last.

But in the midst of all this, as the Mars' crew listened to the scratchy, voice-only connection with NASA, came the wondrous story of Ben Allspot—the man who stopped at nothing to save his children—the man who attempted the impossible and succeeded where all others had failed—the man who had single-handedly saved the entire world, and who had been saved from certain death only by the efficiency of an alien rocket that could operate without turbulence and backscatter.

He was listed as being in extremely serious but stable condition in a Chinese hospital, suffering from multiple fractures and internal injuries, radiation sickness, and some other complication the Chinese doctors seemed reluctant to discuss. His family had been flown to his bedside and in an unprecedented show of cooperation, President Bremmer had been allowed to go with them. The President was now in discussions with Chinese officials regarding the joint retrieval and dissection of the last alien object.

Regardless of all that had happened and despite concerns over the weather, it seemed the world was on the brink of an unparalleled opportunity for peace, and world leaders, perhaps in shock over recent events, appeared eager to embrace it.

So the Mars crew might have had mixed feelings if they weren't preparing to return to the permanent living quarters, and solid food, and a hot shower. As it was, the irritations of the last week were fading quickly with the anticipation of simple comforts. Even Carlos was in a decent mood, and the rest of them were jubilant.

Radiation levels had finally dropped to acceptable levels, and Tom and Evelyn had returned to the base camp yesterday to start the fusion generator and repair a few small holes in the living quarters. It waited for them now—warm and pressured up—a place where they could shed their suits, wash their bodies, and sleep without being stacked like cordwood.

"I tell you it's incredible," said Ki as the rover carried them back home.

Melancon was driving with Kaitlin in the passenger seat. Commander Thon was in the back seat with Tom. Evelyn sat crammed between them, and Dr. Krazinsky rode on the wagon with Carlos.

"Look at this." Ki gestured at the blowing dust and sand. "This was from just one of the objects. Can you imagine the effect if all four had struck Mars? It explains so much about the geology of this planet. All of the anomalies begin to make sense when you consider what must have happened two million years ago. The loss of water, the loss of atmosphere, the strange rock formations."

Tom rolled his eyes and looked at Evelyn who bit her lip to stifle a giggle.

Commander Thon was just building up steam, and he hardly seemed to take a breath as he continued. "Olympus Mons! What a mystery it has been. Why is it that Mars should have the largest volcano in the entire Solar System? It makes no sense unless you consider the effects of an object striking Mars with a direct hit at 100,000 miles per hour. Then you begin to understand that it might have buried itself deep in the Martian crust. Can you imagine what would have happened? Why the explosion would have come close to shattering the planet, and a volcano such as can be found nowhere else could be born. Even Earth's last ice age. I don't think the explosions started the ice age, but I'm willing to bet the dust and water vapor blown away from Mars produced a haze that affected this entire region of the Solar System. Just imagine explosions on Mars large enough to prolong and intensify cold weather on Earth more than one million years ago. It affected our entire evolutionary history."

It might have been interesting if the crew hadn't been listening to endless versions of the same thing for over a week. Tom had had enough, and he reached across Evelyn as Ki looked off to the side of the rover. His hand flicked the radio control on the arm of Ki's suit, and the monologue abruptly ended.

Evelyn made a snorting noise and quickly turned her own radio down to hide her laughter. Tom was forced to do the same thing, and they sat giggling like mute schoolchildren. Melancon sensed that something was not right and turned to look over his shoulder. Tom and Evelyn came to attention and stared back at him, wide-eyed with mirth. Melancon noticed the silent movement of Ki's lips and quickly assessed the situation. "Am I gonna have to pull this thing over?" he asked.

Tom and Evelyn shook their heads in unison, faces contorted with the pressure of withheld laughter. Melancon raised an eyebrow and returned to his driving, but Ki realized something was going on and turned to look at Tom. Evelyn looked away and leaned into Tom as her body shook, and Tom gave Ki his most innocent smile.

Ki frowned for a moment. He knew Tom was up to something, but the enthusiasm for his subject was so strong and the need to talk about it so compelling he decided to ignore them and began gesticulating in silence once again.

Tom and Evelyn collapsed into each other with gales of unheard laughter that went on till they were both gasping for breath and wishing they could wipe the tears from their eyes.

They topped a rise, and the lights of the living quarters came into view, barely visible through the swirling dust. Tom leaned down to Evelyn till his faceplate touched hers. Their eyes were just inches apart, and he raised his voice slightly so she could hear him through the helmets. "I was kind of wondering what you were, you know, planning on doing later on tonight."

Several emotions flicked across Evelyn's face, and she finally dipped a quizzical eyebrow at him. "Are you asking me for a date?"

"Oh yeah," said Tom. "Dinner, dancing, maybe a movie."

Evelyn laughed softly. "You can dance?"

"Well, no, but I might be willing to try something new. You know, with the right kind of girl."

"And I am the right kind of girl?"

"I wouldn't consider asking anyone else on the planet."

Evelyn doubled her fist and planted a solid roundhouse in Tom's stomach.

"Oof," Tom grunted. "Solar System, I meant Solar System, but you've got to quit hitting me."

Evelyn smiled up at him. "Then you need to quit being such a smart ass."

"Hmm, I see many bruises in my future."

"We'll work on it," said Evelyn with a smile and a slow, guileful blink. "I suppose I might let you buy me a drink."

Tom grinned at her. "Great. Anything you want as long as it doesn't taste like cherries."

Evelyn laughed. "I guess it's a date."

"I guess it is."

The lights grew brighter as the rover descended the last hill before the living quarters, and the crew leaned into their seatbelts with anticipation. They would soon be home.

Chapter Fifty-two
The Planet Harmony
Time Unknown

The old Tree looked out over the gathering of children and pondered once again the actions he about to take. It was a huge undertaking. Decades might pass before its completion, and he could not yet see the final stages. He was purposely moving from a solid and predictable future into a malleable and unknown chaos.

Already he longed for the days when life had been simple and the complex philosophies of his ancestors had revealed with such clarity the difference between right and wrong. Would he ever again look at children with pure feelings, or would joy and love be forever shaded by concern and guilt? Would the time ever return when he could be as solidly rooted in his beliefs as he was in this piece of ground? His mind whirled with feelings and thoughts. What was solid before was now fragile and soft. What had been level ground and easily understood was now wildly tilted and dimly complex.

His ancestors had recorded billions of words explaining the concept of an abstraction they called the Cycle of Life, and it had seemed so right and true—the idea that Trees should never interfere in the workings of the Universe or attempt to change that which was meant to be. It was a philosophy purposely constructed in isolation from the material world, and it befit a species evolved from impotent adults who might die with food in plain sight. The old Tree saw it now as an elegant justification for a people mired in their own primeval perspective. The Tree metaphysics had made beautiful sounds reverberate through the land for millions of years but had less substance than the songs of a Skarj Beast in rut. And like the music of the Skarj Beast, the Tree beliefs were marvelously complex, fascinating in their diversity, captivating in their splendor, but deadly in their reality.

It was reality that had toppled the twig house of Tree philosophy from his mind. One brief glimpse of the truth at the center of Koombar thinking had brought it all tumbling down. Within the dark and twisted underbelly of the Koombar reasoning, he had found a mirror image of the convoluted Tree logic, and nothing, not even the simplest act, would ever be the same for him again.

He looked with all his eyes at the children gathering around him. He could not remember seeing so many at once. Some of them were approaching adulthood, and he would later talk to them separately, interviewing them to see which ones might make the best adults. He would then choose their mates and instruct them carefully on what they should do when the time for fusion arrived. It was an incredible, most would say blasphemous, idea. His brothers would think him insane, but what would they do about it? He smiled sadly at the question.

The crowd of children spread out before him in a melee of activity down the hill and past the road. They climbed in the brush at the edge of the clearing and scampered over the rocks behind him. Perhaps a thousand or more called by him from miles around with the promise of a new story—a story such as had never been heard before.

Tree raised his arms and the crowd stopped its motion, coming to rapt attention within the space of a single breath.

"I have called you today to hear a story never before told. It is a special story, and it carries with it a special responsibility. It is a story that must never be told or talked about with anyone who is not here now. If another adult should ask you about it, you will tell them to speak to me. If someone should pressure you to speak of it, you must hold what you know even in the face of death.

"This is but the first small step in a long journey. Many of you will find their final dream before it is done. Others will fuse and grow to adults, and I will not live to see its completion, but it is the most important undertaking in the history of Trees."

The children looked up at him with unblinking trust, and Tree felt his heart might break from what he was about to do. They would remember, these children, they would obey, and many of them would die as a result.

Tree dropped his arms and took a deep breath. There was no going back from this first step. "This is the first of many stories I will tell you, and all of them are new and different, but this one contains perhaps the most important lesson of all. It is a lesson that may allow you to live when others would die. It is called 'The Telling of an Untrue Story,' and in exploring deceit, we will reveal truth—the truth of the Tree destiny."

~

Skrin stood outside the Great Hall with his guards and the draped "gifts" he would give to his father at the beginning of the Feast of Ascendance. His unarmed guards shuffled nervously about. Within a few minutes, they would be allied with the new Supreme Watcher, or they would all be dead.

Skrin peeked under the cover of one of the boxes. After months of working with them, they still made his skin crawl—the beady, flat eyes, the scaly talons, the covering that was not fur but something else. He dropped the flap as one of his father's guards approached.

"Master Skrin," said the guard, "your father awaits you."

Skrin's guards lined up in a double row, twenty in all, and followed him through the tall doors of the great Hall. Each of them carried nothing but a draped box.

His father sat at the far end of the large room on a dais. The air was redolent with the odor of well-aged meat, and his father sat finishing the last of his meal. As always, he was the last to eat. His guards lined the walls, picking at their teeth and caressing their guns.

Skrin approached to within five feet of his father and prostrated himself. "This one is greatly honored to be in the presence of such a fine specimen of the Koombar heritage," he said.

"Yes, yes," his father said. "Stand up, Skrin, my oldest son. Today you will become an adult, and I see you have brought gifts. I hope they are adequate to the occasion."

"I'm sure you will find them interesting," said Skrin. "Would you receive them now?"

His father raised a hand to the guards against the walls, and there was a shuffling noise and the soft click of guns being readied as rifles were brought to the shoulders of the Supreme Guard and aimed at Skrin's small compliment of soldiers.

"Yes," said his father. "Let us see what you have brought me."

Skrin raised a hand without turning around, and his guards bent down to open the sides of the cages concealed by the covers. Nearly one hundred birds flew out and began circling the Great Hall, frantically seeking escape. Skrin's guards ran to the sides of the room in a well-rehearsed move and pulled the guns from the frozen hands of the Supreme Guard. Shots rang out as Skrin rushed forward, grabbing a knife from the table and plunging it without hesitation into his father's neck. He jerked viciously to the side, nearly decapitating the Supreme Watcher, and then stood back as his father fell forward, smashing his face on the table and spilling blood across the floor.

Skrin turned around. Half of the Supreme Guard lay dead in spreading pools of blood. The rest cowered at the point of their own guns. Skrin leaned down to pull the bloodstained cloak from his father's still body and picked a small portion of meat from the table as he ascended the dais.

He took a bite of the meat.

"Delicious," he said. "Let the celebration begin."

ABOUT THE AUTHOR

Gregg Overman was born in New Orleans and spent most of his life in Louisiana, graduating quite some time ago from LSU with a major in zoology and a minor in chemistry. He remains interested in many areas of scientific endeavor and considers himself to be an armchair physicist. This was his first major in college. Gregg has worked as a chemist for most of his life.

In 1987, his career brought him to Memphis, TN where he started The River City Soap Co., a small manufacturing firm specializing in industrial detergents. Gregg now lives in a suburb of Memphis with his wife, his teenage son, four cats, a dog, two turtles, and a guinea pig. He allows that the turtles are almost no trouble at all.

Gregg R. Overman

Made in United States
Orlando, FL
25 September 2025